Marlboro Man

About the author

M. G. Sanchez is a Gibraltarian writer based in the UK. He studied at the University of Leeds, where he obtained BA, MA and PhD degrees in English Literature. He is the author of fifteen Gibraltar-themed books, among them novels, journals, memoirs, historical studies and collections of short stories. He has spoken about his writing at different universities across Europe and more than a dozen articles on his work have been published in scholarly journals. His novel *Jonathan Gallardo* was chosen by Alastair Niven of *Wasafiri* as his personal highlight for 2015 in an article celebrating the iconic magazine's thirty-five-year publishing history. More information about Sanchez's books can be found at https://www.mgsanchez.net/. He also posts regular updates about his writing on a Facebook page: https://www.facebook.com/mgsanchezwriter/.

Marlboro Man

M. G. Sanchez
The Dabuti Collective
2022

For N & N.

'A ghost never dies, it remains always to come and to come-back.'

Jacques Derrida, *Spectres of Marx* (1993)

Marlboro Man

I always knew I'd end up back here – here, where it all started – staring at the same old walls and breathing the same old smells, trapped somewhere between the past and the present.

The cracked pavement tiles, the rotting Persian shutters, the narrow lanes robbed of sunshine, the stink of dog piss souring random street corners – I somehow knew I'd come back to it all sooner or later.

Maybe it was not a conscious thought – one of those unshakeable certainties that burrow their way into your head and never leave you alone.

But nonetheless the gravitational pull was always there – floating in the ether, following me like a curse, an umbilical cord stretched to the span of two oceans but still elastic enough to snap back at any moment and send me tumbling violently to my birthplace.

***

If I open my bedroom shutters, I can see the door of my old school, Saint Bernard's First School, less than ten yards away. Not the main door up on Castle Road, but the side entrance on Chicardo's Passage. The door hasn't been painted for years and these days there is only a derelict building behind the doorway, but it is still there, still bearing the same hand-painted sign saying 'Saint Bernard's Primary School for Boys and Girls', a perfect example of how physical objects often outlive the purpose for which they were created. The whole area up here is littered with similar monuments to mutability. Crumbling bollards and bannisters. Obsolete TV aerials poking out of tin roofs. The fire hydrant against which I once crashed my 'Tomahawk' bicycle (and which nowadays is encased in a carapace of flaky orange rust.) The busted lampposts which currently serve as sniffing and pissing places for every mutt in the neighbourhood. The electrical enclosure which Manu prised open with one of his mum's screwdrivers (he wanted to use it as a hiding place for his porno mags, *el muy cabrón!)* and which now lies enveloped in a cocoon of black and yellow hazard tape. Mementoes from an all-but-forgotten past, rupturing into the present. Meaningless, except for those like me who use them as plumb-lines to trace out the contours of their fading memories.

———————

Remarkable how I can feel Manu's imprint everywhere around me. I see him in doorways, in street corners, waiting at the bus stop opposite Arengo, crouching behind parked cars. Just yesterday, for example, I was returning home with the shopping from Morrisons. I was tired and out-of-breath and couldn't wait to get back to my flat at 13 Chicardo's Passage so that I could put down the bags and rest my weary arms. 'This is no place for the old and the infirm,' I thought, stopping to lay the groceries on the ground, cursing the health problems that have brought me back here. It was during one of these moments of forced respite, as I stood there panting and massaging my palms where the bag handles had been cutting into them, that my eye fell on the residential building which stands – empty and abandoned – on the corner of Chicardo's Passage and Abecasis's Passage. Against the façade of this building Manu and I played a form of 'football-squash', kicking the ball against the wall and then getting out of the way to let your opponent kick it in turn. Standing there with the shopping bags at my feet, it all came back to me – the way our trainers squeaked and skidded on the uneven cement paving, the diapason-like hum issuing out of the bricks every time the ball hit the wall, the irritation we felt when the ball ricocheted off the wall and tumbled down Pezzi's Steps, the way our sweat drops flew off our foreheads and hit each other in the face, the time the ball bounced awkwardly off the wall and broke the wing mirror of a Vespa motorbike parked nearby, Manu shouting 'time-out' whenever an old granny or a pregnant lady appeared at the top of Hospital Ramp, the cries of Mr Marelli (or whatever the guy who lived in the building was called) urging us to go and play somewhere else: *'Pará ya, coño! Qué me estáis volviendo loco, joder, con tanta puta pelota!'* [1]

There is hardly anybody left in this part of the Upper Town. Its former residents departed in the mid-to-late Nineties, when the government built Harbour Views, Montagu Gardens and Gib Five, and our Upper Towners – most of whom had lived here for decades – upped sticks and moved into new flats erected on reclaimed land, swapping a life of overflowing drains and constant parking problems for one of lifts, sea views and underground garages. I've heard that the authorities are in the process of regenerating the district, but I'm not buying it. Yesterday a drain burst at the top of the passage and it was just like in the old days: a torrent of drain water and shredded toilet paper came cascading down the steps, filling the entire neighbourhood with an almighty stink.

---

[1] 'Stop it, damn it! You're fucking driving me crazy with that fucking ball!'

That does not mean, of course, that the streets and alleys up here are completely denuded of people. Many of the buildings are evidently derelict, but one or two individuals have somehow trickled back into the area. It's one of those indisputable life rules, isn't it? A void opens and slowly but surely it starts filling up again with noise and movement. In the flat opposite mine there is Marek, a Pole who works as a barman at the Rock Hotel. And two doors further down, in the modest building facing the back entrance to the old school, there's Borislava Shikalova, the sad-eyed brunette from Bulgaria who has a PhD in Astrophysics from the University of Veliko Tarnovo but works as a cleaner at the Bristol Hotel. And higher up the passage, at the point where it branches off in two directions, there's the Al-Maghribis, the family of Moroccan-born Gibraltarians who, the father tells me, have been nine years on the housing list without ever being offered a government flat. Migrant workers, lonely widows and widowers, the odd *llanito*[2] who failed to play their cards in life right – these are the people who populate this once-thriving but now curiously neglected locality.

***

On the journey into town this morning, I saw some young Moroccan lads playing football in New Street, the long alley connecting Hospital Hill with Hospital Steps. It was the first time since moving back here that I have seen children playing outdoors, and it really cheered me up to think that, while most kids are stuck at home staring at their iPads and

---

[2] *Llanito* can refer either to a Gibraltarian or the vernacular mix of English and Andalusian Spanish spoken in Gibraltar.

iPhones, there are still one or two who play in the same sites where Manu and I messed about all those years ago, and where my father and my maternal grandfather in turn played before us.

Back in the late Seventies, New Street was one of the best places to play football in the entire Upper Town. Tucked out of the way and rarely frequented by pedestrians, it was flanked by a series of steep stone steps at one end and a partially railed entrance at the other, and could easily be converted into a football pitch at a moment's notice. The trick was to head there after school, 'claim the pitch' and then enjoy a game of street football with whoever turned up next – running from one end of the passage to the other, dribbling around our opponents, pausing for some seconds to let an elderly pedestrian pass on their way down to Governor's Street, wincing whenever the ball bounced off one of the shuttered windows lining either side of the alley. We must have irritated the hell out of the neighbours – with our shrieks and our curses and our constant celebrating! – but people were either very tolerant in those days or didn't have the heart to tell off a bunch of happy and excitable kids. Once, I remember, an English ex-military guy came out with a bread knife and threatened to slash our ball if we continued playing outside his ground-floor flat. But when his Gibraltarian missus appeared at their kitchen window and told him to 'stop being *tan cabrón*,' the poor sod lowered his head, turned around and shuffled back indoors with a look of resignation on his pasty-white face, and that was that....

I've made a decision: I'm going to start writing about Manu and everything that happened all those years ago. I will still include the occasional entry *about what's out there* and *how it is affecting me,* but from now on my main focus will be on the past and on the circumstances that compelled me to leave and – after twenty-one years – return to Gibraltar. I know it will be hard and that I will end up picking at wounds that have long since turned into scars, but I have no other option. I am being smothered by memories up here; they encircle me wherever I go – taunting me, calling out to me, projecting half-forgotten images into my head, reminding me of the good times and the bad times, disturbing the stillness and the zombie-like resignation that has reigned inside me since the day I left Dr Grierson's office with the news of my diagnosis. Against my will I stay up late at night; I think about things I haven't thought about for years; I agonise over decisions that cannot be undone; I dialogue with the returning ghosts of the past. I know that by writing a memoir I may end up ushering in even more terrible and grotesque spectres (ironic, seeing how much I crave a full-blown exorcism), but this is a risk I must take. Disowned and rejected, the past is almost like an unexploded WW2 shell buried yards away from a modern motorway bridge abutment. Left untouched, it might grow rustier and rustier and its demonic power might never be unleashed. But it is only by unearthing it and physically handling it – by tinkering around with its internal wiring – that you can truly render it safe for posterity. Besides, I am conscious that I am probably the last person alive who can tell Manu's story. This places an additional – and onerous – burden on my shoulders. If I don't write about these things, it will be as if they never happened. And if there is no written record of our doings, then what would be the point of everything that Manu and I went through?

Okay, let's start at the beginning. I used to live at 24 Castle Road, less than a hundred steps from where I now reside. I lived there with my father, John Dennis Leslie Pereira, in a tiny two-bedroom flat. The property was owned by Mrs Berio, an elderly widow of Italian descent who visited us once a month to collect her rent. The apartment was damp and stuffy and, like all the others in our residential block, infested with *curianas* and *cortapichas*. It also stank of cigarette smoke thanks to my father's incessant smoking. To go from the two bedrooms and living room to the kitchen and toilet, you had to open a door, walk down four steps, cross a miniature patio lined with plastic flower pots, climb five steps and open a second door that led into the other half of the apartment. Saucer-sized patches of mould covered the kitchen walls and ceiling, but this – given the age and state of the property – was not unusual. What was unusual was that, right at the back of the room, directly behind the fridge and cooker and surrounded by a disintegrating plasterboard screen, there was a toilet and shower cubicle. This was where we washed, shaved, brushed our teeth and performed our daily necessities. In spring and summer it was relatively pleasant to walk from the bedrooms to the kitchen/toilet. But in winter, when the rains came and the patio flooded, you often had to wade through a small pond strewn with plastic pots and bedraggled hydrangeas. 'For fuck's sake,' my old man would groan on opening the living room door and seeing the dirty, sloshing rainwater. *'Cómo odio este puto boquete!'* [3]

* * *

It pains me to say that I cannot recall when or where I first met Manuel Gonzalez. Perhaps he approached me one day in the playground at Saint Bernard's. Perhaps he was coming around one of the blind corners in Abecasis's Passage and we crashed into each other – and, just like that, discovered that we were practically neighbours. Perhaps his ma knew my pa and, as the two adults were standing there chatting outside Mrs Pozo's convenience store, he tapped me on the shoulder and asked me if I also collected Panini football stickers and whether I had a Thomas N'Kno to swap for a Uli Stielike.

The simple truth is I don't know. I have tried again and again to unearth that first encounter, but it keeps eluding me, refusing to budge from wherever it lies buried. And yet it must have been a fateful meeting, mustn't it, because even in my earliest memories Manu is there beside me, tousle-haired and out of breath, one or two dirt streaks on his face, the usual collection of scabs and scratches showing through the holes in his torn schoolboy trousers. He is there and we are running together – down Castle Street after finishing school, maybe, or up Tank Ramp after ringing some doorbells, or down Pezzi's Steps chasing a miskicked football, or away from some doorway after going for an emergency piss, or down Lower Castle Road after taunting one of the old drunks sitting outside the Artillery Arms....

---

[3] 'How I hate this shithole!'

9

Movement, laughter, swirls of motion blur. If there was a machine that printed out childhood memories, mine would probably come out more blurred than the sea on a day of heavy Levanter.

───────────◆───────────

My father could have bought earthenware flower pots instead of plastic ones for our patio, but something in him rebelled against the idea of spending money on decorating what, after all, was somebody else's property. In this sense at least, John Dennis Leslie Pereira was like most men of his generation – wilful and a tad stingy, always watching his pennies. He was born on the island of Madeira in August 1942, one of the so-called 'evacuation babies.' He was the unplanned fruit of the union between a forty-five-year-old Gibraltarian ex-nurse called Dolores Remedio (I'm not kidding – that was my granny's name!) and a Madeiran postman, twenty years her junior, by the name of Rafael Pereira. His formative years were spent in the fishing village of Câmara de Lobos, just outside Funchal. *'Tirando piedras al mar y corriendo detrás de las cabras,'*[4] as he used to say – by which I think he meant he didn't do that much at all. In 1948 his parents' marriage broke down and the heartsore Dolores returned to the Rock with the six-year-old John Dennis Leslie in tow. She had hoped to move back into the Remedios' family apartment in Town Range, but her elderly mother still hadn't forgiven her for getting knocked up by a common *cartero* and so she was forced to settle instead in the South District, taking over one of the Nissen huts built for Gibraltar's returning wartime evacuees. John Dennis Leslie

---

[4] 'Throwing stones in the sea and running after goats.'

attended Plata Villa School and then the newly constructed Technical College down at Queensway, but learned precious little in either establishment. At the age of fifteen, he got a job as a labourer at *el Rolli,* which at the time used to be a victualling and repair yard and which, according to legend, was where Nelson's body was brought ashore in a barrel of brandy after the Battle of Trafalgar. There he worked for the next sixteen years, fitting valves and welding hull plates and stealing as many tools as he could from his slightly racist, but somewhat scatty English superiors. Two dates, he always said, changed the course of his life: 3 March 1969, when he married my mother Connie Anne Maldonado. And 12 December 1973, when a strong Levanter wind toppled a jetty crane at the dockyard, where he was temporarily posted to work on the hull of a destroyer, and threw some heavy steel cables on top of him, trapping him for forty-five minutes and permanently crippling his right arm. To these two dates it is necessary to add an unacknowledged but nonetheless very important third – 10 February 1975 – when his wife ran away to the UK with her youngest child (my brother Kenneth) and an English soldier by the name of Wayne Reginald Roscoe. Already taciturn by nature, my father became even more stolid after this double disappearance. In fact, henceforth he had no meaningful communication with anyone or anything – save, possibly, the plants he kept in our yard (which he addressed as 'my little beauties') and the counter clerk at *el Social Security* (where he went every fortnight to collect his disability allowance). When I think of him all these years later, I do not see a person before me, but a series of 'absences', of 'behavioural deficiencies.' After all, he never drank, never took drugs, never read, never listened to music, seldom swore, rarely laughed and – as far as I could tell – never had sex with anyone after my mother's departure. I suppose he wasn't a happy person, but I never thought of him as a particularly sad individual either. He was just what he was: a quiet and introverted man who, when he was not having one of his complaining fits, couldn't be arsed with anyone or anything around him.

Very good news. I have bought a second-hand printer for twenty-five pounds. It is an old HP Deskjet 895 Cxi and I saw it advertised on Thingsforsale.gi. When I called the guy selling it, I asked him if he could bring it up to Chicardo's Passage for me, but it turned out that the chap lived in Benzimra's Alley, just two minutes away from here – so we met and sealed the deal at the top of Pezzi's Steps. It is a clunky, noisy, old-fashioned thing, but it works perfectly well when connected to my laptop, and Charles (the Englishman who sold it to me) even threw in a couple of reams of A4 paper which he no longer needed. I am so, so pleased!

At first sight Manu and I shared almost identical home backgrounds – his parents had split up just like mine and he lived alone with his mother in an equally pokey Upper Town flat. Like me he also suffered from bad asthma on account of the mould in his apartment. But that's as far as the similarities between us went. For a start, Manu lived with a charming, confident, exceptionally attractive woman in her mid-twenties – and not a rundown, morose waste of space like my old man. Tall, proud, always dressed in the latest glad rags despite working as a cleaner at the NAAFI store up at

Europa, Mariadelaida Gonzalez had a long mane of straight blonde hair and a husky feminine voice that could have tempted Saint Anthony out of his desert cavern. You'd frequently see her walking up and down Castle Street with her chest thrust forward and her chin raised high, a woman who'd trigger palpitations and *piropos* wherever she and her legendary figure transported themselves. Watching her, it was hard to imagine that any guy with sense could have willingly jettisoned such a gift from heaven. But the arsehole who had done the dirty on her twice – getting her pregnant when she was sixteen and then ditching her shortly afterwards – was none other than *el Pantera,* a notorious middle-aged *contrabandista* and tough guy whose three main pastimes were sniffing coke, impregnating women much younger than himself and smuggling cigarettes and hashish by sea into Spain.

Neither Manu nor his mum had anything to do with *el Pantera* when they came to live in Macphail's Passage, a stone's throw away from Castle Road, but it could be argued that his shadow always loomed over his son and for this reason I'm going to include a few words here about him. His real name was Johnny Rogelio and he lived in a detached house on Engineer Road, just past *el Casino.* He must have been forty-six or forty-seven when I first saw *el muy cabrón.* Paunchy but stocky dude, one of those guys who are unprepossessing from a distance, but from up close give you the creeps. He had a nose like Doña Rogelia's and a face as furrowed as a *Spitting Image* puppet. He also owned a gigantic head of grey hair that fell in greasy, yellowing locks onto his denim-jacketed shoulders – giving him the appearance, when you saw him riding through Queensway on his Harley Fat Bob, of a superannuated but sexually promiscuous rock star. Like many tough guys of his generation, he wore pointy cowboy boots and he loved nothing better than to strut up and down Main Street or Irish Town in those wooden-heeled size twelves, sowing terror and alarm just with the sound of that metronomic clickety-clack. Fellow hoodlums lowered their eyes in his presence. Grown men grew pale and crossed the road. Middle-aged women dragged their teenage daughters aside, instinctively interpolating their matronly bodies between their darlings and the eyes of the *sinvergüenza* prowling before them. He was known as *'el Pantera'* because he had a tattoo of a panther etched on his lower abdomen, the tail of which, allegedly, was painted on a long but disproportionately thin penis. In summer, when he used to sit with his *contrabandista* mates knocking back Heinekens and smoking sneaky *porros* at the Dolphin Bar in Camp Bay, getting more and more smashed as the afternoon wore on, you could see the head and shoulders of the panther snaking out of his half-unbuttoned jeans, its open jaws and tongue visible beneath a thick tangle of abdominal hair. It was one of the most ridiculous things imaginable, but it was also his personal talisman, the semi-mythical emblem that turned him into a larger-than-life figure and – together with his dough and his fearsome reputation – rendered him into an object of sexual fascination. We all know how this story goes, don't we? *'La tiene tan larga, o no la tiene?'* [5] 'Tis a question, my dear reader, that must have tipped more than one inebriated damsel into those giant *gitano* arms.

---

[5] 'Does he really have such a long one?'

Another curious thing about those early childhood years: I cannot remember much about what Manu and I did together in school. I remember running with him into Saint Bernard's in the mornings, yes. And I remember running out with him in the afternoons. And I also remember, strangely enough, that he once made Raju Ramchandani cry when he told him that he had a face like a plate of *calamares*. But if I try to go beyond these carefully preserved images, I find myself grasping at shadows, searching for a leading man who has wandered off camera. Blackboards, cloudlets of chalk dust, milk poured in large-handled plastic orange cups, teachers who smiled at us but secretly despised our guts, the smell of freshly-cut carnations in the school chapel, the gently flapping soutane of the priest (Father Calleja was his name) who came every Thursday to give us religious instruction – I remember all this, but without Manu by my side. For him to be there at school next to me I need to mentally fast-forward a few years – to when we were in Saint Mary's Middle School, up at Johnstone's Passage. In those classrooms with the flaking gypsum cornices, he emerges from the shadows – flinging a pencil case at Mr O'Hagan, our PE teacher; getting walloped by Miss Perez for sticking his hand up Emma Graviotto's skirt; fighting with Stuart Cribbs, the toughest boy in the school, and Cribbs later saying that he had never fought 'such a hard case'; breaking his left wrist after tripping during a game of British Bulldog; scrawling obscenities on the plaster cast they placed on his hand; smoking discarded butts (which he collected and kept in a crumpled Lipton's shopping bag) behind the shed where Mr Lyons, our caretaker, stored his trowels and his bags of cement. Which reminds me – that's something else I'll never forget about

Saint Mary's: we were always fagging it! I can't remember how or when this habit of ours started. Quite possibly it was towards the end of the second year ... or in the long, lazy, summery interlude between the second and third. I suspect there must have been a trigger for it, some event or random alignment of circumstances that convinced us that smoking was the coolest, most fabulous thing in the world. One of those ads they screened halfway through the Saturday matinee in the Regal 2, perhaps. A bus shelter poster showing a beefcake sharing a cig with a stunning blonde. All I know is that from one day to the next we were smoking like a pair of chimneys! We smoked in the toilets at school, in my place when my father was out, at Manu's when his mother was scrubbing floors for *los ingleses* at *el NAAFI*, behind the rubbish bins at the bottom of Tank Ramp. All we needed was a box of matches and our trusty bag of fag ends. And maybe a little ingenuity in case we got caught, that was all.

I haven't been feeling well for the last two days. The stiffness in my fingers is making it hard for me to type and knife-like cramps keep tearing through my legs. Yesterday I called the Health Centre to tell them I need to see a doctor, but they informed me that in Gibraltar you can only see a GP if you (a) are working and paying social insurance (b) are a child or dependent of someone paying social insurance; or (c) have accumulated enough social insurance credits during your working life to become a fully paid-up member of the Group Practice Medical Scheme. If you don't meet the qualifying criteria, they said, then you can go before a board which convenes twice a year at the John Mackintosh Hall and considers granting healthcare access to the chronically sick, the long-term unemployed, the physically and mentally disabled and other categories of 'non-contributors' – but the last meeting was only held two weeks ago, the phone operator explained to me, and there won't be another now till the first week in May next year. When I told her that I could not wait so long to see a doctor, the woman exhaled in a way that suggested she was *getting tired of me* and then, after a five-second pause, asked me if I had a British passport. '*Po claro,*' I answered, unable to hide my vexation. 'Can't you tell from my accent *que soy llanito?*'[6] 'In that case,' the woman replied curtly in English, 'you can present yourself with your passport at Saint Bernard's Hospital, where you will be entitled to receive free emergency healthcare. However, if your emergency treatment requires transfer to Spain and you are not a member of the Group Practice Medical Scheme,' she continued, reciting the words as if she were reading a pre-prepared script, 'then you will be charged for any medical fees incurred.'

Civil servants, I thought, pressing the end call button on my UK mobile. Same everywhere.

Our favourite smoking place was under the stone bridge spanning *la alcantarilla,* as we called the half-submerged Victorian storm drain that runs all the way from Castle Road to Castle Street and divides Castle Steps from Ansaldo's Passage, Macphail's Passage and the other even narrower passageways behind them. Technically, it wasn't an *alcantarilla*

---

[6] 'Of course. Can't you tell from my accent I am a *llanito?*'

– that is to say, a cesspool or sewer – but this is what Manu and I called it back then (what can I say, when it comes to malapropisms and mistranslations, we Gibraltarians are without peers!) and I am not going to rename it now. To get to *'el refugio'* (as we dubbed our hiding place under the bridge), you had to enter the gutter through its open entrance at the top of Castle Street and then scramble up a slope that took you into the heart of our domain. Once in the hideaway, it was always better to sit on the far side of the barrel arch and with your back turned to Castle Steps, as there you'd be sheltered from the vicious *poniente* wind which sometimes funnelled its way up the storm drain. Manu and I would sit on this spot most afternoons with our bag of fag ends – telling jokes, grading the girls in our classroom from one to ten, laughing at those guys we knew had really small dicks, thinking about September (when we were due to start at Bayside Comprehensive), sniggering at the gossiping folk crossing the bridge above us, imagining what that ugly fucker Mr Johnson looked like with a hard-on and wondering whether Mrs Jimena's nipples were as big as their outline under those translucent lacy blouses of hers suggested, debating whether Santillana was a better header of the ball than Joe Jordan, armpit-farting and then farting for real, spitting, belching, scratching our noses and our arses, eating *pipitas*,[7] occasionally pissing in unison so that our trickles of urine crisscrossed each other as they flowed down the cracked concrete channel....

---

[7] Pipitas – dry roasted sunflower seeds (llanito).

Manu and I started at Bayside Comprehensive School in September 1983. We had been hoping to end up in the same class, but right from the beginning they separated us and put us in different bands. Manu was in 1 Red X, supposedly the lowest academic band in the entire year; I was in 1 Red Y, the one directly above. The school was larger than Saint Bernard's Primary and Saint Mary's Middle put together and, for a week or two, while we got used to our new surroundings, our paths didn't coincide that much. The weird thing about this Bayside place was that some of its classrooms were built into the ground floor of a residential block. Known as 'the voids', these classrooms were cold and draughty and you could often hear people coughing or dragging furniture upstairs. Funnier still, from the playground you could see into many of the apartments themselves. Now and then you'd spot a bald guy by one of the windows with his morning coffee, or an old crone in her pyjamas, or some buxom lady lolling about in a bra and knickers, unaware (or perhaps all too aware) of the commotion she was triggering thirty or forty yards below.

That first year at Bayside was one of those periods in life where things seem to be stuck in neutral gear. We were the youngest kids in the whole school, so we laid low, tried not to bring too much attention to ourselves. Manu couldn't help fighting a couple of times with some of the older boys, but these skirmishes were short-lived and inconclusive and never got him the playground cred he craved. These were the days, too, when we started pinching tapes from Vijay's and other Main Street music shops and listening to them at home. We did this partly out of boredom, partly because we felt frustrated being right at the bottom of the school dung heap.

We listened to these ill-gotten cassettes at Manu's place rather than mine, mainly because my dad grumbled a lot whenever we played heavy metal bands like Rainbow or AC⚡DC, but also because Manu's mum had a much better stereo system than the shitty Sanyo with one working speaker and the taped-up battery compartment that my dad had bought off one of his old *Rolli* colleagues. Sometimes, when Mariadelaida Gonzalez came back from work with a bad migraine, we'd nip down to *la alcantarilla* and continue with our smoking, which these days was not just limited to discarded butt ends, but also included the packets of Marlboro and Winston and Benson & Hedges which the guy at Chippy Stores on Cornwall's Parade – a very cool Indian dude – happily sold to us. Occasionally, we'd even fortify our cigarettes with a few grains of hashish that Manu had scored from some older kids at school. There was never enough of the stuff to get us properly high, but it was a grand thing all the same – sitting there under the stone bridge and puffing away at those crudely reconstituted cigarettes, feeling like a right pair of rowdies, shouting 'fuck the police!', 'down with the pigs!', 'smoke pot and fly!' and other cringeworthy shit like that....

Yesterday I walked past Manu's old place in Macphail's Passage. Unlike most homes in this part of the Upper Town, it is still occupied. The new owners have ripped out the old Persian shutters and replaced them with blinded double-glazed windows. They have also cemented blue tiles with *cartoony* motifs onto the external walls. A beach umbrella by the sea, a crab clambering out of a plastic bucket, an octopus with a tentacle curled around an ice cream cone, and so on.

It's curious how people try to expunge all traces of the former tenants when moving into a property, isn't it? Carpets must be replaced, walls retiled, new furniture brought in. It is just like an exorcism, I suppose, except that what is being exorcised is not an evil spirit, but the property's *genius loci*, those lingering and sometimes uncomfortable 'resonances' that have somehow survived the departure of the previous occupants.

Back in the Seventies, number 3 Macphail's Passage was like a sanctuary to me, a place to which I could escape whenever my father was in one of his bad moods. Like our flat, it was infested with damp and cockroaches, but Mariadelaida's elegant touch ensured that you barely noticed the mould or the little critters. Its curtains and windows, for one, were almost always open and there were always fresh flowers on the window sills, everything arranged with Feng Shui-like simplicity decades before anybody in Gibraltar had even heard of Feng Shui. Then there was the always charming presence of Mariadelaida herself, who, without doubt, was the nicest, kindest, most stylish, best dressed, best smelling person I had ever met. Because that's the other thing about number 3 Macphail's Passage – it was here, and only here, that you saw Mariadelaida Gonzalez in her true element. If you spotted her out in the street, for instance, she always looked aloof and unflappable, a beautiful but permanently sneering *llanita* Brigitte Bardot. In the apartment, however, she was warm and gentle and would often do unladylike things like belch or giggle helplessly over the silliest of stuff. I was always fascinated by this seeming duality in her nature – by the fact that she could be so remote in one setting and so engaged in another – as if she were saving her best side for when she was back at home. Only later – much, much later – did I realise that her street demeanour was just a mechanism of self-defence, a mask she put on to ward off those men who wolf-whistled at her and made crude comments in her presence....

Number 3 Macphail's Passage, then, was Mariadelaida Gonzalez's domain, the place where she could truly be herself. Pottering around the flat, she always had a contented look in her eye, a relaxed air about her. 'Kids,' she'd cry, gathering Manu and me around her and pointing at a paper bag on the coffee table, 'guess what I saw today and couldn't resist buying.' And out of the bag would appear this gigantic *flan de vainilla* or one of those Black Forest arctic rolls that were all the rage in those days. I'm not saying she was perfect – for one thing, she wasn't always aware of the mischief Manu and I got up to – but she was so joyful and spontaneous, so generous and pure of heart, that none of that mattered. At the time, I worshipped her and thought she was the nearest thing on earth to one of God's angels. But really, thinking about it all these years later, she was so much more than an angel. She was a hard-working single mum who, despite being abandoned by her ex and landing in an Upper Town shithole, kept a tidy home, looked like a million dollars and made sure that her son was well-fed and presentable – all of this on the paltry sixty or sixty-five pence an hour she earned as a NAAFI cleaner....

On the way back home, I used my iPhone to count the steps from Manu's old place to my former dwelling at 24 Castle Road. I had counted them manually in 1979 or 1980, and ended up with a figure of 128 steps – a sum that I've always remembered over the years because my father's birthday fell on 12 August – and I was curious to see how close or how far I'd now be from that total. Throughout the exercise I walked with an upright carriage and at what I thought was a good pace, doing my best to ignore the discomfort that lodges under my left ribcage whenever I overexert myself, my walking stick stoically tucked under my arm. Before setting off, I calculated that I'd be needing 200, perhaps 220, steps at the most, but it soon became clear that this was an overoptimistic assessment. Reaching Abecasis's Passage, I was already up to 158 steps. And by the time I approached the rear entrance to Saint Bernard's First School, I had clocked up 207. Some two or three minutes later, as I got to Castle Road, I looked at my phone and saw the figure of 302 steps flash up on its screen. Yes, that's right: what in 1980 I could cover in 128 easy strides now takes me three hundred and two bastard fucking steps.

We finally came out of our mini crisis of confidence in 1985, at the start of our third and final year at Bayside. Maybe it was because the kids in the years above us no longer seemed that big and menacing. Maybe it was because we only had a few months left before we could officially leave school. Once again – *no sé* – it's difficult to ascertain at which point it all picked up. All I can tell you is that we were once more at the centre of things – fighting, swearing at our teachers, getting thrown out of class, being repeatedly marched over to the headmaster's office.

Did I learn anything during those turbulent years at Bayside? I suppose I did – although as ever I struggle to recall what subjects and books we were exposed to. The only episodes in class that I can summon up are a handful of isolated lessons in Year 3, when class Red X and class Red Y merged every Wednesday due to staff shortages for Beginners' French. The guy running our grotesquely overinflated group was Mr Paolo, a dapper young Gibraltarian who had just finished teacher training in London. He was a decent enough bloke – patient and considerate and trying his best to communicate his passion for all things Gallic to the little savages before him – but he possessed a critical, some might say fatal flaw: he had a lisp that made Kenneth Williams sound like a paragon of maleness. 'Pleathe, kidth,' he'd say in front of the class, pronouncing his s's like his tongue was welded to the back of his front teeth. 'Thtop mithbehaving or I will thtop this clath immediately and report you all to the headmather.'

If it had been any other male teacher standing in his place, this warning would have been taken with the seriousness that it deserved ... but because it was *la Paolita* doing the talking everybody in class acted like it was a big joke, hooting and jeering and chucking pencils in the air, spouting one-liners about *maricas* and *maricones*, pulling faces and throwing *cortes de manga* at each other, belching, farting, blowing raspberries, clapping and cheering like it was the final day of the school year....

John Dennis Leslie had this really awful habit: when you least expected it, he would snap out of his apathy and start grumbling about how life was much better in the old days and how nowadays, by contrast, *todo era una mierda*. He must have only been in his mid-forties, and yet there he lay slouched on the sofa – nattering about the past as if it were a long-lost chivalric age where men worked their guts out and women respected the holy vows of matrimony. Talking like this always depressed my father, put him in a foul mood. As I watched him warily from my armchair, I'd feel a mixture of disgust and pity for the guy. The pity stemmed from the fact that life had dealt him two bad hands – crippling him at the age of thirty-one and then robbing him of his wife less than two years later. The disgust came from seeing how he sporadically revelled in his *miserias* and used them as an excuse to justify everything from his stomach ulcers to our state of near indigence. More than anything else, I remember that I didn't want to end up like him – one of those prematurely aged guys whose lives are poisoned by grudges and past failings. And yet here I am at the age of forty-nine, looking back and thinking how much *everything has changed* since the days of my youth. Because things have radically altered in this place, there's no denying it. Not so much up here in the Upper Town – which by and large looks like it did in former times – but in Westside, Ocean Village and the other areas outside the old city walls, where there are now huge office blocks, multi-storey car parks and luxury properties for foreign tax-dodgers. There is also the fact that young people barely speak *llanito* any more. Can you believe this? They go around using expressions like 'I'm buzzing!', 'Shut up!' and 'That's proper minging!' – the sort of English idioms and colloquialisms no self-respecting Gibraltarian kid would have dared use back in the Eighties and Nineties.

But don't worry: I am not as bad as my dad when I think about 'the good old days.' Yes, there are many things about the present that irritate me, but the past was no golden age either. We lived in crappy flats, ate crappy food and – for kids at least – there was not much to do during the weekends. If you were a fourteen- or fifteen-year-old lad and not old enough to gain admission to Cornwall's or Penelope's, you'd have no option but to walk up and down Main Street, eyeing up the teenage girls who promenaded in tightly huddled groups, stopping at *la Jirafa* to buy crisps and chewing gum, laughing at the drunk *guiri* sailors staggering around on shore leave, admiring the local guys (who in some cases were just four or five years older than you) driving past with Bob Marley or AC⚡DC blaring from their clapped-out Peugeots and Citroëns. What I most remember about these Saturday and Sunday afternoon jaunts is that we always seemed to be in a state of great tension. Or perhaps tension is not the right word. Perhaps it would be more accurate to say that we were *waiting impatiently for different things.* Waiting to turn fifteen and leave school. Waiting to be old enough to apply for a learner's driving licence. Waiting for the day you'd be allowed into Penelope's Discotheque. Waiting to reach *la Piazza* to see if the bird that Manu fancied was still sitting there beside Mr Blackshaw's kiosk. Waiting for summer to arrive so you could go down to *el Quarry*. Waiting to be able to legally buy fags and booze. Waiting for your first job, your first pay packet, your first motorbike, your first blow job, your first fuck. Waiting, waiting, waiting and nothing ever bloody happening, time moving as slowly as it always does when you are fourteen years old, thwarting your ambitions, frustrating your longing for experiences, making you wish you could press life's fast-forward button in much the same way as one day, one day, before you know it, just like that, you'll be wanting to hit rewind....

━━━━━━◆━━━━━━

It was on our way back from a careers fair in the school library that Manu first told me he was going to become a *contrabandista*. It was one of those miserable events where a couple of desks are laid out with brochures and one or two ex-pupils are brought in to expound on the joys of making tea for a senior accountant or sitting in a bank counting other people's money. I had no interest whatsoever in listening to any of the 'work-hard, put-up-with-shit' team, but somebody had told us there was *un bombonazo* manning one of the makeshift stands and so, obviously, in keeping with his reputation as one of year three's most avid skirt-chasers, Manu decided that we needed to go and have a sniff around. Arriving there, we quickly realised that we had been conned: *el bombonazo* was a middle-aged civil servant with long grey hair and scornful beady eyes, balls of crumpled tissue poking out of her upturned cardigan sleeves. Knowing that we couldn't just turn around and skedaddle, we walked up to some of the stands and reluctantly asked a couple of questions, all the while thinking about how to get the hell out of there without attracting too much attention. Most of the answers we got were dreary old horseshit, but the last guy we spoke to – a burly fireman with puffy cheeks – was reasonably friendly and even made the prospect of riding around in a fire engine sound quite exciting. When we finally left the library some ten or fifteen minutes later, I jokingly commented to Manu that this was something I wouldn't mind doing – driving around all day in a fire engine with its siren wailing.

'*Pero,* man, what are you talking about?' Manu frowned. 'Have you gone mad or something? You can't seriously be thinking of joining the fucking fire brigade!'

'But why not?' I asked, slightly irritated by the way he had pounced on my semi-serious remark. 'We'll have to get a job somewhere when we leave this place, don't you think, bro?'

'Because there's no *floosh*[8] in that game, *pishón,*[9] that's why! What we have to do is get in with the Winston guys and start earning some real money – not get a job where you'll get treated like shit!'

'And how exactly are you going to do that?' I asked. 'To be part of that racket, you need to know somebody who knows somebody who knows somebody else. That's how it's always been with *el contrabando, colega....* Unless you've come to an arrangement with your dad *el Pantera...?'*

Manu stopped in his tracks and raised his eyebrows in a gesture which suggested he had something to confide.

'No way, man!' I cried. 'You and *el Pantera...!'*

'No, man, no,' he chuckled back. 'I'll never go anywhere near that fucker. It's *el Michael* who's gone into the trade. He bought himself a second-hand Phantom three months ago and just yesterday offered me *un shapucito*[10] as a loader and unloader.'

---

[8] Floosh – money (llanito).
[9] Pisha, pishita, pishón – affectionate (though often sarcastically employed) terms for a youth or young man (llanito).
[10] Shapucito – job (llanito).

'You mean your half-brother Maikito? The one who works in the dockyard and sometimes comes up to your place?'

'Yup,' he confirmed with a smile. 'Some old guy who works with him – and who's been smuggling Winston for yonks – recently did *el Cursillo* and has gone full-blown, I-repent-everything-I've-done-in-my-fucking-life Catholic. Says he's found God, and all that bullshit, and that he wants nothing to do with his dodgy past. Michael bought one of his Phantoms for peanuts, and then got in touch with one of his mates in La Línea, who then introduced him to *el Pelúo,* a guy from Los Junquillos who'd been looking around for a *llanito* to start smuggling Winston cases for him. Anyway, one thing led to the other, brother, and Maikito and this *Pelúo* character have now been in business for the last few months.'

'And you've kept this a secret from me all this time?'

'Man, I only found out about all this when Maikito asked me yesterday if I wanted to work for him.'

I looked at my friend with my thumbs hooked in my pockets. 'I don't get it, Manuel. You say that Maikito's been doing this for months, but only offered you a job yesterday. Didn't he already have his own guys working for him?'

'Well, that's where this story goes a bit nuts. *El Michael* already had four guys working for him. Derek "*el Barriga*" Durante and Stevie Bonifacio, two dockyard electricians, and a mate of his called Freddy Malaspina and his son Freddy *el*

Chico. Freddy '*Chico*' bought a Beeweez[11] last week and straightaway crashed it head-on against the little sentry hut just behind Prince Edward's Gate. Total loss *dejó la moto, compá,* but the worst thing is he broke his right leg in three fucking places, man, and he's going to have to spend at least three months on crutches. But, you know what they say, don't they ... one man's fucking loss is another man's fucking gain.'

'No way,' I blurted with a tinge of jealousy.

'What's wrong, man?' Manu (alert and tuned in as always) replied. 'Aren't you happy for me, or what?'

'Of course I'm happy, *coño!*' I assured him. 'What a question to ask me! It's just that ... well ... you know....'

'Yeah, man,' he butted in before I could articulate what I felt. 'I know, man. You also want a piece of the action, don't you, man?'

'Well, if you put it that way, bro....'

'Fucking hell, Alex, do you really think I'm going to leave you behind just like that. Man, *somos colegas, no?* Blood brothers, and all that shit. I've already spoken with Maikito,' he added, placing an arm around my neck, 'and he's told me that if one of the others falls ill some day or if they go on holiday, we'll give you a call and pay you to help us shift a few boxes. And

---

[11] A Beeweez – a two-stroke scooter popular in Gibraltar in the Eighties and Nineties (llanito).

not only that, *compá*. If Michael's plans work out and he gets to buy a second Phantom before the end of the year, *pó* there's no messing about – you can join us straightaway. So don't look so sad, Alex, *pisha,* please,' he said, removing his arm and patting me affectionately on the head. 'I'm not going to let you join the fire brigade and grow all fat like that *gordinflón* at the careers fair, you know what I'm saying, bro?'

One of the oddities of having *el Pantera* for a father was that you had a shedload of half-brothers and half-sisters scattered around the Rock. Manu had at least fifteen of them, and they came in all shapes, ages and sizes – a gallery of assorted waifs and cast-offs that popped up at random intervals all over town. 'You see that lad/lass over there,' my friend would say, tapping me on the arm and gesturing with his eyes towards some young guy dressed in a bellboy's uniform, perhaps, or a ponytailed schoolgirl riding on the back of a motorbike. 'I think we're related.'

Manu never once told me what he felt about these estranged blood relatives of his, but there was always a wistful look on his face as he followed them with his eyes down Main Street, Irish Town and other locations. Was he maybe wondering how things might have turned out had he been on speaking terms with his *hermanastros* and *hermanastras*? Was he regretting that he had never approached them in the past? Or was it more along the lines of: 'Fucking hell, Dad, did you *really* have to fuck everything in sight in a small, overcrowded place like Gibraltar?'

The only sibling Manu had any real contact with was his half-brother Michael, the eldest of *el Pantera's* sons. Michael, or *el*

Maikito as those closest to the lad knew him, was a stocky, handsome, dark-haired fellow who, like Manu and most of his half-brothers and half-sisters, had nothing to do with the randy old fucker who begot him. He lived in the South District – in a shabby alleyway that bordered the back of Saint Joseph's Church and whose most distinguishing feature was the shard-like brown glass that some *hijo de puta* had sprinkled over the top of the wall separating it from the church grounds. He was a confident, streetwise kind of guy and, like many other poorly educated young Gibraltarians of his generation, trod a fine line between legality and criminality, topping up his £57-a-week salary as a dockyard machinist with a bit of dope-dealing on the side. Once or twice a month he'd tramp up to Macphail's Passage with a bag of *japonesas*[12] or some *churros* for Manu's mum. My mate – usually so switched on – had got it into his head that Maikito visited Mariadelaida to talk about *el Pantera* and what a bastard he had been to them both, but from the uncomfortable looks on their faces whenever we chanced upon them in the flat (and their habit of frequently barricading themselves in the main bedroom) it was clear that there was more to it than that. Still, valuing my life as I did, I never voiced any of my suspicions to my friend and let him believe whatever he wanted. So his mum was fucking her ex's son and running the risk of presenting her own son one day with a weird-as-fuck amalgam of brother and nephew? What

---

[12] Fried, cream-filled doughnuts popular in Gibraltar and the Campo de Gibraltar.

the hell did it have to do with me? At least there was no blood tie between her and her secret boyfriend (which was more than could be said, incidentally, for *el Pantera's* relationships, a substantial number of which – if we are to believe those wagging Gibraltarian tongues – were consanguineous). Besides, there was something endearing *'y super nice'* about the dockyard machinist and part-time drug pusher. Easy-going and innately friendly, a sucker for talking about football, boxing and Formula One, he was one of those salt-of-the-earth types whose lives are so uncomplicated and easy-to-read, so devoid of pretence and malice, that it is hard to hold a grudge against them. Always upbeat and smiling, determined at all costs to see the best in people, he was the sort of bloke who'd do anything for a mate, the kind for whom no favour was ever too big or too small. Naturally, I didn't like that he was sleeping with the woman who – at this stage in my life – I took to be the incarnation of physical perfection. But the more I got to know him, the more pragmatic I became about the whole affair. If someone's got to be doing it, I reasoned philosophically, it might as well be *un tío canela* like Maikito Canilla.[13]

If something is cheaper on one side of a border, sooner or later someone is going to smuggle it across to the other side and flog it for a profit. This is one of the cornerstones of borderland life, an unwritten rule that comes with the territory. Because the border between Gibraltar and Spain is

---

[13] Un tío canela – a top bloke (llanito).

short and well patrolled, Gibraltarian smugglers have traditionally avoided the overland route, preferring instead to ferry their illicit cargo by sea. In the Forties and Fifties, it was chopped tobacco (commonly known in this area as *picadura*) that formed the bulk of this maritime Hispano-Gibraltarian trade. Later, as the Spanish economy picked up and the Andalusian smoking palate became more refined, the preference was for pre-rolled American cigarettes, especially Winston and Marlboro. The main way of transporting these cigarettes was in low-hulled, British-made speedboats known as Phantoms. Before the border fully opened in 1985, only *el Pantera* and a handful of other Gibraltarian guys were involved in this smuggling game. They went around town low-fiving each other and mocking *los majarones* who had to do a nine-to-five job for a living, bragging that they were the only ones with *cojones* on the Rock. 'Nobody here can touch us!' was something you'd hear them say in bars like the Bahía or the Venture Inn. 'We are the owners of this fucking place!'

The truth, however, was slightly more complex than all that. To set up a cross-border smuggling gang you needed contacts on the other side – solid, dependable contacts who wouldn't leave you in the lurch when the chips were down. Establishing these sorts of connections is not easy at the best of times, but when you have an eight-foot, barbed wire-topped fence separating you from your potential business partners it becomes distinctly complicated. That is why dudes like *el Pantera* – old hands who were around before the border closed and who already had their contacts in Spain from this period – had a near-monopoly on smuggling during those years. Not only did they have the know-how and the balls to carry out the job; they also had their *socios* on the Spanish side who would receive the smuggled boxes of tobacco and then pass them on to their clandestine network of distributors and retailers across the rest of the peninsula.

But then came 5 February 1985 – the day when the frontier gates were thrown open and the old system collapsed. Henceforth any Gibraltarian could drive across the border and speak to his neighbours in La Línea and other parts of *el Campo*. Which, of course, was tantamount to saying that anyone could form a cross-border smuggling gang. This is exactly what Manu's half-brother Michael did one wintry afternoon in March 1985, shortly after buying the Phantom from his born-again dockyard colleague. Fortified by three pints of Stella and half a tab of Ritalin, the twenty-three-year-old walked into *el Bar Finlandia* on *la calle Castellar* and met up with Juan '*el Zurrapa*' Avellano, a small-town *linense* hoodlum who was a distant relation of Nuria Canilla, Maikito's half-Spanish mum. *El Zurrapa* put him in touch with *el Pelúo,* a friend of his from his schooldays and ex-*Cruz Roja* volunteer who had been kicked out of the organisation for embezzling funds destined for the famine victims in Ethiopia. The would-be smugglers met three days later at *el Bar Manolo,* in the La Línea neighbourhood of La Atunara. *El Pelúo* had booked the private dining room at the back of the establishment, and it was there that the two men shook hands, spoke for some moments about their mutual acquaintance *el Zurrapa*, ordered some tapas and beers and – while making chitchat about women, football and cars – discovered that they shared a passion for *el Real Betis Balompié*. 'Well, fuck me,' *el Pelúo* chuckled in Spanish, holding his glass an inch or two under his mouth, 'don't tell me you have *béticos* in Gibraltar as well!' 'Of course we do,' Maikito responded good-naturedly, 'and *madridistas* and *sevillistas* and *culés* and all the others too. We are not all Liverpool or Manchester United fans on the Rock, *amigacho!*'

Maikito and *el Pelúo* spent the rest of that first evening talking about football and smuggling matters, their conversation swinging more and more towards *temas beticistas* as the night wore on in a thickening fug of cigarette smoke and alcohol fumes. When Manu's half-brother finally stepped out of *el Bar Manolo*, it was close to midnight and *la calle Santa María*, the street dividing the beach from the buildings behind him, was totally deserted. A thin mist had drifted in from the sea, adding a supernatural tinge to the surroundings and muffling the sound of his own footsteps. Hiccupping drunkenly, not even bothering to put on the helmet he kept clipped to his rear panniers, he jumped on his motorbike – an old Honda XL250 – and rode off in the direction of the frontier gates, swerving around speed bumps and hitting others full-on, beeping his horn at the seagulls resting on the tops of lampposts, shouting 'yes yes fucking yes!' and '*de puta madre, compá!*' to himself as he veered away from the seafront and approached the roundabout connecting *la calle Torrijos* with *la avenida Príncipe de Asturias*.

When Maikito woke up in his flat in Gibraltar's South District the next morning, there was a pile of puke beside his bed and his lower and upper eyelids felt as if they had been stitched together with invisible thread. He also had dozens of tiny red marks around his left eye – something which puzzled him at first, but which became less of a mystery when he remembered that, trying to regain control of his bike after a failed wheelie attempt near La Línea's municipal football stadium, he had jolted forward and hit his face against one of the Honda's wing mirrors. 'Jesus fucking Christ!' the dockyard machinist yawned, climbing out of bed. 'I must have been more pissed than I thought!'

The first thing Maikito did after a quick shower was to call his mate Keith *el Penique* and ask him if he was still selling his VW delivery van. *El Penique*, a hard bargainer if ever there was one, said he could have the vehicle for three hundred quid, but that he'd have to buy his own tax disk and jump-start the old girl himself at Grand Parade, where she was currently stranded with a flat battery. Michael grudgingly agreed to his conditions – and then set about gathering the team for the Gibraltarian side of the operation: an all-important *copiloto* who would ride with him in the launch, a lookout with a walkie-talkie who'd radio the guys from his perch at the top of the Rock if he spotted anything dodgy out at sea, and two general dogsbodies, or *cargadores,* who'd drive the tobacco from the bonded store opposite North Front Cemetery to wherever Maikito and his *copiloto* were waiting to load up the Phantom.

Now, here's where things got a little surprising. In the calculations he had drawn up weeks earlier, Maikito had anticipated that it would take him a minimum of two or three weeks before he could find the right guys for the new outfit, but such was the desire back then among young Gibraltarian men to be part of the contraband scene that, by one o'clock that afternoon, before he had even shaken off his hangover or collected his second-hand van, he already had his four blokes and three others prepared to replace them in case they dropped out of the project. 'Well, I'll be damned,' Maikito reflected, plopping a couple of Alka-Seltzers into a glass of tap water. 'Who'd have thought that forming a smuggling gang would be such a piece of piss?'

———— ·•━◆━•· ————

I quit school on 10 December 1985, two months after Manu and two days after my fifteenth birthday. Those eight weeks without Manuel at Bayside Comprehensive were incredibly dull and uninspiring, but I told myself I would soon be treading in his footsteps and joining his half-brother's smuggling ring. That's how things would surely proceed: *El Maikito* would buy a second boat, *el Manu* would persuade him to take me on, and I'd shortly be with them *echando cajas*.[14]

Fate, however, had different ideas. Just three and a half months after *Freddy el Chico* wrote off his motorbike and Manu replaced him in the gang, *el Pelúo* rang Maikito to tell him he was finding it hard to shift the forty to sixty boxes of tobacco that his partner was bringing him each week. 'It's just that everybody and his bleeding dog is bringing Winston into La Línea these days, Michael,' he said apologetically in Spanish. 'And I don't have access to the heavy-duty buyers that some of these *cabrones* have. I'm sorry, Maikito, *pero* we're going to have to limit ourselves to fifteen or twenty boxes per week until I find some better contacts.'

---

[14] Echando cajas – working as a loader in a tobacco smuggling gang (llanito).

El Pelúo's lack of selling power effectively torpedoed Michael's dream of buying a second Phantom and, by extension, any chance I had of joining the brothers on a full-time or even part-time basis. Manu, seeing how disappointed I was, tried to cheer me up by again suggesting I could stand in for the other gang members when they fell ill or went on holiday. But I already knew enough about the contraband trade to realise this was never going to happen. Limping, with a bad back, with a bad case of the shits, *con un* hangover *tremendo* – not one of these predicaments would've stopped those bastards going out on the boat and making easy money.

And that's how it was for nearly six months. No illnesses or holidays, no unexpected telephone calls, no doorbells ringing in the middle of the night. Instead – a venomous silence, a steadily widening rift between Manu and me. Now and again, yes, I'd see him strutting down Main Street or Irish Town in his flashy Billabong jacket and Caterpillar boots, a couple of heavy gold chains hanging from his neck. Sometimes I'd be on my way home from the Employment and Training Board, where I would go every Tuesday and Thursday for the sake of *doing something*. Other times I'd be heading down to my maternal grandparents' place in Glacis Estate, where I went to watch football matches from their tenth-floor, Victoria Stadium-facing bedroom window. *El Manu* had always been a sturdy and thick-set fellow, but now that he was spending most of his spare time at the Ocean Heights Gym he looked like a teenage Conan the Barbarian, his biceps bulging like overripe *chirimoyas* from under his sleeves. He also seemed brasher, louder, more cocky than ever, as if being *liado con el*

Winston[15] compelled him in some way to act like a stereotypical hoodlum. '*Quillo, Alex!*' he'd roar, disengaging from whatever girl was hanging on to his arm. 'Long time no see, brother! Let's go and have a few games of Space Invaders at the Arcade, *anda!*'

But I always refused. Pretended I had to help my dad with one thing or the other. Would have been like a dagger to the heart, after all – sitting next to him with all his muscles and his fancy medallions.

Ironically, what brought us back together in the end were not words of friendship or even the memory of better days, but the vacuum left behind by another person's misfortune. Remember how Freddy *el Chico* had crashed his Yamaha Beeweez against the old stone hut past Prince Edward's Gate? Well, that family must have been labouring under some gypsy malediction, because nine months later *Freddy el Mayor* fell from a scaffold tower at Coaling Island and shattered his pelvis. *El Maikito* wanted to replace him with another of his work colleagues, some guy called *Jason el Chato,* but Manu argued that *el Chato* (who apart from being snub-nosed was a chubster weighing about twenty stones) was too fat and out of shape to be lugging Winston boxes in the dark. That same evening I got a call from my mate on my father's house phone. His voice sounded unsteady and steeped in saliva, as if he had smoked three or four joints. *What the fuck does he want?* I thought, listening to him rabbit on about a new

---

[15] 'Involved in the Winston trade.'

pair of Levi's 501 jeans and a parrot he was thinking of buying for his mum. Is he winding me up? Has he called me just to fuck with me? Standing there with John Dennis Leslie watching me from the other side of the living room, I felt pissed off and offended and was on the point of sending him to hell and putting the phone down. Then he blurted out the words I thought I'd never hear:

'Anyway, bro, enough bullshit: the reason I'm calling you is because it's all sorted. Yes, man, it's finally happening! I've spoken with *el Maikito* and he's given me the go-ahead for you to come and join us. What do you think, bro? You're one of the boys now!'

For a moment I held the phone against my ear, wondering if I had heard right. Then, turning my back on my father to stop him scrutinising my features, tightening my grip on the plastic receiver, I smiled like a kid who has just seen his greatest Christmas wish come true.

At the height of the smuggling boom, there must have been seven or eight hundred young Gibraltarian men involved in the covert transportation of tobacco from the Rock to Spain. The Government of Gibraltar knew what they were doing, but didn't ask too many questions – the sale of duty-paid tobacco providing the administration with an estimated £90 million a year at a time when the privatisation of the dockyard was threatening to deal a knock-out blow to the local economy. The smugglers called themselves the 'Winston Boys' and were, by and large, a colourful lot. Sure, one or two of them kept their heads down and avoided the limelight, but the majority of those guys couldn't resist flaunting their new-found wealth. Everything they did – from the way they cut their hair (piled high on top, but with a mantle of curls tumbling onto their necks) to the sorts of cars they drove (Celicas, Preludes and American imports like Ford Mustangs and Pontiac Firebirds) – was designed to impress, to arouse envy, to let people know they were members of the tobacco 'fraternity.' Coming in most cases from deprived or working-class backgrounds, having been told at school they would never amount to much, the 'Winston Boys' were on a mission to show off, to let their former critics and doubters know that they were now rolling in cash. During the summer months they'd strut around with T-shirts or singlets draped over their bare pecs and shoulders, sporting Ray-Bans and *chanclas moras,*[16] togged up in skin-tight Levi jeans worn so low you'd often catch glimpses of fluffy pubic hair. Listening to them speak, you'd hear words like *keo,*[17] *papiti*[18] and *floosh* – a snarly, gangsterish argot that was more or less understood by everybody under thirty, but never failed to rile those in authority. Almost all the guys wore thick gold chains adorned with *medallones* – big, showy pieces cast in the likeness of keys, coins, pistols, daggers, treasure chests, boxing gloves, crucifixes, and, of course, the ubiquitous *Virgen del Carmen* and *Virgen del Rocío* figures – and carried inky profiles of Jesus Christ, Che Guevara or Camarón de la Isla tattooed on their backs and chests. Behaviourally, they oscillated between hippie-like lethargy and sudden spurts of hypermasculine aggression – arguing loudly with each other, getting violently

---

[16] Chanclas moras – Moroccan babouche leather slippers (llanito).

[17] Keo – home (llanito).

[18] Papiti – food, especially takeaway food (llanito).

drunk, beeping their car horns at the slightest hold-up, calling other drivers 'cunts', 'shitheads', '*hijoputas*' and '*cabrones de mierda*', wanting to get out of their cars and fight with anybody who dared remonstrate with them. A favourite macho speciality of theirs was to drive up and down the length of Eastern Beach with their windows down and flamenco blaring from their Pioneer car speakers. If they saw a pretty girl walking past, they'd slow to a crawl and, leaning out of the window, ignoring the beeping cars behind them, sliding their Ray-Bans rakishly down their noses, start taunting their 'prey':

'Where are you walking so fast, *shoshito mío?*'[19]

'Me? Nowhere.'

'Then why don't you jump in my car and come with me for a spin?'

'Because I don't want to, that's why!'

'Come on, *shoshi,* don't be like that. I know this really amazing place you're really going to love.'

'And how do you know I'm really going to love this really amazing place?'

'I know because, when I take you there and do the things I'm going to do to you, *te vas a quedar en la mismísima gloria, chiquilla!*'[20]

---

[19] Shoshi, shosho, shoshito – affectionate (though in certain cases sexist or derogatory) terms for a girl or a woman (llanito/Andalusian Spanish).

[20] 'You are going to be in seventh heaven, darling!'

On Saturday and Sunday afternoons you'd see big groups of them sitting with their pints of snakebite at *el Seawave* in Catalan Bay or *el Dolphin* up at *el Quarry*. Banded together in this way, they always became noisier and more animated, more likely to poke fun at waiters, waitresses, *maricones, gordos,* young girls, disabled people and other passing soft targets. Once, as I was walking down the ramp leading to the Dolphin's outdoor terrace area, I saw one of them arguing with Larbi, the bar's middle-aged Moroccan waiter. Larbi – who had a cast in his left eye and looked like a cross between Super Mario and a sumo wrestler – was complaining about having to pick out chewing gum and cigarette butts from their pint glasses; he was saying how much it all repelled him. *'Po, safi,'* the nineteen- or twenty-year-old kid before him responded, picking up a glass full of butts and calmly letting it smash on the ground. 'That's the end of your problems, isn't it, *compá!'*

I used to hate all this shit before joining Maikito's lot. I hated the loudness, the bluster, the undertones of menace. However, once I was part of Michael's gang, all these reservations evaporated and I began to act just like the other smugglers. In only a matter of weeks, I was dressing like them, talking like them, wolf-whistling at girls, frequenting *el Bahía* and *el Seawave* and *el Dolphin* and their other favourite haunts, using the same names they employed when referring to each other (*el Kiki, el Ginger, el Fred Astaire, el Matón, el Lionheart, el Chaqueta Cuero, el Pishposh*), as well as to different members of the local police force (*la Bombi, el Mojón, el Mister Magoo, la Charlie, el duo Sacapuntas*). Most comically of all, I even got myself a huge medallion carved in the shape of *la Virgen del Rocío.* I bought it in Joyería Matías, a jeweller's in the centre of La Línea, as all the local jewellery shops had run out of *Virgen del Rocío* and *Virgen del Carmen* medallions due to the unprecedented demand for them! It was heavy and finely decorated, and when I rolled onto my front in the middle of the night (like all good 'Winston Boys', I didn't even take off the damn thing to go to sleep!) the Virgin's crown would dig into my chest, causing me to wake up in the mornings with a series of tiny, semi-circular bruises on my pecs.

But I'm getting ahead of myself. Let's go back to June 1986, shall we, when Manu called me on the phone to let me know there was a place for me on the gang. When I met him a couple of hours later, he explained that everyone in the outfit had a code name for when we spoke with each other over the radio. He said his code name was 'Scarface' and his brother's '*el Lover Boy*.' Derek, our lumbering fatso of a lookout, went by the name of '*el Flaquito*'; and *el Stevie*, the copilot, was 'Mr Coppell'. These names, he made clear, were only to be used for 'work purposes' and never in public. 'Anyway,' he continued, grinning mischievously, 'I spoke to my brother last night about you and we've decided to call you *el Ojo Tuerto*.'[21] '*El Ojo Tuerto*?' I asked, pulling a face. 'But there's nothing wrong with my eyes!' '*Precisamente*,' Manu replied with a beaming smile. 'We don't want anything which sheds too much light on who you really are, do we, bro?'

---

[21] 'The one-eyed one.'

And so it was that I joined Maikito's gang under the rather unflattering code name of *el Ojo Tuerto*. My role was that of second loader, working alongside my mate in the VW van. Whenever *el Pelúo* radioed through from La Línea saying he was ready for another fifteen or twenty boxes, the two of us would head down to the warehouse at North Front and buy the goods with the money that Maikito had previously given to us. We'd tie each box with a length of strong twine, leaving a loop on top to use as a handle, and then carry the merchandise, two cases at a time, into the van. We'd then sit in the front seats, waiting to receive the call on our FM transceiver from Maikito's *copiloto* Stevie to get going. Once this came through, *el Manu* (who didn't even have a learner's licence!) would drive the boxes to one of our usual loading places: Eastern Beach, Sandy Bay, the rocks to the north of Catalan Bay, or, during times of raging *levante,* the local boatowners' pier known as *el Camber*. Every so often, when the weather was about to change for the worse and we needed the Phantom to set off as soon as possible, we loaded up at our own special, semi-private 'mooring': the short landing jetty beside Western Beach, the MOD-controlled beach just south of the frontier gates and adjacent to the airport runway. Only people working for the MOD could berth their boats in this fenced-off, padlocked area, but Maikito had acquired a copy of the passkey from Charlie Canilla, an uncle of his who worked as a GSP officer and kept a small pleasure boat moored next to the Gibraltar Security Police's RIBs at Western Beach.

How Maikito came to obtain this all-important key, incidentally, is a story worth telling in its own right. Tramping up Main Street one Friday afternoon, he spotted his uncle

Charlie sitting with his copper mates at one of the tables outside the Piazza Grill. Some were having coffees and some were having *chicos*,[22] but all, without exception, were in that hyper-animated state that middle-aged Gibraltarian men slip into when arguing about football and local politics. Thinking 'here's my chance,' *el Maikito* sat next to his uncle, had a coffee with him, picked up a copy of the *Chronicle* lying on the table and, while the oldies were busy arguing about *el 'Manshehta'* and *el Barça*, nicked the bunch of keys *el Charlie* carried attached to one of his belt hoops. He then got up and, after excusing himself with the minimum of fuss, took the entire set to Mister Minit in the Arcade, where he told the Scottish guy behind the counter that he'd give him three hundred pounds on top of what he normally charged if he copied all the keys for him in under half an hour. 'Aye, fella, not a problem,' the big man in the green apron said, 'you'll have yer keys in twenty minutes for that amount of money, son.' As soon as the duplicates were ready, Maikito paid the guy the promised sum and then made his way back to the Piazza Grill, where Charlie and his mates were now debating whether Bryan Robson had a greater sense of tactical awareness than Gordon Strachan. Retaking his seat, he ordered a coffee, listened to their conversation for a few minutes, took a sip of his beverage, and then, just as the oldies were 'transitioning' from football to local politics, leaned forward and adeptly clipped the purloined bunch of keys onto the same cotton hoop from which they had been hanging earlier. '*Pues bueno*, gentlemen,' he said, taking a last slurp of his coffee before getting up. 'Politics is not really my

---

[22] Un chico – a half-pint of beer (llanito).

thing, so I'm off to do a couple of errands. Let's see if one day we get together and go out on your boat, uncle Charlie,' he added, affectionately placing his hands on his *tío's* shoulders. 'Would love to spend an afternoon fishing with you in the bay!'

When I first started working as a loader, Maikito was paying Manu and me six quid per delivered box – two-thirds of what his lookout earned, and half of what his *copiloto* was receiving. Some weeks my mate and I were raking in close to four hundred quid; other weeks (and there were more bad weeks than good ones during those early days) we'd be lucky if we went back home with sixty pounds in our pockets. Considering that we only worked a handful of hours each week, it was not bad money – but when viewed as a regular income ... well, it wasn't that great either.

The fluctuating size of our weekly pay packet in many ways mirrored the roller-coaster nature of our working routine. When we were driving the van from the warehouse to wherever we were loading up the Phantom, things were reasonably exciting – but for the most part we simply sat in the stationary vehicle, smoking, chatting, listening to the radio, waiting to get the all-clear to set off from the retailer's depot. The loading itself, however, was always a frantic, short-lived, adrenaline-filled affair – with constant stumblings, boxes flying all over the place and lots of grunting, shouting and swearing. Once this stage was complete, it was back to sitting in the van again – this time in case Maikito and 'Mr Coppell' encountered complications out at sea and the boxes needed to be taken off the launch and brought back into Gibraltar for storage and safekeeping. Maybe, for instance, the weather was too rough for them to circumnavigate Europa Point. Maybe there was a Spanish customs boat sitting off the beach at La Atunara, preventing them from unloading the merchandise. Whenever something like this happened, we'd have to drive down to one of the local beaches and carry the boxes from the launch back to the van. This was an easy enough operation, but we always had to be cautious in case the Gibraltarian police swooped down on us and arrested us on the technicality that we were *importing cigarettes without a valid import permit*. It was not a common occurrence, but it did happen from time to time – the resident constabulary eager to prove to the world that, despite Spanish and international press claims, they were not giving the local smugglers *an entirely free ride*. The consequences usually weren't severe – a verbal warning, or, if you were really unlucky, a trip to the magistrates' court and a twenty-quid fine – but they'd almost always confiscate the tobacco cases, which meant that we'd end up paying for the impounded consignment out of our own pockets, *un verdadero coñazo*, as Maikito would have said.

Once – the episode is still vividly engraved in my mind – we had to fetch the boxes out of the Phantom because *la Turbo*, one of the high-speed interception boats belonging to *el Servicio de Vigilancia Aduanera*, Spain's Customs Surveillance Unit, was sitting off the first buoy at Eastern Beach and there was no way that *el Lover Boy* and 'Mr Coppell' could have navigated past her on their way to La Atunara. As we stood on the shore hoisting the cases out of the vessel, we suddenly got a call on the radio from Derek our lookout saying that a couple of cop cars were racing down Winston Churchill

Avenue with their sirens on. Agitatedly, not wanting to be caught red-handed, we put the boxes back into the boat and pushed her out to sea. By the time the cops got to the beach fifty seconds later, *el Maikito* had taken the launch to a position sixty or seventy yards offshore, halfway between the stationary *aduana* boat and the shoreline, and Manu and I were sitting with soaking wet trousers in the empty VW van. 'Good evening, officer,' Manuel smiled when the first cop knocked on the van window with his torch pointing down at us. 'You've also come to enjoy the lovely sea view?'

What did my father think of my nocturnal pursuits? Well, judging from the look on his face whenever he caught me creeping back into the property at an ungodly hour, he couldn't have been very happy about my doings – his bloodshot eyes made that abundantly clear. On one occasion he even swore at me from his bedroom and shouted – in a croaky, half-asleep voice – that it was about time I got 'a normal job like everybody else.' Nevertheless, it would be a mistake to think that he frequently voiced his displeasure in front of me. Take the days I had breakfast at the Market Tavern and wouldn't come back home until nine-thirty or ten in the morning. As often as not, he'd be sitting there immobile before the television, his right hand resting like a dead crab on his pot belly, his eyelids drowsily veiling most of his eyes. He'd grunt a quick hello and then focus back on the screen, his posture radiating an almost comatose indifference. Possibly his reluctance to comment on what I was doing had something to do with the cash-filled envelopes I left for him now and again on the living room coffee table – but, having said that, I do not think that John Dennis Leslie was a man to be bought off with on-and-off hundred-quid payments. Pessimistic by nature, convinced that life was no more than a long series of trials from cradle to grave, he was one of those men whose lives are so disconnected from their surroundings, so crushed by their own cynicism, that they can't even summon up the energy to verbalise their feelings. Occasionally, yes, he'd spiral off into fierce torrents of indignation, loudly declaiming how much better things were in the old days ... but you always had the sense that these outbursts were more of an attempt to explain – and justify – to himself how and why he had fallen so low, than an effort to engage directly with whatever was happening around him.

Our biggest problem during those first couple of years, however, was not what my father or even Manu's mother thought about our nightly activities; it was that *el Pelúo* was still finding it hard to sell the boxes we delivered to him. Other gangs were smuggling 100, 150, maybe 200 cases of Winston a week; we were lucky if we managed 20 or 25. Maikito raised the issue a couple of times with his counterpart across the border, but the Spaniard kept fobbing him off with different excuses – assuring him that he would be driving soon to Sevilla to meet up with a new buyer, blaming his lack of selling power on the *Ministerio de Sanidad's* latest anti-smoking campaign, complaining about the exorbitant amounts he was having to pay his own loaders. Towards the beginning of 1989 things got so bad that Maikito and Stevie were only going out on the launch once or twice a month. Those were the worst days by far – stuck at home waiting to hear from *el Pelúo*, knowing that there were other guys out there making money while we sat on our arses watching TV or listening to music. 'Trust us to end up lumbered with that useless fucker as our contact in Spain,' Manu would say to me, pulling a sour face. 'That idiot couldn't get his shit together if his life depended on it!'

Manu may have exaggerated a touch, but there was still something depressing and disempowering about those long periods of inactivity. It wasn't just that we were hanging around like mugs and earning far less than the loaders in some of the stronger outfits; there was something about being stuck at home that undermined our confidence and sense of self-worth, that threatened our 'bad boy' identity. Though we strutted and swaggered like the best of them, we somehow felt inferior to the other 'Winston Boys', not quite the real McCoy. To compensate for these feelings of inadequacy, Manu and I went into town every Friday afternoon and squandered every last penny in our possession. We'd snap up all kinds of crap: leather jackets, jeans, gold earrings, cowboy boots, Calvin Klein perfume, football tops, trainers, bandanas, *medallones,* Whitesnake and Camarón de la Isla LPs and CDs. We bought these items not because we wanted or needed them, but because buying stuff somehow brought structure to our patternless lives. 'Come on, Alex!' my friend would shout from outside my front door every Friday afternoon. 'Get a move on, will you – we've only got two hours left before the shops close!' 'Coming, bro,' I'd reply, popping my head out of the living room window. 'I'm nearly ready. *Solo me falta ponerme un poco de* gel *en el pelo.*' [23]

---

[23] 'Just need to put a little gel on my hair, that's all.'

By the start of 1990, three and a half years had passed and precious little had changed – we were still earning a reasonable amount of money, but spending it all on needless trifles. Manu had usurped Stevie's copiloting role by this stage (*el Stevie*, a rarity among smugglers, had quit his dockyard job and gone to study Chemistry in the UK) and was regularly accompanying his half-brother on the launch. For me it was a bit disappointing to be working alongside somebody else in the van, but the new guy – a scrawny ponytailed plumber called Richita Desoiza – was not a bad sort. With the extra money he was making as a copilot, Manu had bought himself a second-hand Pontiac Firebird that Gerry Bonfiglio, a 'Winston Boy' turned *gayumbero*,[24] wanted to get rid of. It was a flashy cherry-red beast with a white strip painted on the bonnet, and we used it to chauffeur *la Susana, la Jennie* and other of 'our bitches' (as my mate unkindly referred to our female hangers-on) from one beach bar to the other. Now that he was officially Maikito's wingman, too, the nineteen-year-old Manu had more influence over the way things were done in the gang, and he and his brother would often find themselves at loggerheads. Usually, the main bone of contention was *el Pelúo's* uselessness as a contact. 'Why don't we find ourselves some other guy to work with, Maikito?' Manu would say, his forehead puckering into a mesh of frown lines. 'Honestly, bro. I don't know why you keep working with that useless *mamón sloppy*[25] *de mierda*.' 'How many times do I have to tell you?' Michael would respond, angrily shaking his head. '*El Pelúo* and I are good mates. I'm

---

[24] Gayumbero – a drug trafficker who ferries drugs in a speedboat (llanito/Andalusian Spanish).

[25] Sloppy – offensive term for a Spaniard (llanito).

not going to drop him just because you fucking feel like it. In any case, he's told me he's got a new buyer in his sights. You need to start cutting the bloke some fucking slack!'

El Manu would usually back off at this point and take his anger with him to *el Piccadilly* or some of the other bars that we frequented during the evenings, where he'd complain for hours that his brother was too nice for his own good. I didn't particularly enjoy listening to him slag off his own flesh and blood in this way, but I had to recognise that he had a point. Maikito's continued loyalty to *el Pelúo,* after all, was costing us a lot of money – and making us bored and restless. Ten, fifteen, sometimes twenty days would pass before the *linense* called us to say he was ready to receive 'the next shipment' ... and it often felt we were being punished because of the guy's ineptitude. Things got so boring that at one stage I even considered taking on a part-time job as a lifeguard – and only stopped myself when *el Manu* caustically told me that lifeguards were nearly all nerdy sixth-formers and first-year university students: 'Can you imagine working with those dorks? *Fu,* man! It'd be like being back at Bayside again!'

As for our increasingly intermittent smuggling runs, they were going well enough. Once, Manu and Maikito got tailgated and almost rammed by one of the Spanish customs boats some two hundred yards off Sandy Bay. Manu joked about the episode once they were back on solid ground, but I could see from Maikito's unsmiling expression that it had been no laughing matter. Another time bad weather forced them to return to Gib with an undelivered cargo. As we were unloading the Phantom at the building site between *el Technical College* and *el Camber* (nowadays the site of the multimillion-pound Cormorant Quay development), a fat policeman suddenly came running down a mound of builders' rubble towards us. 'Right, lads!' *el gordinflón* cried in a strong Gibraltarian accent. 'The game's up!' I'm not kidding – that's what the lard-arse shouted! Laughable, really – although he and his mates still ended up pulling us to one side and confiscating all twenty of our Winston cases....

But these were exceptions to the rule, relatively minor blips. Most of the time we loaded the launch, delivered the tobacco to *el Pelúo's* minions in La Atunara and had the vessel berthed at Sheppard's Marina within ninety minutes. The only shame, as Manu never ceased to complain, was that we had a fucking useless cunt – and not *un hombre de confianza* – working with us on the other side of the border.

This, then, is the way that things went for a number of years – and this is how they would have continued had it not been for one of those unexpected rotations of Fortune's wheel. Actually, it was not one but two sudden turnings of the old Big-Sixer. The first of these came on 23 March 1990, when a Moroccan-born Spanish national crossed the border into Gibraltar from Spain and made his way to the Bahía Bar, just opposite the Waterport Roundabout. The name of this man was Abdullatif Al-Jaouhari and he had travelled to Gib from Ceuta. A brooding, square-jawed fellow, somewhat pale for a Maghrebi but with the build of a javelin thrower or a nightclub bouncer. He wore blue-lensed sunglasses and a fur-trimmed leather bomber jacket and had what looked like a hammer and sickle (but was in fact an AK-47 laid over a double-headed arrow) tattooed on his left earlobe.

Smoothing back his thick black hair, he walked into the bar, ordered a coffee, then picked up the copy of the *Gibraltar Chronicle,* the Rock's only daily newspaper, lying on the counter before him. When the coffee arrived, he pushed the paper aside and asked Mehdi the barman if he was Moroccan. Delighted to hear somebody speaking Arabic, *el Mehdi* replied with something like, 'Well, of course! You wouldn't find any of these Gibraltarian lazy arses working behind a bar, would you!' Anyway, it turned out that both of them were originally from the Souss-Massa-Drâa region in central Morocco ... and soon the two *compatriotas* were chatting about the great earthquake of 1960, how much Agadir had changed over the years and whether King Hassan – may Allah bestow blessings on him and his family! – would live much longer. This carried on for ten, maybe fifteen minutes; then the Spanish-Moroccan fella told the barman he had come to *el Bahía* because he had heard that the place was popular with 'the local tobacco people.' He said that he wanted to see if any of these guys were interested in a little proposition he had for them. 'You wouldn't know if any of these *muchachos* are here in this establishment today, would you?' Al-Jaouhari asked, switching at this point from Arabic to perfect Castilian Spanish. Mehdi replied that he doubted it very much – it was only eleven in the morning and most of the Winston guys, being lazy arses, only came to the Bahía after three. 'But let me have a quick look,' he added in his throaty Moroccan-Gibraltarian Spanish, 'you never know with these *niñatos!*'

Now here's where things get interesting. Mehdi scans the faces on the streetside terrace and, just as he fears, sees only old men and one or two drunken bums hunched over their beers and long-empty coffee cups. Then he notices Manu sitting among them, having a Heineken with yours truly. 'Isn't that *el Pantera's* son?' he thinks, momentarily forgetting that *el Pantera* has little truck with his own children. *Of course he is,* he answers his own question. Breaking into a smile, happy to help his new mate, he points at Manu and tells Abdullatif that the kid's father is one of the big capos of the local contraband scene. 'Maybe he can put you in touch with his dad,' he says, taking the empty coffee cup from the counter and wondering if the guy will leave him a nice fat tip.

And so, next thing you know, Abdullatif is sitting at our table, telling us in Spanish that he has heard about Manu's father and wants to meet him to discuss a business proposition. Manu replies that his father is semi-retired and no longer interested in 'pursuing new business opportunities.' 'But don't worry,' he adds, smiling amiably. 'My brother Maikito – no, not this guy; this is just my friend Alex – and I own a Phantom and we're always eager to discuss new ideas with different people. What do you have in mind, *amigo?'*

Abdullatif takes off his sunglasses and looks at the nineteen-year-old kid for a moment, his hawkish eyes immobile within their sockets. 'I want someone to start bringing cigarettes for me,' he says, still staring at Manu. 'Into Ceuta. Not Winston, but Marlboro. This is what people smoke down there.'

'How many cases are we talking about?' Manu asks, trying to camouflage his excitement.

'I don't know at this stage. Maybe 100 a week, maybe 120, maybe more. We'll have to see how it goes.'

'What price are you willing to pay for the boxes?'

'Same price as you're getting for them in Spain,' *el ceutí* replies. 'With another five thousand pesetas per box to compensate for higher petrol costs and the extra time you're spending on the boat.'

'And when do you want to start all this?'

Abdullatif replies that he is ready to start now. He has got it all planned out, he says: where to bring the tobacco in, where to store it, who to sell it to. All he needs is a reliable Gibraltarian contact, he continues. Someone who won't let him down. That's why he has come on the Ceuta-Algeciras ferry, driven around to Gibraltar in a rented car and booked himself into a hotel for two days. *Would you and your brother be interested — or, if not, would you know somebody who is?*

Of course, Manu is not going to recommend somebody else, is he? Thinking that this is the big break he and his brother are waiting for, he leans forward and tells Abdullatif to look no further. He and Maikito will bring the cigarettes for him. 'Consider it done, *hermano*,' he says. 'I'll speak to my brother this afternoon and I'll bring him down here tomorrow morning to meet you and shake on it.'

But when Manu broaches the subject with Maikito that evening in his mother's living room, the older brother is not interested. Those Ceuta guys are dodgy, Michael tells him. They're real mafiosos. You start by bringing cigarettes across the Straits for them and in no time they've got you hooked by the balls and smuggling drugs for their organisation. *'Además,'* he says, 'crossing the Straits is not like going around the Rock to La Atunara. You get heavy shit storms out there.

And if *la Turbo* suddenly appears before you, or *el Pájaro*[26] starts hovering above you, you're fucked, man. You can't just swerve and come inshore like we do on the way to La Línea. Besides, I'm not going to do the dirty on *el Pelúo* and ditch him for *un moro*. Some things in life are more important than making loads of money, *hermanito*.'

'But – can't you see? – this is the chance that we've been waiting for for years,' Manu pleads, tears of frustration welling up in his eyes. 'The guy says he wants 120 boxes of Marlboro a week!'

'*Qué no, coño, qué no!*' Maikito half-shouts. 'It's not going to happen, Manu! I'm not getting involved with those dodgy fuckers, *y eso es lo que hay!*'

Rising to his feet, Michael makes a shooing gesture with his hand and walks out of the living room. Manu follows him with his eyes, tears of rage sliding down his cheek. He retrieves a partly crushed cigarette from his packet of Benson & Hedges and places it in his mouth, letting it dangle uselessly from his lips. '*Cristo Dios,*' he thinks, shaking his head, not bothering to wipe away his tears, 'how am I going to tell that Abdullashit fella, or whatever his fucking name is, that we're not going to work with him after all? The guy's going to think I'm a right bloody fuck-up!'

Everything should have ended like that – with a shamefaced Manu murmuring his apologies and excuses the next day in front of an irate *ceutí*. But Fate had a *second surprise* for us, another of those bolts out of the blue. Just hours later, see,

---

[26] El Pájaro – nickname for a Spanish customs helicopter (Spanish).

while Manu writhed and wriggled in bed and wondered how he'd talk his way out of this mess, Maikito got arrested for assault. Yep, just like you hear it – Michael Canilla of 9/A Rodger's Passage, Mr Nice Guy himself, ended up detained and behind bars!

The sorry fracas happened at the Gibraltar Arms, one of Maikito's favourite watering holes, a little before midnight. A couple of hours earlier, HMS Invincible had sailed into port along with three or four destroyers ... and, as a result, Main Street was crawling with English sailors. Brawny, tattooed types, singing football songs and heckling passers-by. Most people would have stayed in on a night like this – but Maikito was not the sort of guy to be intimidated by a few *guiris* and, in any case, after falling out with his brother and rowing with Mariadelaida about the scene in her living room, he felt like going out and having *un par de* drinks. Around eleven-thirty a drunk Englishman staggered into the bar. He must have been six two or six three, a ginger-haired wonder with cauliflower ears and more freckles than a seagull's egg. He sat by the counter, ordered himself a beer, and there he remained, staring as if mesmerised at the bottles and plastic optics on the other side of the bar, a vacant look on his flushed face.

Ten minutes, maybe fifteen minutes pass. Occasionally, Maikito and some of the other regulars crack jokes about the Englishman's ears and his *cara de subnormal,* but the jibes are all in Spanish and nobody really bothers the guy. Then all of a sudden the drunk jerks upright on his stool and says to Noemí the Spanish barmaid: 'I'll give you twenty quid for a blow job, luv.'

Exclamations of surprise, one or two sharp intakes of breath, stool legs scraping noisily against the terracotta floor tiles.

'Eh, man, *que dices?*' Manu's brother shouts over the commotion. 'Show some respect, will you?'

The sailor looks scornfully at Maikito, then in a slurring voice says, 'Fuck off, you spic bastard! No one's talking to you, you greasy dago cunt!'

'Man, you better leave *thees* place,' Maikito snarls back, his Gibraltarian accent thicker than ever. 'This place no good for you, *compá!* You're going to get in big trouble if you carry on *thees* way, *amigo.*'

But the sailor doesn't pay heed to Maikito's warning. Instead he slides off his stool and clumsily makes his way to the other end of the counter, chest puffed out and chin thrust forward, his eyes reduced to two bleary slits.

'I've got a question for you, laddie,' he growls, stopping so close to Maikito that their bodies are almost touching. 'Do you consider yourself a white man, or a nigger with that shitty brown colour of yours, pal?'

Without taking his eye off the sailor, Maikito shakes his head and utters a long sigh, the kind that says, *fuck me, why do I have to get embroiled in shit like this?* Then he looks over to Noemí, who is pleading with her eyes for him to ignore the man's provocations. Not wanting to cause her any trouble, he swivels on his stool and rises to his feet, ready to walk away – but at that moment the Brit lunges forward and tries to ram his head against the underside of Maikito's chin. It is a sneaky and aggressive manoeuvre, but the guy's movements are so steeped in drink that Michael easily evades the headbutt and puts the sailor in an armlock, forcing his crew-cut head onto the imitation marble counter.

'I told you to get the fuck out of here!' Maikito screams, punching and re-punching the counter just beside the man's face with his bare knuckles, particles of spit flying like a hail of arrows out of his mouth. 'Why can't you *bastardos ingleses* ever just listen, eh?'

With these words he releases the sailor from the armlock and bundles him away from the counter. That's all he does – lift him by the shirt and push him towards the bar's entrance. But the Englishman is so drunk that his knees buckle and he falls to the floor, hitting his head with a dull thwack on the metal footrail running along the edge of the counter. It is a sickening noise – part-thud, part-crack – and for a second all eyes in the pub are on the curiously inert body and the puddle of blood already haloing its head. Then, from the other side of the room, tearing the silence like a knife slicing through a shower curtain:

'Coño, llama la ambulancia, Noemí! Qué el puto guiri se no ha desnucao!' [27]

Maikito was arrested later that night and charged with assault and causing grievous bodily harm. Under normal circumstances he would have been held overnight and bailed out first thing in the morning, but the sailor's condition was deemed so serious that no bail was granted. When Manu

---

[27] 'Fuck, call the ambulance, Noemí! The fucking *guiri* has broken his neck!'

went down to the station at nine o'clock after hearing about his brother's arrest, he was told that the Englishman was still in a bad way in hospital. 'That's why we can't release your *hermano* just yet,' a tall cop with a kind face said to him. 'He's going to be here until next week *como mínimo*. Sorry, *pisha*. That's all I can tell you for now.'

Swallowing hard, torn between feelings of gratitude for the copper on the one hand and hatred of the system on the other, Manu nodded stiffly and left the building. Once out in the balmy March sunshine, he remembered he was supposed to be meeting Abdullatif in just over fifteen minutes' time at nine-thirty. Quickly, with his hands in his pockets, he made his way down Irish Town and Fish Market Lane, his intention at this stage being to get the meeting over and done with and then drive across to *el NAAFI* to speak with his mum. But when he arrived at *el Bahía* and saw Abdullatif seated at one of the streetside tables with his coffee and his pack of Gitanes, something must have short-circuited in Manuel's brain – because, as soon as he sat down, he told *el ceutí* that he had spoken to his brother last night and that everything had gone well, both of them having agreed to start bringing cigarettes over to Ceuta straightaway.

'Then why hasn't your brother come with you?' Al-Jaouhari asked in Spanish, raising his sunglasses above his eyes.

'He had a bit of a scrap last night with *un inglés* in a bar,' Manu responded awkwardly, 'and got arrested. But don't worry: he'll be out of jail in a few days.'

'So he had a bit of a scrap, eh?'

'Come with me to *la estación de policía* if you don't believe me. I'll ask a cop about my brother in front of you.'

'Easy, easy,' Abdullatif answered with a full smile. 'I was just screwing with you, kid. Grab yourself a beer or a coffee and chill out, will you? We have a lot to discuss and agree on in your brother's absence.'

———————

So this is how our Ceuta adventure began – with a mad gamble, a spontaneous moment of recklessness. The gamble was born partly out of circumstance (the fact that Maikito was not physically there to stop him) and partly – Manu later liked to claim – out of a feeling that our destiny lay with Abdullatif Al-Jaouhari and not with *el Pelúo*. A blend of opportunism and instinct, you might say – helped along by the innate greed and ambition which coursed through the kid's veins.

One thing's for sure: when his brother was released on bail that Sunday, it looked like the game was up, that Manu would have to come up soon with some serious excuses and apologies.

But just seven hours later our hapless sailor passed away at the Royal Naval Hospital and Maikito was rearrested as he was coming out of his residential block at Rodger's Passage. 'I'm arresting you for the murder of Able Seaman Michael John Birstall of HMS Broadsword,' a copper with a peaked cap declared sombrely, clapping a pair of handcuffs on him.

And then (in a much quieter tone): *'Agacha la cabeza antes de entrar en el coche, anda, pishón.'* [28]

Maikito's second arrest was the start of a long and tortuous legal process that was only resolved on 7 January 1994, when Manu's brother was acquitted of that ridiculous murder charge and sentenced instead to four years for constructive manslaughter (reduced to eleven weeks on account of the time he had already spent in custody). If it had been a Spaniard or a Moroccan who was accidentally killed, the whole thing would have ended after two or three hearings. But because Michael John Birstall was an Englishman (and a Royal Navy sailor to boot) the Gibraltarian judiciary went out of its way to please their colonial masters, trying every trick in the book to prove there had been 'wilful intent' when Able Seaman Birstall was pushed to the floor, desperate to show the MOD and the wider British authorities that they were impartial enough to convict – and impose a tough sentence on – a native Gibraltarian.

Back in March 1990, though, we had no idea of what lay in store for e*l Pantera's* eldest son. We knew that his predicament was perilous and that it would be a while before he was granted bail – he had, after all, unintentionally wasted a guy – but we felt that there was sufficient circumstantial and eyewitness evidence to prove that he had never meant to seriously harm Birstall. Manu himself was convinced that his brother would be out in just six or seven weeks. 'They can't leave him there locked up like *un animal*,' he once said in his

---

[28] 'Lower your head before getting in the car, will you, my lad?'

living room in Macphail's Passage. 'Everybody knows he's a great guy who wouldn't hurt a fly.' He also got it into his head – I don't know how – that we needed to smuggle as much Marlboro as possible into Ceuta during Maikito's short absence from the scene. It was the best way of honouring his brother, he said to me one morning at the Royal Calpe. A tribute to his fighting spirit and his *cojones*. Once *el Maikito* came out and saw how much money we were making, he'd quickly change his mind about the entire business and ditch *el Pelúo* for *el ceutí*. 'Of that I am completely sure,' he snarled, looking me straight in the eye.

Later that day *el Manu* gathered Richita, *el Barriga* and me at the Piccadilly Gardens and told us we were going to start smuggling Marlboro cigarettes into Ceuta and, in the process, make shitloads of money. He added that he was temporarily bringing a new guy into the gang – a seventeen-year-old tearaway called Francis Molinari – and that from now on I'd be working as our *copiloto*. When *el Derek* mentioned how frustrating it had to be for Maikito not to be involved in all this, Manu asked the three of us to swear on our *madres* not to breathe a word about the Ceutan racket to his half-brother when visiting him in prison, his intention, he explained, being to surprise Michael with the good news once he was out.

'You sure we shouldn't be telling *el Maikito* what we're up to?' Derek asked. 'Isn't the Phantom registered under his name and all that?'

'*No,* man, *no,*' Manu insisted, solemnly shaking his head. 'He's already got enough to worry about as it is. The last thing I want is to give him another fucking headache. Better just to keep quiet about it for the time being.'

And so it was settled: we'd start smuggling for Abdullatif, and Maikito wouldn't even have to know what we were doing. Except that ... well ... this wasn't quite how things turned out. Because on his second or third visit to *el Castillo*[29], seeing his brother so downcast, and already sensing that events weren't going to be as straightforward as anticipated, *el Manu* had a dramatic change of heart. Fighting back tears, stammering his words, he told his half-brother that he had disregarded his advice and agreed to work with *el ceutí*. He said that he had never intended to go against his wishes, but that when he saw *el moro* sitting there looking so confident and relaxed, he just couldn't help himself. 'I-I-I don't know what go-go-got into me,' he blubbed. 'I just lost it for a mo-moment.' He then drew away from the scratched plastic screen separating them and gazed down at his interlaced hands, expecting a major bollocking from his *hermano mayor*. For ten, maybe fifteen seconds there was no sound to be heard except the hum of the ceiling fan suspended directly above the see-through partition. Then, with a cold gleam in his eye which suggested that Maikito was no longer the same Maikito that we all knew, the dockyard machinist and ex-dope dealer inclined forward and muttered the following words:

'Go for it, bro. Do what you have to do.'

We started smuggling boxes of Marlboro into Ceuta a couple of days after Manu and Maikito's heart-to-heart. The brothers had never carried much with them in the boat in the past, but conscious that our new route pulled us further out

---

[29] El Castillo – the local prison (llanito).

to sea, Manu now added a torch and some flares to the stash of chocolates, cigarettes, chewing gum packets and woolly balaclavas in the Phantom's glove compartment. He also decided that we needed to carry our passports with us in zipped-up waterproof bum bags – just in case we were forced off the boat in Ceuta for one reason or another and had to return home on the Ceuta-Algeciras ferry. The crossings themselves were something of a mixed bag. On a night of so-called *levante calma*, when the wind was at a standstill and the sea smoother than a piece of polished limestone, you could get to *la ciudad autónoma* and back in eighty minutes without a hitch. On those sorts of trips, you could relax, you could mess about, you could discuss last weekend's football results or what we'd be ordering from Gilbert's Takeaway later that morning. Sometimes we'd even stick a tape in the old cassette player under the ignition panel and start singing together, our voices barely audible above the whir of the Yamaha outboard engine:

> Mister catch me if you can
> I'm goin' down in a blaze of glory
> Take me now but know the truth
> I'm goin' down in a blaze of glory
> Shot down in a blaze of Glory!

By comparison, when the wind was up and the waves were crashing against the Phantom's fibreglass hull, things could get *really, really tricky*. Soaking wet, rendered speechless by the icy cold, eyes and face stinging with sea spray, we'd have trouble seeing more than twenty yards in front of us, let alone contemplating whether we'd be having a 'Gilbert Special' or a kebab and chips hours later. Now and again, too, when you least expected it, a sudden swell would propel the Phantom high into the air and you'd briefly catch sight of the Rock's lights above the waves, appearing and fading like some passing meteor shower. Each time this happened, you thought of your friends and relatives back home, sitting in front of their TV sets in Glacis or Varyl Begg or *el Upper Town,* wrapped in their dressing gowns or already in their beds, just a few miles away but completely unaware of what was occurring out at sea, living their lives in an entirely separate temporospatial dimension....

Not that our crossings only took place at night. Every so often there were no patrol boats out in the Straits and we could navigate to Ceuta in broad daylight. Maybe Verdemar, the San Roque-based environmental activists, were blockading the entrance to the CEPSA Oil Refinery in Puente Mayorga. Maybe an oil tanker had caught fire as it lay anchored in the port of Algeciras. Whenever something of this sort happened, all the law-enforcement boats would be pulled from their usual duties and told to head straight to wherever trouble was brewing, leaving the coast clear for us. It was on one of these occasions that my pal put on a remarkable display of masculine bravado for me. We were about seven miles south of Europa Point that afternoon, roughly halfway between the two continents. It was a warm, sunny day – *un día de película*, as we say in Gibraltar. Pressing the play button on the cassette player, Manu smiled, asked me to hold the Phantom's steering wheel, stood up on his seat, climbed over the low plastic windshield and stepped, slowly and unsteadily, all the time leaning into the breeze, onto the vessel's delicate fibreglass prow. He remained in this half-crouched position for some moments, swaying from side to side, his arms held out like those of a Californian surfer, Jon Bon Jovi playing all along out of the launch's speakers. Behind him loomed Mount Jebel Musa – a giant dollop of blue on a palette of differently hued blues, increasing in size, it seemed, with every passing second. Despite the lack of *guardia* or *aduana* boats around us, we were still travelling at forty knots and the slightest ripple could have sent Manu tumbling into the sea. 'Get back down here, you fucker!' I cried out. 'Stop messing about, *cabrón!*' Finally, after another twenty or thirty seconds, just when you thought he'd never rise from his stooped position, he straightened up and, raising his arms in a V above his head, shouted 'Out with the Winston Boys and in with the Marlboro Men!' That's all he shouted – 'Out with the Winston Boys and in with the Marlboro Men, motherfuckers!'

Though nearly thirty years have passed since Manu yelled those words, I can still see him standing there with his arms in the air and Mount Jebel Musa towering over him in the background. The image is impressed in my mind – as iconic, in its own way, as that of *la Virgen del Rocío* or *la Virgen del Carmen*. Manu, my best mate and business partner, erect and shouting at the top of his lungs, his sinewy arms stretched out towards the heavens. Yes, I will always remember that crazy stunt. Just as I'll never forget how furiously my heart pounded against my ribcage. Because even though I laughed, even though I fleetingly let go of the steering wheel to also lift my arms above my head, deep inside I was absolutely petrified. 'What if he loses his balance and falls into the sea?' I thought. 'What if he lands badly and breaks an arm? What if I end up having to pilot the boat myself?' While I was reasonably familiar with the workings of the Phantom's outboard engine, my experience of navigational matters was limited to the few times Manu and I had borrowed his brother's boat in summers past to 'go for a ride.' It was something we used to do when we were bored – mainly on Sundays and bank holidays. The shops being closed, not having much else to do, we'd steer *la nena* (as Manu affectionately called the Phantom) all the way around the Rock to Catalan Bay, where we would drop anchor off the large, tit-shaped rock known as *la Mamela*. There we would chill out with our reefers and our bottles of Heineken – lying on the prow in our Speedos and with the sun beating down on our naked limbs, only bestirring ourselves to apply some more sun lotion or to pull up the string-tied plastic bag with our beers from the sea. For a laugh I'd sometimes take the wheel on the way back to Sheppard's Marina and follow Manu's shouted instructions, trying to avoid the wavelets breaking around us, merrily shrugging off my mate's complaints about my poor piloting. But that, would you believe, was the sum total of my navigational experience at this stage, the pitiful entirety of my seafaring know-how. No wonder Manu caused such an impression on me when he climbed out of the cockpit that day and stood on that juddering prow. If the crazy cunt had lost his balance and fallen into the sea, we'd have been *totally fucked*.

In all the years I knew him, I never once saw Manu run away from physical danger. He was always so bold and heroic, so keen to sniff out and go charging towards trouble. But it is not true that Manu was completely fearless either. He may have been blessed with a legendary pair of *cojones,* but certain things still irked him, even unnerved him. One of these was the possibility of being arrested in Spain during a smuggling run. Once the *guardias* got wind of whose son he was, so his theory went, they would either beat him senseless, or else frame him for some horrendous murder or sex-crime. The fact that Manu didn't share his father's surname, looked nothing like his old man and hadn't had anything to do with *el Pantera* for years suggested that this was a fairly irrational fear – but he clung to it all the same, convinced that the full weight of the Spanish state would come down on his shoulders because of his infamous crook of a father. As a result, every time we came within two or three miles of the African mainland and began the 'final approach' to Ceuta, you'd notice a subtle change in his demeanour. It wasn't that he became outwardly nervous or agitated – no, that wasn't his style. But there was something about the tone of his voice, something about the deliberateness of his movements, which indicated that he was now fully alert and mindful of what lay around him, in no mood for the usual scrapes and *chulerías*.

With me, it was the other way around: I felt calmer and less vulnerable when we left the open seas, less prone to sudden rushes of panic. I'd go further and say that landing the merchandise was always my favourite part of the night's operation. Al-Jaouhari's drop-off point was on *la calle Recinto Sur,* at the southern end of the enclave. Anybody travelling there by boat in 2019 would have to sail around the eastern coast of Ceuta and then swing westwards towards *el Fortín de la Palmera.* But back in those days, when there was no SIVE and no CCTV, you could actually cut through *el foso de San Felipe,* the high-walled medieval canal which flows through the centre of Ceuta's old town and takes you from the port of Ceuta at the northern end of the territory all the way down to its meridional beaches, thereby avoiding the treacherous waters off Punta Almina. Our destination was a rocky prominence about two minutes from *el foso's* southern entrance and just opposite *el Museo de la Legión*. On this stony outcrop stood a crumbling beachside discotheque – Club Náutico. Enclosed by a low wall surmounted by rusty railings and bamboo panels, and lying semi-abandoned during the winter months, this ramshackle structure shielded us from the main road as we were coming in and also provided cover for Al-Jaouhari's 'unloaders.' Usually, we'd sail to within twenty yards of land and then switch off our engine in about five feet of water. One of Al-Jaouhari's men would then jump into the sea and wade out to where our boat was waiting. Grabbing the rope thrown in his direction, he'd slowly tow us inshore, avoiding the many beer crates, boulders and iron beams which littered the seabed, and tie us to a 'Danger. No Diving' sign planted on the tip of the outcrop. Once our vessel was secure, a small army of kids and youths would come scrambling down the rocks and before you knew it, in less than a minute, the twenty cases of Marlboro would be out of the Phantom's hold and on their way to their next destination. After that, the same guy would haul us out to where he had collected us and, throwing the mooring rope back on board, raising his hand in a sign of farewell, watch us zoom off in the direction of *el foso*.

I won't lie: those first few months working with Al-Jaouhari were pretty awesome. On average we'd be out on the Phantom four times a week, transporting anywhere between twenty and thirty cases of Marlboro per trip. Some nights, when we knew from our North African associate that

something big like a minister's visit was going down in Ceuta
and that most of the *guardia civil* guys had been pulled off their
boats to provide extra police cover on the mainland, we'd do
two, three, sometimes as many as four trips in a single night.
On one of those 'golden weeks' we could rake in as much as
10,000 or 11,000 smackers between us. But these were
exceptional weeks: normally we'd reach the weekend with
around two grand in our pockets. Once – after a
consignment of twenty-five cases was intercepted by *la policía
local* after the drop-off near Club Náutico – we didn't make
anything at all: on the contrary, we ended up giving Al-
Jaouhari two grand of our own money to help him cover the
loss of the confiscated boxes.

Now think about all this for a second. Here are two kids,
aged twenty and without qualifications, earning a minimum
of two and a half thousand pounds a week. If nowadays you
can live very, very well on this sort of *floosh*, back in 1991 it
was an astronomical sum, the kind of dosh that top doctors
and lawyers were on. 'Surely, two rough and uneducated
hoodlums wouldn't have known what to do with all that
money?' I can almost hear you thinking. 'Surely, they would
have struggled for ideas!' Well, think again. Like most young
kids who suddenly get their hands on a fat stash of cash,
Manu and I had no problem finding things to buy. Gold
chains, sovereign rings, medallions engraved with *la Virgen
del Carmen* and *la Virgen del Rocío,* Nike and Adidas tracksuits,
football strips, Caterpillar boots, earrings for Manu's mum,
leather jackets for my dad, tons and tons of CDs (most of
which we never listened to, or listened to just once and then
never played again), headphones, Walkmans, hi-fis,
Gameboys, Gameboy cartridges, ghetto blasters, Armani and

Calvin Klein shirts, expensive perfumes and colognes from Hotu and Star of India. And that's not counting the vast amounts we were frittering every day on coffees, fry-ups, cheese toasties, *pinchitos, gambas al pil pil, calamares, boquerones, choquitos, churros,* fish and chips, curries, pints of lager, pints of bitter, chocolates, sweets, cakes, crisps and other titbits for ourselves and for our growing circle of hangers-on, smuggling buddies, friends of friends and Manu's on-and-off girlfriends.

It was during this time, too, that I bought my first sports car – an army green Honda Prelude VTEC Coupé. I had been meaning to buy a quality motor since turning eighteen, but my excessive spending had never let me save up for a decent model and forced me to drive a succession of second-hand Fords and Fiats. At the beginning of 1991, however, so much money was coming into my hands that, little by little, the unspent notes started accumulating all over my father's flat – in socks and old trainers, behind sideboards and chests of drawers, even in the cavity housing our misfiring kitchen boiler. One day, when my dad wasn't in the apartment, I retrieved the elastic-tied bundles from their hiding places and counted eighteen thousand pounds – enough to buy a cracking sports car. Carrying the notes in a plastic bag, I walked down to Bassadone Motors on Devil's Tower Road and ordered the flashiest car from their Honda catalogue, asking them to accessorise it with alloy wheels, a high-rise spoiler and a large *Starsky & Hutch* white vector stripe on both sides. When the vehicle arrived seven weeks later, I wasn't too keen on the stripes, so, without a second thought, I paid another five hundred pounds to have them removed and painted over in green. 'Make sure your guys do the job properly,' I haughtily told the salesman dealing with me. 'I don't want to see any trace of those shitty *rayas blancas* when I come back to collect my car. Understand?'

Driving the Prelude out of the showroom six days later was a moment of real magic for me. Ever since the days of my childhood, I had dreamt about owning a nice set of wheels; it had been one of my greatest ambitions. In this respect I was no different to the other kids at Bayside – with their Top Trumps cards and their Panini stickers and everything else that conditioned them to slather over convertibles, dragsters and pickup trucks. What can I say? Cars were cool, cars were fun, cars were what separated the big boys from the also-rans. And now it was my turn to own a proper car as well and do all the things that other smugglers did. Overtaking vans and lorries in Dudley Ward Tunnel, slowing down to a crawl along Eastern Beach Road, performing wheelspins and screeching handbrake turns on the flatlands next to the Rosia lighthouse, driving up to the North Mole to watch the evening sun sink behind the mountainous Tarifa horizon.

My only misgiving about the Prelude was where to leave it parked at night. In the past I had always left my clapped-out Pandas and Fiestas on Tank Ramp or Willis's Road or Hospital Hill, often double-parked or carelessly stretched in front of doorways or across pavements, not caring if in the morning I'd wake up to find a scratched bumper or a dented fender. But now that I was the proprietor of a brand-new sports car ... well, I could no longer afford to be so reckless, could I? So almost from day one I began to leave my beauty at Grand Parade, a twenty-minute walk from my father's flat, where all she risked collecting were splashes of seagull shit and the sticky, orangey-red sap that, during the hottest months of the year, dripped off the dragon trees in the nearby Alameda Gardens....

———————

In November 2011 my father, who throughout his life had smoked between sixty and eighty Rothmans a day, was diagnosed with lung cancer. I was not in Gibraltar at the time, but I learned of the situation via a letter from my father's cousin Matilda McComb. Over the next sixty months Matilda sent me regular letters explaining to me how my father was coping and what the medics were doing to keep him comfortable. I never answered any of these dispatches with the full-length replies that they deserved, but I did send her the odd postcard from time to time thanking her for keeping me updated and asking her to pass on my regards to the ailing John Dennis Leslie. One of her last missives arrived together with a Polaroid snap of my dad sitting in his pyjamas in the living room of our old Castle Road flat. I haven't kept any of Matilda's letters or the blue airmail envelopes in which they were posted, but I still have that photograph. It is scratched in places, already fraying around the edges; scrawled in thick orange felt pen on the back are the following words: 'John Dennis Leslie, 12/12/2016.'

This morning I took the photo out of the folder where I have stored it for the last three years and studied it for some moments. My father is staring at the camera with his pyjama top undone; he is trying to smile, but the creases around his eyes and mouth suggest he is in considerable pain. His oxygen mask has been pushed down his face and onto his neck, its valves and tubes sitting like a life-sucking robotic spider on his bony chest. The rocket-like shape of an oxygen bottle can be glimpsed – scuffed and patinated with rust – behind his armchair.

I don't know why I have kept that photograph among my papers. There is something incredibly pathetic about that feigned smile, something that captures the awful predicament of a sick man waiting to be torn away from the land of the living. Here is a guy who spent his adult years bitching about his bad luck – who through the Eighties and Nineties often remarked how good it'd be if he just dropped dead one day – who had even shrugged his shoulders and dubbed Manu 'one of the lucky ones' when we came to learn of my mate's tragic fate. And yet, for all that, there is fear in those 'Chinesey' Pereira eyes, there is real vulnerability. It is the first thing you notice when seeing him there with his pyjama top open to his waist, his once plump belly reduced to a few flaps of stretch-marked skin, his eyes staring out of their virtually fleshless sockets. There is a sense of helplessness, a frantic desire to continue living despite the humiliations and the discomforts his disease is visiting on him. 'Show some mercy,' he pleads with his eyes to the Grim Reaper. 'Grant me that little bit longer before you drag me away.' Or maybe, who knows, maybe I am only transposing my own feelings onto what I am seeing, and my father wasn't depressed or thinking about death at all. Maybe he was tired and needed to go to sleep. Maybe he wanted Matilda to leave the room so that he could bring out the plastic bowl where he did his '*necesidades*'. Or maybe he was neither tired nor in need of a piss or a shit, the only thought crossing his mind at that particular moment back in December 2016 being something like, 'Hurry up and take that photo once and for all, woman, will you? It's not as if my fucking son ever gave a damn about me anyway!'

I don't know why I've written all this down. I guess I had to get it off my chest.

***

A year passed. Manu's half-brother was still in jail, his trial having been delayed several times by the Gibraltar authorities under pressure from the MOD's solicitors. I now owned two cars – the Prelude and a Z28 Chevrolet Camaro – both of which I kept parked on the south-eastern flank of Grand Parade. Mariadelaida Gonzalez was still mopping canteen floors at the NAAFI – albeit with diamond-studded earrings hanging from her ears and a heart-shaped pendant, hewn out of 22-carat gold and the size of a quail's egg, sitting on the cleft between her breasts. John Dennis Leslie, taciturn and ill-humoured as ever, no longer gave me dirty looks when I came home in the middle of the night, but instead complained about the CDs, Gameboy cartridges and other clutter strewn across the flat. As for Manu and me, we continued ferrying boxes of Marlboro to Ceuta and frittering away our ill-gotten gains in the Main Street shops and in La Línea's jewellers. If any police detectives had taken it upon themselves to follow us after one of those reckless blow-outs, they'd have been surprised to see where we took our shopping bags every evening – me to that crumbling shithole on Castle Road, and Manu to his even smaller place on Macphail's Passage. But such was the bizarre situation we found ourselves in during those days: on the surface we appeared to be rolling in money, but behind that misleading veneer we were just as wretched and *desgraciados* as ever.

If all that wasn't enough, Manu was now going through a rough time on account of his brother's prolonged incarceration. He kept saying it was all a fix and that the Gibraltar authorities were determined to keep *el Maikito* locked up till his dying day. He'd also do stupid things – like get completely shit-faced during the morning and then stagger around town *cagándose en la madre* of anyone who so much as glanced at him, or sit on one of the rickety benches overlooking the NOP sports pitch, throwing pound coins, cigarette packets, matchboxes or whatever was in his pockets at the hockey and football players. In January or February 1992, he started joining *el Kiki,* an old smuggler whom we sometimes bumped into at the bonded warehouse opposite the cemetery, on trips to the Club Flexo brothel in Fuengirola. There he'd go on crazy all-night sprees, blowing hundreds and hundreds of pounds on girls, *cocaína* and the flat, tasteless cava they served at champagne prices. A couple of times he actually asked me to lend him some money, promising to reimburse me with interest as soon as we got paid by Al-Jaouhari again. 'Don't you think you're going a bit overboard with all this brothel business?' I once asked him, grabbing him by the arm after giving him twenty fifty-quid notes. Manu's response was to grin and tell me that his visits to the *puticlub* were helping him keep his shit together. 'It's just my way of dealing with things,' he said, escaping my grip and moving away. 'Once I know what's happening with Maikito, I'll quit going with whores, don't worry, brother.'

Maikito's trial was finally fixed for 7 April 1992, a week after the opening of the much-touted Expo in Sevilla. Al-Jaouhari was asking for more and more boxes around this time, no doubt wanting to take advantage of the lower number of coppers in and around Ceuta due to their being drafted into the Andalusian capital. This increase in business suited us fine; it meant more ready cash and it allowed Manu to forget, if only temporarily, about Maikito's impending trial. One night, after we had delivered a record-breaking ninety boxes in four consecutive trips, our *ceutí* associate told us that he wanted to talk to us in person; he said he had something important to propose. His request caught Manu and me by surprise. Though we had spoken to Al-Jaouhari countless times over the last two years, it had always been over the radio or on the phone, never face-to-face. This might seem strange, considering the amount of business between us, but this is the way experienced smugglers operate. You don't get too close to your contacts and you don't allow the buggers to get near you – nobody wanting to drop their guard in the fickle and often cut-throat world of organised cross-strait smuggling.

It was a Friday evening when we met up with Al-Jaouhari in Ceuta. Following his instructions, we dropped off the Marlboro cases at the usual place and then took the Phantom to *la playa Tramaguera,* a small manmade cove two miles further down the coast, where we sidled up to some rocks and entrusted the vessel to a couple of his guys. We then jumped into a waiting car – a battered black 1970s S-class Mercedes that for some reason made me think of the Libyan dictator Muammar Gaddafi – and were driven through a tangle of labyrinthine streets not dissimilar to those found in La Línea. Manu was in one of his awkward moods, staring silently through the passenger window, bands of orange and yellow transiently lighting up his eyes and face every time we passed a shopfront or a streetlight. I suspected that he was thinking about our meeting with Al-Jaouhari – either that, or about the delights the Ceutan police would spring on him if they nabbed us and discovered that he was *el Pantera's* son. Not long afterwards, we alighted at a street corner, where another guy was waiting for us. Urging Manu and me to follow him, he turned around and guided us through a series of badly paved alleys, never once looking behind him, occasionally unlatching and pushing aside creaking *rastrillos*.[30] The flat he led us to was located on the ground floor of a two-storey block; it had patches of damp oozing out of its walls and at least half an inch of water on the floor. A solitary light bulb hung from the ceiling, strips of black insulation tape wrapped untidily around its drop cord. Cigarette packets, pizza boxes, Rizla papers, Styrofoam containers and – most surprisingly of all – five or six mildewed telephone directories lay scattered in a soggy mess on the half-submerged floorboards. In the least flooded corner of the room were three wooden chairs and a small coffee table. Al-Jaouhari was seated on one of the former, wearing the same fur-trimmed bomber jacket he had sported two years earlier at *el Bahía*. Whereas that day he had been cleanly shaven, two finely trimmed sideburns now extended all the way from his ears to the corners of his mouth.

'Ah, my *llanito* buddies,' he said in Spanish, beckoning us towards him and gesturing at the chairs. 'How nice to see you in person. Come and take a seat, *amigos*.'

---

[30] Rastrillo – gate (llanito).

Manu and I nodded uneasily and sat down. Al-Jaouhari then clapped his hands and some scruffy, pointy-headed bloke walked in through the doorway with a battered aluminium teapot and three glass tumblers.

'And how's the big brother back in *Jabal Ṭāriq?*' our host asked – half in earnest, half-sarcastically – as he accepted a glass of mint tea from his man. 'Still locked up on account of his "little scrap"?'

Manu looked at him for some seconds, then raised his own tumbler and took a long and disconcertingly loud slurp. 'He's doing fine,' he said, smiling with his teeth bared.

I can't remember what we talked about for the next fifteen or twenty minutes – probably football and *las hijaputadas* of the *aduaneros*. Bored shitless, Manu and I shot repeated glances at each other, wondering what all this was about and how long we were going to be kept there listening to Al-Jaouhari spouting his bullshit. As we pondered the problem, *el ceutí* brought out a bag of dope and rolled himself a joint. He then extended the bag and some rolling papers to Manu, who followed his example and rolled two more joints – one for me and one for himself.

'Lovely *hashisha*,[31] this, *compá*,' Manu said shortly afterwards, a thin trail of smoke escaping from one of his nostrils.

We continued chatting and smoking spliffs for another twenty minutes to half an hour, the room slowly becoming

---

[31] Hashisha, a Gibraltarian corruption of hachís, the Spanish word for hashish.

saturated with cannabis smoke. Once again I cannot remember what we talked about – although I do recall Al-Jaouhari bringing out his wallet and showing us a photo of a smiling, dark-haired woman with a strong jawline. I also remember the little fellow with the pointy head walking in with a tray of *chuparquías,* the ever-popular Moroccan dessert made with fried dough, honey, sesame seeds and rose water. He trudged around the room with the deep-fried delicacies, but only Al-Jaouhari took one of the rose-shaped pastries.

'This *hashisha* is fucking amazing,' Manu reiterated after a while, holding the spliff in front of him and looking at it through half-closed eyes.

'I'm glad you like it, *hermano,*' Al-Jaouhari replied, wiping a few crumbs off his chin. 'Because I have something to propose to you and it's sort of linked to what you're smoking. What do you think if, from now on, instead of paying you in cash, I start giving you three-quarters of a kilo of *hachís* for every Marlboro case you bring to me?'

I lowered my spliff and turned to look at Manu, but he was already staring straight ahead at Al-Jaouhari, his eyes suddenly alert and focused. 'What you're proposing, *amigacho,* is quite interesting. But if Alex and I get caught out at sea with a cargo of hash instead of tobacco, we'd be looking at four years in the slammer instead of the couple of months we'd get for smuggling cigarettes. Explain two things to me, *amigo:* what's in it for you, and what's in it for us and our guys in Gibraltar, if we switch over to this new arrangement?'

A wry smile alighted on Al-Jaouhari's spade-shaped face. 'For me, it's very simple – I've inherited some business interests across the border in Morocco and it's now actually cheaper for me to pay you in *hachís* than in cash. And for you, well, I think the advantages are pretty obvious – you could be earning considerably more than you're earning now if you sell the hash I give you to a Costa del Sol dealer.'

Manu held his spliff between his fingers at chest level for a few seconds, then brought it to his lips and took a slow drag. 'A kilo,' he said.

'*Cómo?*' the Moroccan-born Spaniard asked.

'A kilo,' Manu repeated. 'If we are going to risk our necks doing this, you have to give us a kilo per case, Abdullatif.'

Al-Jaouhari looked at the joint clutched between his thumb and forefinger, then nodded. 'Okay, okay, I'll give you a kilo. Last week my daughter had a baby girl and I want Allah to see that I am generous with my business associates, so that one day, *inshallah,* he too will look out for my little Amira. I guess it's your lucky day, isn't it, *amiguitos?*'

When I woke up in my own bed around three in the afternoon the next day, I had a sensation that something bad had happened the previous night. I searched my memory banks for the origin of this feeling, but all I could come up with was the *seasickly* malaise that had overcome us both as we sailed, completely drugged out of our heads, across the Straits eight or nine hours earlier. Then, as I rolled out of bed and grabbed the packet of Du Maurier on the bedside table, it all came back to me. *El cabrón de Manu* had agreed with Al-Jaouhari that from now on we'd get paid in drugs instead of cash, hadn't he! Bolting upright, swallowing back a spurt of stomach acid that had come surging up my throat, I rushed out of my room and, with my packet of Du Maurier tucked in my waistband, called Mariadelaida's son from our house phone.

'*Quillo,*' I hollered edgily into the receiver, 'why did you tell Al-Jaouhari that we'd be happy to receive one kilo of *hashisha* for every case delivered to him? *'Ta tú loco o algo?'*

'*Tranqui, colega, tranqui,*' Manu replied in a mock-Madrid accent. 'Haven't you heard the expression "Fortune favours the brave" before?'

'You what?'

'Take a chill pill, will you, *Ojo Tuerto?* Calm the fuck down, man!'

'But, Manu, *coño,* if we get nabbed with a shipment of drugs, we'd be totally fucked! Besides,' I added in a slightly calmer tone, 'don't you remember what *el Maikito* once said about these guys? That they start you off bringing cigarettes for them and before you know it they've got you smuggling drugs for their organisation?'

'*Anda, anda,*' my mate replied. 'Don't be so dramatic. Al-Jaouhari is a family man, not a fucking character in *el Godfather!*'

'What about Richita, Derek and *el Niño*? Have you spoken to them about all this?'

'I've spoken to *el Flaquito* and he's all for it. And you know what the other two are like: they'd jump off the top of the Rock if Derek told them to.'

'Also,' I continued, not quite done yet, 'we can't just bring the shit back to Gibraltar, can we? We'd have to sell it to some *sloppy, no?* How are we going to find a contact in Spain willing to pay for the drugs?'

Manu made a sound halfway between a belch and a chuckle. '*Ya 'ta tó arreglao*, man.'

'What do you mean – *tó arreglao?*'

'This morning I called *el Pelúo.*'

'What?' I cried in shock. 'You spoke with *el Pelúo?*'

'Yes, haha. He was a bit pissed off with us for ditching him two and a half years ago, but once I told him about the new arrangement with Al-Jaouhari you could almost hear *el cabrón* salivating on the other side of the line, haha.'

'And you trust a guy like him with all this?'

'Well, we've got to give him a chance, *no?*' Manu replied, suddenly sounding grown-up and formal. 'The same as Maikito and I gave you a chance, bro, when *Freddy el Mayor* fell from that scaffold thing in Coaling Island. Anyway, Alex, *el Pelúo's* problem is not that he's completely useless; it's that every fucker and his dog is currently bringing in Winston into *La Atunara y Los Junquillos.* Give him a few bundles of good *hashisha* and you'll see how quickly he sells the stuff. So what do you say, *pishita* – are you with me on this?'

Coincidentally, at that very moment jangling sounds came from the street and our front door opened. Startled, I glanced across the room and saw my dad standing there with his keys in his left hand and six or seven Safeway plastic bags on the ground before him, a look of intense weariness contorting his features. 'Let me give you a call later,' I said, turning my back to the door and whispering into the receiver. 'My old man has just arrived with the shopping and I don't want to speak about this with him here.'

We spent the rest of that weekend arguing about what to do, but in the end I caved in and went with it: from now on we would start accepting a kilogram of hash per case. Part of the reason I gave in was that Manu was my best mate and I'd have walked through fire if *el cabrón* had asked me to. But I am not going to lie: I was also suckered into it because of the greater sums of cash involved. Sitting together with me and the others at the Piccadilly Gardens that Sunday, *el Manu* calculated that we'd be making almost twice as much money under the new arrangements. 'Women, *coches*, jewellery – we'll be able to afford the best of the best,' he said, scanning the expectant faces around him. 'And it's not as if a lot has to change for it to happen either. After all, we are already heading there with the Marlboro. All we have to do is bring back *la hashisha* and drop it off in La Línea. Easy as fucking pie, my friends.'

Manu was right about the money side of things. Taking boxes of Marlboro over to Ceuta and coming back with modest packages of hashish saw our income double on some weeks. Moreover, word got out that we were now running drugs and all of a sudden people in Gib were looking at us with different eyes. Women who until then had given us a wide berth started cosying up to us. Car dealers were now telling us they could import any American car we fancied, *you just let us know and we'll arrange it all for you, amigo, no problem.* Even *el Pantera* himself must have been aware of what we were doing, judging from the half-smile creeping across his face whenever our paths crossed in town.

But Manu got it wrong in another sense: smuggling drugs came with its own set of complications. Whereas previously, for instance, we had collected our payment as we handed over the cases of Marlboro, now Al-Jaouhari insisted that we drop off the boxes at the usual place and then head up to the northern end of Ceuta, to an area known as El Quemadero. There, squeezed between the N-354 dual carriageway on one side and the treacherous waters of the Alboran Sea on the other, stood the enclave's *desalinizadora,* or desalination plant, a sprawling complex of water tanks, warehouses and overground pipes that from a distance looked like something out of *Blade Runner.* Sticking out of its western flank was a fenced-off and gated jetty built in the late Seventies, when the Spanish authorities had hoped that the *desalinizadora* would one day form part of a multi-faceted development supplying small and medium-sized vessels in the area with water, provisions and fuel. This jetty had never been employed for its original purpose (on account, it was said, of the Gibraltarian monopoly on bunkering services) and now only remained operational in case there was an accident at the plant and it needed to be used by *el servicio de ambulancias marítimas.* One of Al-Jaouhari's men, a burly Catalan known as *el Petonet,* worked as a night-watchman at the *desalinizadora* and, whenever we came up to El Quemadero after dropping off the Marlboro cases on the other side of the enclave, he'd open the jetty gates, guide us into place beside the pier and then hand over the hash in small packets carefully wrapped in black bin liners and tied together with brown parcel tape.

Something else that got tricky was our relationship with *el Pelúo*. Manu had contacted him weeks earlier because he genuinely believed that the dude would find it easier to shift hash than cigarettes, but *el linense* was once again proving an unreliable sod, coming up with all sorts of excuses to justify his slow disposing of the merchandise. Things were going so slowly, in fact, that sixty kilograms of hash were soon gathering dust in his garage in Los Junquillos – a highly frustrating state of affairs, seeing that (a) police crackdowns in Los Junquillos were a regular occurrence, and (b) in the world of drug smuggling, the more 'shit' you are caught with, the more trouble you will be in. In a bid to break the growing impasse, Manu spoke to his mate and fellow Costa del Sol brothel aficionado 'Kiki' Alman, who put him in touch with Alfredo *'el Lucky'* Ruenda, an ex-associate of Kiki's who was supposed to have shipped containerloads of Colombian coke into Galicia in the early Eighties and who, apparently, was the brother-in-law of the famous crook *el Zancudo de Málaga*. This Ruenda chap called *el Pelúo* on the phone a few days later and told him he was sending a van down to Los Junquillos to collect the unsold drugs that same evening. When *el Lucky*'s men got there at nine, they paid *el linense* a quarter of what he would have made had he shifted the merchandise for us and then ordered him to stand to one side, stick his nose up his arse and *forget about the entire matter if he knew what was good to him*. (*El Pelúo*, for what it's worth, was so scared of his visitors that he didn't utter a word, only opening his mouth when he asked the two muscleheads if they needed a hand loading the taped-up bales into their van.) The minute Ruenda got his mitts on the drugs, he had the consignment sent over to Bobby Matković, a twenty-eight-year-old ex-Balompédica Linense footballer who was studying to be an accountant and who, more importantly, was the fiancé of his daughter Sonia. *El Lucky* had for some time now been wanting to introduce Matković to the family business, and he figured that it would be a good idea to partner young Bobby – a newcomer to the drugs trade – with a small-scale smuggling outfit like ours. Ruenda's instincts proved largely correct, too: though our relationship with the spoiled brat Matković was never comparable to the one we had enjoyed with the hapless but easy-going *Pelúo*, we no longer had any problems disposing of the hashish we were bringing over from Ceuta.

The third and final thing that Manu didn't anticipate that night at the Piccadilly Gardens was that in smuggling, as in business and life in general, the higher the risk, the greater not just the reward but also the potential fall-out. While sticking exclusively to Marlboro cigarettes, you see, we had never had that much trouble with the Spanish authorities. Once, I remember, as we were coming out of *el foso de San Felipe* on a return journey, *la Turbo* planted herself in front of the canal mouth and we had no option but to turn back, sail down the canal and navigate all the way around the eastern end of the enclave, keeping about five miles off the coast in case the law enforcement vessel had turned around and was now sitting somewhere opposite *el muelle de la Puntilla*. On a couple of occasions, too, we were chased by *la Dos Motores,* as the smaller, but more manoeuvrable of the two Spanish *aduana* boats was widely known – but these pursuits had always taken place in the comparatively safe waters off Europa Point and never out at sea, where we would have struggled to outstrip the powerful engines of the Spanish vessel. Now that we were carrying hash, however, and dropping off the drugs on Spanish soil, we repeatedly encountered the *aduana* and *guardia civil* vessels out on our smuggling runs. Part of it was down to us spending more time in Spanish waters and thus being at greater risk of running into their boats. But part of it, too, I'm convinced, was due to the simple fact that – by virtue of carrying drugs – we were tempting Fate to ensnare us. How else could you explain the sudden upsurge in breakdowns and mechanical problems, the unexpected rise in navigational cockups and miscalculations? Jetting out of La Atunara one night at three in the morning, we were even shot at from *la Turbo,* two bullet holes in the fibreglass gunwale and one in the aluminium-plated transom showing just how close to the wind – if you'll excuse the pun – we were sailing.

With minutes to go before the start of Maikito's long-delayed trial, Manu did a very curious thing: he unbuttoned the top three buttons of his shirt, slipped his hand inside the garment and pulled out the cluster of pendants and medallions sitting on his chest. At the time we were in the lobby of the Gibraltar Law Courts – a semi-closed space paved with ancient black and white marble slabs that had something weirdly funerary about them. Around one hundred people were there with us waiting for the Supreme Court's doors to open at ten. Many of them were big shots from the military establishment – tall, florid-faced, bemedalled guys who kept harrumphing and bursting into manly laughter. Manu took one look at the Army and Navy men, shook his head and, pursing his lips together, spat a filament of saliva without anybody noticing on the floor. '*Si estos guiris van a vacilar con todas sus medallitas,*' he said, wiping his mouth with the back of one hand and unbuttoning his shirt with the other, '*po ná – yo me saco las mías también.*'[32]

When the buzzer rang at five to ten, we went inside and took our seats in the courtroom. Panelled throughout in light teak, it was fitted with wall-mounted speakers and tabletop microphones and had a gilded Royal coat-of-arms set above the judge's bench. Manu was sitting right at the front, in one of the spaces reserved for the defendant's family members; I was three or four rows further back. From my position I scanned the length and breadth of the public gallery, slightly taken aback by the heterogenous mix on display. Plain-clothed policemen, earringed 'Winston Boys', black-gowned court ushers, gum-chewing GBC cameramen, Michael John Birstall's relatives, dowdy-looking *reporteros* from the Campo de Gibraltar – they were all crammed in there cheek by jowl. Most interesting to me was the small group of tabloid hacks that had flown over from the UK to cover the trial. One of the men was wearing a double-breasted blazer and the other two sported linen suits with damp patches under their arms. All three of them looked pale and bleary-eyed – suggesting they had spent most of the previous night propping up the bar at the Holiday Inn. When the trio were obliged to stand

---

[32] 'If these *guiris* are going to show off with all their medals, then fuck it – I'm bringing out mine as well!'

up to allow a long-haired smuggler to take his seat further down their row, the oldest of the journos shook his head and rolled his red-veined eyes – as disgusted as a Victorian tourist stepping on a sand-encrusted camel turd.

The trial started ten minutes later. I tried my best to follow what the judge and the others were saying, but their words went over the top of my head, reminding me of the time one of our teachers at Bayside had chided me for switching off in class and I had bad-temperedly thrown my pens and pencils on the floor. Feeling similarly frustrated, I clenched my fists and focused on my knees for a while. Then I looked up and studied the three British journalists in front of me, in particular the guy who had been so put out by the smuggler walking past him. Balding and overweight, with one or two concavities in his cheeks marking out the presence of missing molars, he had a small, misshapen head and close-set 'monkfish' eyes. I found myself wondering where the dude came from, what he thought of Gibraltar and the Gibraltarians, how much he had drunk the previous night to look so fucked-up. I also pondered what he was planning to write about the trial. Although I had never read a British tabloid before and had no idea at this stage of their rabble-rousing journalistic methods, I somehow felt in my bones that the fella's article wouldn't be very complimentary to either the defendant or Gibraltar as a whole. Intermittently, too, I wondered what sort of sentence would be imposed on *el Maikito*. Rushing down Castle Street earlier that morning, Manu had mentioned that Michael's lawyer believed his client would either be released or handed a token two- or three-month sentence – but I wasn't buying any of it. Before taking my seat, I had overheard two local barristers discussing the case in the lobby and they hadn't seemed that convinced of our boy's chances. 'But my dear Bhambhani,' the shorter of the pair – a slim, tanned dude with tufts of greyish-black hair sprouting from the back of his hands – said in a flawless Oxbridge accent, 'don't you remember what happened at the IRA inquest? They used all the leverage at their disposal to either get the witnesses to retract their original statements or to discredit and malign them in the media. I realise that having just received a gong you will be reluctant to say a bad word about the British legal system, but you and I know that justice is never served equitably when the verdict might compromise or reflect badly upon the establishment. Mark my words, dear fellow: they are not going to let this *golfillo* off the hook, even if it seems obvious that there was no malicious intent behind his actions. The lad will be under lock and key for a very long time, I dare say.' 'I am not so sure about that, old chap,' his companion – a dapper Indian gentleman in a pin-striped suit – replied in an equally posh tone. 'Back in 1988 it was the reputation of the British Army and its Intelligence Service that was at stake. Now all we have on our hands is a hard case from Derby who was known for picking fights with his fellow sailors and for once calling his commanding officer a "soft southern tart." I agree that they'll make an example of this Canilla kid – you know, just to put the frighteners on any other Winston lowlifes thinking of trying it on with one of Her Maj's boys – but I doubt he'll get more than a year or two for his handiwork. *Fair's fair*, old chap.'

Picture a long stretch of coastline. At one end there is point A, at the other point B. You are in a launch. You have just dropped off your load at point A and now need to sail thirty miles to point B. Suddenly, a larger, faster, more powerful boat appears behind you intent on stopping you by any means. How do you manage to reach point B without getting forced ashore, shunted aside, or rammed and sunk? Well, the first thing you do is you pray. To Jesus, to Allah, to *la Virgen del Carmen*, to Neptune, to Nemo the fish – to whoever, in other words, might be out there and prepared to lend you a hand in this terrible hour of need. Then you play to your strengths, you capitalise on whatever advantages you have over your pursuers. The boat behind you may be faster than you and have a bigger engine, but you are in a smaller, more manoeuvrable vessel, with the ability to swerve and take sharper corners. If you veer off at the right moment, you will be able to wrongfoot your pursuer, to send him in the opposing direction for a few precious seconds. Normally, what you do is you wait until the son of a bitch is just behind you. You wait and wait and wait, keeping calm, holding your nerve, resisting the temptation to do anything stupid. Then – when his bow is practically scraping against your stern – you pull out the throttle and turn your steering wheel rapidly to the left or to the right, causing the awkward, clumsy beast to briefly lose its bearings.

Ideally, though, you don't want to be performing last-moment manoeuvres of this sort. Ideally, you want your chasers to keep their distance, to treat you with respect. The only way you can do this is by travelling as close as possible to the shoreline, in just a few feet of water. It's all about brinkmanship, about utilising your strengths and exploiting your adversary's weaknesses. Phantoms have a V-shaped, but essentially flat keel and can travel in very shallow water; *la*

Turbo and *la Dos Motores* – big lumbering bastards that they are – will run aground in depths of less than seven or eight feet. Of course, if you draw too near the shore, you yourself will come a cropper and end up stranded there like an injured seagull floating in front of a killer whale. This is why the *guardias* and the customs men sail as close as they can to the shore themselves – waiting for you to slip up, hoping to cajole you into an error of judgment. But here's the thing: just as you can run aground or hit a submerged shopping trolley, they can also come to grief on an uncharted sandbank or get their propellers tangled in a fisherman's net. What kills your enemy, as the old saying goes, can very well end up killing you too.

Especially hazardous for pursuer and prey alike are the piers, jetties and assorted breakwaters which dot the length of the Costa del Sol and the Costa Tropical beyond it. Smugglers will tell you that there are two types of projecting structures: the makeshift, low-budget sort, usually made out of rubble or interlocking tetrapods, which protect a nearby marina or a beach from incoming winds and waves; and the more solid concrete constructions which serve as berthing places in their own right. The former are ringed by submerged terraces of rock and cannot be approached by deep-hulled vessels. But the latter have been specifically designed as mooring points and have no protective buffer around them. If you are staying close to the shoreline and see one of these fixed berthing piers before you, not only will you have to pull out to go around it; you also know that, because the water surrounding them is so deep, the vessel chasing you will be able to plonk itself right on your arse. In metaphorical terms, this is the point when the mouse turns a corner and finds himself staring right into the eyes of the waiting cat, the moment of maximum danger. There will only be an armspan or two between you and your pursuers and, as you go around the pier, you will hear their taunts and insults, you will be blinded by their glaring searchlights. Never mind. Take a deep breath. Be positive. Continue focusing on what you are doing. The bastards will want to force you against the pier, but they won't be taking too many risks either, knowing that the slightest slip-up on their part could see them crash against solid concrete. Use that knowledge to your advantage. Treat their hesitancy as a defensive weapon. Think – as Manu used to say – like the mouse in *Tom and Jerry*. If you can anticipate what your enemy's next move will be, if you can already visualise it in your head, you'll nearly always – like Jerry – find a way of squirming out of trouble at the last moment.

A quick word about our pursuers. People in Gib have this idea that the *guardia civil* are all jackbooted, para-military ultra-*fascistas* directed by Franco from beyond the grave – sneering, moustachioed, anti-Gibraltarian bullies who will go out of their way to target and intimidate anybody coming from the Rock. But this was not the impression Manu and I got while battling it out with them in the Straits and the Alboran Sea. Apart from one or two rogue elements within their organisation, we are talking about professional and highly trained guys who follow the rules and know at all times what they are doing. For instance, you very rarely see *la guardia* indulging in dangerous or *chulo de mierda* manoeuvres out at sea, or goading you with insults whenever they break into your radio channel. With *el servicio aduanero*, however, it was a different matter. Ageing, world-weary officers plucked from far-off places like Galicia and Asturias, most of them already in the final stages of their careers, they came to the Straits with a real sense of vindictiveness and malice, convinced that *contrabandistas* – especially *contrabandistas llanitos* – were vermin to be exterminated. These were the guys who tried to chase you into the path of submerged rocks, who didn't think twice about shooting a flare at your face. *'Hijoputas malnacidos llanitos de mierda!'* you'd hear them taunting you via their megaphones and onboard loudspeakers. *'Dejad que os coja. Les vamos a follar el culo tantas veces y tan duramente que vais a terminar más jorobados que la puta vieja esa de vuestra reina!'* [33]

Here's a curious anecdote for you. When Manu was seventeen years old, he climbed the cliff between the two little tunnels in Rosia Bay. Handing me his towel and his *chanclas moras,* he stretched his arms behind his back, slapped his cheeks, cracked his knuckles, then began scaling the rock face, looking all the time for handholds and clumps of weeds, resting here and there on the odd rocky overhang, pulling further and further away from the ground. Before long a modest crowd of beachgoers had assembled below on Camp Bay Road. *'Ay, ay, qué se va a matar!'*[34] cried an old lady in a sunhat. 'He's got to be as high as a kite!' a middle-aged man in Speedos snorted beside her. 'Spiderman, Spiderman!' a small kid yelled, laughing and shaking his head. Meanwhile,

---

[33] 'You fucking Gibraltarian bastards! Wait till we get our hands on you! We are going to fuck you up the ass so hard and so many times that you are going to end up more hunchbacked than that old whore of your queen!'

[34] 'Oh my God, what if he falls and breaks his neck!'

Manu continued climbing higher and higher, never once looking down or behind him, unaware, it seemed, of the uproar he was causing. Very soon he was within reach of the summit. Holding on to a projecting ledge, his sinewy arms glistening with sweat, he kicked out with his right leg so that his foot hooked over the top of the cliff, and that was it: he had managed to scramble on to the peak. Swivelling around, displaying no emotion, he sat down with his legs hanging over the edge of the precipice and brought out the lighter and packet of Du Maurier tucked in the waistband of his swimming trunks. He lit a cigarette. He puffed at it tranquilly, all the while staring at the far horizon, never acknowledging the group of spectators gathered fifty yards below. When the cigarette was about to die between his fingers, he stubbed it out on a rock, slipped the packet and lighter back into his trunks, and started making his way down the cliff. He descended slowly and cautiously, stretching out his right leg to test for potential footholds, occasionally hanging from his fingertips as he struggled to find suitable projections on which to rest his weight. Several times he made the assembled audience gasp or bring their hands to their mouths, but he carried on without a word, showing no panic. When he at last alighted on solid ground, he walked through the crowd of stunned spectators to where I was standing and, slipping on his *chanclas* and throwing his towel over his shoulder, urged me with his eyes to follow him in the direction of the second – and longer – of the two Rosia Bay tunnels. 'I knew he was zonked,' Mr Speedo snickered before we entered the tunnel and disappeared from the scene. 'Did you see those crazy *porrista* eyes?'

But Manu wasn't drugged or even drunk; Manu was just being Manu. Even back in our middle school days, he had oscillated between periods of glacial calm and sudden rushes of excitability, baffling teachers and educational psychologists alike. One moment he would be sitting there with his pens and protractors ... and the next he'd have half his body out of the window, trying to jump onto the roof of the outhouse adjacent to our classroom. Nowadays they'd probably call it bipolarity or attention deficit hyperactivity disorder, but at the time there was no such terminology and Manu was just known as a problem or difficult child, the sort of kid that teachers feared and hoped would never land in their class. But was he really bipolar? Did he suffer from some undiagnosed mental health affliction? If you ask me, he simply had a hunger for intense experiences, a need to continually test himself. Quite possibly it had something to do with the absence of his father; it may even be that he was born with abnormally high levels of testosterone. With mercurial, 'predictably unpredictable' characters like Manu, it is always hard to map out behavioural origins, always difficult to identify the motives behind their actions. What I can safely say, though, is that over the years this appetite for danger became more and more pronounced, leading him into all kinds of wild, fuckwitted scrapes. One day he'd climb the cliff between the two tunnels at Rosia; another time he'd go up to some couple and tell the bloke he wanted to fuck his girlfriend in the arse; later that same day, he'd overtake a car while going past *el Black Spot*[35] near Catalan Bay, risking a head-on collision with whatever was coming towards him

---

[35] A dangerous bend on Sir Herbert Miles Road.

from the other side of the bend. It was as if he couldn't help himself, as if he needed to keep topping up his adrenaline levels.

The most dramatic expression of this behaviour came when we were out at sea battling with the Spanish law-enforcement agencies. Other pilots dreaded being chased by *la Turbo* or *la Dos Motores*, but Manu Gonzalez relished these skirmishes, got a real kick out of the bruising encounters. More than that, I always felt that he secretly hankered for them. The moment we spotted one of the enemy vessels, you could feel this current of expectation emanating from him, a sort of invisible force field. Yes, it was true that he had a paranoid fear of being apprehended and recognized as *el Pantera's* son – but once the Spaniards latched themselves behind us all that was forgotten and he'd be catapulted into a high-octane frenzy, revelling in the swerving manoeuvres, the sputtering engine noises and the ice-cold splashes of seawater. Again and again he'd shout, he'd laugh, he'd throw *cortes de manga,* he'd let go of the steering wheel to clap or raise his arms, he'd even get up on his seat and bare his buttocks at our pursuers, not giving a shit whether he'd lose his balance and topple overboard. Once he whipped himself into these moods, too, it was impossible to determine when he'd snap out of them. Sometimes we got off the boat at Sheppard's Marina and he was as calm as if he had been sitting cross-legged for hours under a Bodhi tree; there wasn't a flicker of emotion on his face. But other times his eyes – which were already large to begin with – were even more flared than usual and his speech was difficult to understand. We'd be sitting there breakfasting at the Market Tavern, say, and he'd be incessantly twirling his knife and fork, speaking at a hundred miles an hour, looking as crazy and fucked-up as Jack Nicholson in *The Shining*. From the expression on the other diners' faces, we could tell they thought Manu was *encocado* or *anfetaminado*, but Derek, Richita*, el Niño* and I knew better than that. *El Manu* was just being *el Manu*.

In the early days of Maikito's trial, Manu was twice removed from the courtroom for causing a disturbance. The first time it happened was on a Friday afternoon, less than a fortnight into the hearing. Launching out of his seat, yielding to a flash of rage, he shouted 'When's this shitshow going to end?' – and was promptly escorted out of the chamber by a shaven-headed security guard. The second incident occurred three days later and came in response to the prosecuting lawyer describing his brother as 'a morally disreputable character.' 'Disreputable *tu puta madre!*' Manu suddenly roared, forcing all heads in the courtroom to turn in his direction, bringing the trial to a temporary halt.

Manu was given a stern reprimand that Monday and told he risked going to jail if he continued interrupting the hearing, but in hindsight the judge needn't have bothered. Although we carried on taking our seats in the public gallery, Manu and I were quickly losing patience with the whole thing, no longer believing that the trial would end in just three or four weeks. Even the atmosphere in the courtroom, it seemed, was changing – with fewer spectators turning up and the exchanges between the prosecution and defence lawyers becoming increasingly dull and repetitive. Soon there were neither 'Winston Boys' nor GBC cameras to be seen anywhere; and out of the three tabloid hacks, only the guy with the monkfish eyes continued sitting there with his notebooks and his pens, looking sicker and sicker with each passing week. We ourselves were only coming to the courtroom every second or third session – and even then it was more to accompany Manu's mum than to follow arguments and speeches that neither of us really understood. By then, too, my mate was a very different animal – sitting there without saying a word, only shifting on his seat to stretch out his arms or to pick his nose and flick a bogey at the floor. Finally, one morning in November 1992 Manu failed to show up at my Castle Road flat before the start of that day's session. Afraid that the lazy arse had slept in, I rang his number from our house phone. When he answered moments later, he told me to wait a sec and then – after unhooking the cordless receiver and taking it with him into the bathroom – said that he was through with the whole charade. 'The judge, the lawyers, the ushers, the British journalists, the smirking coppers, the *guiri* big shots with their medals,' he hissed venomously, not wanting his mother to hear what he was saying, ' – they can all go to hell! They are going to do with my brother whatever they fucking like, and I'm not going to sit there like *un cabrón* waiting to hear a verdict that was decided ages ago.'

The way we stopped attending Maikito's trial a third of the way through the hearing still pains and embarrasses me, but this is what Manu and I were like back then: impulsive and scatter-brained, unable to concentrate on anything other than what was easy to understand and directly in front of us. This was especially the case when we were in the boat and our whole world somehow ended up contracting into the space of that cramped damp cockpit. Stationary oil tankers, cruise liners, patrolling warships, traditional fishing boats – we passed them all as if they were cardboard cut-outs in a game of paintball, not for one second thinking they contained real flesh-and-blood human beings. It was the same with the illegal migrants crossing the Straits in their pathetic dinghies. We had heard about the recent spate of drownings and knew that they were out there somewhere, but their invisibility rendered them distant and abstract, less real than the cigarette packets, chocolate wrappers, bottles of Heineken and other rubbish we kept tossing overboard during our journeys. If either of us ever brought up the subject of the dinghies, the other would immediately cut in, complaining that it was too early in the morning to be dealing with that shit. 'Talk to me about football or women or how high we're going to get this Saturday night, *anda, compá,*' was a typical rejoinder. '*Qué* the last thing I want to do is think about those poor bastards!'

Sometimes, however, it was impossible to shut out all that *realness*. Take the night we saw the floating corpse. For most of the evening we had sat in the van with *el Richita* and *el Niño,* waiting in an alley near Saint Theresa's Church for the weather to improve. 'Fucking shitty rain,' Manu kept saying, biting his nails and spitting the bits out. 'Why can't those *inservibles* at GBC ever get the weather forecast right?' When we finally set off from Sheppard's at three, the storm surge had caused the level of the water to rise by about twelve inches – an unusually large amount for the predominantly tideless Mediterranean. Not just that, a stiff wind was blowing from the direction of Algeciras, shrieking eerily as it skimmed the surface of the water and causing the sorts of dips and swirls you only encounter far out at sea. Loosening the mooring ropes, I swivelled on my haunches and gave Manu the thumbs-up sign, letting him know that he could start reversing out of the berthing bay.

For the rest of the night I focused on the tasks at hand – navigating across the Straits, sailing down *el foso de San Felipe,* dropping off the Marlboro cases by Club Náutico, receiving the taped-up bales from the Catalan at the desalination plant. The sea levels were still very high in Ceuta and at *la playa del Peñoncillo,* just off Torrox Costa, where Matković and his men were waiting for the merchandise – but the wind and rain had abated considerably. That must have been one hell of a squall earlier, I told myself, remembering how the elements had battered our van down at North Front. Relieved to be on our way home, I ducked under the windshield and asked Manu if he was still interested in coming to the *Market Tavern* with *el Richita* and me for an early-morning breakfast. '*Po claro,*' he cackled over the breeze. 'When have I ever turned down a nice, greasy fry-up?'

Ten minutes later, as we were approaching the Detached Mole, I saw the body floating there in front of us. From a distance it could have passed for a half-submerged oil drum or a dead dolphin entangled in a drift net. But as we got closer I noticed what looked like an outstretched arm and the contours of a grey-haired head.

'Stop, stop!' I shouted. 'What's that over there?'

'That's just a dead tuna,' Manu cried, closing the throttle.

'No way, man! That's not a dead tuna. Go back so that we can have a look.'

Shrugging, Manu turned the Phantom around and steered to within a couple of yards of the buoyant mass. It was a corpse all right. Male. Middle-aged. Half of a flip-flop clinging abjectly to one of its feet. Floating facedown and with its arms extended beyond its head, it made me think of an emissary lying prostrate before a petulant King-Emperor, a condemned man waiting for the fall of the executioner's axe.

'What shall we do?' I asked, looking anxiously at Manu.

'What do you mean – what shall we do? We'll go back home and have breakfast with *el Richita* as agreed, *que si no.*'

'But the body...'

'He's dead, man,' Manu responded, shaking his head. '*Al mutawafaa,* as they say in Ceuta. Forget about the poor bastard, will you, *Ojo Tuerto?* If we don't get a move on, the dining room in the Market Tavern will be full and we'll be waiting all day for our fucking all-day breakfasts!'

And so we turned around and jetted off towards the Detached Mole, leaving the body floating there with its arms outstretched and its face in the water, the tatty flip-flop now swirling about in our frothy white wake.

I've spent the last few weeks taking pictures of Upper Town houses with my phone. I photograph the most decrepit and neglected, the ones in the worst condition. Just down the road from my place, for instance, there is the former dwelling of Mrs Alice Peña, one of Mariadelaida Gonzalez's fellow cleaners at the NAAFI and the mother of Felicity Peña, one of our old classmates at Saint Mary's. Once a bright and cheerful marigold yellow, its walls have faded over the years to a dirty diarrhoea-brown and are now supported by a combination of planks and rusted acrow props. Every time I walk past this building, I am fascinated by the archipelago of loose plasterwork clinging to its façade; I am mesmerised by the untidily laid cables and pipes wrapped like a moth-eaten corset around its decaying shell. What is it about old buildings that so grip me? Why do I keep photographing them? Could it be because they remind me of my own fragile condition? Because I somehow see them as the last standing witnesses to my childhood?

I am especially drawn to old doors. Graffitied doors. Rotting doors. Doors with old-fashioned rim locks. Doors with wrought-iron lunettes. Doors without numbers. Doors without locks. Doors that have been bricked up. Doors hanging from a single hinge. Doors where the paint is coming off and you can see earlier textures and colours.

Photographing these Upper Town entranceways, I can't help thinking of all the people that must have walked through them in former times, each of them saddled with their own worries and concerns, focused on their here and now. Did these folk ever pause to think of those who had lived in their buildings before them? Did they wonder who'd take their place once they were gone? Or were they like most people nowadays – uninterested in anything except their own comfort and convenience?

More time passed. On 7 January 1994, as Manu and I were swilling Heinekens at the Bahía's outdoor terrace, our lookout Derek came running towards us from the direction of Corral Road. I haven't talked much about *el Derek, alias el Barriga,* alias *el Flaquito,* so far in the course of this story, but let me tell you that he was one lazy son of a gun, the sort of *llanito* who gets into his car to drive from Glacis to Marina Bay, all of five minutes' walk away. He had a chin the size of a tennis ball and was permanently unshaven, a combination of attributes that made it look as if he carried a baby hedgehog curled up on his neck. On his trips up to Governor's Lookout and O'Hara's Battery he always took with him a plastic bag filled with Maltesers, Mars Bars, Galaxies, Aeros, Twixes, Murray Mints, Rowntree's Fruit Pastilles, Fruitellas, Jelly Babies and other goodies. He'd set the crumpled Safeway's bag beside his binoculars and his walkie-talkie and start munching away, going from one treat to the next without interruption, chucking the chocolate-stained and sugar-encrusted wrappers into the nearby bushes. Sometimes, when you talked to him over the radio, you could tell that he had a sweet or a piece of chocolate in his gob; it wasn't that you could hear munching or swallowing noises, it's just that his voice *sounded different*, as if there was half a Mars Bar stuffed between his tongue and the side of his mouth.

El Barriga, in short, was your typical couch potato, the kind of bloke whose idea of heaven was to sit at home watching TV and cramming his face with sweet treats. And yet there he was that day – running past the Waterport Roundabout with his cheeks aflame and his belly wobbling under his XXXXL T-shirt, looking like he could collapse at any moment. Anybody with a normal brain would have sussed out that something serious was afoot, that the guy must have had some important news to communicate. But, half-pissed as we were, tickled pink by the sight of all that juddering fat, we watched him come closer and closer without once thinking what could be wrong. 'Look at this one,' Manu jested with the neck of his beer bottle almost touching his lips. 'I bet he's run out of Mars Bars and he's going to Ramson's to top up his supplies, *el cabrón gordinflón!*'

'What the fuck is wrong with you two arseholes?' was the first thing that Derek, breathless and bent-double, blurted out on reaching our table. 'I've been sending messages to your pagers for ages without getting a reply.'

'What's up, *compá?*' Manu said, quickly sobering up.

'Your brother, that's what's up.'

'What about my brother?'

'He's just been sentenced to four years for manslaughter.'

'What the fuck are you on about – my brother hasn't even been convicted yet!'

'They convicted him this morning and because of the special circumstances of his case he was sentenced straightaway.'

'What the fuck!' Manu cried, leaping out of his seat with his fists clenched. 'You're telling me that Maikito's going to have to spend another fucking four years in jail?'

'*No, no,* man,' Derek wheezed out placatingly. 'Let me finish, *tío*. They've given him four years, but they've taken into consideration that he's already done nearly four years in the nick.'

'And what does that mean?'

'What do you think it means, brother?' *el Flaquito* grinned. 'In eleven weeks Michael will be a free man!'

Manu stared at *el Barriga* for a moment, trying to process what had just been said, then threw his arms around our lookout and kissed him on the neck. Whooping, laughing, screaming with delight, he attempted to lift the twenty-two-stone Derek but discovered he was too heavy to budge. 'You fucking fat bastard,' he muttered sheepishly but good-naturedly, then grunted aloud and tried again – this time managing to hoist *el Flaquito* a couple of inches off the ground. He then punched the air in a gesture of triumph and made his way around the different outdoor tables, high-fiving unemployed drop-outs and geriatric domino players, hugging disabled ex-smugglers and widowed *pensionistas*. In this jubilant mood he strutted up to the bar and asked Mehdi to bring everybody whatever they wanted 'plus a little bit extra' – two pints if they were on the beer, a bottle of wine if they had asked for *un tinto*, a coffee and a brandy if they were having a *café con leche*. Once he had provided for his fellow *'Bahieros'*, Manu invited Derek and me to move with him to a spot next to the low wall separating the outdoor terrace from the public pavement. A tattered Heineken sun umbrella shielded the table in question from the sun, but Manu reached out and undid its clasp, allowing the green and white canvas flaps to whoosh to a close.

'*Pues ná*,' he said, sitting down on one of the plastic white chairs and propping his boots on the seat beside him, 'let's celebrate, lads!'

Snapping his fingers, he called over *el Mehdi* and asked him to wipe down the table and bring us an ashtray. When everything was to his satisfaction, Manu gave the Moroccan a twenty-quid tip and then sank even deeper into his chair, all the time keeping an eye out for friends, relatives and acquaintances walking past the front of *el Bahía*. 'Have a drink with me, *anda,*' he would say to these passers-by, waving them over to our table. 'Come and celebrate with us our Maikito's release!' Most people said they were in a rush and didn't have time to waste, but one or two stopped and had a quick whisky or a brandy with us. Soon Derek, Manu and I were so drunk that we could hardly remember why we were drinking or what we were celebrating; all that mattered was to keep ordering drinks and knocking them back. We laughed; we belched; we stomped our feet; we banged our fists on the table; we skinned up; we broke glasses – most of the time accidentally, but once or twice just for the hell of it; we argued; we arm-wrestled; we wolf-whistled at girls; we made fun of queers and fat birds; we kept rising to our feet and hollering at other 'Winston Boys' driving past, encouraging the dudes to park up and come and join us, in the process attracting reproving looks from families and *gente del pish.*[36] At one point things got so animated that Manu jumped up on our table and began tap dancing between the empty bottles and glasses, knocking several of them to the ground, tipping an imaginary hat in Mehdi's direction every time one of them smashed to pieces. Laughing, I looked up and saw that the afternoon sun – now on the latter stages of its parabolic journey towards Algeciras and the hills behind Tarifa – was suspended directly above my mate's head, encircling his upper body in a luminous golden halo. For a moment I continued hooting and clapping, tears of laughter now streaming down my cheeks. Then something strange happened: as I was sitting there raising my bottle of Heineken towards him and squinting against the sun, I had a feeling that things were about to go seriously wrong for us. It wasn't a premonition or a vision or anything as dramatic as that; it wasn't even the thought that the soon-to-be-released Maikito might end up usurping my place on the boat. I just felt that something, somewhere was stirring malignly into being, ready to pounce on us and upend our present state of rapture.

Ironically, nothing of any significance happened over the next month. For a while it even looked as if we were on a lucky streak – with not a single Spanish law-enforcement vessel to be seen on three consecutive runs. However, this must have been Providence's way of messing with us, one of those unnatural lulls preceding a violent storm. Our problems started on a Thursday night/morning, as we were

---

[36] Gente del pish – snobby or affected people (llanito).

bringing a shipment over to a beach near Marbella. Earlier that same week we had made a drop-off in the Atunara area of La Línea, right in the shadow of the Rock, but due to increased police patrols in that neighbourhood we were now unloading twenty-five miles further up the coast, at a beach in Nueva Andalucía. Since the guys on shore hadn't radioed us for twenty minutes, we sailed in slowly and with our balaclavas on, making as little noise as possible, relying on the glow emanating from the nearby N-340 highway to draw out the one or two rocks poking out of the sea. Suddenly, when we were about thirty yards offshore, two giant searchlights were switched on somewhere on the beach and the entire bay was flooded with light. 'Hands up, *cabrones!*' an angry Spanish voice crackled out of a megaphone. 'Hands up!' Instinctively, Manu slipped the throttle into reverse and we backed out of the cove as best as we could, scraping the side of the Phantom against some rocks that would have surely sunk us had we hit them head on. Bullets pinged like snapping guitar strings around us; pieces of limestone broke off the half-submerged rocks and then splashed into the water. 'Are they following us?' Manu shouted after a moment. 'I don't think so,' I replied, twisting my neck to look behind us. 'I think there were only two jeeps on the beach!'

We must have been half a mile offshore when Matković called us on the radio. He explained that the *guardia* had pounced on his men and confiscated their transceivers. 'The bastards had the beach under surveillance,' he rasped out in Spanish. 'Never mind. I've got some other guys waiting for you at our usual spot near Saladavieja. Let's get this fucking job done, boys!'

Acting on the Serb's instructions, we made our way inshore to Saladavieja and this time unloaded our cargo without any problems. Manu even jumped out of the boat to smoke a cigarette once the bales had been spirited away by Matković's men. 'Have a cig with me, *anda, Alex*,' he shouted from the shoreline, playfully waving at me to join him. 'Look at the full moon – *mira como brilla!*'

The last thing I wanted was to get out of the Phantom and smoke a cigarette with him on Spanish soil, but I still climbed out of the boat and let him light a Du Maurier for me. I remember feeling a terrible sense of unease as we stood there smoking in silence, an almost dizzying awareness of the pulse in my ears. It was a similar sensation to the one I had experienced at *el Bahía*, but sharper and more intense, even more disorienting. The lapping of the waves – normally so calming and restful – sounded sinister and threatening; the Phantom's engine growled like a psycho murderer's chainsaw. 'Something is not right,' I thought, looking at my moon-lit companion. 'Something bad is about to happen.' As I reached this worrying conclusion, Manu tossed his cigarette butt on the sand and walked through the ankle-deep waters to the boat. 'Let's get going,' he said, throwing a leg over the gunwale. 'All this sea air is making me fucking bloody hungry, man!'

Five or six minutes later we saw *la Turbo*. She was just off Casares Costa, tucked behind the larger of the two sea rocks opposite La Punta del Salto de la Mora. In less than thirty seconds she left her place by the rocks and latched onto us, forcing us to change course and hog the shoreline. The only thing we could do was to ignore her and continue as we were doing, knowing that the *Turbo's* deep keel wouldn't allow her to enter such shallow waters. After a while, just to add to our difficulties, a customs helicopter appeared above us. Up and down the chopper went, rolling from side to side, tracking us with its powerful searchlight, hovering above us for a second and then swooping down to within two or three yards of our heads. Nearing El Puerto de la Duquesa, we had to swing out to avoid the first concrete jetty forming part of El Puerto's *Marina Deportivo*. At that moment the helicopter started shooting at us. Not fucking flares, but live fucking bullets. *Plop-plop-plop* was the sound they made as they landed on the water around us. *Plop-plop-plop*. 'Why are they shooting at us?' I shouted at Manu. 'Can't they see that there's nothing in our hold?' But I don't think he heard me. Or if he did, he chose to ignore me. Through the breathing vent in his balaclava, I could see that his mouth was twisted into a smile, his teeth glinting like bone showing through a wound. *El muy cabrón's* enjoying this shit, I thought. He's fucking getting off on the whole thing! Shocked, I grabbed the aluminium handrail to my left and forced myself to look ahead. Just then a bullet hit the Phantom and the engine began making an ominous whirring sound – like that of a washing machine about to conk out. I tightened my grip on the handrail and for a moment rocked backwards and forwards, as if willing the boat on with my own momentum – but it was no use: smoke was now pouring out of the engine and we were rapidly losing power. Glancing over my shoulder, I saw that the Turbo was coming towards us and had no intention of stopping. *'Qué se nos echa encima!'* I shouted, preparing to leap overboard. *'Qué se nos echa encima!'*[37] For a fraction of a second

---

[37] 'She's going to hit us! She's going to hit us!'

I looked at Manu and to my consternation saw that he was still seated behind the wheel, either oblivious or not caring about the threat now yards behind us. Then, stepping on the gunwale and thinking *suit yourself*, I closed my eyes and jumped into the sea.

Our Phantom was rammed from the side that night and broken into two separate pieces, the larger of which landed upright on the seabed and ended up poking like a shark fin out of the water. Having survived the collision unscathed, I was fished out of the sea and driven to the *guardia civil's* headquarters in La Línea, where, after being furnished with shoes and dry clothes, I was examined by a doctor. Once I received the all-clear, I was given something to eat and put in one of the holding cells. For the next two or three hours I lay on an uncomfortable mattress bed, staring forlornly at the ceiling and wondering what on earth had happened to Manu. Moments after jumping into the water, I had shouted 'are you okay?' and he had yelled back 'yes, yes, all good!' – but that was all I heard before getting scooped out of the sea and bundled into a jeep waiting by the pier. En route to *la jefatura*, I had repeatedly asked the *guardias* about my mate, but they had ignored each and every one of my questions, their eyes focused sternly and unblinkingly on the road ahead.

At eight-thirty in the morning, I was escorted out of my cubicle and led into a small, windowless office that reeked of cigar smoke. Stacks of elastic-band-tied folders jutted out of cardboard boxes; a ring of used foam cups surrounded an old-fashioned vacuum flask. High on the wall hung a framed portrait of Juan Carlos I just after his coronation – the purple of his sash having faded over the years to a sun-bleached, almost translucent shade of lavender. 'Stay right here,' my warder said, turning around and leaving me alone in the room. After a few minutes a tall guy with fancy epaulettes came into the office and sat down on a chair across the table from me. Big, bandolero moustache. Sideburns practically touching the sides of his mouth. From the medal ribbons pinned on his jacket, I knew that he was a *guardia civil* big shot, one of their top ranks for sure. With a politeness and *cortesía* that took me by surprise, he asked me what my friend and I had been doing on a fast launch in Spanish waters at four o'clock in the morning.

'Nothing,' I replied in Spanish, 'just going for a ride.'

'Just going for a ride, eh?' *el comandante* repeated my words in a world-weary tone.

'*Sí.*'

'Are you sure you weren't on your way back to Gibraltar after unloading a shipment of Winston or cannabis somewhere on the Costa del Sol?'

I nodded.

'And that you had nothing to do with a little, shall we say, incident that occurred some hours ago on a beach at Nueva Andalucía?'

'I don't know what you're talking about.'

'Are you sure?'

I leaned back and nodded again, then asked if he knew anything about Manu.

'Your friend is okay,' the big guy said, placing a hand on the desk and (it seemed to me) staring at his own fingernails. 'You don't need to worry about him.'

'How do I know you're telling me the truth?'

He looked at me with a sad sort of expression and then got up and walked out of the office. At this juncture I thought I'd be marched straight back to the holding cell, but instead I was led to a jeep and told to get in the back seat. I assumed they were going to transfer me from the *guardia's* headquarters to the main police station in Algeciras, but when we reached *la avenida Príncipe de Asturias,* the road running parallel to the frontier fence, the vehicle suddenly drove over a pedestrian crossing and switched onto the opposite lane, pulling up with a jerk in front of the border gates. 'Clear off!' the driver snarled in Spanish, unlocking the back door and throwing my passport at me. 'Go back to your shitty Rock!'

I got out of the car, walked up to the passport control kiosk and showed them my passport. Without even looking at the document, the *policía nacional* nodded and waved me through. From there I made my way to the Gibraltar Immigration post, some twenty or thirty yards away, and into the building the Immigration people share with their colleagues in Customs. I was relieved to be back on Gibraltarian soil, but I was also worried sick about Manu, fearing he had been seriously hurt in the collision. Desperate to find out what was going on, I went into the payphone just behind the 'Visit

Gibraltar' kiosk and called Matković, but he told me he hadn't heard anything, his words punctuated by a series of highly irritating yawns. Before hanging up, he promised me he would ring *Rafael el Tortuga*, one of the local cops on his father-in-law's payroll, and ask him to make some enquiries on his behalf. '*Vale,* Bobby,' I mumbled into the phone. 'Give me a call if you hear something, will you?' I then made my way across the runway towards the town centre, dog-tired but sick at heart, struggling to hold back my tears. Approaching Casemates Square, I saw another payphone and decided to call Manu's mum. I realised it would be a risky manoeuvre – after all, how can you ask a mother if the *guardia civil* has been in touch about her son? – but the uncertainty was killing me. Tensely, I dialled Mariadelaida's number ... and nearly dropped the receiver when I heard that fucking rascal on the line.

'*Quillo, quillo,*' I choked out in relief. 'I thought something bad had happened to you!'

'I'm okay,' Manu replied feebly.

'When did you get home?'

'This morning at nine.'

'Did they also drop you off at the border?'

A long pause followed, at the end of which Manu mouthed an almost inaudible '*Sí.*'

'*Qué suerte que nos han soltao, no?*' [38]

---

[38] 'How lucky they've let us go, don't you think?'

'*Cómo que suerte?*' Manu shot back angrily. 'What happened last night was attempted fucking murder – and they fucking know it! Shooting at us from the helicopter and then driving *la Turbo* at maximum speed towards the Phantom! Who the fuck does that kind of thing? And then the Spanish tell us *llanitos* that we have no reason to fear them! Fucking hell, man, no wonder they washed their hands of us as soon as possible. That bastard *guardia civil* with the moustache must have known that the *aduaneros* crossed a line last night. Best get rid of the two *llanitos* before they become a problem, he must have thought!'

———————◆———————

The ramming of the Phantom affected Manu and me in very different ways. My friend hated *los sloppies* for what they had done and vowed he would get even with them one day, regarding the whole episode as a state-sanctioned attempt on our lives. 'Those fuckers will pay sooner or later,' was a phrase he often said during those days. 'If you fuck with me, I will fuck with you ten times worse.' How exactly he proposed to 'fuck' with a national law-enforcement agency like *el servicio aduanero* was, unsurprisingly, not something he went into detail about. But the need for revenge was still there. You could see it in the glimmer in his eyes when he talked about the incident off La Duquesa, in his facial contortions, in the way he'd spit out a gob of phlegm and then do a brusque *corte de manga* in the direction of the border, as if he could somehow transmit his anger and his hatred telegraphically across the frontier fence.

For me, on the other hand, what happened that night was a wake-up call. For close to two years now we had been tempting Fate with this kilo-of-hash-for-a-case business; we had really, really – and I mean, *really, really* – pushed our luck. 'This shit cannot carry on,' I thought. 'This shit has to stop. As soon as we get a new boat, we need to ditch the drugs and start getting paid in pesetas again. We have to get back to basics and stop being so fucking greedy!' Guessing that Manu wouldn't be too pleased to hear all this, I internalised my feelings for a couple of days, all the while wondering how to broach the subject. When I finally spilled the beans, my mate got so worked up that he stomped up to a Main Street rubbish bin and – *cagándose en la puta madre de la Turbo y en el cabrón que la había estado pilotando*[39] – kicked the plastic container out of its cylindrical metal bracket. I waited for him to calm down, then restated my case, telling him that I would quit if we kept getting paid in drugs. Manu closed his eyes at this point and exhaled through his nose. 'Let me think about it,' he muttered in a much quieter voice, flipping open his packet of Du Maurier and throwing a cigarette into his mouth. 'Maybe you are right.' A day or two later, when we went down to the ship brokers at Marina Bay to check up on how our order for a new boat was progressing, he told me he had thought *en serio* about the matter and realised I was right: we weren't getting paid enough for the risks we were taking. Al-Jaouhari needed to understand this, he said; it was necessary that the fucker started seeing things from our perspective as well. Thrilled to be hearing all this, I suggested going to the nearest payphone and communicating our decision to the *ceutí* there and then – but Manu said this

---

[39] 'Goddamning *la Turbo* and the fucking bastard who had been piloting her!'

wasn't his style of doing things. 'No, no,' he insisted, shaking his head. 'These matters need to be settled in person. Face to face like men. We'll tell him once we get the new boat, on our next run to Ceuta. He won't be too impressed – neither will Matković when he hears what we've decided – but fuck them: what has to be done, has to be done.'

For the next few days I did not see or hear anything from Manu. I knew that he was receiving physio treatment for some ligaments he had damaged jumping out of the boat (and aggravated kicking that rubbish bin), so I didn't bother too much about our lack of contact. On top of that, the guy at Peninsular Sailing had told us that the new Phantom wouldn't be with us till the end of the month at least – so it wasn't as if we could plunge straight into work either. Late one evening, though, *el Manu* called me on the house phone and asked me if we could meet up. 'You want to go out at ten on a Sunday?' I whispered into the receiver, gazing at my father watching TV on the other side of the room. 'Everything will be dead at this time.' 'So much the better,' my mate replied mysteriously. 'We have things to talk about.'

We met at the Old Vic, a Main Street pub long closed down. It used to be located just up from the Post Office, between Cloister Ramp and Bell Lane, and was said to be Gibraltar's second smallest bar (after Ye Olde Rock on John Mackintosh Square, another pub that no longer exists). To reach it you had to go through an ordinary residential doorway, climb a flight of uncarpeted wooden stairs and turn right into a cramped room fitted with a counter, a few tables and a padded bench that ran along three of its four walls. Manu was the only person in the pub that evening, the barman having retired to the small kitchen unit behind the bar. Two crystal flutes and a bottle of fancy champagne rested on the table in front of him.

'Everything's sorted,' he said, pouring me a glass of fizz and one for himself.

'What's sorted?' I asked, sitting opposite him.

'Al-Jaouhari,' he responded, taking a sip of his drink. 'I've already spoken with him.'

'But I thought you wanted to speak face-to-face with the guy!'

He looked at me for a second with the rim of his flute held under his lips. 'I went to Ceuta yesterday on the Algeciras ferry,' he said.

'You went to Ceuta yesterday,' I cried, wanting to add 'without me?' but instead mumbling out 'with your bad leg?'

'I knew you were a bit upset about the ramming and I didn't want that *moro de mierda* to wind you up.... But don't worry,' he said, putting down his glass. 'Everything's sorted now.'

'Really? Al-Jaouhari didn't take it badly when you told him what we've decided?'

'Well, there were one or two bumps along the way, bro, but we got there in the end.'

'And how did you manage that?'

'Well, I told him it was not on that we were risking our necks in *aguas sloppy* just so we could earn a bit more than in our Marlboro-for-cash days.'

'And he agreed we could go back to payment in pesetas *just like that?*'

'Not exactly.'

'What do you mean?'

Manu smiled mischievously and retrieved a polaroid snap from a jacket pocket. 'Have a look at this baby,' he said, extending the photo in my direction.

I took the picture in my hands and found myself looking at a rigid-hull inflatable boat, the type of large powerful vessel known by smugglers as *una goma*. 'It's a zodiac tied up in some crumbling marina,' I said, putting the photograph down, ' – so what?'

'Not just a zodiac, *Ojo Tuerto*. Our zodiac, *compá.'*

'I don't follow you, man. What about the new Phantom we ordered?'

'The RIB is a present from Al-Jaouhari.'

'A present?'

Manu's eyes contracted and acquired a glazed, far-off look – the way they sometimes did at Bayside whenever he got asked a question in class. 'Okay, okay. How can I put this, Alexito? I went to see Al-Jaouhari, right? And while there I told him we were not happy with how things were going, *no?* Well, when I finished speaking, he made me an offer I couldn't refuse.'

'And what was that?' I asked suspiciously.

'He proposed we should forget about the Marlboro and just run drugs for him.'

'What the fuck, Manu!'

'I know, I know,' he said, shifting uneasily on his seat. 'At first I was pissed off too. *Cabrón moro,* I told myself. Up to his tricks again. But when I looked at the figures, I thought, "Fuck, man. If we play our cards right, we could make a killing with all this." Do you know how much *floosh* we could make per trip if we were just smuggling hash?'

'But I don't want any more cash, Manuel!' I cried. 'I just want us to go back to how things were!'

'Twenty grand per trip!' he went on excitedly. '*Veinte de los grandes, compá!* Nearly four times what we're earning now!'

I swear to you: I could have punched *el cabrón* as he sat there with that greedy leer on his face. Yes, he was bigger than me and yes, I had always felt slightly intimidated by his larger-than-life presence, but, boy, did I come close to lumping him one on the chin just then!

'It's like Al-Jaouhari said to me,' Manu continued, ignoring my obvious displeasure. 'You guys are already taking the same risks as the *gayumberos,* he said. Why not take advantage of the situation and take things up to the next level?'

'But I don't want to take things up to the next fucking level! I've already told you a million times.... Anyway, don't you think it's a bit weird that Al-Jaouhari has made you an offer like this? It all sounds a bit ropey, if you ask me.'

Manu picked up the polaroid snap from the table and put it back in his pocket. 'Man, Al-Jaouhari is a businessman with fingers in different pies. If anything, he's doing us a favour by giving us this fucking amazing chance.'

'What the fuck, man?' I replied, feeling the colour rise to my cheeks. 'Do you really think that Al-Jaouhari is doing us a favour? What that fucker wanted from the very beginning was to get us smuggling big quantities of drugs for him!'

'Come on,' Manu said, dismissively shaking his head. 'We've been working with the guy for nearly four years. If his plan was to get us smuggling hash for him, he hasn't exactly gone balls to the wall about it, *no crees?*'

I looked at him and saw that most of his teeth were visible in his mouth, a thread of spittle stretching like a strand of spider's web between his half-open lips. 'Is this something you planned with *el Maikito*?' I asked.

'Lo qué?'

'Maikito and you. Planning all this together so that when he comes out of jail he's back on the launch and making big money. Is that what's behind all this?'

'Ohu, ohu, you're really off your head, mate! How many times have I told you that Maikito is no longer interested in

smuggling or anything else that could land him back in jail. He's a changed man.'

'Yes, yes, I know,' I countered sarcastically. 'All he wants to do when he comes out is to smoke joints and eat fillet steaks – like you keep telling me.'

'And it's the fucking truth, man!' he hissed angrily and with his fists clenched. 'That's what he's always saying!' And then less vehemently: 'I arranged all this for you and me, Alex – not for anybody else!'

'What about Richita, Derek and *el Niño?*' I spat out, ignoring his attempt to butter me up. 'What happens with them? If we go ahead with all this, we won't really be needing them, will we?'

'We'll keep using Derek as our lookout,' he answered with the aplomb of someone who's already got everything worked out in his head. 'The other two we'll have to palm off somehow.'

I continued looking at him for some moments and then averted my gaze. 'Man, you're a fucking bastard. You really are.'

'*Venga ya, Alex,*' he said, leaning forward and grabbing me lightly by the arm. 'Don't get like this. Al-Jaouhari is giving us an opportunity to hit the big-time. This is what we've been waiting for all our fucking lives!'

'No, man,' I said, getting up from the table, 'this is not what we've been waiting for; *this is what you've negotiated behind my back.* Do you really for one moment think I believe that you asked Al-Jaouhari to pay us in pesetas again? Come on, man – you take me for a fool or something? You went to Ceuta especially to ask *el moro* if we could ditch the Marlboro and just start running hash for him, didn't you? That's why you did everything behind my back, why you cut me out of the whole fucking negotiating process. Well, what can I say, mate – congratulations. *Ponte un* badge, *colega*.[40] As always, Manu Gonzalez ends up getting what he wants. Except that this time I'm not going to form part of it. This time you're on your own, you bastard.'

And with these words, I turned around and strode out of the Old Vic, leaving him sitting there with his bottle of Dom Pérignon and his fancy crystal glasses, his eyebrows knitted in a sulky frown, the thread of spittle once again visible between his partly open lips.

Manu must have called me a dozen times over the next ten days. Every time the phone rang, I asked John Dennis Leslie to take the call, reminding him not to tell anyone I was home. 'No, he is not here, Manuel,' my old man would bark into the receiver moments later. 'He's just gone out. I'll get him to call you when he's back, okay, *pishón*.' Finally, around five o'clock one afternoon, someone knocked on our front door and from the living room window I saw my mate standing on the raised kerb bordering Castle Road. Gritting my teeth, I tiptoed over to the sofa and asked my father if he minded opening the door and telling Manu I had just set off towards

---

[40] Ponte un badge – pat yourself on the back (llanito).

el pueblo.[41] But this time John Dennis Leslie (who always had a soft spot for *el Manu*) refused to cover for me. 'I'm sick of lying to the kid,' he said, turning around and shuffling off in his carpet slippers towards his room. 'If you've fallen out with him and don't want him to come here any more, go and have it out with him yourself.'

When I opened the door, Manu was standing there with his hands in his pockets and a lit cigarette in his mouth. He wasn't smiling, but he wasn't pissed off either. All his medallions were tucked into his sweater except for his *Virgen del Carmen* piece, which now rested like an Olympic gold medal atop his chest. 'We've got to talk,' he said, spitting out the cigarette and crushing it with the heel of his boot. 'Things cannot continue like this.'

We went to our old hideout under the stone bridge. I hadn't been there in years and everything around us – the bulging abutments, the span and height of the vault, the space where we used to sit – looked smaller and less impressive than I remembered, imbued with all the strangeness of a half-forgotten dream. Lowering himself into a cross-legged position, Manu pulled out his packet of Du Maurier and lit another cigarette. I remained standing for a moment, then also sat down.

'Do you remember the time you were shitting yourself and you took a shit right there?' he asked, pointing with his

---

[41] El pueblo – the centre of town (llanito).

cigarette to a spot presently covered with fag butts and *pipita* shells.

'Yeah,' I replied, smiling reluctantly. 'Yeah, I remember.'

'It looked like a NASA rocket, the way the fucking thing came out pointing upwards!'

I shook my head and helped myself to one of his fags.

'Mira, Alex,' he said, lighting my cigarette for me, 'I've been thinking about things and you were right, man: I was out of order when I went to Ceuta to discuss things with Al-Jaouhari without you. But I acted the way I did because I smelled an opportunity, man, because I didn't want us to keep taking all those fucking risks without getting paid what we deserve to be paid, know what I'm saying, *compá?'*

'Yeah, I know, brother. You and that fucking nose of yours, always on the hunt for bigger and better things. But what can I say, Manu – I've got a bad feeling about all this and I can't go against my instincts. That's why I'm pulling out, man. Don't take it badly, dude.'

'Don't worry, Alex. I respect your decision. If you want out, you want out – that's how it is. All I'm asking is you don't leave me this very second. Wait until the end of the month at least, so that my brother can come out of jail and take your place as *mi copiloto.'*

'But didn't you tell me a million times that all Maikito wants to do once out of jail is to eat fillet steaks and get as high as a kite?'

131

'Yes. And I wasn't fucking lying either. But I got a message through to him yesterday via *Justin el Cara-Sieso* (you remember *el Cara-Sieso,* don't you, that half-English guy who was with us at Bayside and now works as a prison warden *en el Castillo?*). *Bueno,* as I was saying – I got a message to him in jail explaining what's been happening, and he now wants to join me on the zodiac. *Dice que* he might as well, seeing how things are going. That's why I'm asking you as your best mate to wait until the end of the month. I don't want to do my first trips on the zodiac without a dude I can trust there beside me.'

I took a long drag on the cigarette and looked searchingly into his eyes. 'You wouldn't be bullshitting me with all this, would you, you bastard?'

'*No,* man. *Te lo juro por mi madre y por tó lo más sagrao que tó lo que te he contao es verdá!*' [42]

'Can't you ask one of the others to give you a hand?' I said, focusing for a moment on the hundreds of cigarette butts scattered around us. 'I'm sure they'd jump at the chance to join you on the boat.'

'I still haven't told Richita or *el Niño* that I'm going to offload them once Maikito is out of jail. Would be a real *putada,* don't you think – taking them out with me on the zodiac, only to ditch them three or four weeks later?'

---

[42] 'I swear on my mother's life, and everything holy, that I'm telling you the truth!'

'What about *el Flaquito*?'

'Have you seen the size of that fucker, *compadre?* What do you want – for the zodiac to sink on its maiden voyage?'

'So I'd only help you out until the end of the month?' I asked, smiling in spite of myself.

'Until the twenty-eighth, when Maikito comes out of jail. Or maybe until the twenty-ninth or the thirtieth, so that he can recover from the party I'm going to throw for him. Stay with me until then and then you're free to do whatever you fucking want.... I'll make it worth your while, I promise,' he added, uncrossing his legs and leaning forward.

'Okay,' I said, stubbing out the cigarette on the ground and rising to my feet. 'I'll do what you want. But don't fuck me around, do you understand? I'll stay until the end of the month with you and then I'm out *pase lo que pase,* okay?'

The next few weeks were among the most stressful in my goddamned life. Manu, you'll remember, had previously argued that we were taking the same risks as the *gayumberos* without earning any of their dough, but this wasn't really true; there was a shitload of difference between smuggling ten or fifteen kilograms of hash and smuggling close to a third of a ton of the stuff. For a start, we were no longer loading up at the desalination plant in El Quemadero, but across the Moroccan border in Belyounech and Lqassarine. This wasn't because it was quieter or less patrolled on the other side – in fact, the coastline to the west of Ceuta was just as developed as in the Spanish enclave – but because the drugs were coming from the Kif-growing regions in Al Hoceïma province, between Tetouan and Al Hoceïma town, and it would have been madness to smuggle three-hundred kilograms of hash across the heavily guarded Morocco-Ceuta border. Also, unlike a couple of weeks ago, we no longer owned what we were carrying onboard; the entire shipment now belonged to Al-Jaouhari and as such we were only workers in his employ. That does not mean, of course, that we were earning any less *floosh* than before. On the contrary, we were making more money than ever. Nevertheless, we were no longer calling the shots – and this meant having to suffer the whims of our capricious *ceutí* boss. Foremost among these were his objections to Matković and the Ruenda clan. Although he had never met or even spoken by telephone with the ex-football player, the fiercely pan-Islamic Al-Jaouhari had always disliked that our *linense* contact was of Serbian descent, believing that all Serbs were Islamophobic pigs who deserved to be wiped from the face of the earth. Now that he was in charge of the whole operation, he yearned to ditch Matković in favour of one of his Muslim associates in Almería – and only came to his senses when, during a heated telephone call with Manu, it was pointed out to him that the Ruenda family were not people you wanted to piss off, let alone walk away from during the middle of a long-term business arrangement.

Another thing that irked us about the new set-up was having Elfatmi travel with us in the RIB from the Moroccan coast to the Costa del Sol or the Costa Tropical. Elfatmi was one of Al-Jaouhari's 'heavies', a lumbering man-mountain with Toby jug ears and a striking resemblance to the WWF wrestler André the Giant. He always sat there behind us without saying or doing much, only coming fully to life when we got to the other side of the Straits and the bundles needed to be shifted out of the vessel. If everything went well, we'd drop him off along with the rest of the cargo ... and the poor fuck would then have to make his way back to Morocco later that morning on the Algeciras-Tangier ferry. But if for some reason the bales couldn't be unloaded, he'd remain sitting behind us, so quiet and uninvolved that we often forgot he was there, watching our every move until we reached Lqassarine or wherever it was that we were taking the drugs back to. '*El Elfatmi* is my human insurance policy,' Al-Jaouhari explained when Manu once asked him over the phone why 'the big guy' needed to come on the RIB with us. 'If something goes wrong and you need to chuck my cargo overboard, he'll come and tell me all the details. That way there's no room for future misunderstandings.'

Al-Jaouhari's words that day encapsulated the difference between the world we were leaving behind and the one we were immersing ourselves in: everything was much tighter when it came to large-scale drug smuggling, subject to greater scrutiny and control. Cops, customs officers, landowners, lorry drivers, crop farmers, shepherds who doubled up as watchmen, warehouse managers in charge of 'kif-beaters', packers and wrappers, street urchins who acted as lookouts, loaders and unloaders – everybody was bound together in a national web of complicity, one that stretched across all levels of Moroccan society and was kept intact by a free-flowing mixture of threats, bribes and easy cash. Just how far this network extended became evident when, on our first trip to Lqassarine, we saw one of the Arcor-53s belonging to the Royal Moroccan Gendarmerie fifty yards offshore, stationary and with its lights switched off. 'How the fuck do you expect us to land on the beach with that fucking juggernaut anchored there before us?' Manu shouted angrily in Spanish into our radio. 'Are you guys off your fucking heads?' '*Tranquilo, tranquilo,*' our Moroccan land contact barked out in response. 'That fucking juggernaut, *amigo,* is on our side. She's there to make sure things run smoothly, *entiendes?*'

We did not know it at the time, but this was how things were done at the Moroccan end of the operation. Maybe there'd be a police car parked just off the beach; maybe a lone cop motorcyclist, bored out of his head and smoking a cigarette, sitting astride his vehicle with both boots on the ground; maybe an army jeep, driven to within yards of the shoreline. 'I've got them all bought off,' Al-Jaouhari once boasted via the radio – and one was inclined to agree, judging from the different law-enforcement types we saw 'overseeing' the loading of the bales during those first trips. Once, would you believe, there was even a copper helping out with the loading. He was a short, dumpy fellow with a pencil moustache and a podgy face rendered spectrally pale by the headlights of a parked squad car; his clip-on tie had popped out of his sweater and was swaying like a pendulum under his fat neck. He reminded me of someone, but I could not put a finger on who. 'Look at that fatso puffing away in a police uniform,' Manu sniggered beside me seconds later. 'He looks like Paul Bearer, the fat little guy who's always with The Undertaker, *no crees?*'

My final stint as a smuggler lasted from 3 March to 26 March 1994. In between these two dates I made 15,750,000 pesetas

– roughly £76,000 once exchanged at one of Gibraltar's dodgy bureaux de change. I had nowhere to put this money, so once again it was stashed away in makeshift hiding places in our Castle Road flat – under the bed, in jacket pockets, in sock drawers, behind the sofa. If you are wondering whether I was tempted to continue in the drugs trade with all this *floosh* coming in, the answer is yes – briefly, very briefly, around 24 March, I almost caved in. 'Are you going to quit now that you are making all this money?' I thought, staring at the wads spilling like hatching chicks out of the socks in my drawer. 'Do you really want to be leaving this racket?'

But a day or two later I was brought back to my senses. We were about five miles off the Moroccan coast at the time – with a full cargo of hash and Elfatmi sitting like a mannequin behind us – when one of the Spanish helicopters appeared overhead and started tailing us. It was one of the blue-liveried *aduana* copters you sometimes saw in the summer from Gibraltar's beaches, and she kept swooping down on our RIB, trying to clip our radio antenna with her landing skids, screaming abuse at us through its megaphones. With a full load and over twenty miles to our destination, all the odds were against us, so we changed course and headed back to the North African coast, knowing that the Spaniards would be reluctant to follow us into Moroccan airspace and territorial waters. However, the bastard stalking us that night was in gung-ho mode – refusing to get off our tail even as we drifted closer and closer to the shore. Straight away we knew we had a problem on our hands. If we turned around and headed out to sea, the chopper would carry on hounding us and communicating our movements to all the *guardia* and *aduana* boats in the Alboran area, coordinating with them and their land-based colleagues in a bid to tighten the net around us and ensnare us. Alternatively, we could land on the beach at Lqassarine and try to get our Moroccan loaders to shift the cargo out of the RIB's hold – but with a full moon in the sky (and the Spanish copter causing such a fuss above us) there was a good chance that the Moroccan authorities (I mean those elements that weren't in Al-Jaouhari's pocket!) would already be there on the beach waiting to pounce on us. Confronted by these two equally unpalatable options, we decided to tuck behind *la Isla de Perejil*, the uninhabited rocky islet which lies two hundred yards off the Moroccan coast and about three miles from the Morocco-Ceuta border. The *isla* is technically owned by Spain, but the Moroccans get really tetchy whenever Spanish law-enforcement vessels or aircraft come anywhere near what they regard, with some justification, as their sovereign territory. *Surely, surely, this prick in the copter wouldn't follow us all the way there, would he?*

But, guess what, this is what the guy did – herding us further and further inshore, reducing our chances of coming out of this one unscathed. Like a rabbit hunted by a low-flying eagle, Manu swerved the boat from side to side, slicing through clouds of stinging sea spray, forcing Elfatmi and me to cling to the zodiac's handrails for fear of being catapulted overboard. Meanwhile, our Moroccan minder began shouting something in Arabic and pointing with his head at the bales in the back of the vessel. Was he saying that we should toss them into the sea? I wondered, staring at his opening and closing mouth. Or was he demanding that we should keep them safe whatever the circumstances? No matter, I thought. Either way we're screwed. As I came to this depressing verdict, I looked to my right and realised that we were now just ten or fifteen yards from the island and getting closer and closer with every millisecond. I could even, thanks to the beam of light trailing us, see the tufts of wild parsley growing out of its birdshit-stained cliffs. '*Quillo, Manu,*' I thought. 'What the fuck are you trying to do? Crash head-on against the fucking *patuca?*'[43] Then I saw the gap in the rocks – a fissure not much wider than your average one-vehicle garage. With consummate skill, ignoring the helicopter floating above us, Manu turned the RIB around and slowly reversed into this tight space, our rubber fenders scraping against the jagged cave walls as we went in, the overworked Yamaha engine coughing up fumes like a consumptive in his death throes.

'Leave the cave right now!' came the megaphoned response in Spanish seconds later. 'I repeat, come out of the cave right now!'

We thought they wouldn't dare try anything beyond a verbal warning, but next thing we knew the helicopter was hovering just inches off the sea and shining its lights into the cave, blinding us with their glare. Not knowing what else to do, the three of us leaned forward and tucked our heads under the plastic windshield, making ourselves as small as possible. Ten, maybe twelve yards now separated the front of our RIB from the helicopter, and the sound of the latter's rotor blades was hitting and bouncing off the cavern's low ceiling, enveloping us in a deafening cocoon of white noise. Also, because we were in such an enclosed space, the air was filling up with the smell of diesel fumes, making it hard to breathe.

---

43 Patuca – rock (llanito).

This is it, I thought. The end is upon us. Mentally, I cursed the bastard beside me for having entered this bloody cave and turned us into sitting ducks. But instead of the expected hail of bullets a startling thing happened: the lights slowly receded into the darkness and the rotor blades lost their threatening rawness. Quieter and quieter they became, until in the end, after twenty or thirty seconds, all you could hear was the lapping of the waves and our fenders being crushed between the gunwale and the cavern walls, a squeaking, high-pitched sound that, of all things, reminded me of the mating call made by a love-sick dolphin.

'How did you know they wouldn't shoot at us?' I asked Manu when I finally dared to look up. 'How were you so certain?'

'I wasn't sure of anything,' he replied, pulling off his balaclava in the darkness. 'I just had a feeling they wouldn't hang around here for long being so close to the Moroccan shore. They're not going to start a fucking war *con los moros* on account of two Gibraltarian lowlifes like us, are they, you know what I'm saying, *pishón?*'

I wonder whether I'll be able to finish this memoir. Once again I am getting strong pains in my arms and legs, and this morning I could barely move my left leg – so numb and bereft of feeling had it become during the course of the night. Also, my heart is now doing this weird thing where it contracts into a tight lump and then suddenly uncoils back into normal position – as if instead of a blood-pumping organ I carried within me a worse-for-wear rubber stress ball. I am of course worried that one of these attacks might see me keel over and slide into eternal blackness, but an even greater fear is that I will depart life's stage leaving this story untold, and that Manuel – brilliant, beautiful, turbulent Manuel – my comrade, my ally, my brother, my main fucking man – the only person I've known in this *puerca puta vida* who always had the balls to look others in the eye and do whatever he fucking wanted – will disappear from people's thoughts for good, erased for all eternity from the book of memory.

I was supposed to go one last time with Manu on the RIB after the incident at *la Isla de Perejil*, but instead I stayed at home with my pager switched off and the phone off the hook. The next time I saw my mate was about five days later at *el Bahía*. He was sitting at one of the outdoor tables with his elder brother. It was just after midday and Manu's new car, an enormous green Bentley convertible with a G666 number plate, was parked on the pavement skirting the bar, forcing pedestrians to walk on the road to go past it. I was worried he'd start recriminating me for the no-show at Sheppard's Marina, but as soon as Manu spotted me he summoned me over and, with a smile which made it clear he no longer gave a damn about Thursday night's non-appearance, created a space for me to sit down among them. 'How great to see you again, Maikito!' I cried, turning to my old boss. 'You look good, man!'

But it wasn't really true: the dude didn't look good. He had put on at least four stones in weight and rolls of flab now bulged out of the arm holes of his vest. Tiny scratches – as small as tick bites – covered his forehead and cheeks; an ulcerous growth had sprouted like a miniature plastic poppy on the edge of his mouth. But it was neither the petal-like ulcer, nor the scratches, nor the unsightly lumps of blubber that most captured your attention as you sat there facing him; it was the sequence of bluish-black teardrops tattooed from his lower left eyelid down to his jawline.

'That's one fucking heavy-duty tattoo, *compá*,' I said, noticing he had caught me looking at his face. 'What's it supposed to mean, man?'

'*Son las lágrimas que mi alma derrama al verse puteada por la diosa malévola de la fortuna*,'[44] he responded in a low, monotone growl, a mad look flaring in his eye.

'Very impressive,' I mumbled back, not sure what else to reply to a statement like that.

We carried on drinking that day till about nine in the evening. Manu was in one of his boisterous moods – cracking jokes with the other Bahía regulars and haranguing passers-by and wolf-whistling at girls and doing his best to be the centre of attention. In the old days his brother would have told him to bring it down a notch, but the new Maikito just sat there placidly and with a half-witted grin on his face, an air of almost bovine tranquillity having descended on him. It was a curious and tragic thing to behold, but it also proved to me that I was right to leave the world of drug smuggling and night-time run-ins at sea with the Spanish and Moroccan authorities. 'Look at the way the fella sits there staring into space,' I thought. 'Listen to the half-assed bullshit

---

[44] 'They are the teardrops shed by my soul when being fucked over by the malevolent goddess of fortune.'

occasionally spewing out of his mouth.' If this was what prison could do to a man after four and a half years, then what would it be like if we were caught out at sea with two hundred or three hundred kilograms of hash and had to do a ten- or twelve-year stretch in a Moroccan slammer? Yes, no doubt there'd be those who'd think I was wasting the opportunity to make a mint. I was conscious of that too. But what did all that mean set beside the possibility of getting killed by a stray bullet or spending years and years rotting away in the clink? Anyway, I already had £123,000 stashed away in different nooks and crannies in my father's flat. 'Enough to buy seven Honda Preludes,' I told myself, staring once again at the teardrops etched on Maikito's face, 'or five E-Class Mercedes, or three Jaguar XJS V12 Coupés!'

Before we left *el Bahía* that day, Manu said it was important we stayed in touch. He spoke these words as he was lighting a cigarette, during a moment when his brother had gone to the toilet. 'After all, we've always been good mates,' he said, allowing a puff of smoke to seep through his nostrils. 'We shouldn't lose touch just because we are no longer working together. I'll call you on Friday so that we can meet up for a few beers, *qué te parece?*' Because he never looked me in the eye during this little speech, I suspected that he was talking nonsense and had no intention of keeping his word. But that Friday at three, while at home wondering what to do for the rest of the day, I picked up the phone and heard those all too familiar roguish tones:

'I'm at the Venture Inn, Alex. Why don't you come and join me for a drink, *tío?*'

From that day onwards Manu and I would meet up once a week, usually on Friday afternoons between two and four. We didn't have a regular meeting place, but instead kept changing venues and heading to wherever the mood would take us (*el Star Bar* in Parliament Lane one week, *el Piccadilly* at the end of Main Street the week after, *el Captain's Cabin* the week after that, and so on). I thought this patternless jumping from bar to bar was very unusual – like most *llanitos*, once Manu and I became fond of a venue, we rarely went anywhere else – but I never questioned the latest arrangements, believing that new circumstances, as the proverb says, or should say, sometimes require radical new measures. Manu always insisted on paying for whatever beers or coffees we ordered, and I, knowing how much money he was making, never objected. By an unspoken agreement, we avoided chatting about tobacco or drug smuggling matters, concentrating instead on safe topics like football, cars and WWF wrestling. If he ever turned to his experiences as a drug smuggler, it was almost always in an oblique manner that revealed little about what he was up to. Once – as we were sitting by the bar at *el Piccadilly* – he started complaining loudly about his Moroccan associates, saying he was sick and tired of their posturing and their false promises. 'If they say *I swear by Almighty God,*' he protested, 'it's like me saying *I swear by Almighty Donald Duck* – as they do not take seriously anything sworn in any language other than Arabic. If you want to know whether they're telling you the truth or not, you need to get the slippery buggers to say *Waheyat Allah*, like they say in Morocco and Ceuta.... Isn't that true, Abdelhafid?' he said, turning to *el Piccadilly's* Moroccan barman. 'If one of you guys says *lo juro por Dios,* it means jack fucking shit!'

For all that, there were times when, all fired up as he was from his escapades at sea, he'd end up revealing some smuggling anecdote he couldn't keep to himself. Sipping coffee with me at Bianca's one afternoon, for instance, he told me that he had been driven aground in Spain the previous evening by *los aduaneros*. Maikito – luckily – hadn't been with him on the boat; feeling unwell, he had swapped places at the last moment with a Moroccan known as *el Estufa*. It was just like the time we ourselves got chased down off El Puerto de la Duquesa, he explained, except that this time there were three of them aboard (Manu, Elfatmi and *el Estufa*) and they had three hundred kilograms of hashish in the back of the RIB. 'Imagine, man,' he said, looking at me archly over the top of his wraparound sunglasses. 'We got driven aground at La Atunara with three hundred k's of *hashisha* in the bloody boat.'

'So what did you do?' I asked.

'What do you think I did? I ran like the wind!'

'But weren't there *guardias* waiting for you on the beach?'

'*No,* man. I could hear them coming along *el Paseo Mediterráneo* with their sirens on, but they were still thirty or forty seconds away and there was also this thick *taró*[45] that made it difficult to see for more than ten yards in front of you. Here's my chance, I told myself. And in a flash I started legging it out of the beach. "*Alto ahí!*" the fuckers shouted from the *aduana*

---

[45] A thick sea mist which occasionally settles over the Straits of Gibraltar.

boat. "*Alto ahí!*" *Alto ahí tu puta madre,* I thought – and carried on running across the beach to the road.'[46]

'And you managed to get away *just like that?*'

He explained that he had crossed the road and plunged into the backstreets behind *el Bar Manolo.* By this stage the entire area was crawling with cops and *guardias civiles*, he said, and the sea mist had acquired an eerie, phosphorescent tinge due to all the flashing blue lights in the vicinity. 'It was like that scene in *Close Encounters of the Third Kind* when the spaceship's doors suddenly open,' he added after a moment's pause. 'That's the kind of freaky shit I'm talking about.' Soon barking dogs could be heard in the near distance. Shouted orders. The crunch of heavy-soled boots. Turning into *la calle Numancia,* one of the narrower streets in the neighbourhood, he saw that there was a roadblock up ahead. He immediately scurried back into *la calle Este,* but to his horror spotted a dog and its handler coming towards him from the opposite end of the lane. Running out of options, still soaking wet, he scrambled up a drainpipe and jumped over a wall into an enclosed patio. Pyramidal mounds of rubble were scattered across the patio tiles and there were three or four damaged Persian shutters – probably awaiting repair – propped up against a wall. Without a second thought, he crawled under one of the broken shutters and put a hand over his mouth, hoping to stifle the sound of his agitated breathing. For the next forty-five minutes he remained secreted in this makeshift bolthole, not daring to move, hearing the

---

[46] 'Stop right there! Stop right there!' – 'Go stop your own fucking mother!'

policemen and *guardias civiles* trooping up and down *la calle Este.* At one point one of his pursuers heaved himself onto the patio wall and a single beam of light jiggled across the patio floor. Through the gaps in the shutter Manu followed the beam as it traced the outline of the yard, its passage reminding him of a firefly in mid-flight. He was sure – he was absolutely convinced – that the light would expose his hiding place under the shutter, but the angle of the slats must have prevented the beam from alighting on him, for a moment or two later the torch was turned off and the *guardia* or copper jumped down from the wall. Finally, close to three in the morning, the manhunt was called off and Manu was able to squeeze out of his refuge. Rubbing some feeling into his benumbed legs, he stood up, took a deep breath, kissed the medallion of *la Virgen del Carmen* dangling from his neck, stretched out his arms, removed his overalls, and, wearing only a T-shirt and underpants, leapt over the wall. He then made his way to the nearest phone booth and called his brother, asking him to bring him some shoes and a fresh set of clothes. 'Please, be quick, Maikito,' he said, struggling to hold the receiver between his fingers. 'I'm fucking freezing to death here!'

'And what happened then?' I asked, visualising Manu standing in his vest and underpants in the phone booth.

'Nothing much,' he replied, lifting his coffee cup. 'Maikito arrived in his car half an hour later with my clothes, I got changed, we drove to the frontier and we went together through passport control.'

'That easy, bro?'

'Yep, that easy.'

I looked at him as he sat there with his *café con leche* held before him and I thought I could detect a flicker of bad-boy arrogance in his eyes. 'What about Elfatmi and the other guy?' I asked, remembering the huge Moroccan who used to sit there quietly behind us in the zodiac. 'Did they also manage to escape?'

'*Po no sé,*' Manu admitted, putting down his cup and bringing out a cigarette. 'No one's bothered to tell me. I think they were both picked up by the cops, but I'm not one hundred per cent sure. All I know,' he said, lighting his fag, 'is that we've lost a shitload of hash and it will take us at least four or five trips to recover our losses.'

It must be one of the saddest human traits – clinging to something that no longer has any meaning. Once-happy lovers, former friends, people forced to leave their jobs after many years – all of them want to hold on, to deny that things have changed and that it is time to move forward. Often this resistance comes wrapped in different fears – fear of the unknown, fear of emotional dislocation, fear of starting all over again. Working in concert with each other, these fears urge you to stay put, to leave things as they are. But the longer you remain passive and in denial, the more bitter and painful the final rupture will be. Because here's the thing about dead and dying things – no matter how much you strive to preserve them, no matter how many times you persuade yourself that there is still life and colour in them and that they will continue buttressing your existence for a while, they *always always always* – as sure as day follows night and night follows day – turn to dust in your hands.

It would be foolish, though, to pretend I had thoughts like these back in August or September 1994. I was just an impressionable twenty-three-year-old, wasn't I, an indolent, self-obsessed kid who knew nothing about nothing and still hero-worshipped his larger-than-life childhood friend. And yet, as the weeks and months went by, something began to change – for I found it harder and harder to sit there with Manu every Friday drinking coffees or pints and pretending that everything was like in the old days. Perhaps it was because of Manu's occasional boasting about his drug runs – but no: that couldn't be it, could it, seeing that, apart from a sudden (and somewhat comical) penchant for Arabic expressions like '*makayen moshkil*' and '*ma'ajbaneesh*', there was little in his speech these days which revealed what he was up to out in the Straits. I think, rather, it had something to do with his changing physical appearance, with the emblems of his growing status. The gem-encrusted rings, the top-of-the-range Patek Philippe and Rolex watches, the smuggling-related tattoos (one of a RIB on his chest; several *cristos* and *vírgenes* on his forearms, biceps and calves) – all of this shit began grating on me, made me feel increasingly uncomfortable in his presence. Additionally, Manu himself appeared to be altering as a person, changing from the reckless, happy-go-lucky scallywag that I had always known into a mafioso-like big shot. Urged on by his brother, he had bought a large plot of land up at Europa and was now arranging to build a detached six-bedroom property on it with a swimming pool, a tennis court and a gym. To get the project off the ground, he was having to deal with lawyers, estate agents, building contractors and financial advisers, and the bloodsucking leeches kept following him wherever he went, even appearing at our Friday-afternoon sessions. Watching him consult with these people was a mad and surreal experience. Ever since our school days, Manu had been the sort of bloke who hated details, who'd run a mile before getting involved in anything too complicated. Yet there he was each Friday surrounded by his new 'advisers' – nodding, rubbing his chin, taking down notes, rattling on about 'property deeds' and 'ceiling joists' and 'asset placement'. Bizarre, bizarre stuff! Not only that, I began to get the impression that he enjoyed spending time with these movers and shakers, that he found their company agreeable and even stimulating. I sensed as much from the warm smiles he bestowed on them, from his respectful handshakes and embraces, from the way he'd enquire about what eau de cologne they were wearing or whether their suits were off-the-rack or tailor-made.

Quite honestly, it was as if the Manu I knew and loved was fading away right before my eyes.

Eventually, something had to give. One day I didn't show up at *el Cannon Bar;* and Manu, for his part, didn't bother calling me to find out why I had stood him up. And, just like that, without any fuss, our Friday-afternoon gatherings were at an end. That does not mean that things suddenly became awkward between us. Spotting me in the street, he'd always call me over and we'd either chat for a while about football and WWF wrestling, or, if he had time, pop over to the nearest bar for a couple of quick pints. One morning – much to my surprise – he even told me that his mother and half-brother were an item again. ('Can you believe that, *compá?* They're back together like in the old days, but this time it's all out in the open! *Qué locura, no, hahaha?*') But the regimented meetings, the brotherly closeness, the making an effort to see each other – all that went by the wayside. Did it sadden me to see us drifting apart like this? I suppose it did – although it wasn't that surprising either. If there is one thing guaranteed to sabotage a friendship, it is a widening status gap between the parties concerned. It's almost an unwritten rule in life. Individuals with money prefer socialising with other monied individuals; they somehow get it into their heads that a man or woman's worth is dependent on what they earn. In the days of his youth, for instance, before his accident with the jetty crane, my dad had a mate called Brian Andrade. It may be hard to believe considering what a grumpy old git my pa went on to become, but John Dennis Leslie and this Brian guy were as thick as thieves, they were *completamente inseparables.* They worked in the same section at the victualling yard, met up every Friday evening for drinks, socialised as a foursome with their girlfriends every Saturday night and even went snorkelling together off *el Rolli* on Sunday mornings. But then one day '*el Andy*' won £355,000 on the Littlewood Pools and all of that came to a sudden end. By this I mean that Andrade quit his job at the yard, moved into a flash apartment on Witham's Road, bought himself a Mercedes, ditched his girlfriend for a much prettier woman, started wearing ridiculous paisley-pattern cravats, plonked a gold signet ring on his left pinkie, tried (but ultimately failed) to stop pronouncing his c's and z's as s's in Spanish, became a member of the Royal Gibraltar Yacht Club, grew a pot belly, developed a partiality for Romeo y Julieta Churchill cigars and – perhaps most disappointing of all, as far as my dad was concerned – never went spearfishing again for squid and octopus by *las Dos Hermanas* and along the western flank of the South Mole.

I am not happy with how this memoir is progressing. I feel as if I am rushing things, as if I am compressing months and years of experience into hurried paragraphs – but what else can I do? Weakened by illness, finding it harder and harder to focus, I need to be selective, I have to ignore the inessentials and concentrate instead on the salient points of this story. If I am not able to keep my narrative taut in this way, if I allow myself to be ensnared by the decorative and anecdotal, then there is a real chance I will never complete this tale of mine and this – the prospect of stalling and running aground, of leaving things undone – is something that fills me with a heavy existential dread. I *must* finish this story, I *must* give written form to my memories. *Experience, once lived,* as all good writers know, *is forever lost unless brought to life on the printed page.*

I saw less and less of Manu over the winter of 1994/1995. He was busy building his new house and sorting out his financial affairs – all this while still shifting the odd two- or three-hundred-kilogram consignment of hashish from Morocco to the Costa del Sol. Driving along Europa Road in my Chevrolet, I could just make out the scaffolding towers and the half-built walls behind the eight-foot fence he had erected around his plot of land; it was impossible to say what the new place would look like when finished, but its scale seemed positively palatial. One day, during one of our increasingly rare get-togethers, he told me that he had bought a laundrette and a PC repair shop in order 'to expand his portfolio of interests.' At first I thought he was taking the mickey out of the lawyers, accountants and other posh types he now hung around with, but the expression on his face made it clear he wasn't joking. 'PCs are where the future is at, *amigo*,' he continued matter-of-factly, handing me a 'Rock Hi-Tech Solutions' business card. 'My financial advisor Mr Noel-Thompson says that by 2000 everybody will have a personal computer at home.'

With Manu rapidly sliding out of my life, there soon came a point where I didn't know what to do with myself. Most mornings I would wake up at around twelve, have a cup of tea with my dad and then, after slipping into some fancy clothes and applying half a tub of gel to my hair, go for endless drives around the Rock in one of my two cars. I drove with either metal or flamenco playing at full blast out of my speakers – always on my own, always slumped back against my seat. If I felt particularly rebellious, I'd head up to Princess Caroline's Battery, or some other secluded Upper Rock spot, so that I could skin up and smoke a spliff – but otherwise I drove without stopping, thinking about things and wondering about the future, overtaking learners and other overcautious drivers, tossing my hair back, smoking countless cigarettes, wolf-whistling unenthusiastically at girls, cursing bicyclists and motorcyclists, beeping my horn whenever I crossed paths with relatives and acquaintances, accelerating wildly along Sir Herbert Miles Road and Dudley Ward Tunnel, desperately trying to conjure up some excitement, *un poco de marcha*, a rush of adrenaline that would temporarily lift me out of my worsening apathy. Various times I thought about calling *el Pelúo* and asking him if he wanted to start smuggling Winston with me. The idea felt curiously tempting. I had both the money to buy a new Phantom and the experience by now to pilot it on my own, and I could easily find two or three young lads willing to help out with the loading and unloading. On the other hand, well, on the other hand, there were rumours going around that the Gibraltar Government was about to turn the screws on the local smugglers, particularly those carrying drugs across the Straits. Something to do with Spanish pressure and the UK not being happy with the image that Gibraltar was projecting abroad, my father told me one day while slurping a cup of tea in our Castle Road living room. 'About bloody time too,' he added, looking pointedly in my direction. 'It's a real disgrace what's happening in this place!'

Months passed and nothing changed. I continued moping around without a purpose, unsure what to do with myself. Occasionally, I saw Manu with his new buddies; less occasionally, we'd go together for a drink. He looked chubbier these days, sweatier, less athletic, a pair of diamond studs having replaced the two hoop earrings that once dangled piratically from his left ear. In addition to the laundrette and the PC repair unit at the Arcade, he now owned a fish and chip shop and a hairdressing salon called Beautique Hair and Nails. Both businesses, he explained, were registered in somebody else's name – but this was just a ruse set up by his lawyer to bypass tax and ownership regulations.

By March 1995 I was so fed up that I went down to the boat dealers in Marina Bay and ordered a brand-new Phantom. During the four or five weeks that it took to be delivered, I made plans for my comeback into the tobacco trade, but when the vessel eventually arrived I could not bring myself to re-establish contact with *el Pelúo* and simply left it moored in its berth at Sheppard's Marina, unused and unloved, a monument to my failed aspirations. That same month, too, I sold my Prelude to Jason Castelnuovo, a second cousin of mine who had quit his A-levels to join a tobacco smuggling gang. I still had a lot of cash stashed away in socks and money bags at my dad's place on Castle Road, but after splashing out on a Phantom and a new engine I needed to 'balance the books' – to borrow the kind of language now employed by Manu and his white-collar mates – and the best way of doing this, it seemed to me, was by offloading the Honda.

Another three or four months went by and we were now in the height of summer. It was an exceptionally humid and *levantery* July, I remember, and, as I twisted and turned at night in my single bed, breathing the warm and acrid air in our Castle Road flat, I wondered whether it would be a good idea to spend a few thousand quid on AC units for the entire property. Over the last three or four weeks, too, there had been renewed speculation about possible changes to Gibraltar's anti-drug smuggling laws. The rumours said that Joe Bossano, the Gibraltarian Chief Minister, had been repeatedly warned by the Foreign Office to do something about the Rock's *narcotraficantes*, but had refused to obey the big cheeses in Whitehall. This was his last chance, people claimed. His final warning. If he didn't clean up his act by the end of the month, the UK would take matters into its own hands and impose direct rule on its colony.

It was on one of those Levanter-ridden days that *el Joe* finally caved in to Whitehall's demands. It was around two in the afternoon when I became aware of the news; I was making my way down Main Street to collect the Chevrolet from Grand Parade. I had just lit a cigarette and was somewhere between Gache the Opticians and the law courts when I heard a cacophony of car horns coming from the direction of Convent Place, the square adjoining the Governor's residence. It wasn't just the three or four odd hooters you hear in Gib when somebody gets married. What I am talking about is fifty, maybe a hundred, car horns blown in unison – a veritable wall of noise. Like everybody else in the street around me, I slowed down to a shuffle and listened to the growing ruckus, wondering what was going on. Then – before I had a chance to gather my thoughts – I saw the convoy spilling into Convent Place from the other end of Main Street. Car after car after car in an unbroken chain – Pontiac Firebirds, Audi S6s, Toyota Land Cruisers, BMW 7-series, Mercedes SL 600s – all of them blowing their horns and revving their engines. From the tinted windows and gold-coloured paint jobs, I knew that the vehicles belonged to the Rock's smugglers. I could also see that their owners were in a state of agitation. Some guys had their heads and shoulders out of their windows; others were shouting obscenities in English and Spanish; others drove with their right arms poking through their sunroofs, fists defiantly clenched. One fellow even had a mate of his – a scrawny, heavily tattooed guy wearing nothing but a pair of Speedos – standing on the bonnet of his Alfa Romeo!

I continued watching the convoy of 'Winston Boys' and *gayumberos* pile into the square. Each car pulled up wherever it could, forcing those behind to mount the pavement or drive onto the tiled area in front of the old regimental guardhouse. Soon there were twenty, perhaps thirty vehicles scattered before the Governor's palace, with an equal number of scooters and scramblers swirling like flies around them. Horns screeched; engines roared; drivers stepped out of their cars. *'Queremos nuestras gomas!'* went up the cry. *'Queremos nuestras gomas!*[47] With a pounding heart, I observed a bearded smuggler run across the road and chuck a tin of paint against the marble columns of the Convent's porte-cochère. Hitting its target with a loud thwack, it left a fuzzy white print on the weathered stone, dirtying the pillar like a gigantic *cagada de pavana*. Meanwhile, the little guy with the Speedos slid off the bonnet and scuttled up to the lone sentry guarding the palace gates. Laughing and pulling faces, conscious, no doubt, that everybody in the vicinity was watching him, the fellow danced around the motionless young soldier, his arms held above his head and his tattooed hands flapping about like castanets. He circled the sentry once, twice, three times – all while giggling like a giddy teenager – then sprinted back to the other side of Convent Place to rejoin his braying companions:

Queremos nuestras gomas!
Queremos nuestras gomas!
Queremos nuestras gomas!

---

[47] 'Give us back our RIBs! Give us back our RIBs!'

In next to no time the square was gridlocked with cars and motorcycles, with almost no room for pedestrians to pass between them. Among the new arrivals I noticed Manu's Bentley convertible. Its roof was down and my mate was standing on the driver's seat, a black-banded boater shielding his eyes and the upper half of his face. He was urging the others to shout louder, clapping one moment and then clenching his fists, now and again pointing accusingly towards the Convent's ceremonial balcony, swaying from side to side to the rhythm of the rough-throated masculine chanting:

Queremos nuestras gomas!
Queremos nuestras gomas!
Queremos nuestras gomas!

While all this was going on, a line of policemen had formed across the front of the Governor's palace. There were only five or six of them, and they were already attracting a flurry of boos and insults. Egged on by his mates, a chubby guy known as *el Captain Caveman* stepped out of the crowd and – in a cockney accent strangely at odds with his dusky appearance – told the cops to 'fuck right off back to wherever you lot 'ave come from,' adding, just to confuse the matter even further, *'pedazos de cabrones hijoputas!'* Despite this, the presence of the coppers had a dampening effect on the protestors, slowly forcing them back into their cars. Doors began to slam shut. Engines revved. Flamenco and heavy metal once again blared through open car windows. 'Let's get the fuck out of here!' one of the guys finally yelled with half his body hanging out of a blue BMW. 'This place is starting to stink like a right old pigsty!'

Shortly afterwards the protestors left Convent Place and turned into Governor's Lane, shouting 'bastards' and '*hijoputas*' and '*cabrones de mierda*' as they drove past the watching police officers. One of the last to vacate the square was Manu in his Bentley. He was hatless now and hunched over his steering wheel. Driving with his arm held out of the window, his left middle finger raised at the coppers by the locked palace gates, he was laughing and shaking his head, a look of fierce exhilaration in his eye. I thought *el muy cabrón* hadn't seen me, but as he came parallel to where I stood he suddenly looked right and skidded to a stop, bringing the tail end of the motorcade to a temporary halt.

'What the hell is happening?' I asked, poking my head through the open passenger window.

'*Quillo,* what do you think is happening?' he shouted hoarsely. 'They've started confiscating our boats — that's what's happening! *Anda,* jump in, *compá,*' he added, leaning over with a grin and opening the door for me, '*qué la vamos a liar!*[48]

Why did I open the door and climb into Manu's Bentley? Was it because of the roguish smile on my mate's face? Because at some subconscious level I craved to be part of the smuggling scene again? Or was it simply because I was bored out of my head and Manuel had presented me with an opportunity to be involved in something transgressive and exciting?

---

[48] 'Come on, jump in, mate – we're going to raise hell!'

I cannot offer a straight answer to these questions.

Looked at objectively, there were many, many reasons why I shouldn't have got into that car. I was no longer a smuggler for one, and I didn't give a damn about their bloody *gomas,* and the last thing I wanted was to get into trouble with the local law. And yet, despite all this, despite knowing that it was in my interests to walk away, despite the resentment I felt towards Manu for gradually pushing me out of his life, I found myself pulling the Bentley's heavy chrome handle and climbing into the car with him. And then something rather peculiar happened, something that I had never experienced in my life before: I had this feeling of 'rightness' in my bones, of deep-rooted certainty. Hanging my right arm out of the window, I tilted my head to one side and, seeing Manu banging his horn, knew that I was exactly where I was supposed to be. Manuel and me, the cream leather seats of the Bentley, Camarón's *cante jondo* issuing from the speakers, the trail of vehicles snaking its way past King's Chapel and into Governor's Lane – everything was as perfect as perfect could be. '*Vamos! Vamos!*' I shouted, drumming my right palm against the outside of the passenger door. 'Let's show those *bastardos* who they're dealing with here!'

The next hour wasn't just the most memorable in my entire youth; it felt like a dream in which everything was turned on its head. Gibraltar, you see (at least the Gibraltar I knew back in the Eighties and Nineties), often resembled a permanently switched-on pressure cooker, its overcrowded streets and high population density made all the more claustrophobic by endless government laws and regulations. Cigarette smuggling, it is true, was condoned by the Gibraltarian authorities because of the revenue the legally imported and taxed boxes of Winston brought to the exchequer's coffers, but beyond this anomaly everything remained as controlled as always, as tightly contained. Nearly half of all land was in MOD hands and closed off to the local population, which meant you grew up surrounded by 'Keep Out' and 'Military: No Entry' signs and effectively knew your place. If that wasn't galling enough, both the civil and military authorities ran the territory with that special blend of paranoia and severity encountered in garrison towns, treating ordinary citizens as potential terrorists and teenagers as hooligans in training. If you sat on a Main Street bench after tottering out of a nightclub, some copper would come and threaten to arrest you if you did not move on. If you stood waiting for more than ten minutes for your mum or dad to pick you up by the Naval Ground's Queensway gates, a *guiri* sentry would pop out of nearby HMS Rooke and order you, a native-born Gibraltarian, to stop loitering outside MOD property. If you went for a spin on a Friday or Saturday evening and pulled up next to the lighthouse to eat a takeaway burger or kebab, a cop car would sooner or later materialise by your side and demand to know what you were doing parked there. If you booed a local politician as he was coming out of the House of Assembly, some heavy-jowled *policía secreta* would take you aside and jot down your name and address, arguing that heckling and shouting at those in authority was not something one did in Gibraltar. This is what it was like back then: there was always someone in uniform bugging you, breaking your balls, trying to control you, to cow you, to mould your expectations and keep you thinking like an obedient little colonial.

For a magical period of around fifty minutes that day, however, none of these constraints existed. We beeped our horns; we mounted pavements; we drove wrong way down one-way roads; we insulted off-duty policemen; we lit up joints and hung them brazenly out of our windows; we threw empty cans and beer bottles at oncoming cars; we stopped at the bottom of Ragged Staff to help an old lady cross the road; we halted in front of *el Camber* to scratch and kick a parked police van; we set a couple of bins alight; we tied a length of rope to a lamppost opposite Chilton Court and tried (but failed) to bring it down; we got out of our cars at the Waterport Roundabout and briefly blocked both the northward and southward flow of traffic; we smashed the windows of an electronics shop belonging to a guy in the Opposition who had badmouthed us in the House of Assembly, then danced on the crunching pieces of glass – all of this without a single bobby or MOD policeman in sight, guided by no other instinct than what we felt to be right.

It may sound extraordinarily stupid and naïve, but for close to an hour we believed we were the new owners of the place and that nothing could stop us. Unused to gathering in such large numbers, our natural brashness bolstered by the continuing lack of policemen, we simply couldn't process what was happening and got drunk on the illusion of invincibility, thinking ourselves completely untouchable. *Ni el Canepa ni el gobernador ni la mismísima reina puede con nosotros – y eso es lo que hay, compá!* [49]

---

[49] 'Neither Canepa, nor the Governor, nor the Queen herself can stop us – you better get used to it!'

Of course, it was all a mirage – and a short-lived one at that. As we went round and round in our convoy beeping our horns and playing loud flamenco, the local police were already shifting into their riot gear and getting ready to confront us. Approaching the Sundial Roundabout, we saw a long line of them, visors down and batons unsheathed, behind a barricade of cop cars. Realising that there was no way through, some of the guys got out of their vehicles intending to square up to the coppers, but before they could group into a protective phalanx, the latter charged at them, hitting our boys with their shields and their batons, bombarding them with taunts and insults. Outnumbered and caught by surprise, having no way of fending off the truncheons save with their bare hands and arms, the smugglers fought back and even knocked down one or two cops, but the riot policemen, alas, were much better organised and slowly but surely got the upper hand.

All during this time Manu and I were sitting in the Bentley some two or three hundred yards further down the length of the convoy – roughly where the old adventure playground used to be – listening to one of his Ketama tapes, totally unaware of what was occurring ahead. When word of the attack finally reached us, we left the car and, together with another fifteen or twenty guys, marched up to the roundabout. By the time we got there, though, the riot police had retreated behind the barricade of cop cars, taking some of our lads with them. You could see the helmeted officers pushing the smugglers onto the ground, holding them by their hair, placing handcuffs on their wrists. Trainers, wallets, flip-flops and gold chains – and for some reason a dog-eared porn mag – lay strewn across the thirty- or forty-yard stretch separating us from our adversaries, curiously enfolded in the shimmering blue haze rising from the baking hot tarmac. Also stranded in this no-man's space was Johnny *'el Merluza'*, one of the most charismatic and *cachondos* of all the 'Winston Boys.' His vest was torn in two and he lay there clutching his knee, blood pouring out of a head wound, his massive belly and man boobs covered in tangles of bloodied hair.

'Are you okay, Johnny, *compá?'* someone in our group shouted.

'Yeah, yeah, I'm fine!' Johnny gamely responded. *'Los hijoputas esos que están allí se aprovecharon de que solamente había unos cuantos de nosotros afuera de los coches pa embestirnos y inflarnos a palos, los hijos de la gran perra puta!... Hijos de la gran perra puta!'* he repeated in an even louder voice, letting go of his knee and turning with a grimace in the direction of the cops. *'Qué sois todos una maná de chulos y hijoputas de mierda!'* [50]

Thirty-five arrests were made that day – eleven at the Sundial Roundabout, seven at Sheppard's Marina, four outside *el Bahía Bar* and the rest in other locations scattered across Gibraltar. The general opinion among those who didn't get arrested was that we would have won the day if the two hundred of us had acted in concert, but this was just a macho delusion, a naïve after-the-event fantasy. If by some miracle we had overpowered the local cops, we'd have found ourselves facing the forces of the Gibraltar Regiment. And if

[50] 'Yes, yes, I'm fine! Those motherfuckers over there took advantage of the fact that only a few of us had come out of our cars to charge at us and lay into us with their truncheons, the no-good, cowardly motherfuckers!'

we had survived their tear gas and their rubber bullets, then the British Army would have stepped in, more specifically the five hundred members of the British Army's elite Parachute Regiment who, according to a report published in the *Gibraltar Chronicle* later that month, had been put on standby by the UK authorities, ready to fly into North Front from Catterick in North Yorkshire at an hour's notice and put us all in our place.

From the very beginning, then, we had misread the situation, overestimating our strengths while underrating our adversaries, having somehow got it into our heads that two hundred guys with long hair and *chanclas moras* could take on and subdue not just the local constabulary, but the might of the extended British establishment.

Even more idiotically, there were those in the smuggling fraternity who – in spite of the confiscated boats and the thirty-five arrests and the six hospitalisations and everything else that happened that July day – continued to believe that things would soon return to normal, who still trusted in Joe Bossano's ability to stop the British 'meddling' in native Gibraltarian affairs. When the local police were forced to hand back one or two of the impounded RIBs due to legal constraints, these die-hards thought that victory was now around the corner, that they'd shortly be free to smuggle again to their hearts' content. 'What did I tell you, eh?' they smirked and laughed in your face. 'Our Joe would soon find a way to get the *guiris* off his back!'

Their hopes proved to be foolishly misplaced. Facing enormous pressure from the UK, Spain and the EU, the

Government of Gibraltar abandoned its laissez-faire mentality and began clamping down on the smugglers, particularly on the drug runners who were such a stain on the Rock's international reputation. Customs officers were granted further stop and search powers; police cars now regularly toured the territory's beaches and marinas. Not long afterwards, emergency legislation was passed in the House of Assembly prohibiting the use within Gibraltarian waters of fast boats over six metres in length or with more than 200 horsepower motors. Some of the *gayumberos* resisted the new measures by buying smaller RIBs and fitting them with specially adapted engines; others went back to using Phantoms. Clearly, a lot remained to be done before the Rock could be described as a smuggling-free zone, but 'the good old days' – those halcyon years when you could smuggle drugs and cigarettes with almost complete impunity – were now a thing of the past.

The riots proved to be a major turning point in my personal life as well. During my fifty minutes with Manu in the Bentley I had somehow convinced myself that the dwindling embers of our friendship were being relit and that from then on everything would be just like in the old days. But in reality the exact opposite came to pass: that fleeting hour in his car was the last we spent together as mates. Ironic, isn't it? You convince yourself you are about to fix things ... when in actual fact you are already writing the last chapter of your story.

Contrary to what you may think, this last and decisive rupture had nothing to do with anything we said or did that day or even with the riot itself. In truth Manu had come out of the disturbances better than most: he hadn't been arrested and his RIB wasn't impounded and – luckiest of all – Maikito was released without charge after knocking off a policeman's hat and calling him '*un puto calvo cabrón.*'[51] But just because he still had his *goma* and his personal freedom didn't mean that things were going well for my old friend. Three days after the riots, his mother came back to Macphail's Passage from Saint Bernard's Hospital looking pale and with creases in her sundress. Unused to seeing his elegant mum in such a state, Manu asked her what was bugging her, but Mariadelaida, knowing her son's tendency to take family matters to heart, refused to say. Again and again he probed, but she kept shaking her head and looking away. 'What's wrong, Mum? Tell me, *anda. No me dejes así,* please.' Not until he sat on the sofa beside her and encircled her with his arms did she finally relent, his physical closeness serving to unlock the previously unmentionable words:

'I've got cancer down there.'

'Down there, Mum?' Manu asked, still holding his mother in his arms. 'What do you mean?'

'You know, Manu,' Mariadelaida said, gazing at the floor.

'...?'

'In my womb, Manu,' his mother grunted through clenched teeth. 'I've got cancer in my fucking womb!'

---

[51] 'A fucking bald bastard.'

Manu didn't say anything in response. He simply released Mariadelaida from his embrace, leaned back and looked at her with a serious and somewhat bemused expression – like a child who's caught his mother using a four-letter word. When he finally snapped out of his shock-induced trance, he cleared his throat and, in a wobbly, emotional voice, told his mum that he'd look after her, that he'd use his money to send her 'to a clinic in Switzerland', that he'd see to it that she got the best treatment that money could buy, that he'd move heaven and earth – *cielo y tierra, te lo juro,* Mummy, *te lo juro por tó lo más sagrao* – to ensure she'd be okay. Mariadelaida listened to this impassioned monologue with a sad smile, torn between self-pity on the one hand and sympathy for her son on the other. 'Stop, Manuel,' she whispered at last, laying her tiny manicured hands over the back of his massive left palm, 'please stop. The cancer is not operable. We have to accept things for what they are. Don't beat yourself up like this, *amorcito.*'

From then on Manu was in a bad way. He barely talked to his brother and he no longer greeted me in the street; he also stopped showing any interest in his entrepreneurial ventures. Shunning nearly all human contact, he spent most of his time wrestling with his pain or raging at the world and its cruel ways. Quite often he was drunk – staggering down Irish Town with his *medallones* jangling on his chest or zigzagging up Engineer Lane in pointy cowboy boots like his dad's, clenching his fists and muttering unintelligible words under his breath, now and then snapping out of his stupor to insult some passer-by or challenge him to a scrap. Previously, whenever Manu and I had come across some overly *'chulo'* type in the street, we would jokingly describe him as *'un puro macho'* – but this, ironically, is what he himself had become with his virile swagger and his loud swearing and his murderous death-stare. One day, as I was returning home from Lipton's with some shopping, just as I was going up the weathered steps between Cannon Lane and *la Piazzela*, I ran into Maikito and he told me what Mariadelaida had said to him about his brother.

'We have to do something to help him, Alex,' Maikito – who was beginning to look more like the Maikito of old – said with a grave shake of the head. 'He is no longer himself. First the riots and my arrest, and now what's happening with Mariadelaida – it's been a rough time for the kid, *sabes lo que te digo?* Why don't you go and try to cheer him up? I think he could do with a mate right now.'

'But every time I see him, the fucker keeps blanking me!'

'That's just Manu being Manu, Alex,' Maikito replied, reflexively shutting and opening his eyes. 'You know what the idiot's like. Loves to project all that hard-man bollocks, but inside he's softer than *un chulacrem*.[52] *Anda,* go and talk with him, Alex. Give him a bit of support. Do it for the sake of his poor mum, *pishón.*'

I shook his hand and promised that I'd speak with Manu soon. I wasn't really planning to keep my word, but when I came across my friend a day and a half later – heckling passers-by from a bench in John Mackintosh Square – strong feelings of pity welled up inside me and I found myself approaching him with a wary smile. As I got closer, I saw a

---

[52] Un chulacrem – a cream cake (llanito).

bottle of whisky tucked between his thighs. Also, the upper half of his trousers was covered in circles of chalky white residue, the sort left behind by sweat, urine or common *salihtre*.[53]

'Well, look who's here,' Manu cried aloud, his red-veined eyes opening wide ' – the lapdog who until recently followed me everywhere!'

Of all the words he could have thrown at me, Manu had chosen the most vindictive and hurtful, the ones most guaranteed to cut me to the bone. Ever since we were children, there had always existed in me the suspicion that Manuel Gonzalez saw me as some kind of hanger-on, a starstruck minion content to follow him wherever he went. He had never explicitly said as much, but certain looks and gestures, certain postures and facial expressions, had left me with this impression. Hearing his words that afternoon at John Mackintosh Square confirmed my suspicions. 'Screw you, Manu,' I thought, stopping in my tracks and telling myself I no longer had to take his shit. 'Just because you are in pain doesn't give you the right to hurt those who want to help you, you ignorant *egoísta de mierda!*'

With these thoughts I turned around and walked out of the square, vowing never to have anything to do with the bastard again. To my chagrin, Main Street was crawling with shoppers and tourists in shorts and flip-flops. A trio of grey-haired bourgeois ladies stood outside the House of

---

[53] Salihtre, a Gibraltarian corruption of salitre, the Spanish word for describing seawater residue.

Assembly, assertively shaking their charity collection boxes in people's faces. A GBC reporter, gaunt and with pimply bags under his eyes, urged folk to 'spare a few pennies for Prostate Cancer,' his voice partially drowned out by static crackling out of a tripod-mounted speaker. 'Stay there wallowing in it, motherfucker,' I muttered to myself, still thinking about Manu, warning off one of the approaching do-gooders with a grim shake of the head. 'Don't think I'm going anywhere near you again!'

Paradoxically, I saw Manu many times over the rest of the summer. We kept crossing paths in town, often in tight corners where it was impossible to avoid the person coming towards you – strolling down the hill between the two Casemates tunnels, walking around a delivery van in Horse Barrack Lane, hurrying along the stretch of flat ground between Boschetti's Steps and Pezzi's Steps. Sometimes he was drunk. Sometimes he was sober. Sometimes he had the vacant look of someone who was mentally elsewhere. For what it's worth, not once did we say hello or acknowledge each other. In the meantime, I started dating a girl from the South District. Filomena Bado-Jenner was her name – a twenty-two-year-old university dropout and gym instructress. She was the wayward daughter of a top-ranking civil servant – freckly, flat-chested, argumentative, hating her parents' conservatism but unwilling to jettison the perks of her privileged upbringing. I can't remember how we met or who made the first move that brought us together. Unlike Manu, I must confess, I had never slathered over the local womenfolk or gone to ridiculous lengths to sleep with them. Three or four times I had copped-off with his girlfriends' mates – and on one distinctly unmemorable occasion I had accompanied him to a Costa del Sol brothel – but that, I'm afraid, was as far as my experiences with the opposite sex extended.

Filomena was good fun to begin with. Loud and outspoken, with a tendency to gobble up her words when nervous or excited, she was one of those women who always need to be out and about, either *tapeando* or going to the gym or strolling up and down Main Street, surveying the world around them from behind their crystal-studded Gucci shades. She was also very tactile – repeatedly laying her head on my shoulder when we were indoors and threading her arm through mine while walking around town. Every Saturday we'd cross the border and go for long drives in my Chevrolet to Tarifa, Bolonia, Caños de Meca and other villages on the Costa de la Luz, stopping en route for drinks and tapas at the Hurricane Hotel, *el Cortijo de Zahara* and other vaguely 'New Age' establishments. 'Flo' knew all these 'little gems' thanks to her previous beau – a burly, twice-divorced forty-nine-year-old cop called Dylan Mallia who had treated her 'like a Queen' – and loved nothing better than to sit there amid the sand dunes and the palm trees, enjoying what she described as the 'Tarifa vibe.' The places we visited were nice enough – '*muy* chilled out *y nada de* commercial', as Filomena used to say – but all that faux hippie bullshit wasn't really for me. The incense burners, the curtained daybeds, the oversized cushions, the looped ambient music – it all weighed down my soul. Once – I think we were that day at *el Meliá Atlanterra* – I was so turned off that I found myself thinking about the dead African migrant Manu and I saw in September or October 1993 by the Detached Mole. Most probably the poor bastard had been trying to land somewhere on this same stretch of coast, I reflected – the Costa de la Luz, due to its proximity to North Africa and its relative barrenness, being the preferred entry point for those wanting to smuggle their way into the Old Continent – before being swept by the current further down into the Straits. For a moment or two I pictured the fellow struggling with the waves, holding his breath every time he went under, seeing his dreams and his hopes, *everything he fucking fought for,* perish just half a mile or a mile from where we were now sitting. Then I focused on Flo reclining there with a Marlboro Light and a Strawberry Daiquiri, looking cool and sophisticated with her sunglasses and her broad-brimmed sun hat, getting ready to call over the waiter so that he could take our picture with the pocket camera (a Pink Canon covered with felt pen-drawn hearts and stars) she carried in her white leather Armani handbag.

Miss Bado and I never returned to Gibraltar from our Costa de la Luz trips later than seven or eight. There was a simple reason for this: we needed to get up early the next morning to drive to Catalan Bay to spend all day stretched out on the beach. It was what she had been doing since she was a toddler, she once explained, saying Sundays never felt like real Sundays for her unless they were spent sunbathing in *la Caleta.* More often than not, we laid our towels at the southern end of the beach, near the Caleta Palace Hotel and *la Mamela.* It tended to be quieter that end than the family-oriented northern side, and you also had the advantage of being next to the village's only two bars. One September morning, as we made our way down the concrete ramp leading to the beach, we discovered that 'our spot' had been commandeered by fifteen or twenty young English blokes.

They had fair-skinned bodies and tattooed calves, their muscular sunburnt thighs almost as red as the cross in their Union Jack shorts. A dark purple T-shirt spread on the sand behind them bore a picture of a roped anchor, together with the words 'Dazza's Breakfast Bash, HMS Sheffield's 1994 World Tour.' Filomena – who ever since her university days had had it in for the English – wanted to move to another part of the beach, but I told her that I wasn't prepared to budge for the sake of twenty *guiri* sailors. So we threaded our way through the mass of tattooed limbs and blond heads and plonked ourselves right among them. For the next four or five hours we sat there hemmed in by a sea of slowly reddening bodies, watching the Englishmen drink their sun-warmed cans of cider and occasionally indulge in high-spirited japes. Appraising glances were now and again cast in the direction of my bikini-clad companion and whispered comments about her arse could be heard whenever she got up to go for a swim, but none of this induced me to move elsewhere. I remember looking at the guys from time to time and thinking how good it must be to have fair hair and milky-white skin and sit there drinking warm cider in a pair of skimpy Ron Hill shorts, laughing and belching and generally lolling about, not having to worry about chronically depressed relatives, unstable childhood mates and high-maintenance girlfriends.

At half past three, just as the sun was disappearing behind the Rock's craggy summit, I went to the little shop in the lane between the Seawave and the Village Inn. There I bought a bottle of mineral water, a packet of cigarettes, some chewing gum and a mint Cornetto for Filomena. While paying for the items, I heard loud hoots and guffaws issuing from the beach. Picking up my purchases, I hurried back to my girlfriend and saw five or six of the sailors standing on the shoreline. They were jeering at some long-haired prick in a RIB who had drifted past the orange marker buoy into the safe swimming zone. The fucking idiot was opening and closing his throttle, casting up waves in his wake, coming perilously near the swimmers and ladies on lilos. In response to his showboating, the young men lined up in a row and – with their backs turned to the sea, at the count of three, laughing and giggling like schoolkids – lowered their shorts just enough to bare their arses. Thereupon the fellow in the RIB slowed down and approached the shore. As he came closer, I began to think he looked familiar and indeed, as the vessel prised its way between some of the alarmed swimmers, I realised, with a combination of shock and horror, that it was Manu Gonzalez. He appeared to be drunk or high on drugs, his eyes rolling back into his head and then popping out again, his windswept curly hair sticking up like that of a pocket troll doll. But this was not all. Coming to a stop directly in front of the sailors – in waters so shallow he could easily have run aground – he pulled down his shorts and waved a huge, curved penis at the Englishmen, daring them to match his shamelessness, not giving a shit about the hundreds of people watching him from the beach. 'So you think it's very brave of you to show me your arses, do you?' he seemed to be saying. 'Show me your fucking knobs if you fucking dare!' Just yards away from him, the sailors looked at each other, not knowing how to react. Then one of them spat on the wet sand and turned his back on the RIB and its pilot. 'Put that little todger away,' he said in an unconvincing tone, already shuffling back to his sunbathing mates. 'Don't be such a fucking arse, pal.'

———————————◆———————————

Like everybody else on the planet, I have different regrets about the past. I regret all kinds of things – not making more of an effort with my dad when he was alive, leaving school at the age of fifteen, frittering away all those thousands of pounds when I was in my mid-twenties, putting off going to the doctor when I first started feeling unwell. But there is one regret that consumes me more than the others, that continues clawing at my conscience to this very day – not seeking out Manu after that shocking beach incident. Everything I saw that afternoon suggested that the poor lad was not well and having a rough time, that he was on the verge (if not already in the midst) of a mental breakdown. The signs were all there. The crazy eyes. The showboating *chulo* manoeuvres. The reckless way he had snaked past all those swimmers. Then, of course, there was what he did in full view of the beach. Let's not forget that, either. True, in Mediterranean countries you will always find one or two *machotes* who cannot keep their dicks in their pants, who need to brandish their willies in order to assert their maleness. That's the way it goes in these Catholic bastions of hot-blooded masculinity, I am afraid. Gender boundaries are so rigidly demarcated, so inviolably carved in stone, that there will always be those who manifest their identity by flashing their dicks. But Manu, let me explain, had never been one of these inveterate penis-wavers. Passionate about the ladies though he was, not averse either to a bit of wolf-whistling and catcalling, he was nevertheless scrupulous and reserved when it came to his sex life, never bragging about his conquests or sexual dalliances, displaying an almost Puritanical reluctance to talk about matters of the body. Perhaps he was like this because he wanted to be different to *el Pantera* and that fucker's much-gossiped-about prick – but it was still something that made him stand out in the bluster-filled world of the contraband trade (and probably explained why he never minded my own comparative lack of interest in women). And yet there he was that day at Catalan Bay, pulling down his shorts and showing off his genitals, waving them about like a stage magician twirling his *varita mágica*. All the families watching him from the beach must have thought he was just another *sinvergüenza contrabandista* – 'one more lowlife out of the many lowlife scoundrels we have in this bloody place!' But I – who had known and been friends with Manu since the age of five – knew differently. I knew that this was not how he normally behaved. I knew that something was wrong. And, what is worse, what is downright unforgivable, I did bugger-all about it.

There are certain individuals who are born with their destinies already mapped out, who cannot escape the tragic end Fate has already woven for them. The odour of doom is there from the very beginning, understated but always present, following the wretches like a curse or a congenital disease yet to mushroom into being, slowly but implacably intensifying around them. Manu, my friend Manu, my dearest childhood companion, witness to all my adolescent highs and lows, fearless captain in our battles with *la aduana* and *la guardia civil,* was one of these individuals; he was the type of difficult and aggressive kid for whom everybody – classmates, teachers, social workers, counsellors, policemen, psychiatrists, justices of the peace, even friends and relatives (but never, mind you, parents and grandparents) – foresees a sticky end. If you had met Manu during his time at school, you'd have guessed that this 'sticky end' would be linked in some way to future criminal activities. Had you seen him that day at Catalan Bay, you would have gone one step further and imagined him being shot by a *guardia civil* or hit on the head by the skids of a low-flying *aduana* helicopter. 'That kid is seriously out of control,' you'd have whispered, watching him brandish his penis in front of the entire beach. 'When we least expect it, he'll be coming back to Gib in a body bag!'

When the end came, it was more or less as anticipated, but with a final absurd twist that nobody could have predicted. Five days had passed since the incident with the British sailors, and Manu and Maikito were out at sea in a borrowed Phantom, their usual vessel having been damaged during the former's stunt at Catalan Bay. Manu had drunk eight pints of beer and four whisky and Cokes earlier that night and Maikito, seeing how pissed his brother was, had nearly called the whole trip off. They had just unloaded a hundred-and-eighty-kilogram shipment of drugs near Balerma in Almería and were on the way back to the Rock. Rounding the southernmost extremity of El Cabo de Gata Natural Park, they spotted one of the *aduana* launches about a mile off Almería harbour. She was sitting there so quietly and peacefully, Maikito later told me – '*como uno de esos* ghost ships' – that for a moment the siblings persuaded themselves that they were about to slip past her without being detected.

But this was just wishful thinking; the customs men *had* seen them and within minutes were following in their slipstream.

Manu and Maikito headed inshore as they always did when tailed, seeking refuge in the shallows. By doing this, they managed to keep their pursuers at bay and even had the time and space to taunt them with a few jeers and hispanophobic insults. But as they were going around one of the many rubble-mound breakwaters that are to be found between Roquetas de Mar and Motril, the engine of the borrowed vessel cut out and they whirred to a sudden and frightening halt. At that moment *la Turbo's* enormous bows closed like a pair of snapping jaws around them and Manu and his brother were sent flying into the air. Maikito landed on the sea, twisting an ankle and badly spraining his neck; but Manu, poor, luckless, wretched Manu, came down headfirst on a wooden pallet that – by a million to one chance – happened to be floating on the water.

Now think about what I'm telling you. Let it sink in. On a night when there was no marine debris to be seen for miles, *el cabrón* had to land right there, *there,* on that floating chunk of wood. Land headfirst, too, not on his fucking back or on his fucking shoulder. Forgive me if I sound crude and overemotional, but it really blows my mind to think that of all the places he could have landed, of all the ways this could have ended, he had to crash on that pallet that had materialised out of nowhere. But no, that can't be right: that pallet *must have come with its own story, too.* Someone must have built it, fixed its wooden pieces together with a hammer or a pneumatic nailer. A poor man's hand, I can see it now – gnarled and leathery, edged with broken, dirt-rimmed fingernails. For two or perhaps three years our pallet bore barrels of oil and boxed electric fans and designer clothes made in Bangladeshi sweatshops and destined for the US and the UK. And then, when the thing finally buckled and it was no longer fit for purpose, someone in a cargo ship tossed it overboard. And there, in the middle of the Mediterranean or the Atlantic, it floated for a while, algae and barnacles slowly gathering on its warping boards. Pilots of small boats saw it and carefully skirted around it. Captains of cruise liners and warships steered towards it for *a fucking laugh*. A coastguard vessel – Spanish, Portuguese, Italian, European at any rate – spotted it and was on the point of retrieving it from the sea – only for an order to come through on the radio asking it to urgently change course and attend to some unspecified emergency. Or maybe, maybe, maybe, who knows, maybe everything I've written here is total bullshit. Maybe the pallet didn't come from the high seas. Maybe it was found by some *golfillo* somewhere on the Costa del Sol and then dragged to the nearest beach. A dirty-faced Andalusian scamp – kicking the pallet into the sea, entering the water moments later to push it further offshore. 'I name this ship *My Beautiful Titanic*. May God bless her and all who sail in her!' And then, laughing and snorting out seawater through his nostrils, imagining that he was a tug pulling a cruise liner, our protagonist would have taken a deep breath and pushed his 'pallet-boat' seaward, watching it drift away on the outgoing tide, raising a hand in a mock-military salute, little knowing that in two hours and two days (or however long the damn thing took to manoeuvre itself into position) that floating hunk of wood and metal would turn into the sacrificial altar, the unforgiving chopping block, upon which my best friend's skull was violently cracked open.

Manu Gonzalez was buried in Gibraltar ten days later. I had meant to attend the funeral – I had even arranged to meet Derek, our former lookout, outside Saint Theresa's Church before the service – but at the last minute I was possessed by a terrible apathy and I couldn't go through with it. John Dennis Leslie, standing by our front door in the threadbare black shirt and trousers he always wore for funerals, urged me to reconsider, telling me it was my duty to be there for my best friend. 'You will always regret not going,' he said, giving me one last chance to get up from the sofa and join him on the taxi ride down to Devil's Tower Road. 'It's the least you can do for a mate.'

But I didn't leave the sofa. I just sat there in the black get-up I had bought the previous day from Marks & Spencer's, playing with the knot on my black leather tie (I had wanted to buy a plain cotton one, but they didn't have any in stock), periodically delving into the tin of Quality Street toffees nestled in the crook of my arm. I didn't feel sad or racked by grief; I just felt incredibly weary. Wave after wave of crushing fatigue kept washing over me, triggering concatenated yawns, making it a struggle for me to maintain my eyes open. I was aware, nonetheless, that the funeral mass started at three – so at five minutes to the hour I rose from the sofa and switched on the television, turning up the volume to its maximum setting. Some wrinkly old Spaniard in a beret and trendy sunglasses appeared on the screen; he was talking about shooting *perdices rojas* in the *Sierras Subbéticas* south of Córdoba. 'We release about a thousand of the birds,' he said, smiling to reveal a gap between his front teeth, 'and that's when the fun begins – not even the Barça-Madrid derby comes close for sheer excitement!' I studied the fellow for a second, then shuffled back to the sofa, intending to fall asleep. But when my head hit the cushion, my eyes inexplicably flared open and I no longer felt tired. Even weirder, I was seized by a tremendous restlessness, the sort that makes it impossible for you to keep still. Clutching the drum-like tin under my arm, I got up and, shrugging off a momentary bout of dizziness, began pacing up and down the room, stopping every few minutes to flick the lid open and help myself to more toffees, stuffing them into my already overfull mouth, distractedly throwing the coloured foil wrappers on the floor. Somewhere in the background the old guy was enumerating the differences between *perdices pardillas* and *perdices rojas*, but it was no longer enough – I needed something weightier and more substantial, something that could fight off the images developing at the back of my mind. Hurriedly I walked to the sideboard and picked up the only book we kept in the flat – a yellowing hardback copy of the *Longman's Family Medical Dictionary*. Laying it on the living room window sill, I opened it at random and read the first entry that appeared before me:

> *Macroglobulinemia, also known as Lymphoplasmacytic lymphoma. A condition in which the blood contains high levels of large proteins and is too thick to flow through small blood vessels. One type is Waldenström macroglobulinemia, which is a type of cancer.*

I had no idea what the words meant, but I read on all the same, stuttering wildly, mispronouncing scientific terms, switching from *Macroglobulinemia* to *Macroglossia* without looking up from the sill, racing through *Macrolides* and *Macrophage Activation,* reluctant to break the incantatory

rhythm of my recitation. Earlier my father had told me that
funerals at Saint Theresa's usually last around an hour – so I
figured that, to be on the safe side, I needed to read until
about a quarter past four. Then, and only then, would I be
safe from these unwanted thoughts; then and only then
would I be impervious to the images threatening to ensnare
me. But when I finally looked up from the book and at my
watch, it was just ten to four – a full ten minutes before the
estimated end of the funeral. Flustered and dismayed,
struggling to get air into my lungs, I peered down again and
almost shouted out the words printed on the page before me
– *The nuclear changes which take place in the last two cell divisions in
the formation of the germ cells! The chromosomes divide once but the cell
body divides twice with the result that the nucleus of the mature egg or
sperm contains the reduced number of chromosomes!* – but it was no
use, the dam had cracked open and I could picture them all
standing still around the burial vault: Mariadelaida Gonzalez,
ashen-faced and frail, held up by her ageing parents; a visibly
bruised and battered Maikito; John Dennis Leslie, glum as
always but with a hint of discomfort in his eyes; Derek,
Richita *y el Niño*, cross-armed and gazing into space, looking
like *cantaores flamencos* with their black suits and their long
curly hair; the pallbearers and the gravediggers, waiting
several yards away with ill-concealed impatience; the
soutaned priest, squat and centrally placed, a blood-red stole
hanging from his neck; the hundreds of other mourners –
some grasping wreaths, some shaking their heads, some
staring at their feet – gathered in concentric circles around
Manu's family and their friends. Even worse – I could see the
coffin sliding into the gap at the foot of the vault, its bottom
end scraping against the edge of the cavity, tiny splinters of

oak breaking off its base and scattering like grated parmesan over the patchy, sun-scorched grass. 'Your best friend is being buried at this very moment,' I thought, suddenly plunged into a maelstrom of guilt. 'And all you can do is stand here scoffing toffees and reading about eggs, sperm and chromosomes!'

———————•———————

When my father at last got back from the funeral, the medical dictionary was still on the window sill and the floor was covered with Quality Street wrappers. It was just before seven o'clock. The television was still on, but the volume had now been turned down. I was sitting on the sofa, one leg hooked over the tattered brown armrest. I had just smoked a joint and I was in a pleasantly disengaged state, able to think about things without letting them gnaw at my insides. 'How did it go?' I asked in a matter-of-fact voice, trying to disguise that I was stoned.

'Not well,' he replied, taking off his tie with his good hand and throwing it over the back of a chair. 'The ambulance bringing him from Spain got caught up in the border queue and didn't arrive at Saint Theresa's until twenty past three. Father Lima wasn't able to get things going until twenty to four.'

'Lots of people?'

'Yes,' he replied, walking up to the television and switching it off.

Without speaking another word, he lifted the dictionary from the window sill and placed it back where it belonged. He then started picking up the toffee wrappers from the floor, but halfway through the task decided this involved too much effort and, straightening up, with a pained expression on his face, began side-footing them into a corner of the room, herding them together for future collection. Once this was done, he brought out a packet of Rothmans and, with the air of a man rewarding himself after a laborious chore, plucked a fag with his lips into his mouth. Moodily he retraced his way across the living room until he reached the door to his room.

'You should have come,' he said, pausing for a moment by the threshold, facing me directly for the first time since entering the flat. 'Several people asked after you.'

He lingered there for a second or two, then exhaled quietly and disappeared into his room. He hadn't spoken to me in an angry or recriminatory tone, but I knew he was disappointed. It was evident from the tired stoop of his shoulders, from the accusatory look in his eye, from the semi-hushed sigh blowing through his nostrils. An all-round vibe of disappointment, the sort he projected when I slept past midday or came back pissed from Cool Blues Nightclub or lied to him about going down to the ETB to look for a job. Staring at the collection of shiny wrappers on the other side of the room, I shook my head and wondered where my dad got his sense of certainty from, how he could be so sure of what was right and what was wrong. But before I had the chance to give the matter further attention, rustling sounds came from his room and my father's voice once again dominated the airwaves:

'By the way, it stinks of *porros* in this bloody place. Open the windows to let some air in, *anda!*'

I can only remember isolated details about the next couple of weeks. I know that I sold my unused Phantom. I know that at some point I visited Mariadelaida to offer her my condolences (and that during the twenty minutes we spent together she barely breathed a word). I also know that I was waking later and later as the days went by. One afternoon – I cannot recall for what reason – Filomena came up to our Castle Road flat. She wore a clingy cotton dress that drew out her legs and bum, and my father kept plying her with chocolate digestives and cups of tea, telling her how beautiful and elegant she looked, secretly checking her out whenever she wasn't looking in his direction. When she finally left our apartment, John Dennis Leslie sat down beside me and – with as serious a look as I had ever seen on that swarthy Pereira face – told me that I should be making more of an effort with 'the girl.' 'You've got a really nice bird there,' he said, winking at me in a way that nearly made me vomit. 'Don't fuck it all up by being so distant with her. Give her some attention once in a while so that she feels wanted. You know where I'm coming from, *no, pisha?*'

I spent the following weeks chain-smoking by our living room window and staring at people, cars and motorbikes going past on Castle Road. I am not sure what thoughts occupied my mind as I sat next to the open Persian shutters; all I can tell you is that I would become fidgety and impatient whenever there were no cars or people out on the road and that I'd get ash-coloured patches on my elbows if I laid them on the rotting wooden sill. On one of these mornings, as I sat there absentmindedly with my cigarettes and my lighter, I saw Maikito trotting past. He was swinging his arms and chewing on some gum, a purposeful look in his eye. Nudged out of my usual apathy, I left my place by the window and rushed out into the street. 'Maikito, man!' I cried after him. 'What's up? Where are you going in such a hurry?'

'Alex, *pishón*,' he said, turning around. 'How're you doing? Long time no see, *compá!*'

'I'm good, brother. Just chilling out at home with the old boy. Going with the flow, you know.... And you, man – where are you going – up to Mariadelaida's?'

'No, man, *no*. I'm on the way to see my *tía Eugenia* in Keightley House.... Mariadelaida and me are no longer together,' he added with an uncomfortable smile. 'Things have got kind of difficult after her illness and what happened to Manu.'

'I'm sorry to hear that, Michael.'

'Don't worry, *pishita*,' he replied brightly. 'I've been talking with a *sloppy* lawyer, you know. Top, top guy with plenty of experience. We are going to sue the hell out of the Spanish government for what they did to my brother.'

'Cool, man,' I said, wondering what a lawsuit against the Spanish Government had to do with him and his old missus.

'*Negligencia criminal en el desempeño de sus funciones como agentes del estado*, that's what we are doing them for.' [54]

'That's great, man. Really great.'

'It won't bring Manu back, but at least it will make Mariadelaida feel that justice has been served, you know what I'm getting at, *no, pisha?*'

'*Sí, claro,*' I said.

'Those fuckers are going to regret the day they murdered my little brother,' he nodded to himself, his eyes moist with emotion. 'I can tell you that much.'

This conversation took place in October or November 1995. Over the next few weeks I sometimes thought about Maikito and his legal challenge against the Spanish Government, wondering if he would ever succeed in his quest for justice and redress. The whole enterprise seemed like a shot in the dark to me, a costly and complicated exercise almost guaranteed to end in failure. If there was one lesson the recent riots had taught me, it was that you cannot take on the might of the establishment. You can question it, yes, you can hold a mirror to it, you can even apply subtle amounts of pressure here and there – but confronting it head-on like Maikito was proposing? Come on, let's be realistic, shall we? Still, having worked with both Manu and his brother, I knew that if somebody could pull it off, that person had to be *el Pantera's* eldest son. Fearless without being impulsive, a lifelong devotee of maps, plans and late-night calculations,

---

[54] 'Criminal negligence in the discharge of their duties as state agents.'

he was the sort of bloke who carefully weighed his options before committing to a course of action, who only launched into a new project if he could visualise a successful outcome. So, while I thought he was on a hiding to nothing, I didn't dismiss him outright either, believing, or at least wanting to believe, that he could – in theory – succeed against the odds.

The weeks passed and I continued to sit by the window looking at people and cars. I won't pretend that I thought much about Maikito or his legal challenge while I sat there – but I did wonder from time to time how things were shaping up for him, unsure whether the ongoing radio silence indicated that the situation was proceeding as expected, or whether it meant that *el proceso* was being stymied by red tape. Finally, one morning, as I was sitting by the window enjoying my first smoke of the day, John Dennis Leslie came back from his fortnightly trip to *el Social Security* with an unusually excited look on his face. 'Guess what I've heard about that Maikito fella who was knocking off Manuel's mum?' he said, leaning against an armchair, trying to recover his breath after the long trek up from Line Wall Road.

'He's got a date for his court case against the Spanish Government?' I asked, desperate to hear some good news.

'*No, hombre, no,*' he frowned. 'He's been nabbed on a beach in Estepona with over three hundred kilos of hash. *Ese cabrón no se salva de la que le va a caer,*' he hissed with uncharacteristic ferocity, '*aunque se vuelva a meter en el coño de su madre.*'[55]

---

[55] 'That fucker won't be escaping a jail term even if he hides in his mother's pussy.'

Maikito's arrest in Estepona led to the collapse of his legal challenge and also aggravated Mariadelaida's fragile mental state. As for me, I now felt less and less inclined to leave the flat – often spending entire days by the living room window. When he wasn't confined to his room with crippling arm and shoulder pains, my father would be right there behind me – smoking cigarettes and watching gossipy chat shows like *Nunca es Tarde* and *Cita con la Vida*. He never commented on the actual programmes, but seemed quite engrossed by them. Sometimes he complained that I kept leaving uncleared ashtrays all over the place, but this was hardly a fair accusation, as he frequently did the same himself. At regular intervals he'd get up and go to our out-of-the-way kitchen, coming back five minutes later with two cups of tea balanced on a tray. I've always disliked strong tea – especially strong tea made with condensed milk – but I masochistically accepted what he brought to me and drank it without complaint, not wishing to be thought ungrateful.

There is one final element that needs to be mentioned about those limbo-like months after the funeral: Filomena and I split up. Actually, you couldn't really call it a *split* – there is far too much energy, too much *drive* and *calculation,* in the term. Our relationship, rather, dried up and faded – losing its scent and its freshness as rapidly as a bunch of wind-dried cemetery flowers. I can't even remember whether one of us instigated the break, or whether the thing just collapsed of its own accord. One week we were calling each other every night; and the next we were no longer communicating. Because I didn't want to furnish my father with further evidence of my practical and emotional shortcomings, I said nothing about our break-up. But after a few weeks even someone as dopey and distracted as my dad sniffed out that something was wrong. 'You really need to be making more effort with that girl of yours,' he said to me one afternoon, lowering the volume of the TV with the remote and gazing well-meaningly in my direction. '*A las nenas hay que mantenerlas contentas y satisfechas,*[56] like my late cousin Jimmy used to say.' 'Can't argue with that, Dad,' I replied from my position by the window, a lit cigarette held between my pinkie and ring finger. 'Uncle Jimmy always knew what's what, didn't he?'

I'd love to tell you that I snapped out of this mini-depression shortly afterwards and was soon back on my feet again, but, alas, it would be a lie: things remained largely unchanged over the next couple of years. I still smoked cigarettes by the window sill, I still hated leaving the flat and – even more depressingly – I still drank that orange tea while John Dennis Leslie watched his chat shows on *Antena Tres* and *Telecinco*. The only thing that changed, thinking about it now, was my father's disposition, which became more morose following the funeral, more miserable than ever. Irritated, I think, by my continuous presence in the apartment, he'd lower the set's volume with the TV remote when you least expected it and throw crazy-eyed hissy fits – berating me one day for not looking for a job, and the next for sitting around on my arse 24/7 and wasting my youth away. 'Do you want to become like me?' he'd suddenly shout. 'Is that it? You want to waste your life like I have wasted mine? If you carry on like this, I'm warning you, kid, you're going to end like me – *con la salud*

---

[56] 'You need to keep the birds happy and satisfied.'

hecha una mierda y sin un puto penique![57] Most of the time I did
not react to these outbursts – but sometimes, seeing him
sitting there unshaven and in that crusty blue dressing gown,
with his flannel pyjamas showing through underneath, I'd
remind him that I was the one paying all the household bills
and that he had no right to talk to me in this way. 'Besides,'
I once shouted back at him in a fit of pique, 'if getting a job
is so important to you, why don't *you yourself* get a job? You
could sell lottery tickets or work in a shop or go around
handing out advertising flyers. It's only your right arm that's
crippled, not the rest of you!'

With hindsight I should never have lashed out at my dad. I
should have remained calm and allowed him to rant and rave,
knowing that he'd soon work all that pent-up frustration out
of his system. But when John Dennis Leslie got a cob on ...
well, it was almost impossible to sit there and bite one's
tongue. In any case, these periodic quarrels of ours had an
unexpected benefit – inasmuch as they forced me to leave
the flat and get some badly needed fresh air. Flushed of face
and emotionally rattled, I'd head down Castle Street and Bell
Lane and walk up and down Main Street, scowling and with
my hands in my pockets, playing and replaying our latest
argument in my mind, already regretting whatever poisonous
shit had come out of my mouth earlier. In years gone by I
would have cleared my head by taking the Camaro for a spin,
but these days I rarely felt like driving, only going to Grand
Parade every few weeks to turn over the Chevrolet's engine
and rub out the 'Clean Me' and '*Soy un guarro*' jibes scrawled
on her dirt-caked windows and bonnet. As a result, more

---

[57] 'Fucked up healthwise and without a pot to piss in!'

often than not, I just walked from one end of Main Street to the other – smoking cigarette after cigarette, looking at my watch every couple of minutes, throwing butts and empty Du Maurier packets on the pavement, exiting Southport Gates through the ancient arch near Trafalgar Cemetery and then, after crossing to the other side of the road, re-entering *la calle Real* via the more modern arch known as Referendum Gate.

One last observation about these walks: I was always hoping to bump into someone who'd have a coffee or a beer with me. An old school friend, maybe, one of my estranged cousins, some mate from my Winston days – it didn't matter who or even what they had to say, as long as they sat there and made me forget about my shitty humdrum routine at home. That's all I essentially wanted – a smile, a face, a pair of eyes to focus on. But sadly no one ever invited me for a *café con leche* or approached me for a chat – the most I got from my acquaintances being a rapidly mouthed *'Quillo,* Alex, how's it going, *pisha?'* (always spoken glibly and with no expectation of a reply) or a brisk raising of the eyebrows (the universally recognised gesture for 'I-am-in-a-hurry, I-have-no-time-to-chat'). Part of this must have been due to my dishevelled appearance and the unhinged look in my eyes after those frantic Castle Road ding-dongs. But being a loner with no friends, let's be honest, couldn't have helped either. In Saint Bernard's, Saint Mary's and later at Bayside, you see, it had always been Manu and me against the world, blood brothers now and forever, both of us united in an impregnable fellowship of two. Enclosed in this protected space, accustomed to keeping outsiders at arm's length, I never had the opportunity to make other friends and now found myself with no one to talk to. In fact, during all those angry, aimless Main Street strolls, I only once had a drink with someone – and that was when I bumped into our former lookout Derek Durante one morning as I negotiated the right-angled corner linking Bell Lane with Engineer Lane. Red in the face, even heavier than in the old days, he patted me on the back, asked me if I was all right and invited me to have *un chico* with him at a nearby bar. 'Sure, dude,' I replied – and was soon sitting with *el Barriga* in the Royal Calpe's back patio, laughing good-naturedly and clinking beer glasses, cracking bawdy jokes and gabbing about past times, not once mentioning Maikito and his incarceration over in El Puerto de Santa María. Before long our talk turned to Manu and what a great, all-round, absolute legend the guy had been. One by one, we dredged up our shared memories – our breakfasts at the Market Tavern, *el Manuel's* mood swings, his fear of being apprehended in Spain and recognised as *el Pantera's* son. For twenty, twenty-five minutes I wasn't bothered by any of this – but when Derek started reminiscing about our late friend's tattoos and *medallones* I was suddenly overcome with sadness, weighed down by the thought that Manu had been wrenched away from us in his prime. '*Po ná,* Derek, brother,' I said, hurriedly draining my beer and rising to my feet, 'I'd better crack on and finish running my dad's errands. We'll have to do this again some other time.' 'Sure thing, bro,' our old lookout replied, his fat cheeks redder and shinier than ever. '*Dame un* call and we'll arrange something. That's what old mates are for, *no?*'

Then I walked out of the bar and dashed across the road into Cannon Lane, where, gasping for breath and blinking away my tears, I went up to a parked motorbike and tore off one of its wing mirrors.

My reprieve came in the form of a greeting card. It was posted through our letterbox in December 1997 – one of those cheap, flimsy-looking cards that come in packs of 50 or 60 and are decorated with flowers, robins and sprigs of mistletoe. I had been receiving similar cards – one at Christmas, and one on my birthday in October – for as long as I could recall, but had never paid much attention to them, mainly because they always carried the same unchanging handwritten message:

> *Happy Birthday/Merry Christmas, Alex.*
> *Love your Mum & Wayne. xxx*

The Christmas card I received for 1981 had contained a doodle of Santa Claus drawn by my little brother Kenneth. And seven years later, on my eighteenth birthday, there had been a five-pound note taped to my card so that I could 'go and buy myself a beer.' But other than that, there was nothing of substance in those envelopes, nothing that ever captured my imagination. That year's Christmas card, however, carried a hastily scrawled postscript under the usual greetings:

> *P.S: Now that your brother has flown the nest, so to say, we have a spare room in the house. If you ever feel like coming to the UK, <u>don't think twice</u>, it's all set – Wayne and I would love for you to stay with us. Mum & Wayne. xxx*

My first reaction was to place the card on the sideboard next to the other Christmas cards and put it out of mind. But as we got closer to the end of the year (and my father, as he did every December in the run-up to New Year's Eve, became increasingly miserable and bad-tempered), I often found myself picking it up and gazing at its accompanying message, wondering if my mother had really meant what she said about me staying in her house. In my heart of hearts I did not want to leave Gibraltar and travel to the UK, but I also knew that I couldn't stay forever at 24 Castle Road. I had already spent £58,000 out of the £123,000 I amassed as a smuggler and – just to add to the whole messy mix – Mariadelaida Gonzalez, poor woman, had passed away a month earlier. Pressured on the one side by John Dennis Leslie and on the other by my dwindling finances, I had started trudging down to the Employment and Training Board in Line Wall Road and asking about jobs – but either they had no vacancies available or (what was even more demoralising) they only offered me shitty, minimum-wage positions (distributing leaflets outside the ICC, collecting glasses at Cool Blues Nightclub, that sort of stuff). Not the most inspiring of scenarios, whichever way you looked at it.

My anxieties reached their peak on New Year's Eve, 1997. My father and I were sitting that evening in the living room, watching RTVE's *Especial de fin de año*. A bottle of Bell's whisky, unopened and with a stack of plastic cups placed like a hood over its neck, stood on the coffee table. Bowls filled with crisps, peanuts, *aceitunas* and sausage rolls were arranged in a circle around it. At a quarter to midnight, just as the comedy duo *Martes y Trece* appeared on the screen dressed as Roman Centurions, my father yawned and got up, saying he had a migraine and was going to bed. 'Why don't you stay up a little longer, Dad?' I asked, lowering the TV volume with the remote. 'The twelve chimes will be striking in just a few minutes.' 'I can't, *pisha*,' he replied, his eyes narrowed to two weary slits. 'I've got a real bastard of a headache. You stay and watch them, Alex.' 'Are you sure, Dad?' I insisted. 'You're going to miss the start of the New Year by a quarter of an hour.' 'Don't worry about me, *pishón*,' he smiled weakly. 'I'm sure I'll be able to hear the chimes and fireworks from my bedroom,' adding, almost as an afterthought, 'Happy New Year, *pishita*.'

It was the look on his face that clinched it. That tired, crushed, down-in-the-mouth, I-am-fed-up-with-everything look that always made him seem much older than his fifty-five years. Seeing it there – with only fifteen minutes left till the start of the New Year celebrations – made me realise that I had to get away, that I could not spend another month cooped up with him in that dilapidated Upper Town flat. *There was just no other way out of this rut.* My father may have been a fairly decent guy – may have even had one or two moments when he was okay company – but he emanated the odour of loss, he breathed out lashings of negativity. And this aura of defeat, this overspill of gloom, was slowly stacking up around me and walling me in, sucking the air from my lungs, threatening to leave me forever immured with him in that tomb-like apartment.

When the shops opened again on 2 January, I headed down to Alpha Travel in Main Street to buy a one-way ticket to London for that Sunday. The guy who sold me the ticket was a very chatty fellow with a collection of elastic bands wrapped around his wrist; as he typed on his keyboard, he told me he had spent New Year in London and had an 'absolute blast' there. 'I really recommend you go and see *Beauty and the Beast* at the Dominion Theatre on Tottenham

Court Road,' he said, brushing a loose strand of hair from his forehead. 'It's an absolute corker, that musical.' When I got back home shortly after eleven, I went into my room, shut the door and filled a rucksack and a suitcase with sweaters, jumpers, scarves, gloves and long-sleeved T-shirts. Once the packing was done, I hid the bags under the bed and returned to the living room. My father was in the exact position he had been when I walked into the flat half an hour earlier – slouched on the sofa and with one leg crossed over the other, the TV remote lying like a codpiece over his groin. 'Dad,' I said, pausing beside the television.

'Yes, Alex?'

I stared at him as he sat there before me and was once again struck by how old he looked, his wispy grey-black hair flattened across his scalp in an untidy '*George and Mildred*' combover, his two-day-old stubble growing in sad patches on his pouchy cheeks.

'I-I was just wondering if you've seen my packet of Du Maurier,' I stammered, unable to deliver the knockout blow. 'I thought I left it on my bedside table, but it's not there.'

It went on like that for the next twenty-four hours. I kept approaching him with the intention of revealing my travel plans, only to lose heart at the last hurdle and ask about the whereabouts of my lighter or our can-opener or whatever other nonsense came into my head. Finally, before long, it was Saturday night and *¿Qué apostamos?*, my dad's favourite weekend evening programme, was coming to an end. Knowing it was now or never, I waited until he rose from the sofa and then, taking a deep breath, stood up myself.

'I've got something to tell you, Dad,' I began awkwardly.

'What's that?' he asked, stopping in the middle of the room with the flaps of his dressing gown open.

'I'm flying to the UK tomorrow to see Connie Anne,' I said in an unconsciously apologetic tone. 'My flight leaves at seven-thirty in the morning.... I'm not sure when I'll be back,' I added softly.

He remained motionless by the coffee table for an instant, his eyes pinned on the floor, his shoulders stooped as usual. I thought he was going to have a go at me, that he was about to start ranting about life's unfairness and how everybody ends up letting you down and all that self-pitying bollocks, but when he eventually looked up I saw neither anger nor resentment in his eyes, just a dim glimmer of sadness, a frail ember teetering on the verge of extinction.

'You're doing the right thing, Alex,' he said, already walking towards his bedroom. 'If you stay here, you'll only end up like me.'

'One more thing, Dad,' I insisted, raising a hand to keep him from leaving the room.

'What's that, son?'

'I'm going to leave fifteen thousand pounds for you in my room. They are under the bed, wrapped in a Safeway's plastic bag.'

'*Gracias, pishita,*' he replied, a smile creeping across his face. 'Say hello to your mother from me when you see her, *anda.*'

And with those words – the last words, as it turned out, that I ever heard him speak in the flesh – he went into his room and shut the door behind him.

———————

Nine and a half hours later I was on a Boeing 737 headed to London. I was seated by one of the windows, drinking whisky and Cokes. By the seventh or eighth glass, I had calmed down sufficiently to sit there staring at the clouds streaming past, thinking about my dad in Gibraltar and my mum in Yorkshire and whether she and her English partner would appreciate me turning up without warning on their doorstep. I had last seen Connie Anne Pereira (now Mrs Connie Anne Roscoe) when I was four years old, back in February 1975. I remembered her not as a whole person, but as a series of constituent parts – hoop earrings, long-fingered hands, a beehive of brunette hair. During the years of my childhood and early adolescence, I often thought of her and was desperate for her to come back to Gibraltar and make up with my dad. I kept telling myself that I really missed her, that things would be so much better if she was there with us in our Castle Road flat, that Dad's mood would improve and he'd stop feeling depressed because of his arm. When I was thirteen or fourteen, however, all that went out of my head and I accepted that Connie Anne would never return to us. From then on my mother occupied a place in my imagination somewhere between the Virgin Mary and a planet in another galaxy – something theoretically good but impossible to reach, only coming to mind when you concentrated on what it represented. And yet there I was in that window seat two days before the Feast of the Epiphany, tanked up to the gills with *whisky colas* and unable to speak without slurring my words, getting closer and closer to the mother I hadn't seen for nearly twenty-three years. 'How will she react when she sees me by her front door?' I wondered. 'Will she put her arms around me? Will she give me a kiss? Will she turn to her English partner and, in a surprised but slightly sardonic tone, mangling her words like a character in *Coronation Street,* say, "Now then, Wayne, lovey, look what we got here – if it's not me old babby Alex?" Will she pull a face and chide me for not having warned her beforehand about my visit? Will she – come to think of it – even recognise the poor fuck standing there nervously in front of her?...'

I pushed the button on the overhead panel and ordered another whisky and Coke – much to the disgust of the portly Englishman sitting beside me. While I waited for the drink to arrive, I focused back on the clouds, but my thoughts were now spinning in the direction of my checked-in suitcase and the £48,000 inside it. Packing the bag two days earlier, I hadn't paid any attention to the sock-wrapped bundles – but it suddenly came to me that you cannot just bring all that cash into a country. No, of course not. There were anti-money laundering regulations, forms to fill in – all that type of stuff. Moreover ... moreover ... moreover ... what if my suitcase had already been x-ray screened at Gibraltar and advance warning of its contents had reached the customs team at Gatwick? *What then?* And why – while we are on the subject – hadn't I thought about something as obvious as this before – an ex-smuggler like me? What in God's name was wrong with this brain of mine? We are not talking about two hundred or three hundred pounds here; we are talking about forty-eight bloody grand. What sort of a dumb prick thinks he can fly with forty-eight of the big ones knocking around in his suitcase? I could see myself standing next to a low counter in the Green Channel, swaying on my feet thanks to all those blooming whisky and Cokes, struggling (as I always do when drunk) to speak good English. *Well, I ... I ... I ... how do you say? ... I sort of ... sort of ... dju know ... forgot about these declaration forms, officer ... dju know what I mean, amigo?* What a messed-up way for this venture to end, I thought, leaning over the guy next to me to grab the *whisky cola* being extended in my direction by the stewardess. Man spends ten years running cigarettes and drugs, quits the whole infernal business, mopes around like an arsehole for over two years, decides to emigrate and start a new life – only to get arrested for trying to smuggle £48,000 into the UK in a suitcase, *el muy idiota cabrón.*

But when I walked through the green channel at Gatwick airport, there was nobody there. Yes, just like you hear it – there was not a customs officer in sight. Maybe the guys were on a tea break. Maybe the security people in Gib hadn't bothered to screen my suitcase. Or maybe ... maybe all this took place before 9/11, when it wasn't mandatory to check every chuffing item of luggage loaded onto every chuffing plane. Anyway, who cares how it happened? What mattered was that I had managed to sneak my way into the UK with forty-eight thousand smackers in my bag! 'Once a smuggler, always a smuggler,' I smiled as I pushed my trolley past the cab drivers, waiting relatives and 'meeters and greeters' in the arrivals hall. Shivering with delight, still pissed out of my head, I staggered to the nearest airport bar and ordered a pint of their finest bitter. (Well, it wasn't going to be another whisky and Coke now that I was in good old London town, was it?) But no sooner had I paid for it than a new thought entered my head: what if the security people in Gib had rifled through my bag and helped themselves to my cash? What if *that* was the reason I hadn't been collared going through the green channel? Perturbed and distressed, not bothering to pick up the handful of small change on the counter before me, I left my pint untouched and rushed into the Fox and Hound's toilets, where, shutting myself in the first empty cubicle, I opened the locks on my case and frantically rummaged through my trousers, shirts and sweaters, only letting up when I realised that the cash, thank fuck, was still there.

I needed to catch two trains and a bus to get from Gatwick airport to Croxby in Yorkshire. I tried talking to the guy next to me on the leg into Victoria Station, but the fellow didn't prove very forthcoming and for the remainder of the journey sat facing the aisle, more or less with his back turned to me. From Victoria I travelled via the Tube to King's Cross, faintly amused at the way people stood so close to each other without making eye contact. At the station I bought an overpriced egg and cress baguette and a can of Fanta, which I drank in small sips while waiting to be served at the ticket hall. By the time I reached Doncaster two and a half hours later, my drunkenness had faded and a pounding headache had settled between my eyes. Stringy bits of phlegm now clung to my throat; my lips felt like they had been dusted with talc. Hiccupping softly, a little taken aback by how cold it was, I stepped off the train and began rolling my suitcase down the platform, wondering how far the bus terminal was from the railway station. Then I realised I had forgotten my rucksack – the same rucksack into which I had previously transferred my money at the Fox and Hound's toilets! – in the train. 'Fuck no!' I shouted, grinding to a stop. 'Fuck no, no, no, no!' Fighting off a wave of nausea, feeling like my heart was squelching its way up my windpipe, I turned around and sprinted back to the carriage. A platform guard had already blown his whistle; beeping sounds were signalling the imminent closure of the train doors. I was a hundred per cent, two hundred per cent sure I was about to say goodbye to my life's savings, but right at the last moment, after a second blast of the guard's whistle, the doors opened and a catering trolley assistant appeared at the top of the aluminium boarding steps. 'Looking for this, mate?' he said, holding up the bag. 'Good job one of the other passengers saw you leaving it behind. Here, matey, catch!'

I was so relieved to be reunited with my rucksack that I forgot about the bus and splashed out on a taxi. The cab driver was an unshaven Asian guy with a tuft of greyish-black hair on his chin. He wore a loose-fitting kurta and a white woollen skullcap brocaded with silver thread. He reminded me of Kayron Martinez, a lad who was in my class at Bayside and whose main talent – I still remembered all these years later – was to let off thunderously loud belches. The bloke before me had the same piercing eyes, the same shade of olive skin, and was only missing Kayron's flowing sable locks and the mole on the side of his neck. Throughout the twenty-five-minute journey he remained largely silent, only picking up his VHF radio microphone to grunt out the odd monosyllable, not once looking at me via the rear-view mirror. To take my mind off my hangover I alternated between staring at the embroideries on his skullcap and looking through the passenger window, trying to make sense of the alien landscape around me. Petrol stations, scrapyards, parks with fenced-in play areas, skips filled with rubble, used-car showrooms, billboards with partly torn-down posters – the overall impression I got was one of underpopulated utilitarian greyness, with the occasional mound of fly-tipped rubbish giving the scene a mildly anarchic flavour. After a while we left the main road and entered a series of wide avenues dotted with speed bumps and priority chicanes. Grey-brick terraced houses lined the streets, their slate-coloured walls blending well with the overcast January sky. Graffiti covered the lower – and in one or two cases, the upper – end of most lampposts. In the parking lot of a boarded-up pub, someone had left a rolled-up carpet, a broken baby walker and a wing-back chair, the entire ensemble looking weirdly apocalyptic in the advancing afternoon gloom. I scanned the streets for passers-by, but I couldn't see anyone apart from an elderly man waiting at a bus stop and a small boy kicking a tennis ball against a wall. The old guy was wearing a leather bomber jacket and his yellow-white hair was combed forward in an Elvis-like quiff; the right panel of his jacket was adorned with what from a distance looked like Coca-Cola bottle tops, but were probably metal lapel badges. The boy had a cigarette tucked behind his ear.

'Well, here we are, fella,' the taxi driver said, pulling up and turning to face me. '23 Churchill Lane, Croxby.'

I peered out of the passenger window and saw yet another dreary, grey-bricked property with crumbling wooden window frames and a small but overgrown patch of garden. Parked in front of the house was a two-door Suzuki Swift and a scruffy white van with flat tyres. A sign on the van said 'Chas and Wayne – Paving and Driveway Repairs.'

'How much do I owe you?' I asked.

The guy with the skullcap looked down as if trying to work out the sum in his head, then very brusquely spat out, 'Seventeen pounds and twenty-five pence, fella. But just give me seventeen quid, yeah?'

I paid the fare and stepped out of the vehicle. I knew I had been ripped off, but more important things were on my mind. Tightening my grip on my left rucksack strap, uncomfortably aware of my rapid breathing, I angled my body to one side so that I could carry my suitcase through the narrow gap between the white van and the battered Suzuki. The house, I noticed, looked even smaller from out on the street. Distinctly grimier. Coke cans, chocolate wrappers and empty crisp packets lay scattered on its overgrown lawn, along with a bamboo birdfeeder that had toppled onto its side. A downpipe fixed to the front of the house was so corroded that it reminded me of a half-eaten *barquillo*.[58] 'Okay,' I thought, opening a garden gate that hung abjectly from one hinge. 'This is it. The moment you've been waiting for for so many years, *compá*.'

It was my mother who opened the door. I recognised her the instant I saw her. She looked tired and slovenly – much older than the idealised embodiment of womanhood that had

---

[58] Barquillo – a crispy rolled wafer pastry popular in Spain.

intermittently broken into my thoughts during the last twenty-odd years. Her hair, once so dark and abundant, was cut short and dyed blonde. Deep, graven wrinkles lined her forehead. From the way she peered at me through her glasses, I thought she hadn't recognised me, but I quickly realised I was mistaken. 'Alex, me boy,' she blurted out in an accent that shocked me nearly as much as her appearance, 'me precious lovely boy!' She then threw her arms around me and hugged me to her bosomy chest, obliging me to stoop forward and let go of my suitcase, squeezing me so hard I almost couldn't draw the air down into my lungs. 'Don't cry,' I said, shyly stroking the back of her head. 'Don't cry ... Mum!'

***

Can you believe this? I saw Maikito earlier today. Or rather I saw the person once known to me as Maikito Canilla. Overweight and balding, wearing a peach-coloured polo neck and a pair of beige chinos, he was walking down Hospital Hill with two children – a boy and a girl – dressed in the colours of Loreto Convent School, Gibraltar's only independent junior school. The kids were twins by the looks of it – and he was holding them by the hand. The lack of tattooed teardrops on his cheek confused me at first, but then I saw the hypopigmented patches on the left half of his face. So *el Maikito* has gone all bourgeois, I thought, observing the way his belly juddered with every step, noticing how his tired, plodding gait contrasted with that of the two lively sprats beside him. The last I had heard of the dude was back in the winter of 1995/96, when, aged thirty-three, he was caught on a beach in Estepona with over three hundred kilos of hashish. He must have gone on to serve five or six years at El Puerto, a bitter pill to swallow for somebody who had already spent four and a half years locked up *en el Castillo* for manslaughter. None of this, however, could be discerned from his current appearance, all slick and pomaded as he was, wearing an eau de cologne that could be smelled from the other side of the road. For a second I thought about calling him over and revealing my identity with a *'Quillo,* what's up, *Maikito,* man?' – but I rapidly decided against this tactic. What would be the point? This guy was not the same Maikito I knew all those years ago, that genial, good-looking rogue who peddled amphetamines and *hashisha* and dated the hottest woman in the Upper Town. That Maikito had disappeared and been replaced by this jowly fifty-seven-year-old bourgeois, father of two snooty kids and husband to some unknown woman. Something must have triggered this metamorphosis, I thought. Maybe he married some lass from a rich family? Perhaps he opened a pharmacy or a photo studio with the money he had stashed away before his capture in Estepona? As he trudged by without giving me a second glance, I couldn't help wondering what this version of Maikito thought about the past he had left behind. Did he think of Mariadelaida and Manu? Did he sometimes wake up in the middle of the night dreaming about Michael John Birstall, the English sailor he accidentally killed? Did he cringe at the naïve optimism that once led him to believe he could take on the might of the Spanish Government? Or had he somehow disassociated from his past like so many people in this town have done, burying his former shortcomings and wrongdoings under layers of denial?

I spent my first night in Croxby on a folding bed in a room that stank of cigarette smoke. There was no cupboard to put my clothes in and no bedside table – not even a bedside lamp. Light was provided by a 40-watt bulb hanging from the ceiling, its glimmering core projecting a blob of luminosity on the part of the window not hidden by the undersized brown curtains. Half of the walls were covered in stripy, fairly new pink wallpaper; the other half was painted in a sickly shade of avocado green that, judging from the dirt marks visible on its surface, hadn't been washed for decades. Where the radiator once stood there was a square patch of unplastered, unpainted brickwork; all that was left of the original panel was a valveless copper pipe sticking like a rude middle finger out of the floorboards. 'This used to be your brother's room before he left to join t'army,' my mother had told me earlier. 'It's in *eh* bit of *eh* state because t'cheeky sod took all his furniture and his belongings – and even his lampshade! – with him to t'flat they've offered him down at Clayton Barracks, but we're hoping to make it more comfy. We've already started wallpapering it and Wayne's best friend, Chas, says he's going to bring us *eh* little bedside table and *eh* radiator and *eh* cupboard what he picked up last month from *eh* house clearance in Burngreave.'

Sleep eluded me that first night. Seated upright in bed and with my arms crossed, I found myself looking around me and remembering those times when I had thought of my mum during my childhood and teenage years. As mad as it sounds, I had always imagined that she resided in some posh house set in its own plot of land, one of those grand detached buildings you often saw on BBC and ITV property programmes. In great part this was due to my father's persistent complaint about his ex-wife – that she had dropped him for an easier and more luxurious life in the UK. But it could also have been, couldn't it, because everything in fair Albion was supposed to be bigger and better than in little insignificant Gibraltar. That, at any rate, is what Miss Tallman and Mr O'Hagan and Miss Perez and Mr Brown and Mrs Avellano and Mrs Jimena and Mr Sandler and Mr Kapadia and Mrs Ethel-Farrugia and all the other teachers at Saint Bernard's, Saint Mary's and Bayside had repeatedly told us. *We are talking about the Mother Country, after all, compá, know what I mean* – home to the best army, the best navy, the best special forces, the best rock bands, the best actors, the best documentary makers, the best capital city, the best policemen, the best hospitals, the best doctors, the best scientists, the best universities, the best national parks, the best writers and – of course, of course, let us not forget – the best football teams and the loudest, merriest, most passionate sets of football supporters....

Anyway, it doesn't really matter why I thought like this; what matters is that I was way off the mark. Swayed by my father's prejudices and hang-ups, having swallowed all the biases of a colonial upbringing, I had created something in my mind that bore no correlation to reality. The proof was there all around me. In the peeling wallpaper. In the broken skirting boards. In the stink of poverty that followed you from room to room. Cramped and low-ceilinged, lit by the faintest of light bulbs, the house in Churchill Lane reminded me in some ways of our Upper Town apartment, but without the fancy LCD TV that I had bought for my dad and without the fresh sea air and blazing Mediterranean light that I had grown up with (and always taken for granted). The bathroom, admittedly, was inside the house and not attached to the back of the kitchen like an unholy appendage – two very big plus points! – but the toilet didn't flush properly and part of the hallway ceiling had come down, exposing the asbestos panels in the gap between the two storeys. And as for the gardens at the front and back of the property – well, they were hardly the neat Arcadian enclosures in which I had once placed my truant mum and her husband. The front garden, as I've already said, was riddled with rubbish thrown by passers-by – fag ends, chocolate wrappers, empty crisp packets, squashed beer cans, spent lighters, medicinal blister packs, plastic bags and even used condoms. Its gate had been kicked down so many times, Concepción explained, that she no longer bothered phoning the council workmen to get it fixed. The back garden, by contrast, was bounded on three sides by neighbouring plots and appeared to be free from the scourge of anti-social littering. But even this seemingly flawless area – I discovered during Connie's introductory tour of the house – came with its own drawbacks:

'Don't walk into t'garden, Alex, luv.'

'Why not?' I asked, halting by the open back door.

'It's covered in Wally's poos.'

'*Lo qué?*'

'*Wally*, not *Wayne*,' she said, guessing what was on my mind. 'Our nine-year-old Rottie. He's down at t'PDSA clinic in Newhall having *eh* tumour removed from his neck, poor bleeder. I'm supposed to be fetching him first thing tomorrow in t'morning, luv. Wayne has this thing about going anywhere near dog shit, see, so I'm t'one what has to pick up our Wallster's muck. Normally, I do it when I come home in t'evenings, but I've been so tired with work this week I haven't had t'chance to go on one of me poo hunts yet.'

Wayne – in case you are wondering – was sitting in the living room watching TV when his wife spoke these words. Like Connie and the house and everything else around me, the fellow looked nothing like I had imagined. In his periodic rants against my mother back at Castle Road, John Dennis Leslie had always called his love rival *'el soldao'* or *'el militar'* – never by his real name. That Wayne had once been a member of Her Majesty's Armed Forces nobody could deny – but there was nothing *remotely soldierly* about him. Fat, bespectacled and heavily bearded, with a head of naturally curly hair that made you wonder whether he had Afro-Caribbean roots, he was originally from Mossley Hill in Liverpool and still gutturalised his k's whenever he got angry or upset (which, in all fairness, wasn't very often). He had joined the army in 1970 after finishing his A-levels – partly because he was bored, partly because he wanted to follow the example of his father who had also been a military man. His first two overseas postings were to Dhekelia in Cyprus and Paderborn in Germany. He found Cyprus too anti-British and Germany too boring, Connie told me, and was mightily relieved when he arrived in Gibraltar in February 1973 and saw how fiercely Anglophilic, how compact and self-contained, the Rock was during the closed-border years. (When I asked Concepción how a married mother-of-two could have met, dated and planned to run away with a young English soldier right under her husband's nose, she smiled and went red in the face – then made a cryptic comment about the Alameda Gardens and its 'cracking little hideaways'. Go figure!)

Wayne's posting to Gibraltar came to an end in February 1975. With his commanding officer's permission, he took my mum and Kenneth to Northern Ireland – first to Bessbrook Hill and then to South Armagh. In 1981 – when two of his best mates were killed in a landmine attack near the village of Camlough – Corporal Roscoe nosedived into a major depression that triggered two suicide attempts and effectively wrecked his army career. Penniless and sick, struggling to see where his future lay, he returned to Mossley Hill with his wife and adopted son, but just three months later – thanks to a job offer that never materialised – the family shifted eastwards across the Pennines to Croxby, a small mining town between Rotherham and Doncaster, where his ex-army mate Chas Slaithwaite was from. Since then, he had tried his hand at different jobs, including fitting and repairing driveways and back patios with 'lazy-arse Chas', but ongoing fits of depression had made it difficult for him to adapt to civilian life – and by the time I reached his house in Croxby in January 1998 he had been out of work for five and a half years, his only income these days being the fifty-eight pounds and six pence he received every fortnight from his small soldier's pension. Like most military veterans, he never allowed anybody to utter a bad word about the British Army – but he sometimes berated his ex-employers for their lack of support, saying that people like Chas and him deserved much more than the state had offered them. Polite and softly-spoken, propped up by morning and evening doses of fluoxetine, he spent his daylight hours either sleeping, watching TV or walking Wally at the local park (where, due to his aversion to canine excrement, he never bothered picking up the ageing Rottweiler's shit). Just goes to show, doesn't it? You can diss a man and blacken his name – like John Dennis Leslie did with Wayne for all those years – without realising that, in essence, you are no different to the fellow you profess to hate.

So Connie was an old frump, Wayne a coprophobic depressive and the house on Churchill Lane a proper dump – but what about my long-lost brother Kenneth? Did he also fail to live up to the mental image I carried of him? Well, from some of the framed photos on the living room sideboard I could see that, unlike my mother and stepfather and their council-owned home, he was *exactly* like I had imagined – a dark and curly-haired kid with downy eyebrows, a square jaw and that shiny, bulbous beast of a nose which John Dennis Leslie, in his better moods, sometimes referred to as the Pereira '*picota.*' Moreover, the photographs showed him doing all the things – riding a pony, paddling a canoe, hanging out with his mates in an indoor shopping arcade – that I could never have done in Gibraltar and which I, for many years, had envisaged my kid brother doing in the UK. That's something else, by the way, I need to mention here. Just as my father had fashioned his ex-wife into a grasping, socially ambitious, *guiri*-loving gold-digger, so too I had moulded Kenneth into a Little Lord Fauntleroy, fitting him with all the trappings accompanying a life of British middle-class privilege. Kenneth – through no fault of his own – got turned by my imagination into a pampered golden boy, *un niño bonito* who was enjoying, and taking advantage of, the opportunities denied to his elder sibling.... But was Kenneth as privileged as I had imagined? Had his childhood really been so much better than mine? Doubts, I must admit, had already been planted in my head when I stepped out of the Asian guy's taxi and saw that ramshackle grey-brick mid-terrace before me. *Nagging, mounting doubts, the kind that make you wonder whether you have judged a person unfairly.* But it was only when I asked Connie Anne about my absent brother later that day that I realised just how off base I had been:

'Well, our Kenneth is finally settling down now he's joined t'army, *in't* he, luv?'

'What do you mean, Mum – finally settling down?'

Concepción looked at me uncertainly for a moment, her eyes flaring behind her square-framed 'Barbra Streisand' glasses. 'Your brother, Alex, is ... well ... *eh* special sort of character, luv.'

'I don't get you, Mum.'

'He is special, *in't* he?' she mumbled, crossing her arms in the manner of someone who's already said too much.

'You mean special as in he is handicapped?'

'No, not that kind of special, luv. *Eh* different kind of special.'

'What do you mean, Mum? I don't get you.'

Uncrossing her arms, Connie Anne exhaled aloud and began telling me a disturbing little story. Its protagonist was my brother Kenneth, the same angelic, chubby-faced Kenny whom I remembered crawling around our Castle Road flat with snot dribbling out of his nose. Until the age of nine, Concepción explained, he was everything that a mother could hope for – '*eh* real cutie-pie' who was always smiling and never got into trouble. All that, however, changed when the family moved to Croxby in 1981 and he enrolled in Croxby Manor Bridge School. First it was a broken fire alarm; then smoking in the toilets; then scrapping with the other kids; then frequent absences from class; then, when he was eleven, the worst thing yet – stabbing a History teacher with a screwdriver he had picked up from the school's woodwork and metalwork workshop. ('Luckily, t'screwdriver only tore off t'little flap of skin between Mr Ashbourne's thumb and his index finger, luv. Otherwise God knows what sort of trouble our Ken would've been in!') From then on it was pretty much non-stop – drugs, alcohol, fights in the street, arguments in the house, sleeping with older girls, petty acts of thievery, continuous altercations with the neighbours. In 1985, aged thirteen, he was placed in a Secure Training Centre on account of his repeated anti-social behaviour. Two years later, he was sentenced to fourteen months at a Young Offenders Unit for beating the owner of a Rotherham curry house with a cricket bat. On leaving Wetherby YOI at the age of sixteen, he went through a relatively trouble-free period, but he soon reverted to type and went back to his bad boy ways – doing time for everything from theft to GBH to the possession and supply of Class A drugs. It was only in the last twelve months, Concepción said, breaking into a weary smile, now that he had joined the Army, that he was finally settling down, that he was finally putting his troubled past behind him. 'It's not that I think he'll ever change completely,' she admitted, looking me in the eye, ' – because knowing what our Kenny is like, he's bound to get into trouble again sooner or later – but I think that in t'army he's found t'discipline what somebody like him needs to keep on t'straight and narrow, know *worrah* mean, Alex, luv?'

My first week in Croxby was spent watching TV in the mornings and afternoons, then chatting with Connie Anne in the evenings. The television watching usually started at seven, shortly after Concepción had gone off to work. Wayne would sit there on the sofa in his dressing gown and slippers, switching every half hour or so between BBC1 and BBC2, frequently dozing off with the remote clutched in his hand. At around half nine he'd get up and, after making a cup of tea and some toast, let Wally out into the back garden so that he could go for a shit. This would be followed by another two or three hours of intermittent snoozing/watching television and a short thirty-minute break to heat up a pair of microwave meals for us. After Channel 4's *Countdown* finished at three, he'd lay the remote aside, slip into his faithful Puma tracksuit and we'd take Wally across the road to Alma Park, a largish municipal area centred around a bowling green and a pond filled with half-submerged shopping trolleys. Syringes, dog turds and broken glass bordered the sinewy path weaving through the park's interior, and, as we followed the gently plodding Rottweiler, Wayne grumbled about the amount of dog shit around us, saying it was a disgrace that nobody in Croxby picked up their dog mess. I thought it a bit strange that he complained so much when he himself never bothered to pick up Wally's

Rottweiler-sized turds, but I did not voice my concerns. 'I'd be the first person doing the bagging and binning,' he told me one day, perhaps sensing my puzzlement, 'if I didn't have this thing about coming near faecal matter. That's why I let Wallace have his first poo of the day – which always happens to be his largest – in our back garden. Some of us around here still have a sense of civic duty, you know,' he added, not realising that his explanation had left me more confused than ever.

Stickler for routine that he was, Wayne timed our walks so that we reached the house just before Connie got back home from her job at the local Nisa store. She always looked exhausted when she walked through the front door and the first thing she did was to slump on the sofa and – still wearing her uniform and that ridiculous blue and yellow visor cap – light a much-needed fag. With the cigarette clamped between her right index and middle fingers, she'd commandeer the TV remote and flick through the channels, at the same time letting Wayne know how her day at the supermarket had gone. She would shower him with all the latest news and gossip – how Briony, the daughter of the store manager Mrs Asquith, was coping at High Weald Hospital; what Kwame, the supermarket security guard, had said about African people who wipe their arse with their right hand; what some drunk old bloke had said to Kwame ('Get yer hands off me, you shit-faced gollywog fucker!') when Kwame stopped him swiping a bottle of vodka. In response to all this, Wayne would sit there either staring at the TV or at his interlaced hands, only snapping out of his trance to utter the occasional grunt or shake his head. He seemed remote, uninterested, less alive than earlier in the day. Not that Concepción minded his lack of conversational involvement. Proving the dictum that nature abhors a vacuum, she continued puffing away at her cigarettes and talking about all manner of things, too wrapped up in her own words to be put off by her husband's taciturnity. In that curious English accent that I could never get accustomed to, she'd alternate between describing her Gibraltarian past and urging me to tell her about Castle Street and Engineer Lane and Cornwall's Parade and all the other places she had frequented in her infancy and youth, avidly asking me if they had changed much since 1975. She said she often dreamt about these streets and lanes, but doubted whether she would ever see them again. The closest she had come to the Rock in nearly thirty years, she admitted, was back in 1989, when she and Wayne went for a week's holiday to the Costa del Sol. On the spur of the moment, they had booked to go on a day-trip from Benalmádena (which, like most English people she pronounced Benalmadeena, with a long second 'e' vowel) to Gibraltar, but in the end she couldn't bring herself to board the vehicle. 'It was just too much,' she mumbled sheepishly. 'I wanted to go, luv. I really wanted to, like. But when I remembered t'nasty letters me mum and me cousins and Johnny's family sent to me after I run off with Wayne – and when I imagined, on top of that, how hard it'd be if I bumped into you or your dad while walking through Main Street or Irish Town – well, it kind of put me off t'whole thing, if you know *worrah* mean, luv.'

I must confess it was a strangely moving experience – sitting there in the evenings with my mother. The stories she told about John Dennis Leslie and my late grandmother Dolores; the way her plumpy, half-frozen fingers closed around her first mug of tea and slowly changed in colour from an abalone grey to a glowing salmon pink; the worry lines that showed up in her forehead whenever she spoke about my brother's brushes with the law; the tiny spots of condensation forming on her glasses every time she blew on her drink; the anecdotes she remembered from her years at Bishop Fitzgerald School and at Saint Margaret's Secondary Modern – it all hit me with the force of a deradicalisation programme, opening my eyes to new facts, stripping away long-established falsehoods from my mind. For years and years, after all, I had known only one version of the Pereira family story – John Dennis Leslie's. Everything I knew about my mother was filtered through his eyes; every event in their timeline together came enfolded in that special Pereira cynicism of his. Malleable child that I was, I had swallowed it all hook, line and sinker, never for one moment doubting that he was telling me *the truth, the whole truth and nothing but the truth*. But as I sat there in that glum living room watching Connie Anne smoking fag after fag and gabbing away in her Nisa overalls, it became clear to me that, from the very beginning, there had been *two truths* – similar in some respects, yes, but not always in accord, weaving in and out of each other like two sets of parallel but continually diverging and converging railway tracks. You could label these two competing storylines *Narrative A* and *Narrative B*. In *Narrative A*, Connie and John Dennis Leslie were a model *llanito* couple who had been perfectly content before Wayne Roscoe entered the scene in the summer of 1974; in *Narrative B*, Connie was an unhappily married woman trapped in a flat with an embittered cripple. In A, she never cared for *el soldao* and only ran away with him because she sniffed an opportunity for material advancement; in B, Wayne Reginald Roscoe was the love of Concepción's life and the man who rescued her from the clutches of a loveless marriage. In A, she never came to visit me on the Rock because she 'didn't give a flying fuck' about me; in B, she stayed away from Gib because of the way both my Dad's family and her own had turned against her. In A, she never sent more than the odd greeting card because she was selfish and fickle; in B, she rarely wrote because she had 'enough on her plate' dealing with Kenneth and his problems. In A, she had left one of her children behind in Gibraltar because she wanted to enjoy life with her *guiri* fancy man with as few burdens as possible; in B, she had only taken Kenneth with her because *all this took place back in t'early Seventies, luv, when women didn't have t'same rights as what they have now and taking you two little mites, Alex, me boy, would have led to an awful awful legal battle which could have gone either way, like.*

Narrative A and Narrative B, then, two versions of the same story, two realities that sometimes coincided and even blended together, but were often at total loggerheads, lunging at each other like two drunk teenagers in a catfight or two middle-aged alpha males rowing over a parking space.

The big question was: which of these two narratives should one believe? Should it be *Narrative A,* with its undertones of misogyny and ingrained sexism? Or should it be *Narrative B,* with its circumlocutious explanations and its underlying subtext of maternal guilt? Well, most of the time I thought that Connie's version of events felt more honest and plausible than John Dennis Leslie's, but that does not mean I believed everything she said either. Like that rubbish, for instance, about not having the time to write more often. That didn't sound legit to me. Actually, it sounded like a cover-up for plain forgetfulness. If you wanted to make time for a kid, you gritted your teeth and 'found time.' Simple as that.

Measured purely in terms of sleep hours, that first week in the UK was probably the calmest and most relaxed I had spent in years. But there was one thing nonetheless that continued to bother me – one issue that bugged me deeply – and that was how to break to my mother and stepfather that I wasn't planning on going back to Gibraltar. I kept agonising over this delicate business, wondering what to say to them, not wanting to give the impression I hoped to remain in the house as an unpaying lodger. But before I had the chance to come clean, Connie surprised me by bringing up the matter herself. 'I've had *eh* good talk with our Wayne,' she said, appearing one night by the entrance to the guestroom in her lilac terry-towelling pyjamas, 'and we've agreed you can stay with us as long as you like, luv. One month, two months, ten months, two years – whatever, luv. I spent twenty-three years regretting I left you behind in Gib and trying to build up t'courage to reconnect with you, and I'm not going to push you out of me life again. Consider this your home, Alex, luv.'

The next morning, I asked Wayne if there was an employment exchange in town and he told me there was a jobcentre on Hinchley Lane, about half a mile away. 'But don't get your hopes up too much, Alex, kid,' he warned me, plonking two cups of tea on the coffee table for us. 'Unemployment is very high in these parts and they won't exactly roll out the red carpet for you when they discover you are not one of their own.'

Two hours later, I found myself standing before the Hinchley Lane Jobcentre. It was an ugly, cuboid building not dissimilar to Saint Jago's Stone Block back in Gibraltar. Everything inside was tired and faded – the desks, the signage, the punters queuing at the counters, even the tie-wearing clerks who sat behind yellowing plastic security screens. After waiting for half an hour to see an adviser, I was given a bunch of forms to fill in and instructed to go to a counter on the second floor. At this new counter I was told that the forms I had just filled in could not be processed as I hadn't submitted any valid proof of address with them. 'Does this mean I can't apply for a job? I asked the clerk before me. 'No, no,' the man replied sourly, 'it just means that next time you come here you'll have to bring us *eh* utility bill or *eh* bank statement with your name on it.' 'But how can I bring you these things when I've just moved to the UK?' I asked. 'How can I bring you something I don't have?'

I continued bombarding the clerk with different questions for the next ten minutes. I could see that he was having trouble understanding my accent and growing increasingly irate. Impatient mutterings, meanwhile, were coming from the queue behind me and, when I briefly turned around, I saw a tall guy standing there with his arms crossed and his eyes bulging out of their sockets, glaring at me as if I were responsible for all his unemployment woes. In the end – having visited another three counters and filled out two further sets of forms – I was able to pick three job cards from the job board and take them to one of the blokes at the main counter. Inputting their reference numbers into his computer, the fellow told me that two of the vacancies had already been filled. 'This one here, though,' he said, picking up the third card, ' – packing operative for Godfrey Holdings – is still open. It's *eh* T and T gig. That means that there is no formal interview,' he explained, noticing the baffled look on my face. 'You just turn up and they'll give you *eh* trial, like, lad. Let me give them *eh* call and ask them when they want to see you.'

The job with Godfrey Holdings turned out to be one picking potatoes on a farm somewhere between Wakefield and Huddersfield. Twelve of us were dumped in a remote field – four 'triallists' and eight 'regulars' – and told to split into twos. The regulars, already knowing each other, formed into their usual pairings, leaving us triallists to stare at one another, unsure who to choose as a work partner. In the middle of the field there was a tractor, a row of skip-sized containers and a sleeping Golden Retriever. For every container filled with potatoes, the foreman informed us, we'd get £8.50, or £4.25 per man. At the end of the working day, he said, there'd be a £6.50 bonus for the duo filling most containers.

My partner for the day was a French guy called Pierre. He told me he was a plumber by trade and that he had been fired from his last job for shitting in the toilet of a showroom apartment in Leeds. 'A right massive shit it *wor*,' he said – either consciously or unconsciously – in a Yorkshire accent. We spent the bulk of the day carrying buckets of potatoes from the field to the collection point, pausing briefly with our elbows on the rims of the metal containers before staggering back, bucket in hand, to the potato beds. It was hard, back-breaking work and by three in the afternoon we had only managed to fill one and a half skips between us. 'Fuck this shit,' Pierre grumbled, resting his black-haired forearms against the rim of a container. 'This shit is no good; this shit is *dégueulasse,* man; this shit is for animals and not men!'

I got paid £8.50 for my efforts that day – plus £1.05 for a container filled to quarter capacity. I pocketed the money without a word and shuffled towards the minibus taking us back to Rotherham, desperate to sit down and rest my aching back. I had already decided that I would not return to the job the next day, but at eight o'clock that evening, would you believe, Mr Bryce, the foreman from Godfrey Holdings, called me on the house phone to tell me that I hadn't passed the trial and not to bother coming to the pick-up point the next morning. 'Okay,' I said, yawning softly into the receiver. 'No problem.'

I continued going every morning to the jobcentre on Hinchley Lane. I'd pick cards from the jobs board and bring them over to the counter clerk, who would then phone the companies I had chosen and find out for me whether the vacancies were still open. A couple of times the clerk got told that the post in question was still waiting to be filled, only for the person on the other side of the line to take fright at my foreign-sounding name and, muttering some excuse or the other, make out that the vacancy had in fact already been taken. 'Have you ever thought of changing your surname to Percy or Perry or summat similar, Mr Pereira?' an employment adviser asked me one morning after one of these telephonic U-turns, covering his mouthpiece with his left palm. 'Just *eh* thought, matey.'

Six, seven weeks passed. Despite applying for all kinds of jobs, I had only been granted three interviews (two of which were over in less than five minutes) and I was beginning to think I was never going to get a lucky break. Then – out of the blue – I was called for an interview with Access-Tec Solutions, a local firm which specialised in building castors and base clamps for scaffold units and who were looking for a machinist for their plant off Wellingham Road. I didn't know the slightest thing about grinders, lathes and micrometers, but back in the day I had always tinkered around with our Phantom's engine and done DIY repairs at home – so I figured that it couldn't be too hard to operate one of these modern machines which, as my father would have said, virtually run on their own.

My interview at Access-Tec Solutions was scheduled for ten o'clock on a Saturday morning. Since there were only a reduced number of buses on a Saturday between Croxby and the Wellingham Road Industrial Estate, I ended up walking the four and a half miles to their factory and warehouse, arriving there at a quarter to ten. Mr Crashaw, the guy interviewing me, was a tall baldy with a glass eye; his work dungarees were pulled up so high you could see the lumpy contours of a testicle resting against his inner thigh. He seemed more interested in hearing why Gibraltar was British than in questioning me about my employment history, and once again I had a feeling I was going to be sent packing. But as we strolled out of his office minutes later, Crashaw patted me on the back and – to my utter shock – informed me that the job was mine if I wanted it. 'It's not t'best paid job in t'world,' he acknowledged, shouting over the clatter coming from a nearby milling machine, 'I'll grant you that, laddie, but *eh* job's *eh* job and they're *eh* friendly bunch down here and in t'warehouse – even if most of them, God knows bloody why, are flaming Sheffield United fans!'

I didn't sleep at all that Sunday night. I kept getting up and going to the toilet, tiptoeing across the carpeted landing, hoping that the creaking floorboards wouldn't wake Wayne and my mother in the room next door. Different fears underpropped my nervousness – fear of being out of my depth in the new job, fear of not being able to hack it as a nine-to-fiver, fear of fucking up this wonderful opportunity to start afresh in life. In addition, there was a corner of my permanently spinning brain that couldn't stop wondering how I would be received by my new colleagues at the factory. Following Crashaw out of his office on Saturday, I had had a quick look at them and been reminded of the blond, big-boned, inherently cocky types that frequently came to the Rock with the Royal Navy. What worried me was not that they would ostracise me or make fun of me – I could handle that kind of shit – but that they wouldn't understand my Gibraltarian accent and be forever asking me to repeat myself. Of all the things that had surprised me about life in the UK, this was the one that most irritated me – the puzzled looks that greeted me whenever I opened my bloody mouth. Wayne, the employment advisers at the job centre, our next-door neighbours at Churchill Lane, the Asian guy in the corner shop at the end of the street, even on occasions my mother herself – it was rare for me to string more than two sentences together without being asked by them to repeat what I had just said!

The nerves and uneasiness were still there when I set off in the morning for the bus stop on Brocklesby Lane. As it was only ten past seven, it was fairly dark and there were hardly any cars on the road. Because I had not slept, my eyes hurt and I had trouble looking up at the sky – patches of which were coming alive with grey light. Walking past a milk float, I thought about my dad and wondered what he was doing just then. Most probably, since it was already a quarter past eight in Gibraltar, he had to be in the bathroom hawking up and coughing his guts out. '*Me cago en la leche!*' he'd be gasping between coughs, his bloodshot eyes rolling back into his head. '*Qué asco de mierda vida!*'.... That grisly morning ritual had always repelled me, made me feel as if my father and I were part of a cursed breed. Nevertheless, as I strode past the red-faced milkman and his vehicle, I almost found myself yearning for its familiar rattle. For an instant, for a crippling moment of doubt, I was even tempted to turn around and walk back to the comfort of a morning cuppa on Wayne and Connie's tatty living room sofa. 'What's the point of all this?' I thought, catching sight of the little troop of men and women waiting by the vandalised bus shelter. 'Why put yourself through all this bullshit for the sake of four pound fifty-five an hour?' But just as I was about to beat an unheroic retreat, an unexpected image came into my head – that of Manu overtaking a Ford Escort at the 'Black Spot' on Devil's Tower Road, risking a head-on collision with whatever vehicle was coming down the hill towards us. I could see him pounding his fists on the steering wheel of his old Pontiac, screaming at the top of his lungs, his teeth bared like they always were during one of his adrenalised frenzies. 'No, no, no!' I thought, digging my hands into my pockets and increasing my pace, ready to take my place in the queue. 'Pull yourself together, Alex, and be a fucking man!'

My first week at the Access-Tec Solutions factory confirmed for me that the working-class English are just as distrustful of outsiders as their proletarian compatriots in the armed forces. Everything was as bad as I had previously imagined – the suspicious looks, the arsey supervisors, the constant requests to repeat what I had just said, the brutal mispronunciations of my surname. Excluding Mr Crashaw and the two deputy gaffers, there were twenty-seven other guys on the shop floor with me, almost all of them ex-miners from the recently closed Blackwood Colliery up in Birkenfield. Taciturn, no-nonsense types, known for their stinginess and their foul-mouthed sarcasm. Behind my back they had already awarded me a nickname – though it took another two weeks before I discovered they were calling me 'Perry the Paki' on account of my black hair and olive complexion. Nonetheless, it would be wrong to make out that everybody was against me and that my fourteen months at Access-Tec Solutions turned into a war of attrition between 'Perry the Paki' and those around him. Though most of the older guys never warmed to me, some of the younger ones, realising that I wasn't all that different to them, soon dropped their hostility and began treating me as one of their own – swapping stories with me about cars, footie and bad hangovers, complaining about Crashaw and his two sidekicks, inviting me to go with them to the George and

Dragon, our local across the road, after clocking off on a Saturday lunchtime. I wouldn't go as far as describing them as my mates, but I still had a soft or softish spot for all those crazy, hard-drinking tykes: Big Phil, Grant the Cunt, Little Bazza, Big Bazza and the forklift operator whose name I can't remember but who had smudgy lipstick traces tattooed around the base of his dick. To those guys I was no longer *eh dirty foreigner* or *an asylum seeker* or *eh pikey bastard;* I was just 'Perry' – the friendly, talkative bloke from Gibraltar who'd be legless after only six pints and was always rabbiting on about not being Spanish. I'm not saying that Big Phil and the others were paragons of broadmindedness or genteel tolerance. The way they spoke about British Asians, for instance – 'real Pakis and not fake Pakis like what you are, Perry, mate' – was almost enough to make you finish your pint in one slug and hotfoot it out of the George and Dragon. What I am saying is that once they got to know someone – once they interacted *meaningfully* with a man or woman from another ethnic or racial group – all that pseudo-racist crap usually evaporated and they saw the person in front of them as an individual rather than as a caricature of another culture. In this respect they were very different to the old guys – angry, hard-bitten near-retirees who clung to their prejudices like barnacles to driftwood and refused to address me other than in the snappiest, most unfriendly terms. For those *viejos bastardos,* a dirty foreigner was a dirty foreigner and that, I'm afraid, *was all there was to it.*

Curiously, I learned more in the Access-Tec Solutions factory than I did during the entirety of my Gibraltarian schooling. On the one hand I learned complex mechanical tasks like die-sinking, contour drilling and how to mount a long casting on a lathe faceplate. At the same time, by observing and listening to those around me, I learned about the miners' strike of 1985, about Margaret Thatcher's battles with Arthur Scargill, about the food parcels sent by the Russian Government to the striking miners and their families, about how the pit closures had torn the heart out of once-vibrant and thriving Northern communities, about how people who had voted Labour all their lives could, thanks to the incessant goading and scaremongering of the British tabloids, end up hating foreigners and people of colour. But more importantly, I learned the ability to think and see beyond what lay immediately around me, to stop regarding myself as the centre of the universe. Credit for this must be given to Mr Alan Patrick Toby, the old boy who taught me how to use the Emuge-Franken NEO, the multi-purpose milling machine in our factory which drilled, bored, cut gears and helped slot together the different pieces that went into the construction of our beam and swivel couplers. Toby had been at the plant since it opened in 1977 and, unlike the other old guys, had never gone down a mineshaft. He was a serious and pale-faced chap who kept to himself and hated being in the limelight; while you never felt he was judging you or looking down on you like his coevals, you also sensed he didn't give a shit about anyone or anything around him. I did not know it at the time, but Alan was part of what, even back in the late Nineties, was a rapidly dying breed – the self-taught, working-class British intellectual. At lunchtime he'd always sit on his own in the canteen with a hand-rolled cigarette in one hand and a book in the other, the briny remnants of a tuna or mackerel salad visible, along with a scrunched paper napkin, in the scratched-to-shit Tupperware container before him. I never gave his books a second look or asked him what they were about, interpreting his constant reading as yet another sign of his all-round eccentricity. But one day, catching him giggling to himself in the canteen, struck by the expression of joy on his normally impassive face, I couldn't help questioning Toby about the volume he was perusing.

'It's *eh* collection of essays by Barry Hines,' he answered, flipping his paperback around so that he was eye-to-eye with the photo of a pint glass printed on its cover. '*This Artistic Life*.'

'And is it really that funny?'

'Well, that depends on who's reading it, don't it, lad? To you it might not seem funny at all, but to me it's freaking effing hilarious.'

I looked at him for a moment, wondering if Toby had just insulted me to my face. 'Why do you read so much, Alan?' I asked. 'What do you get out of it?'

'Have *eh* look around you, lad,' he said, putting down his book.

'What do you mean?'

'Have *eh* look around you and tell me what you see.'

'I don't know,' I replied uneasily, ' – what am I supposed to see?'

'I'll tell you *what I see*. I see *eh* canteen stuffed to t'brim with guys who barely wash, revel in their own ignorance, treat their own farts as wisecracks and only talk about football, women, gambling and t'pleasures of drinking till they are 'paralytic'. I read to escape this grim reality, lad, to remind meself that there is an exciting, ever-changing world out there beyond these four walls. But I also read because I owe it to meself and to me political beliefs, because I don't want to be kept tractable and manipulable, like, because I don't want to end up like me esteemed colleagues at Access-Tec Solutions who never question the status quo and believe everything they read in t'freaking, effing *Sun*. That, in *eh* nutshell, is why I read, lad.'

I didn't respond to this surprisingly impassioned declaration, but from then on I was very curious about the books he brought to work, furtively gazing at their covers and spines, reading their blurbs whenever he left them lying on the canteen table, wondering if they really helped him disconnect from the daily grind. Toby, what is more, must have cottoned on to what was happening, for one morning around the middle of June he appeared before me with a crumpled plastic bag and a smile on his face.

'I've got something for you, lad,' he said, pulling out a Junior Classics copy of Robert Louis Stevenson's *Treasure Island* from the bag.

'I'm not going to read *that*.'

'Why not?'

'It's a children's book, *in't it?*' I replied, involuntarily adding a Northern edge to my words.

Toby shook his head, more amused, it seemed, than irritated. 'Okay, okay, what was t'last book you read?'

'You what?'

'What was the last book you read, lad?'

'Err ... I don't know.'

'You don't know?'

'No, I can't remember.'

'Not even what it was about?'

'No – my mind's gone blank.'

Toby smiled the smile of a vindicated man. 'Might that be because your last book was read while you were at school, like?'

'Maybe,' I conceded with a nervous shrug, 'maybe.'

'Then why, if you want to reconnect with t'world of reading – which presumably, judging by t'way you keep looking at me books, is what you want to do – would you start anywhere other than where you left off?'

'Err ... I don't know.'

'Here lad,' he said, pressing the book into my hands. 'Take it home and give it *eh* go. You might find it more interesting than you think.'

The novel remained untouched on my bedside table for the next five days. Looking at it, I kept thinking about what Manu and the other kids in my class would have said had they seen me in 1982 or 1983 with a bleeding book in my hands. Back then, we had all worn our ignorance like a badge of honour, bragging non-stop about how we didn't give a shit about Mathematics or English or History or any other subject that could be learned from books. Reading was for nerds, for wimps, for *niños del pish* like Georgie Francina or Tommy McGlanny-Garcia – not for *chulillos* who were desperate to leave school and *lick the cunt-flaps of the world*, as my late friend, with his talent for crude hyperbole, used to say. And yet, despite all this, here was this book sitting on my bedside table. *A novel. A fucking novel!* Though I kept ignoring it and telling myself that reading was for losers and geeks, the damn thing continued prising its way into my thoughts, bringing Alan Toby's words to mind, filling me with an unsettling combination of guilt, confusion and embarrassment. One evening, after a shitty day at the factory that saw me clash several times with the racist old guard, I went into the bedroom and picked up the book. It looked shabby, well-thumbed. On the cover there was a picture of a long-haired pirate pointing a flintlock pistol at a glowing orange horizon. Absurdly, this pirate reminded me of Michael Xicluna, a cigarette smuggler from Glacis Estate who was in the year above me at school and whose nickname was *el Chupatetas*. Startled by the mind's ability to bring disparate things together, I opened the paperback and studied its first page, my eye drawn to the elaborate drop cap at the beginning of the chapter. I was convinced that this 'Treasure Island' story had to be a pile of horseshit and to prove this, to demonstrate that Manu and the others in Red X had been right and Alan Patrick Toby was wrong, I forced myself to read a couple of pages, mouthing most words over two syllables under my breath, wanting to chuck the novel aside every time I stumbled upon a term I didn't recognise. 'What a load of shite!' I thought with a frown. 'What a waste of fucking time!' But as I reached the fourth or fifth page and came to the fight between Billy Bones and Black Dog, as the former swung his cutlass at his enemy and, with a resounding thwack, hit the signboard of the Admiral Benbow instead, something weird occurred: I started growing curious about what was going to happen next. 'No way, man,' I thought, putting the book down and frowning again. 'You can't be getting into this silly rubbish!' But even as I mentally berated myself with these words, even as I shook my head at the 'uncoolness' of it all, I kept thinking about those two angry pirates, wondering why there was so much bad blood between them, trying to work out why Captain Bones had been so freaked out by the sight of Black Dog. In short, though I'd have swallowed my tongue before admitting to it, I was already hooked.

———

Did Alan Toby choose *Treasure Island* for me because he had heard from some of the younger machinists that I once smuggled cigarettes (I never, of course, said anything about the drugs) on a fast launch from Gibraltar to Spain? Or was it just a coincidence that he happened to pick a story about the sea, daring outlaws and the lure of ill-gotten gains? Either way, it proved to be an inspired choice – Stevenson's elegantly written but pacy storyline serving to demolish all my former prejudices against books, readers and reading. Yes, there were many words in the novel that I didn't know and yes, I had to read certain passages two, three and even four times before I fully understood them – but my English teacher at Bayside, Mr Dobson, must have done a better job than I imagined, seeing that I had no trouble visualising Ben Gunn, Jim Hawkins and Long John Silver in my mind's eye. Once I finished the novel, I asked Toby if he had any more books I could borrow and he responded by bringing in a dog-eared copy of *Lord of the Flies* which, despite the picture of the unappealingly fat boy on the cover, I managed to read in all of two and a half days. From this point on I spent a good chunk of my wages on books and never went anywhere without a paperback in my pocket. I started off by following Toby's advice and sticking to young adult fiction titles, but I soon got tired of their sexless storylines and switched over to sleazy, mass-market horror novels by the likes of Shaun Hutson, James Herbert and Clive Barker. I liked the amount of graphic sex in these penny-dreadfuls, their obsession with flesh-eating rats and decomposing corpses – and I got a real kick from looking up words such as 'heinous', 'primal' and 'anthropophagy' in my pocket Collins dictionary. My 'mates' in the factory – noticing how I never joined them any more on their Saturday afternoon piss-ups – thought that I was 'losing the plot' and tried tearing me away from my reading, saying that only faggots and 'boring old *fookers*' like Toby read books. But I never took them seriously and always found an excuse not to go to the pub. 'I'll try and join you guys later,' I'd shout, jogging through the factory gates. 'I just need to go into town to run a few errands. I'll see you lads at around three, all being well.'

Another two or three years had to pass before I progressed to the biographies, histories and literary novels that Alan Patrick Toby read in the Access-Tec Solutions canteen, but make no mistake about it: once introduced to books, I was never the same person again. By forcing me to engage with abstract concepts and ideas, by helping me understand that behaviour is almost always directly influenced by social background, by allowing me, in effect, to transcend the here-and-now, books changed the way I saw the world, they enabled me to identify patterns in situations and actions that, until then, I had assumed were governed by patternless chance. Reading, in other words, permitted me to stand back and point an interrogatory torch light at all the previously cordoned-off areas of my past – my relationship with my father, my friendship with Manu, my lack of interest in all matters academic, even my desire to escape the Rock and start afresh in the 'Mother Country.' Nevertheless – as profound and life-altering as this process was – as much of a spiritual and intellectual kick up the arse – it was nothing compared to what was about to happen next. Life, alas, can sometimes be like that – lulling us into thinking that we are finally on the path to self-mastery, when in reality all we are experiencing are the birth pangs of an even greater existential crisis.

It all started in the changing room at Access-Tec Solutions. A small, stuffy, windowless chamber attached to the back of the canteen, it contained three rows of lockers, the last of which served to screen off a medium-sized shower area with urine-yellow floor tiles and dirty grout lines. During weekdays only Simon Marsden, an ex-Army guy who came running into work all the way from Conisbrough, used the shower room, but at Saturday lunchtimes it was filled with the boys as they freshened up for their afternoon 'sesh' at the George and Dragon. Though by this stage I was no longer going to the pub, I still enjoyed showering with the others before heading back home on a Saturday. It had the air of a minor ritual, something that both marked the end of the working week and heralded the start of the weekend. On one of those Saturdays, as I was lathering up under one of the four fixed shower heads, I became aware of Gary Scissett, one of our two YT lads, standing behind Big Bazza in the shower room. 'About time you came to t'pub with us, Gazza lad,' Big Bazza was saying to him. 'Sharon t'barmaid will cream her knickers when she sees a handsome young devil like you.' I had noticed Scissett once or twice before, but it was only as he stood there naked and enfolded in cloudlets of rising steam, with his arms held limply by his sides, that I realised how much he resembled my late buddy Manu. He had the same shoulder-length curly hair, the same V-shaped back, the same lack of proportion between his muscular thighs and his slender girlish calves. He even had the same long, curving leathery penis, its glans bulging conspicuously under the unretracted foreskin. Looking at him filled me with a belated sense of grief for my departed friend, a cutting sadness. Steadying myself against the protruding lip of the metal soap holder, I remembered the afternoon we had spent together in his Bentley during the riots, the way he had drummed his forearms against the steering wheel, the impish smile on his lips. As I thought about these things, my throat went dry and an electric spark buzzed through my loins. Aware that something was terribly wrong, I looked down and saw my prick extended in a full erection. *What ... the ... ?* Fortunately, because I was standing at the far end of the room, I was able to turn around and face the wall, thus hiding my embarrassing bulge from the others. With my eyes fixed on the soaking wet wall tiles, I threw my arm to the side and groped blindly for the cold tap, finally managing to turn it on after four or five bungled attempts. I wanted to scream, to stamp my feet, to punch the walls to warm up my trembling limbs – but I kept the tap open and allowed the icy water to flagellate every inch of my body, not content until the ogre between my legs had retreated into its cavern. When after a minute or two I gazed down, my erection had dwindled to a mere smidgen and my feet were almost the same colour as the veins threading through them. In a state of near-exhaustion, feeling like I was going to vomit, I turned off the tap and walked past Big Bazza and the seventeen-year-old Gary Scissett, keeping my eyes on the soapy puddles forming on the discoloured yellow floor tiles, my smacking lips replicating the pitter-patter of my frozen feet....

Sitting at the back of the bus on the way home was a depressing experience. I couldn't stop thinking about what had happened in the shower room, replaying it again and again in my mind, wondering if the fact that I got an erection while staring at a naked teenager proved that I was what Manu, in the old days, would have described as *un maricón de mierda.* When I finally reached the house, I rushed to my room and picked up the book I was currently reading – *Weaveworld* by Clive Barker. I read a few pages, then shoved

it aside and got in bed. I yawned out loud. For five, maybe
ten minutes I stared at the ceiling and chewed the tips of my
fingers, ignoring the smell of aluminium lodged under my
nails. Then I jumped up and went downstairs. Connie and
her husband were in the living room, watching an old black-
and-white film on Channel Five. Tiptoeing across the floor,
I grabbed a cushion and sat down on the armchair beside
them. Some fedora-wearing actor was walking along the
Thames Embankment, the smudgy form of Tower Bridge
suspended like a dark cloud behind him. I watched the man
for a while, slightly creeped out by the movie's scratchy 1940s
soundtrack, then got up and asked if anyone fancied a cuppa.
Wayne said *that'll be grand, Alex, thanks;* Mum *I'm okay, ta, luv.*
Glad to escape the stifling atmosphere in the living room, I
went to the kitchen, switched on the kettle, prepared a mug
of tea for myself and another for my stepdad, returned to the
front room, handed Wayne his mug, then told the pair I was
going upstairs to read. Moments later, as I made my way up
the carpeted stairs trying not to spill any tea, I came to a
decision: I was not gay. I could not be. I had gone out with
Filomena for four months and when I was a kid, remember,
I had lusted like a little brute after poor Mariadelaida
Gonzalez. That wasn't gay behaviour, was it? If I had got an
erection looking at that kid, I told myself, it was only because
I was still grieving for my late friend. Because even now,
almost three years since his passing, I was still fucked-up
inside. Eros and Thanatos, those two closely related
incarnations of the human instinct, must have become
entwined in my brain and triggered this weird reaction. Most
likely, that's what it was – a mix-up, a crossing of wires, a by-
product of intense loss. These things happen all the time

when people are grieving, don't they? Look at my father's cousin Matilda, and the way she alternated between tears and fits of hysterical giggling during her mum's funeral. 'Sorry, John Dennis ... sorry, Uncle ... sorry, Titi,' she had apologised to my dad and the other members of the family around her. 'I don't know what's wrong with me. I really don't.' That was what grief was like – it singed your insides, it threw you off balance, it messed with your internal wiring and made you act in crazy, irrational ways, replacing tears with laughter and brotherly feeling with counterfeit sexual desire....

When I got to my room, I put the mug on my bedside table and tumbled onto the bed. Closing my eyes, I tilted my head back and tried to mentally recreate Filomena's nakedness. It was difficult at first – because I had all but forgotten what my ex looked like – but after a while a reasonable impression lit up in my mind. At this point I unbuttoned my fly, took hold of my cock and stimulated it with angry, vigorous strokes. I hadn't masturbated in a long, long time, and this, coupled with the fact that I had been sexually excited just hours earlier, ensured that I came quickly and strongly, overlaying the chequered quilt cover with a trellis of sticky white fluid. For at least ten minutes I gazed at the closed bedroom curtains, aware of my slowly decelerating heart. Then I got up, opened the bedside table drawer and, taking out some tissues, faintly disgusted with myself, wiped the already liquefying trails off the duvet. 'You can't be a fucking poof,' I thought, speciously interpreting sperm volume as proof of heterosexuality, ' – no poof would have come so strongly thinking about his ex!'

I was calm and collected on the way to work on Monday morning. I had buried most of my doubts over the weekend and no longer felt that everything I took for granted about myself hung by a thread. All this fake serenity ended, however, when I got to the factory and saw that young Scissett – who for the last few weeks, as part of his work experience, had moved from one machine to the other – had that morning been assigned to the workstation opposite mine. *Maldito sea el demonio*, I thought, sighing so loud that more than one head on the shop floor turned in my direction. Filled with despair, I decided to focus on my work and put the kid out of mind – to avoid looking at him for the rest of the morning. But you know what it's like: the more you tell yourself not to look at someone or something, the more you are drawn to them, and at a certain point I found myself staring at his handsome boyish face. This time I wasn't cursed with the crude excrescence of an erection, but was instead gripped by a dreadful lassitude, the sort of giddy, anxiety-driven paralysis felt by a shy girl when coming before a boy she secretly fancies. Powerless to avert my gaze, forgetting all the vows and promises I had made at home the previous day, I saw that he still resembled Manu, but not as much as I had thought when studying him naked in the shower. I also noticed something that had previously escaped my attention: Scissett, bless him, shuffled around with a bit of a limp. In a moment which couldn't have lasted more than three or four seconds (but which all these years later has somehow acquired for me an epiphanic film-like intensity), I realised that I wanted to hold the precious boy, to cradle him in my arms, to possess him and make him mine. Even more damnably, I wanted to be possessed by him, to be held in turn. Of all the novel feelings coursing through my veins that morning, this surely had to be the most incriminating, the most compromising. As someone brought up in the *binarily* gendered world of a Mediterranean port town, I knew that there was a chasm of difference between wanting to possess and wanting to be possessed – between *dar por culo,* as my sniggering schoolmates used to put it, and *tomar por culo.* The former, though sickening and something of an abomination, suggested domination, subjugation, the blunt imposition of the male will; the latter, by contrast, spelt out weakness, submission, a state of eye-rolling, nancy-boy pliancy. Furthermore, there were certain situations when, as a heterosexual man, one could get away with looking at, desiring and even possessing a male body. Perverts, island castaways, prisoners who for years are deprived of female company – all these specimens of beleaguered masculinity could, in a moment of weakness, fuck another bloke and nobody would think them any less male for it. But submitting to another man, allowing oneself to be possessed, longing to be used and then discarded like a dirty dishrag – that, on the other hand, *was plain fucking disgusting.*

Switching off my machine, I removed my safety goggles and told Mr Pilkington the foreman that I was going out for a bit of fresh air. He started muttering something about 'lazy fuckers who keep taking the piss', but the pained expression in my eyes must have got to him, for he cut his words short and nodded, diplomatically looking in another direction. Given the all-clear, I went through different swinging and sliding doors until I found myself standing outside the factory's back entrance. It was only twenty past eight – and still quite dark. Reaching into my top overall pocket, I brought out my bag of Golden Virginia and rolled a fag. I lit it with my disposable lighter. I felt tired and overwhelmed, tortured by alternating currents of shock and relief. Bringing the cigarette to my lips, I took a deep puff and looked back on my relationship with Manu, searching my memory for prior evidence of dodginess. If you only focused on the physical side of things, then it was clear that there had never been any direct contact between us, nothing, at any rate, that could be described as untoward behaviour. At the same time, I had always felt a strange glow of pleasure in his presence, hadn't I? During our Winston and Marlboro days, I continually longed to be at his side – and, whenever circumstances drew us apart, I often counted the hours and minutes left until we were together again. Yes, I fretted, I sulked, I descended into what my father would, innocently and without irony, deride as one of my 'drama queen moods.' Conversely, when I found myself sitting beside Manu in his car, it was as if unseen celebratory trumpets were blowing around us and nothing mattered except our shared reality, both of us united against a hostile and unfeeling world, *blood brothers now and forever.* Because here's the thing, here's what I haven't told you until now, I didn't simply admire Manu's fearlessness and his impulsiveness and his refusal to play by the rules. No, it went much further than that. I also loved his muscles and his machismo, the U-shaped ridge swelling up on his arms whenever he flexed his triceps, the way his dark brown hair separated after a swim into a mantle of individual curls – so tiny and yet so perfectly formed – on his shoulders, the vicious flame that lit up in his eyes every time somebody disrespected him. The truth is I had loved Manuel Gonzalez completely and unconditionally, recognising his faults but unable to stop worshipping him, as constant in my devotions as the quiet, well-bred *niña del pish* who, despite knowing that her family is right and she is doing herself no favours, cannot bear to ditch her roughneck boyfriend from *los Glacis*. He had been my sun, my moon, the one star bringing a gleam of joy to the otherwise starless expanse of my childhood, and though we never kissed or held hands or lay together as lovers, though I'd have surely baulked at the idea of getting close to him in this way, hardly a day went by when I didn't look forward to the double pleasure of *being with him* and *being seen with him*.

***

Growing up in the Gibraltar of the Seventies and Eighties, you'd never have guessed that one out of every ten people is gay. At school there were two or three *pencos* – geeky, limp-wristed kids shunned or mocked on account of a purring lisp or their lack of interest in football. And occasionally, while walking down Main Street, you'd cross paths with *el Azuquita* – a colourful local eccentric, over six foot tall and fanatically pro-British, who paraded around in floppy sun hats and bright red summer dresses, cheerfully ignoring the cries of *maricón* and *mariquita* trailing in his wake. But that was it – there was almost nothing around you to suggest that Alfred Kinsey was right or that our Rock was anything but a breeding ground for hot-blooded *hembras* and *machotes*. Hermetically sealed off until 1985 from the rest of the world, our political and judicial systems built upon decades of solid Catholic dogma, we lived in a city where the thought of a pride march or a gay club or – *qué horror!* – gay rights was enough to send most folk into a furious, sign-of-the-cross-making tailspin. Discovering that you were gay in this sort of environment was not just challenging; it was a real test of character. If Fate lumbered you with such a terrible curse, you had one of three options:

(1) betray your innermost impulses and live as a straight man or woman;

(2) quietly court those of your own sex, but without ever confirming or denying you were gay, enfolding your movements, as it were, in a cloak of protective vagueness;

and, finally, the most drastic but effective option of all:

(3) pack your bags, bid a teary farewell to Mummy and Daddy and relocate to the UK.

Legions of young Gibraltarians have over the years undergone this brutal rite of passage – swapping small-town certainties for big-city insecurities, saying goodbye to their friends and family just to be true to themselves. A few, a very lucky few, would reach their destination and straightaway hit the job and accommodation jackpot. Others, poor sods, ended up fighting long-running battles with unscrupulous bosses, small-minded neighbours and gangster landlords. Others still, sick of commuting from one side of London to the other, missing the energising blessings of the al fresco Mediterranean lifestyle, would one day pack it all in and, with their tail between their legs, return to safe but ultra-conservative Gibraltar, their dream of escape evaporating like a fast-fading *Levante* before their eyes.

I know, I know – I've gone off on a tangent here. But I am only so animated because I understand what those reluctant exiles went through. Because I know from personal experience how hard it is to start your life all over again as a gay man in a foreign land. Admittedly, I did not have to find a job or a place to live – all those elements, thank God, had already been taken care of. But I still had to deal with the idiosyncrasies of the place I had landed in. What do I mean by this? Well, let me put it this way. If you are a gay man or woman planning to leave Gibraltar for a new life in the UK, you need to be aware that there is a hierarchy of gay-friendly places in the Mother Country. At the top of this pyramid rests London, queer capital of the world, a sprawling megalopolis holding all manner of nationalities and races, everybody living cheek by jowl and trampling on each other's toes, too preoccupied with important matters like knife-crime, terrorism and the daily commute to give a shit about trivialities like gender and sexual orientation. Behind big beautiful London are the great liberal British cities of Brighton and Manchester, places with recognised gay quarters and a thriving gay subculture where no one will bat an eyelid at two women holding hands or a fella wearing eye-liner. If you can't afford to live in these bastions of broadmindedness (and let's face it, it isn't cheap to rent in these areas), then your next best option is to find a large city. Birmingham, Leeds, Newcastle, Liverpool, even a no-nonsense, working-class city like Sheffield will do. In these places you will discover at least two or three gay pubs, possibly a whole street of them. Attitudes to gay people will be relaxed; big stores like John Lewis and Debenhams will periodically decorate their windows with pink triangles and rainbow flags; every June you will be able to join your gay brethren in a heavily policed but always festive pride march.

Moving further down the ladder, we come to that famous topographical feature in the British landscape – *the nondescript town in the middle of nowhere.* Here you will find one lone gay bar, its windows discreetly tinted, temporary squares of cardboard occasionally making an appearance in place of some panes. Failing that, you might hear of a certain pub (like the Old Millhouse in Rotherham) that doesn't tout itself as a gay bar, but still attracts LGBT types. Finally, at the bottom of the scale we have the traditional British village/small town – an umbrella term that covers everything from leafy hamlets in rural Dorset to joined-up council estates in Sunderland and Middlesbrough. Here is where the gay dream dies, where all one's hopes and desires are put through the mincer of chauvinism and self-righteousness. For as the Bible tells us, 'no human being can tame the slanderous, gossiping tongue. It is a restless evil, full of deadly poison.'

Anyway, what I am trying to say is that, even though I didn't face the usual problems encountered by my compatriots in the capital and other large British cities, I didn't exactly have it easy either. If London was the Mecca for Gibraltarian queers, then Croxby, with its cadre of single mums and its out-of-work miners, its prefabricated health centre and its concrete 'pit houses', its fly-tipped streets and its turd-strewn parks, was right at the bottom of the gay-friendly league, a place where nobody came out and the worst thing that could happen to a man, barring him being found guilty of bestiality or paedophilia, was for him to 'turn' queer. In the fourteen months that I worked at Access-Tec Solutions, I never once came across anyone 'that way inclined', the closest thing to any sort of LGBT awareness among my colleagues being the constant stream of homophobically inspired insults and slurs *(you poof, you fag, you faggot, you fairy, you fudgepacker, you bumboy, you batty-boy, you dirty cocksucker, you shit-packing homo, you good-for-nothing shirtlifter, you sausage jockey,* et cetera, et cetera) which every day rebounded backwards and forwards across the shop floor. It was much the same, I'm afraid, in the other places I frequented – the George and Dragon on Wellingham Road; the Mecca Bingo Hall on Overton Lane, where Connie and I would sometimes go on Friday evenings; the Croxby Working Men's Club and Institute, where Wayne, despite being on a cocktail of antidepressants and painkillers, would now and then take me for a pint and a spin on his favourite fruit machine. *Men were men* in Croxby and *women were women*, and nothing, neither pride marches in London nor rainbow flags in Leeds nor the bombing of the Admiral Duncan nor even Todd and Nick sharing a chaste kiss in *Coronation Street* – I repeat, absolutely nothing – could convince its inhabitants otherwise.

I was still in the middle of this 'Scissett' mess when I came home one Saturday and saw a silver Ford Capri double-parked next to Wayne's van. Two fluffy red dice hung from its rear-view mirror; a large sticker on its rear bumper said 'I'm only speeding cos I have to poo.' From the moment I set eyes on that stupid phrase, I knew I was looking at Kenneth's car, and as I turned the key in our front door lock I felt dizzy and weak in the knees, having a fair idea already what to expect, but also wondering whether reality would match my expectations. Less than twenty seconds later I saw him on the sofa before me – a tall, strapping lad with long legs that reached almost to the fireplace. He reminded me of John Dennis Leslie – or rather of John Dennis Leslie when young – his relaxed posture bringing to mind an old photo I once saw of my dad in the days he used to go snorkelling with his mate Brian Andrade. 'Ey up, Alex, lad,' Kenneth said, throwing me a rascally wink. 'Nice to meet you at last, bruv.' Seeing he wasn't going to get up, I shuffled across the room and extended a hand in his direction. He took it without bending forward, a not unfriendly look on his face. Now that I was closer to him, I noticed that his Adam's apple protruded in the same way as my dad's and that the backs of his hands were overlaid with tangles of wiry black hair – another John Dennis Leslie characteristic. 'Nice to meet you too, Kenneth,' I said, releasing his hand and sitting down on the armchair opposite the sofa. 'Our mum's told me loads about you.' 'Has she?' Kenneth laughed, turning to Connie Anne with a mock reproving look. 'That's no fookin' good is it, Ma? You don't want to be scaring t'poor fella off back to Gibraltar with your stories, do you, Mrs Roscoe, luv?'

We didn't talk much after that. Kenneth continued sitting there with his legs stretched, telling his mum and stepdad about his new mobile phone – '*eh* Nokia 3210, Ma. Best phone money can buy, according to t'papers' – and his coming deployment to Bosnia with the SFOR peacekeeping corps. His accent was much stronger than either my Mum's or Wayne's mild Liverpudlian intonation, and it amused me to think that someone as dark-skinned and Latin-looking as my brother sounded just like one of our ex-miners up at Access-Tec Solutions. Sporadically, he'd glance over in my direction and either wink or knowingly raise one of his eyebrows – but other than that he barely brought me into the conversation. If it had been anybody else sitting there before me, I'd have assumed that the bloke saw me as a threat or even as a competitor for our mother's affections. But I quickly realised that Kenneth was one of those fast-talking, solipsistic types whose focus rarely shifts away from their own interests and concerns. Sheffield United's crappy run of form at the start of the new season, a dodgy curry that had given him 'the shits' for three days, the scandalous £2.65 he recently forked out for *eh chippy tea* down in Aldershot, the twenty quid won last week on a scratch card – everything was grist to the mill, everything part of the Kenneth Roscoe one-man comedy show. Watching him in action gave me an indication of the upbringing he must have had – put on a pedestal by his doting mother and stepfather, socialised from an early age to be the cynosure of all eyes. 'Guilt has to be at the heart of all this,' I thought. 'Guilt for separating two young brothers. Guilt for leaving me behind in Gibraltar. Guilt for never reaching out to the abandoned one. Yes, yes, that's what all this is surely about.' Connie's smiles and acquiescent nods, the way the normally prudish Roscoe ignored Kenneth's repeated use of the f-word, the laughter greeting every piece of bullshit coming out of my brother's mouth – all of it smacked of sublimated remorse, of contrition for unfixable past actions, and suggested that for years and years Concepción and Wayne had capitulated to Kenneth's every whim, buying him Christmas and birthday presents they couldn't really afford, never laying down behavioural boundary lines, allowing him, in a sense, to get away with blue bloody murder.

At ten past seven, Jace Morden, Kenneth's best friend from school, turned up at the house. Connie introduced him to me as Kenneth's 'old partner in crime', and before long the two mates had relocated to the kitchen, where they sat sniggering like a pair of schoolboys, slapping each other on the back and occasionally exchanging high fives, enjoying the bowls of crisps and mini sausage rolls which my mother kept bringing to them. From my place on the living room armchair, I stole periodic glances at my brother, fascinated by the change that had come over him. Whereas a few minutes ago he had lain slouched on the sofa like the world's laziest teenager, he was now sitting up and waving his hands like he was off his head on speed, his eyes bulging like colour-drained gobstoppers. He was also swearing even more openly than earlier, peppering his words with 'cunts' and 'spliffs' and 'tits' and 'arses' – not giving a damn that his parents and I could hear everything he was saying. Discomfited and embarrassed, I turned towards Connie Anne and saw that she was standing there between the kitchen and living room with the same slightly imbecilic look as before, the very picture of maternal complaisance. At that moment I understood something about my mother that had all along been staring me in the face, but which somehow hadn't yet crystallised in my head. My brother Kenneth wasn't just Connie's son; he was the sacrificial altar upon which she was still atoning for her historical sins.

***

Kenneth drove back down to Hampshire that Sunday evening. The next day I went into town after work and bought my first-ever mobile – a Nokia 3110, the model below my brother's 3210. The gadget took my mind off my problems for a while, but once the novelty faded I was back in the same quandary as before, trying to figure out what to do with my growing sexual urges. The break that I was looking for – if you could describe it as a break – finally came on a Saturday lunchtime in November, as we were approaching the end of yet another hard week's slog at the Access-Tec Solutions Factory. Little Bazza and Big Bazza, our resident loudmouths, were having one of their pantomimic ding-dongs, just as they always did before clocking off for the weekend. 'Did you hear that, lads?' Big Bazza was saying, swivelling around so that everyone on the shop floor could hear him. 'Did you fookin' hear that? Queer boy here is gonna take his gran for *eh* fish supper in Thurcroft instead of coming down to t'Easel with us for some bevvies, t'fookin' goody two-shoes little poof!' 'Don't fookin' call me *eh* fookin' goody two-shoes little poof, you fat homo shithead,' shot back an irate Little Bazza. 'I'm not t'one what walks t'dog near Roundacre Wood at night just so that I can cop *eh* look at t'gay doggers rimming and felching each other, am I, you filthy arse-bandit!'

I had, of course, heard about this Roundacre Wood place before – in a workplace as sex-obsessed as ours it would have been impossible not to – but never given much thought to it, dogging, in my mind, not being any different to Morris dancing, bank holiday binge drinking and other British eccentricities. All that changed, however, the moment I heard Little Bazza accuse Big Bazza of walking his dog near the wood to spy on 't'local gays and arse-bandits.' During my fifteen-minute bus ride back to Brocklesby Lane, I kept thinking about the guy's outburst, trying to recollect his exact words, wondering where Roundacre Wood lay in relation to Croxby, asking myself if it really attracted gay doggers or whether my colleague was spouting hot air as usual. When I got home a short while later, I saw that Mum was out shopping and only Wayne was in the house. Deciding this was too good an opportunity to miss, I took off my work jacket and asked my stepdad if he fancied a cup of tea.

'Yes, please,' Roscoe mumbled from his customary spot in front of the TV. 'A cuppa would be lovely, Alex, thanks.'

I went to the kitchen and made him a mug of tea, bringing it to him with two ginger snaps on a side plate. As I set down the refreshments on the coffee table, I casually – and without looking him in the eye – asked him if he knew anything about a place called Roundacre Wood.

'Roundacre Wood,' my stepfather replied, stirred out of his afternoon trance. 'That's where the degenerates round here go to *mingle*, if you know what I'm getting at.'

'The degenerates?' I asked, feigning ignorance.

'You know, gays and whatnot,' Wayne answered, picking up the remote and switching over to Sky News. 'I've got a mate who lives just opposite the wood and he says they are there nearly every night, the shameless meffs.'

'Is it very far from here?'

'Not that far, but not that close either, thank God.'

'What do you mean?'

'It's on the far side of Rotherham. Sort of overlooking the M1.... Why do you ask, Alex?'

'Oh, it's just that two of my colleagues, Big Bazza and Little Bazza, were insulting each other like they normally do every

Saturday lunchtime, and Little Bazza accused Big Bazza of walking his dog in Roundacre Wood just to spy *on all t'filthy action*. I was wondering where the place was and whether it was as bad as Little Bazza made out.'

'Well, I've never been there myself, but, like I say, I've got a mate who lives near there and he is pretty scathing about the area! Says he'd move out tomorrow given half a chance!'

<hr>

I mulled over Wayne's words for the next few days. I knew that here was the break I was looking for – the chance to meet and 'mingle' with like-minded people – but I also feared the backlash that would follow if anyone at Access-Tec Solutions sniffed out that there was a queer in their midst. The shame, the insults, the shocked looks – it wasn't too difficult to imagine how it would all pan out. Finally, after nearly a whole week of this mental flagellation, some of the old 'Winston Boy' bravado reignited within me and made me catch the X1 night bus to Rotherham. It was a Thursday, I think. Possibly a Friday. A cold night. Leaden-skied. Apart from the driver and me, the only other person in the vehicle was an oldish guy with tattooed knuckles who was dressed entirely in denim and wolfing down a kebab. When I got off the bus at Rotherham Central Station, I walked through a concertina-like glass corridor and emerged into a wide dual carriageway. Thanks to Wayne's *A-Z for Rotherham, Mickelthorpe and Wath Upon Dearne,* I knew that Roundacre Wood was on the other side of town, about three-quarters of a mile away from the bus and coach terminal. All I had to do was walk straight ahead for eight hundred yards, turn left at the second of two roundabouts, skirt the edge of a council estate and – if everything went as it should – *I'd be there.*

For the next twenty minutes I marched past council offices and overfilled bottle banks, past pound shops and bingo halls, past banks and kebab houses, past culverted sewers and rusting street lights – everything well-lit and visible at first, but becoming more and more spectral and desolate as the number of lampposts diminished. Piles of uncollected rubbish lay on both sides of the road. A lone drunk pissed against the back of a bus shelter. Two construction workers sauntered along in their fluorescent orange safety jackets, helmets placed over drawn hoods, their oversized headgear reminding me, most ludicrously, of the *ninots* in the Valencian *fallas*. Roundacre Wood was not really a wood at all, but a largish bosky hill adjacent to a small council estate and a set of playing fields. At its foot there was a tiny car park with a single lamppost and a vandalised pay meter. There were no cars to be seen anywhere, but close to the meter, behind the low timber railing enclosing the empty quadrangle, someone had dumped an electric cooker with old-style coiled hobs, the battered thing resting on its side like a scuttled battleship. It was impossible to gauge the exact height of the hill from where I stood, but the roar of motorway traffic suggested that, if you jumped over the knee-high fence and started climbing up the slope, it wouldn't take long before you reached the summit and found yourself looking down the other flank at the southbound lanes of the M1. Disheartened by the lack of vehicles in the car park, feeling colder than I had bargained for, I looked around me and, after an initial tremor of hesitation, hurdled the rail and sat down on the cooker. I felt stupid and vulnerable, brimming with self-hatred. I also wondered if anybody from Gibraltar had ever strayed into this shithole in the middle of nowhere. *Probably not*, I thought, rubbing my arms. *Probably no other Gibraltarian has ever been here.* With the help of the nearby lamppost I could make out some of the items of rubbish strewn beyond the railing – a handful of beer cans, a few chocolate wrappers, a squashed KFC bucket, a small mattress, a strapless hard hat, an empty bottle of HP sauce, a suitcase, a traffic cone, the crumpled, jelly-like form of a used condom. Spotting the latter, I thought of the absurdity of my plight – turning up at random to a gay dogging venue, expecting to encounter some clandestine action on the exact day and time I had come here, on such a cold fucking evening too. *Really, Ojo Tuerto,* I muttered, watching my breath condense into a vapour. *You are something else, dude.* Bizarrely, it was at that moment that I heard the voice coming from the bushes behind me:

'Ey up, fella, what you're doing there?'

'Me,' I replied, too dazed to think properly, 'nothing, nothing.'

'What do you mean, nothing? You're not *eh* cop, are you, fella?'

'No, I'm not a cop.'

'How do I know that?'

'Because I'm not.'

A ten- or twelve-second pause, as if my unseen companion were mulling over my words. Then, just as I thought I had scared him off for good with my unthinking remarks:

'You're here for some fun, then?'

I slid off the side of the cooker and turned around. A man about my height was standing there in a hooded top and tracksuit bottoms, his features obscured by the peak of a baseball cap. I couldn't see much of him in the dark, but from his build and voice I guessed he had to be about forty. When he saw me bob my head, he nodded and then plunged into the wood behind him. I followed the guy with my hands in my pockets, wishing I had brought a baseball cap with me. The air was charged with the smell of bracken and damp soil, and, as we went up the hill, the sound of motorway traffic became louder and louder, rebounding unnervingly off the closely packed boughs and branches. Pinning my eyes on my guide's back, I wondered where we were going, who would be there to meet us, what those people were already doing. As I wrestled with these thoughts, we reached the brow of the hillock and then began shuffling our way downhill through an ankle-deep layer of dead leaves. When we eventually came to a stop, I found myself in a clearing which, judging from the deafening roar of speeding cars and trucks, could not have been more than twenty or twenty-five feet above the M1. Part of a motorway gantry could be seen suspended above the treetops, its big, bulky form silhouetted against the overcast night sky like the bow of an alien spaceship. In the middle of the glade, six or seven semi-naked figures were engaged in homosexual acts. *Old guys* – or old at least in the eyes of the twenty-nine-year-old I was back in those days. Boldly, without waiting to be asked, I unzipped my trousers and jumped straight into the mêlée. What I experienced then is almost impossible to put into words. I felt pleasure, yes – but I also felt disconnected from both my immediate and distant past. More strangely still, I could feel a rush of purificatory energy flowing through me, chipping away at my core, shattering taboos and self-imposed interdictions, opening my eyes to the cold, marmoreal beauty of male thighs and buttocks, reshaping my sense of what was right and what was wrong. If you are disgusted by what I am relating, then think how *shocking and astonishing* all this must have been for me – brought up in a tradition where homosexual urges were regarded as proof of moral corruption, conditioned to think that there was nothing more disgusting, *nada más puerco y más degenerao,* than to caress, and be caressed by, another man. It was as if thirty years' worth of psycho-sexual mores were gushing fiercely out of my system; as if every poison fed into me, every last moral and psychic contaminant, were being dislodged by a harsh and bitter-tasting emetic. It was, you could say, as if the old Alex Pereira had died and was now being replaced by another Alex Pereira, someone braver and purer, no longer in thrall to the tyranny of convention, capable of recognising the double-standards of bourgeois morality, unwilling to submit to any form of justice other than that dispensed in the courtroom of his own conscience. It was – if you'll forgive the rather sacrilegious comparison – as if I had been crucified and then brought back to life in the shadow of the M1.

Last night I printed out everything I have written so far.

It was most odd – seeing the papers arranged in a pile before me and thinking that my life story somehow lies woven into them, something not touchable and yet there all the same.

Writing truly acts as a resurrector of past experiences, doesn't it? If we don't write about our trials and tribulations, we risk leaving nothing of ourselves when we eventually disappear from this world of *substanceless* shadows.

In a lot of ways the next six months mirrored the roller-coaster highs and lows of my old smuggling days. Operating at night, using nicknames for each other, being continually on the lookout for the law – there were so many elements that reminded me of our former cat and mouse dodges in the Straits of Gibraltar, so many moments that mimicked my transgressive Mediterranean past. What was different, however – what came as a bit of a surprise – was the lack of interaction between the various pleasure-seekers, the way that everybody just toddled off after our sessions without so much as a word of goodbye. The main reason for this, I suspected, was the sheer turnover of participants, the impossibility of knowing who'd be showing up on the night at Roundacre Wood. But it must also have had something to do with the fact that – unlike the swashbuckling business of making money on a fast launch – having gay sex with strangers was not exactly an endeavour to brag about. On the contrary, it was something that could wreck your street cred, that compromised your manhood and which – in places as close-minded as Croxby or Mickelthorpe – could turn you into a lifelong pariah. If you were going to assume these risks, then obviously it was best to stick to the matter at hand and minimise all unnecessary contact with the others. Get in, get out *and then forget about the whole sordid affair until the next time you came to Roundacre Wood.*

That is not to say there was no camaraderie among the anonymous desperadoes who every few days gathered for sex a stone's throw away from the M1. Although great advances in gay rights had been achieved in the UK in the last ten or fifteen years, section 13 of the 1956 Sexual Offences Act still rendered it illegal for more than two men to have sex together and this, coupled with the fact that hounding and harassing 'poofters' was one of the favourite pastimes of the South Yorkshire Police, made queer dogging much more hazardous than its heterosexual variant. Everybody, in this sense, knew the risks they were taking; each of us realised how close to the wind we were sailing. One false move, one foolish mistake, and all of us would've ended up in jail and ostracised for life by our family, friends and work colleagues. This feeling that we were all in it together was not something articulated in words, but it was there just the same – floating in the spaces between our perspiring bodies, enveloping us in a web of silent collective complicity.

Winter soon arrived – a savage, snow-filled winter that caused fishing lakes to freeze and water pipes to burst, but seldom stopped us from attending our sessions at Roundacre Wood. Instead of travelling to Rotherham by bus, I was now driving there in my mother's Suzuki Swift, which I borrowed every few nights for a couple of hours and parked under a rust-eaten pylon behind the nearby council estate. To throw Connie and Wayne off the scent I invented some cock and bull story about attending adult classes in pottery and media studies at Rotherham College. Though nobody at Roundacre Wood knew my real name and I never referred to my accomplices other than by their chosen (and sometimes quite absurd) nicknames, I was now receiving a steady stream of text messages on my mobile from the other regulars – mostly about timings and weather conditions and the always agreeable news that fresh faces would soon be joining us. The main organiser of our meetings was a guy everybody knew as Scragsy – a short, balding dude with a Geordie accent, a cleft lip and the well-padded figure of a pub darts player. I had no idea where he lived or what he did for a living, although once, as he was pulling up his trousers following a mid-week session, I saw a laminated security pass on a lanyard drop out of his pocket.

The gathering themselves were always frantic, jittery affairs – and it was not uncommon to come out of them with bruises, scratches, bite marks and even black eyes. Until March we kept our jackets and sweaters on, but once the weather improved one or two of the guys peeled off their tops and started operating in the buff, the scent of spring having inured them to the knife-like winds occasionally blowing through the clearing. Incidentally, while we were 'at it', a bomb could have exploded nearby and nobody would have noticed a damn thing – but both before and after the orgies everybody was in a state of hyperawareness, alert to the slightest rustle in the bushes or the faintest glimmer of lights down in the car park. In one of my rare conversations with Scragsy, I found out that the police had broken up three of our get-togethers in the last three years, but that so far – touch wood – nobody had been charged with any offences. He also told me that in September 1997 the guys had clashed with some teenage yobs from the neighbouring council estate who had rushed into the clearing armed with baseball bats and chanting 'death to gay scum', their bodies reeking of alcohol and cannabis smoke. 'Nasty little scratters,' Scragsy said, spitting out a gob of saliva and then wiping his mouth with the back of his hand. 'You'd think they'd 'ave other more important things to worry *aboot* than *eh* group of us lads meeting up for *eh* bit of rough and tumble, like, but evidently not, the shitty little scrotes.'

Freud calls it repetition compulsion – *the tendency to repeat earlier experiences or to recreate previous psychological states.* According to his theory, some of us do not really learn from our life mistakes; rather, we unconsciously – and sometimes consciously – put ourselves in situations where we are likely to make the same errors. We don't do this because we are gluttons for punishment or because we like to create trouble for ourselves; we do this because, at some deep, subconscious level, we find comfort in old addictions and recurring patterns of behaviour. Eight years in the drug and cigarette smuggling trade, after all, had taught me that crime never pays, that if you keep transgressing, sooner or later you are going to come a cropper. I knew this from what had happened to Manu and Maikito, as well as to the dozens of other 'Winston Boys' and *gayumberos* who had been arrested, jailed, shot at and even killed. But did this stop me from repeatedly breaking the law just a handful of years later in South Yorkshire? No, of course not. I continued playing with fire, I recklessly ignored the warnings, until in the end – surprise, surprise – I got my fingers burned.

It happened on a bank holiday weekend in April 1999. England was playing Hungary that evening in an international friendly and the match was being shown live on ITV; as a result, only five people had bothered coming to the clearing that Saturday. Earlier in the afternoon there had been a serious traffic accident near junction 34 of the M1, and ambulances and police cars could still be heard careering up and down the highway, the whirr of sirens ricocheting uncannily off the trees around us. Suddenly a twig snapped behind a thicket and in a trice we were surrounded by a band of men in dark uniforms and square-visored baseball caps. 'Stay right where you all are!' a male voice shouted in a gruff Northern accent. 'Don't you fookin' move!' 'Bimbo', the shortest and most insignificant-looking guy in our group, somehow managed to slip unnoticed into the woods, but the rest of us could only stand there with our hands cupped over our private parts, our pale bodies skewered by a multitude of crisscrossing torch beams, wisps of condensation spewing like ectoplasm out of our panting mouths.

We were taken to Rotherham Police Station and locked up in separate cells. I briefly glimpsed my cell's interior when they opened the door and some of the frail corridor light seeped in, but once they shut me inside everything became dark and featureless. For a while I was under the illusion that I was being held on my own. Then – horror of horrors – I heard a rustling sound from the other side of the room. *Mierda puta*, I thought, feeling my heart wobble in my chest. Moments later, as my eyes, ears and nose attuned themselves to their new surroundings, I realised that there was someone there on a bench. A big fellow. Lying asleep under a pile of blankets. He was making smacking sounds with his lips and letting off squeaky farts, the pungent smell of which was already pushing up my nostrils. I wondered why I could see his clothes and not his face, then I realised I was looking at a black man. Now that I was aware of his presence, I was more nervous and self-conscious than ever, not wanting to move in case I woke up my cell companion. I also kept wondering what the guy had done to end up there in the cell beside me. Had he mugged somebody? Had he beaten up his wife? Had he been nabbed selling drugs? Or was he, in his own way, just as blameless as those of us busted at the wood – arrested merely for the crime of being trapped in his black skin?

———————

I don't know how long I remained in this state of heightened anxiety. Maybe it was an hour, maybe two, maybe three. Somewhere along the line I found myself thinking about *The Dark* by James Herbert, one of the horror novels I had read in the last few weeks. I thought about the way the 'darkness' spreads in the novel – first affecting a single street, then a district, then the whole of London. I thought what a twisted but clever idea it was to write about darkness as a kind of sentient, malevolent presence. When the cell door finally opened and a beam of light poured in, I saw that it was indeed a black man lying there asleep beside me. He was, however, much older than I had imagined – well into his seventies or even his eighties, with a long mane of grey hair braided into thick, tentacle-like dreadlocks and a set of painfully cracked and overgrown fingernails. Before I had time to examine him any further, though, I was ushered out of the cell and taken to a big room with bright fluorescents. In this room there were loads of chairs and a large projector screen; there was also a poster on the wall with a waterfall and the words 'Evil is powerless if the good are unafraid'. I was ordered to sit down on one of the chairs and then a man about my age – wiry, ill-shaven with a variety of pimples and blackheads on his face – entered the room through a

different door to the one I had used. He said his name was
Paul and that he wanted to help me, although his voice and
the expression in his eyes told another story. Twirling an unlit
cigarette between his fingers, he asked me what my name
was, where I lived, who I worked for and other formulaic
questions that I answered honestly but without much
conviction. Once these were out of the way, he began asking
more personal questions, such as whether I was a practising
homosexual, whether I had AIDS, whether I enjoyed anal
sex, and whether I had performed any sex acts on the other
men arrested that night. I knew that he was trying to get me
to incriminate myself, so I answered no to everything he
asked, insisting all along I had only turned up at Roundacre
Wood to see what all this fuss was about dogging and only
joined the others – wait for it – out of 'a sense of peer
pressure.' 'Okay, fella,' Paul said, bringing the interview to a
close. 'It's time for me to go and question your friends.
You're free to go pending further investigations.... But don't
think you're off t'hook, matey,' he scowled unpleasantly,
perhaps noticing the look of relief on my face. 'With what we
got on you guys, there's every chance you and your bum
chums will be charged with indecent exposure, public
lewdness and gross indecency under section 13 of t'1956
Sexual Offences Act.'

Dawn was breaking when I left the station at seven in the
morning. As I stood there checking that nothing had been
taken out of my wallet, I remembered that I had left my
mother's Suzuki parked under the pylon behind Roundacre
Wood Council Estate. Fighting off a yawn, I pocketed my
wallet, walked up to the nearest taxi rank and asked an Asian
cabbie if he could take me where I needed to go. 'No *problemo*,

fella,' he said, unlocking the back passenger door. When I reached the pylon ten minutes later, I saw that one of the Swift's windows was smashed in and there was glass all over the driver's seat. Where my Mum's Aiwa cassette radio player had sat six or seven hours earlier, there was now a gaping rectangular slit, its lower edge draped by a spaghetti-like tangle of cables. A sticky brown substance covered the bottom half of the windscreen, and some of it had trickled into the gap between the window and the bonnet. Touching it with my finger and holding it under my nose, I was relieved to discover it was mud and not shit.

Over the course of that Sunday and bank-holiday Monday I received two texts from Scragsy on my mobile. The first said 'Don't worry – everything will be fine.' The second 'Don't forget: no one was technically caught having penetrative sex – we'll all be fine.' Early on Tuesday, though, while I was away from my workstation on a smoke break, I picked up a copy of *The Sheffield Star* that someone had left in the canteen and saw my name in a piece about the recent arrests at Roundacre Wood. There it was, black on white – a public outing with all the gory details thrown in. Now, if my name had been Barry Johnson and I resided in Central Sheffield, or Colin Smith and I came from Seacroft in Leeds, then maybe, just maybe, I could have pretended that it was somebody else named and shamed in that provincial rag. But my name was Alex Pereira, wasn't it? Alex fucking Pereira from fucking bloody Croxby – the only fucking Pereira, more than likely, in the whole of fucking bloody South Yorkshire. So far, it was true, nobody on the shop floor had given me any funny looks or made any disparaging remarks – but it was only nine-thirty in the morning, wasn't it, and chances were that none of them had even looked at the paper yet. Depressed and distraught, feeling like the new life I had fought so hard to establish was collapsing before my eyes, I glanced around me and, seeing that the coast was clear, tore the offending page out of the paper, crumpled it into a ball and stuffed it into one of my overall pockets.

I stayed at home for the rest of the week with the excuse that I had a bad flu. I was feeling anxious and demoralised and more than once I was tempted to pack my bags and do a runner back to Gibraltar. Then on Friday morning, as I was lying in bed struggling to get up, Wayne knocked on my door and told me I was wanted on the phone. I thought it'd be Crashaw moaning his head off about my prolonged absence from work, or maybe the Suzuki dealers telling me that Connie's car was fixed and ready to be collected, but it turned out to be somebody from Rotherham Police Station informing me that no further action was being taken against me and the other men arrested at Roundacre Wood. My first reaction was one of elation – expressed, somewhat embarrassingly, in my punching the nearest wall! – but when I calmed down and reflected on the matter I rapidly sobered up. *I had been publicly outed, hadn't I, and I still had to go back to a factory full of homophobic brutes.* No amount of backtracking from the police could change these hard facts. Lamenting my earlier moment of exuberance, I returned to my room and clambered into bed, too dispirited to decide what I was going to do next.

Throughout that weekend I wrestled with the different options open to me. One moment I was convinced I could return to Access-Tec without anybody batting an eyelid; the next I'd see myself squirming over my workstation, all sweaty and stressed, struggling to block out the torrent of insults and mocking innuendoes. I could imagine the things that Big Phil and Grant the Cunt – and especially Big Bazza and Little Bazza – would say, the sheer spite in their eyes. *So Perry the Paki has gone queer, has he? What do you expect with these dirty foreign fookers? It's in their nature, in't it? – And to think we invited t'cunt to come down with us to t'George and Dragon! Lucky t'cunt didn't slip some roofies into your pint, haha. You'd have ended up with eh right pain in t'arse t'next day! – Give over, you fat homo shithead! You and him were besties right from t'beginning. Bet you sucked each other off every day in t'bog, didn't you? That's why you been looking so chirpy in t'mornings, innit, you dirty fookin' perv!*

By Sunday night it was clear to me that I couldn't continue at Access-Tec. In fact, I couldn't even remain in Croxby. If I stayed there with my mum and stepdad, I'd be forever stigmatised and made fun of, I'd never be able to shake off my reputation as 'the poofter son of her what works down at Nisa on Mill Lane.' So it was decided, it was all settled: I would leave town. I would hand in my resignation at the factory, tell Wayne and Connie that I was moving out of their place and then shift my meagre belongings to some other more gay-friendly location. The first part of the plan was just about doable (though it pained me very much that I'd never see Alan Patrick Toby again), but the second and third parts ... well, the second and third parts were bound to be tough. To strengthen my resolve I thought about all the good things that awaited me away from Croxby and all the bad things I'd be leaving behind, but it didn't really help, the one issue dominating my mind being how hard it'd be to abandon my mum after spending so many years separated from her. I was also worried about how Connie herself would take the news of my departure, particularly since neither she nor Wayne appeared to have any idea of what I had recently been through. When I finally mustered up the courage to tell her that I was moving out of Croxby, my mum looked at me for some time without saying a word, an ember of distress flaring in her brown Mediterranean eyes. 'It's not because of that silly gay thing what were in t'papers,' she said at last in a voice that almost broke my heart. 'That sort of thing doesn't bother me or Wayne, you know, luv. We'd accept you whichever way you're inclined, me boy.'

I caught the 10:35 am service from Sheffield Central to London Saint Pancras two days later. I didn't even have to go into work to formally hand in my resignation – Wayne having kindly decided to phone Access-Tec and deal with them himself. Low-lying clouds banded the sky that morning, throwing a patchwork of moving shadows on the rural landscape. A tractor with a George Cross painted on the back of its cabin was ploughing a field somewhere between Derby and Leicester. 'Teas, coffees, crisps,' an obese man in a blue uniform droned as he pushed his trolley down the carriage aisle. 'Wine, beers, peanuts.' The previous evening Wayne had told me of an old army mate of his who now ran a B & B in Newham and, as I sat there holding on to the note bearing his friend's address, my thoughts turned to London and the challenges I'd soon face there. Specifically, I found myself thinking about men – gay men, that is – and what they'd be like in the capital. At Roundacre Wood they had all been rough, blue-collar types – the sort who got drunk with the lads, belched, farted in public and laughed uproariously at sexist or misogynistic jokes. Obviously, their counterparts in London would be freer and more self-assured, less afraid of revealing their gayness to the world. On paper this seemed like a good thing – a positive thing – but what would it be like in practice? Would I lap up all that in-your-face campness? Would it scare me off? Would it make me pine for my undemonstrative beer-bellied Northern roughnecks? In addition, there was the increasingly problematic matter of my finances. Although I hadn't spent a lot on myself since coming to the UK, I had felt so sorry for Wayne and Connie's straitened circumstances that I had steadily haemorrhaged money on their property, buying everything for them from televisions to a new bathroom suite to a display unit for Wayne's military badges and medals. This had left me with £12,200 of savings, or just over a quarter of the money I brought with me from Gibraltar. In theory this was more than enough to see me through until I found a place to rent and settled down – but I was also conscious that London was a very expensive city and that I needed to get a job as soon as possible. As I turned these thoughts over in my head, I noticed a copy of the *Sun* that had slid between my seat and the vacant seat beside me. Seeking an escape route from my worries, I stuck two fingers into the gap and pulled out the paper. It was yesterday's edition, but I began reading it all the same. Most of the articles were typical tabloid pieces – the usual garbage, in other words, about gays, immigrants, foreigners, feminists and other minorities – but towards its back pages I came across a large advert showing a handsome white-jacketed waiter attending to a middle-aged lady on the deck of a cruise ship. She was wearing a straw hat and a stylish summer dress; a string of pearls adorned her tanned and creaseless neck. He was one of those biracial types who, depending on which context they are in, could pass either for European or Asian, his lidless but intensely bright eyes pinned suggestively on the woman's legs. Printed underneath the pair were the following words:

Are you able to read, write and speak fluently in English? Are you hard-working, self-sufficient and reliable? Do you enjoy making new friends from different countries and meeting interesting people? If you've answered YES to all these questions, then come and work for us at MSC Cruises, Europe's largest cruise operator. We are currently looking for stewards, waiters, cleaners, and other essential service personnel. Please call the number below to arrange for an immediate interview. If you are the kind of person we are searching for, we promise a range of benefits, including:

* 4 weeks of vacation for every 15 weeks onboard.

* Free accommodation and meals while aboard.

* Paid flight tickets to and from our ships.

* The opportunity to make friends from all nationalities in a safe and modern environment.

I don't know whether it was the waiter's smile that did it, or the idea of living in what sounded like Croxby's antithesis, but by the time I had finished looking at the advert I was already reaching into my pocket and bringing out my mobile, ready to phone the number printed at the bottom of the page.

What happens next is that twenty years come together and hurtle past like a fleeting meteor shower. Twenty years full of friendship, fun and love affairs; twenty years crammed with books and autodidactic learning; twenty years which at the time seemed so solid and so enduring, so rooted in permanency, so woven into the rip-proof fabric of the present – in a flash they were all gone, wiped out, tossed out of sight like particles in the Hadron collider.... Such is life – a vale of shadows shot through with longing for lost things, as I think the Roman emperor and Stoic philosopher Marcus Aurelius once said.... But wait, wait: this won't do. I cannot just describe *how quickly* and *how fugitively* those two decades have gone by. I need to rummage through my memories, to conjure up some recollections so that I can at least trace out the inglorious arc that took me from that London-bound train to this cramped Upper Town apartment.... That is what good storytelling is about, is it not – dredging up selected memories and arranging them in sequential order....

My first job at sea was on the MSC Melody, a medium-sized cruise liner with a crew of 500 and a gross register tonnage of 35,000. In that ageing French-built ship sailed by men and women from twenty-three different nationalities, something altogether magical happened: I finally came upon a place where I wasn't regarded as an outsider, where I didn't have to disguise who I was or what I felt inside. When those first exhilarating fifteen weeks were over, I said goodbye to my new friends and dragged my two suitcases to a small bedsit in the Portswood neighbourhood of Southampton. It was on the fourth floor of a *liftless* block and as sparsely furnished as a prison cell, but it overlooked a quiet park and was only a thirty-minute walk from the harbour – useful for when my work tours started in Soton itself.

From then on it was all *hustle and bustle*, boarding and disembarking, jetting off to foreign ports and then flying back to London, travelling from Waterloo Station to Southampton Central, doing the same journey in reverse fifteen weeks later, going to bed in mid-ocean and then waking up the next day in a new country, waking up to a raging storm and going to bed with an eerily becalmed sea, every week an odyssey, every day filled with the promise of adventure – a continually spinning carousel of faces, places and new experiences, sometimes turning fast, sometimes slowly, only stopping during those long, torpid weeks in between tours when I divided my time between my Portswood bedsit and the Edge and Box, Southampton's only gay bar, smoking Marlboro Menthols and downing shots of Sambuca, reading books and watching crap TV, thinking how bad it was, how absolutely disgusting, that yet again, yet again!, I had broken my promise to Connie to go and see her and Wayne up in Croxby. That is something else I need to mention here: in the twenty years that I worked for MSC Cruises I only visited Croxby on seven or eight occasions. Each time I went there intending to spend the weekend with my mum and stepdad, and each time I left after the first night, unable to deal with the provinciality of the place and the boring, half-assed shit the oldies talked about.

The last time I saw the pair was in 2016, just after the Brexit referendum. Wayne was more depressed than ever and my mother – who back in 1998 had been considerably overweight – now waddled around the house with the aid of a walking stick, her legs as thick as Victorian elephant foot stools. There was no Wally by then – and hence no dog shit in the back garden. Both of them had voted to leave the EU and Concepción spent most of the weekend telling me how important it was for the UK to control its own borders, arguing that there were too many people already in the country. Wayne, for his part, sat there without moving a muscle, his vacant stare suggesting he had no interest in the matter and had only voted Leave to please his missus. When I asked my mum how a poor town like Croxby could possibly benefit from the UK losing fifty per cent of its export markets, she mumbled something about 'overseas aid' and 'European health tourists', saying it was time to wipe the slate clean and 'once again start doing things with pride.' I was tempted to ask if she had read all this nonsense in the *Sun* or the *Daily Express*, but instead I bit my tongue and reached for my mug of tea, deciding to postpone the 'great Brexit debate' until my next visit.

But I never again caught the two trains and three buses I needed to go from Southampton Central to Croxby in South Yorkshire. Maybe I didn't want to hear any more of those shitty Brexiter opinions. Maybe by this stage Wayne reminded me too much of my own sick and depressed father. Or maybe it was just that Croxby was a parochial backwater and no place for an increasingly camp gay man. To make up for the lack of direct contact, I'd skype Connie twice a month from Cozumel or Port Canaveral or wherever I happened to be and we'd chat about *The X Factor*, Wayne's worsening depression and the new dog they were thinking of getting ('a little Sheltie or some other breed what's low-maintenance, luv, seeing that neither Wayne nor meself are in *eh* fit state to go for knackering long walks, know *worrah* mean, luv?'). But even this proved too much of an effort and around November 2017 I ditched the Skype calls in favour of monthly postcards. Yep, I know – pretty reprehensible. Downright callous. But what could I do? Our paths in life had diverged so much that even making small talk was a struggle.

But let's get back to my early years with MSC Cruises. By late 2002 I had served on all the major ships belonging to our line: the MSC Symphony, the MSC Capriccio, the MSC Rhapsody, the MSC Fantasia, the MSC Magnifica. I was also busier and happier than at any point in my life before or since. At Access-Tec Solutions, remember, I had been more or less glued to my workstation all day. But now I prepared and served meals to passengers, I set tables and buffet lines, I washed laundry and made beds, I vacuumed floors and cleaned toilets, I ran souvenir shops and creches, I worked as a barman and as a casino croupier, I took passengers on tours of our ships as well as of the destinations we were visiting. Most of my colleagues came from Indonesia and the Philippines, but there was also a large contingent of Europeans, North Americans, South Americans and Africans – ranging from students on their 'gap year' to grizzly old hands who were hooked on life at sea. Among them, of course, there were a number of gays and lesbians, and these folk became my friends and surrogate family, the people with whom I shared my meals and in whom I confided my deepest hopes and fears. There was Bodashka Marchuk, the body-building Ukrainian sommelier who never smiled or laughed, but who'd cry like a baby when reciting the poetry of Ivan Kotliarevsky, Ukraine's national poet. There was Alejandro Manuel Martínez, the Mexican deckhand from Monterrey whose silly bugger antics made me giggle and with whom I gossiped bitchily in Spanish about our bosses and some of our less amiable colleagues. There was Belhassen Al-Hamami, more commonly known as Mimi, the muezzin's son from Tunis who was mad about Warhammer boardgames and Abba. There was Achille Pelletier, the ultra-camp French Canadian with the Marcel Marceau face who loved his expensive Bally shoes. There was Mary Adekugbe, the Nigerian pastry cook who was 'cut' as a child of three, but who still cheered everybody up with her positive attitude and her infectious laughter. What struck me about these people was just how different to each other they all were, how unique in themselves. Brought up in Gibraltar, you are brainwashed into believing that gay folk are either limp-wristed, hip-waggling pansies or butch, short-haired lesbians with contralto voices – but, after only a few months at sea, it became clear to me that gays and lesbians, as well as bisexuals and transexuals, were just as ordinary, just as boring, just as brilliant and messed up, just as adept at self-sabotage and just as shameless at self-promotion, *just as fucking normal,* in other words, as their straight brothers and sisters.

Anyway, I won't bore you any more by talking about my job duties or the people I shared them with out at sea. Suffice it to say that finding that day-old copy of the *Sun* on the Sheffield-London train brought purpose to my previously directionless life and helped me explore facets of my character and sexuality that would have otherwise remained uncharted. Of course, I'm not going to make out that it was all – to use a cliched but in this case fairly apt phrase – *plain sailing*. With a name and a physiognomy like mine, it was inevitable that, from time to time, I'd bump into some American or North European passenger who felt empowered to talk to me as if I were a piece of shit. But I'm happy to report that these incidents were rare and seldom taken to heart. I had friends and I had lovers and I was having an absolute whale of a time. So what if some stuck-up Texan or Viennese thought he was better than me because he had money and his skin was a shade lighter than mine? At least I was at peace with myself and I was sexually fulfilled – which, judging by how miserable they all looked, was more than could be said for those middle-aged, gringo cunts.

One final anecdote about my MSC days. During my twenty years with the company, I docked at Gibraltar some eighteen or twenty times, but not once was I brave enough to disembark and visit my old hometown. I was tempted, yes – there was a part of me that was *very, very curious* to see the changes wrought in my absence – but, try as I may, I couldn't walk down that gangway. I preferred to stay onboard instead and gaze at the Rock from the safety of the passenger deck, mentally running through the highs and lows of my Gibraltarian past but securely detached from the birthplace of my memories. Perhaps I was scared that, coming face to face with the landscape of my youth, I would end up reigniting the unhappiness and the sense of unbelonging that had stalked me as a young man. Or perhaps I was worried that I'd meet somebody from my Winston days and that they'd blanch at what – in recent years – had become my very evident gayness. It is difficult to pinpoint what it was. All I know is that I felt caught between two contradictory pulls – the urge to go ashore and the urge to stay onboard – and that the latter urge always won. Even when my father was in his death throes less than a hundred yards away from the harbour in Saint Bernard's Hospital, I remained cooped aboard – feeling like an utter shit, true, but unable to do anything about it. I wanted to go and see him, to hold his hand and stroke his cheek, to let him know I had forgiven him for the way he lashed out at me when I told him, via the phone in 2009 or 2010, about my homosexuality, to ask him to forgive me, in turn, for never phoning him again after this call and only keeping in touch by means of postcards – but, as fucked up as it sounds, I couldn't summon up the energy and resolution to leave the vessel.

And yet the moment our ship pulled away from the North Mole, I always felt a stab of longing, a dizzying, maddening yearning for the streets and alleyways I was leaving behind and which, back then, I thought I was destined never to behold again with my own eyes. In my mind I could see all the places where I had lived out my infancy and early adulthood – Castle Street, with its broad stone steps and its amphitheatre-like amplitude; *la Piazza*, with its coffee-drinkers and its Friday morning flag-day sellers; Catalan Bay and Eastern Beach, where I spent summer after lazy, sun-drenched summer; the Alameda Gardens, where as a boy I sat astride the stubby, ten-inch howitzers guarding Eliott's Column; *la Piazzela* and the Jewish Boulevard, mute witnesses to countless scraped knees and games of 'One, two, three, *taco* [59]; Princess Caroline's Battery, where, under cover of decommissioned WW2 anti-aircraft guns, slouched on the front seats of his Firebird, Manu and I smoked our *porros* and occasionally snorted *un par de rayitas*; Grand Parade, where every July the authorities held the annual fair in the Seventies and early Eighties, and where later, as a young man, I parked my Honda Prelude and my Chevrolet Camaro; Casemates Square, Irish Town and City Mill Lane, those mid-town locations where for years and years one kept bumping into friends, relatives and folk you'd rather avoid; and last but not least, most poignantly of all, the winding, labyrinthine alleys of the Upper Town, our refuge and our sanctum, part-playground, part-sports arena, stinking of damp, dog piss and drain water, its rough-cut, limestone steps often made slippery by *el Levante*, its unforgivably steep hills and potholed ramps cursed by delivery drivers and the elderly alike. I saw all this and more in my mind's eye, a whirlwind of scenes and moments that had come and gone and – like all earthly happenings – summarily vanished into thin air.

Time is a fickle creature, isn't it? When you are young and desperate for things to happen, it stalls and slows down to an uncooperative crawl. But when you are old and worried about your future, it hurtles by faster than a pair of runaway horses. I have this theory, see. I believe that we all carry the equivalent of an aeroplane's black box inside us, something which registers the passing of time. In our teenage years and our twenties, this device functions with Swiss-watch

---

[59] A Gibraltarian version of hide-and-seek.

precision, ensuring that we are aware of every ripple and quiver in life's unfolding continuum. This is why summer holidays always drag on forever when we are kids, why Christmases and birthdays always seem so remote and far off, why it feels like there's an eternity left until you are eligible for a learner's driving licence. But as the decades pass and we grow older, this delicate mechanism rusts and warps, impeding us from registering all those subtle gradations and making it seem as if time were flowing mercilessly past us. Now the reverse happens. Christmases come around with frightening rapidity, years merge like rivers at a confluence, summers are over in the blink of an eye.

The cruise ship activities described in the last seven or eight pages took place when this time-registering device was in relatively good order. Now we must enter a new and very different stage in this story, a time marked by loss and physical decay. From this portentous description, you might think that a line was suddenly crossed after which nothing was the same again. But no, for me the decline was gradual and stretched out, so much so that, for a long time, I didn't even realise that my world was falling apart around me. Yes, it is true that in late 2016 my father died and that in February 2018 Wayne was institutionalised on account of his vegetative depression – but as sad as these events were, they never distracted me from either my onboard duties or the pursuit of various romantic liaisons. In fact, during those crepuscular years before the darkness of terminal night set in, I lived more or less as I had done in the last decade – but without the freshness and the *joie de vivre,* admittedly, that had characterised my early days in the cruise industry. Worn down by years of sexual and alcoholic excess, getting balder and *wrinklier* with each passing season, finding it harder and harder to stomach my drink, I still managed to have a good time, but everything now felt cheaper and tawdrier, dressed in less vibrant colours. Soon I was one of the oldest stewards in the MSC fleet, a trusty old-timer to be sought in moments of crisis. Like most ageing gay men, I wasn't at first ready to accept the changing status quo and, for a while, I went out of my way to prove to my colleagues that I could still party with the hippest, giddiest youngling. As a result, I dyed my thinning hair platinum blond; I started going to the gym twice a week; I added nipple piercings to the five earrings and two nose-studs that I already sported; I obsessively followed the UK charts, wanting to show the young ones that I also listened to Clean Bandit, Rag 'n' Bone Man and Dizzee Rascal. But – what can I say – it was a losing battle, wasn't it? I could not keep up with the youngsters. I tried and tried and tried, *God knows how much I fucking tried,* but all I reaped for my pains were pitying half-smiles and apocalyptic hangovers that put me out of action for days on end. When I finally realised I couldn't turn back time, I ditched all that silliness and acted as others saw me. Kindly, avuncular, a dependable, rock-like shoulder to cry on. I also became increasingly disconnected from my past, less inclined to commune with its ghosts. I no longer thought about my father or about Manu, for instance, and I never went on deck when we docked at Gibraltar, preferring to stay in my cabin reading history books and novels. Occasionally, very, very occasionally, I'd find myself thinking about the day Manu and I had sailed past a dead man just off the Detached Mole, a mere two or three hundred yards from where my ship lay currently berthed. I'd wonder what his name was, where he was from, what he had hoped to achieve, what impact his death must have had on his relatives – all the things I hadn't paused to think about when I was a self-obsessed twenty-three-year-old. But other than that my past was dead and buried; it had become a part of my life that no longer meant anything to me.

Then something happened which wasn't supposed to happen. One morning in January 2019 I woke up with stiffness in my left hand and wrist. Since 2017, I should perhaps explain, I had been waking from time to time with minor aches in my hands and fingers. However, that morning the soreness was on another level and bordering on actual pain. For ten minutes I lay there on my narrow bed with my palm against my chest, wondering why my wrist and fingers had become so swollen and red. Then I remembered that two days ago I had spent five hours cleaning food-holding cabinets with Rocky Narváez, a Puerto Rican colleague of mine. 'It's just a bad case of delayed onset muscle soreness,' I told myself, jumping out of bed and opening the hot-water tap in my washbasin. 'It will go away before you know it.' And sure enough: a day or two later the stiffness disappeared and I could hold things properly once more. 'Talk about being a drama queen,' I thought, looking back on the incident that same weekend, amused at how worried I had been days earlier.

But three weeks later it happened again. And this time it not only affected my wrists and fingers; this time the stiffness had spread to my arms and shoulders. And it wasn't just simple tenderness either; it was tenderness mixed with numbness and intermittent tingling. 'Something's got to be wrong,' I

thought, wincing with pain as I tried turning onto my side.
'This feels very odd.' Then it dawned on me that earlier in
the week I was asked by Monsieur Alphonse, the head chef
of Bistro Saigon, the Vietnamese restaurant on deck 9 of the
MSC Splendida, to bring ten crates of vegetable oil from the
storeroom to his galley. 'That's got to be it!' I decided. 'I must
have strained some muscles carrying those bloody boxes of
KTV Cooking Oil!'

I know, I know – it was stupid and irresponsible of me to
think like this. But because these early flare-ups never lasted
more than a few days, I was able to continue in a state of
denial – latching onto all sorts of explanations to justify what
I was going through. Meanwhile, the gaps between the
attacks became shorter and shorter. Before long I entered a
new level of denial, telling myself one moment that I was
rundown, and the next that I was suffering from nothing
worse than sleep deprivation; then later changing my mind
again and ascribing all my problems to an ordinary vitamin
deficiency. Finally, shortly after switching from the MSC
Splendida to the MSC Meraviglia for a new tour of duty, what
I most dreaded occurred: the pain-free periods disappeared
altogether and the discomfort and stiffness became
unwavering constants in my life, the flare-ups having
somehow merged into one solid block of ongoing pain. Yet
even then I pretended that everything was all right, even then
I utilised every trick in the book to disguise my difficulties
from my colleagues. 'Do you mind carrying the second tray
of lemon yoghurt cakes, Zoran?' I'd say to one of my fellow
stewards. 'I hurt my shoulders yesterday doing lat pulldowns
in the gym and I'm really struggling today.' Or: 'Got an awful
hangover this morning, Catalina, *mi amor*. Really overdid it

last night drinking applejack shots. You wouldn't mind helping us out with the bed linen for deck 8, would you, *querida*?'

More excuses followed, more bouts of self-deception. Then one day, as I was serving high tea in the Meraviglia's Tropical Palm Court, I suffered a terrible cramp in my right leg and crashed to the floor with a tray of lemon drizzle slices. I could not move nor could I be helped up, the slightest motion in my legs bringing on multiple stabs of pain. 'I'm sorry, Jonas,' I kept saying to Jonas Lindstroem, the restaurant manager, as I lay there on my back unable to rise to my feet, 'I'm sorry. I don't know what's come over me. Truly I don't know.'

With the assistance of Lindstroem and two of the waiters, I was bundled onto a wheeled trolley and then taken to the ship's doctor on deck 3. I had only been there once before – to obtain some antibiotics after a bad case of the clap! – and I felt as uneasy as can be imagined. 'I'm just a bit rundown,' I said to Dr Ling as he stood there listening to my heart with a stethoscope. 'Nothing to worry about, doc. Been burning the candle lately at both ends, that's all. You know what it's like.' But the doctor, a tall, taciturn Singaporean with the build of a marathon runner, did not look convinced. 'I'll have to run some blood tests,' he muttered, removing the bell of the stethoscope from my back and pulling down the tail of my shirt. 'We need to rule out there is no serious underlying disease behind all this. We'll have the results first thing tomorrow.'

Dr Ling's preliminary tests revealed that my erythrocyte sedimentation rate was high and that I was suffering from anaemia. I thought all this could be fixed with some rest and a few vitamin pills, but the medic said I needed further tests – the kind that could only be done in a hospital. 'But I am fine,' I protested to the poker-faced Asian dude. 'Honestly, I am! Look, doc,' I said, extending my hand and holding it with my fingers spread, 'my hand doesn't even tremble any more!'

I spent the next five days arguing with the doctor and the health and safety team about my physical condition, but my protestations fell on deaf ears: they decided that I needed medical tests and that I had to leave the ship as soon as possible. And so, on 15 June 2019, shortly after we moored at Naples, I was forced off the MSC Meravilglia and bundled into the first EasyJet flight from Naples International Airport to London Gatwick. I remember the day as if it were yesterday – mainly because of the extraordinary kindness shown to me by my younger colleagues. Knowing that I was going away for some medical tests, they had all gathered in the principal lobby of the Meraviglia and lined up in two rows beside the main disembarkation door. 'Best of luck, grandpa!' some young kid teased as I made my way past this impromptu guard of honour. 'Remember you need to buy loads and loads of chocolate,' somebody else guffawed, ' – and not any more blooming books – before you come back to us!' *'Venga, ánimo, Alexito!'* Alejandro Manuel, my Mexican friend and former lover, cheered and patted me on the back. 'You'll be in tip-top shape before you know it!' Touched by the display of solidarity, I thanked the guys for the gesture and told them that I expected similar VIP treatment when returning to the ship in a couple of weeks' time. But even as I laughed and joked with them, even as I shook hands and accepted their hugs and kisses, even as I stood there promising that I'd be back on the Meraviglia before the start of the autumn season, I knew deep down that I was only deceiving myself and that I'd never set foot on a cruise liner again. 'This life is over and done with,' I thought, anxiously stepping over the six-inch gap between the side of the ship and the connecting jet bridge, '*este cuento ya se acabado*.'[60]

Four months passed and I still had no idea what was wrong with me. This was not because my condition was difficult to diagnose or because the doctors at the Belmont Road Surgery in Portswood didn't know what they were doing, but merely because the NHS is a slow, lumbering beast plagued by a Brobdingnagian bureaucracy and the need to keep costs down. First, I had to wait ten days to see a GP, then six days for some blood tests, then two weeks to see the same GP again, then another week for the results of further blood tests, then two months to see a rheumatologist, then two weeks for a chest X-ray and a CT scan of the spine ... then, finally, when I phoned Southampton General Hospital to get my results, I was told that the rheumatologist would soon be contacting me to discuss my diagnosis. In between these widely-spaced developments I stayed at home watching TV and ordering books from Amazon. Over the years I had read hundreds, if not thousands of novels, but because I had started relatively late as a bookworm and bibliophile there were still many titles on my 'to-read' list – and it was to these books I now turned, hoping that their sweeping storylines would help me forget about my mounting troubles. Robert

---

[60] 'This tale is at an end.'

Musil's *The Man Without Qualities*, Marcel Proust's *Remembrance of Things Past*, Andre Gidé's *The Counterfeiters*, Thomas Mann's *The Magic Mountain* — these and other mammoth volumes began arriving at my little bedsit in Portswood, rapidly taking up the limited space left on my packed bookshelves. But there was a problem, an unexpected hitch: I couldn't read any more. Or rather I could read, but often had trouble building mental pictures in my head, the cramps and stiffness in my limbs rarely allowing me to forget my condition as *a body in pain*. So while there were one or two days when I'd be mentally transported to Hans Castorp's Alpine sanatorium or Proust's *Château de Guermantes,* there were plenty of others, too, when I felt trapped in my own skin, as vexed and burdened as someone carrying a dead weight on their shoulders.

It was on one of those dreaded, impossible-to-read days that I picked up the phone and called my mother for the first time in two years. For around twenty seconds I sat there with my mobile held expectantly to my ear. Then a voice — frail, weary, shockingly old — could be heard on the other end of the line:

'Hullo.'

'Hello, Ma.'

'Who's that?'

'It's me, Ma.'

'Who's that? Kenny lad? Is it you?'

'No, Ma, it's me, Alex.'

'Who?'

'Alex, Connie. Your son Alex.'

'Alex?'

'Yes, Alex, your other son, Kenneth's brother.'

'Ah, Alex,' Connie Anne said, wetting her lips like an old woman brought back to her senses, 'me boy – what a long time it's been! How are you these days? Are you keeping well, luv?'

I had been planning to tell her about my undiagnosed illness and my permanent return to the UK, but I quickly changed my mind and started rattling on instead about Cuba and Barbados and Saint Lucia and the other places I had visited just before falling ill. I told her about the young boys who put on diving shows for tourists in the Malecón in Havana; about the quaint cobbled street in Bridgetown named after the pop singer Rihanna; about the time I was invited with my Nigerian friend Mary to the ultra-posh Saint Lucia Golf and Country Club at Cap Estate, where we ordered afternoon tea and chanced upon the actress Liz Hurley sunbathing topless on the beach. She listened to this rambling monologue of mine without breathing a word, then – once I had run out of things to say – told me that her boiler had conked out a day earlier and that she was waiting for Rotherham Council to send somebody over to fix it. It was a right pain in the arse, all this boiler business, she said, sounding a little more like the Connie Anne I had lived with for a year and a half, but at least it had happened in September and not in January or February, when everybody's boiler, you know, is on the blink and you'd need to wait at least a week before the Council sends someone round to have a look at it. 'Why don't you come up to Croxby one day for t'weekend once it's fixed, Alex luv?' she finished by saying, a quiver of expectation in her voice. 'I haven't been able to visit Wayne now for t'last six months because of his bad spells, and as for your brother Kenneth, even though he is no longer in t'army and living just down t'road in Killamarsh, he never bothers coming to see me any more. Too busy living it up at t'pub and t'bookies – that's what our Kennie's like!'

'That's a good idea, Ma,' I said softly. 'I mean – me coming to visit you.'

'Well, you know you can come whenever you want, Alex. You're always welcome here – just like your brother is.'

'Thanks, Ma. I'll come and see you soon, I promise.'

For once I really meant what I said. For once I wasn't fazed by the thought of having to catch two trains and three buses and then listening to Connie Anne ramble on about *The X Factor, Britain's Got Talent* and all her other favourite TV programmes. But when the day of my journey arrived, disaster struck – I felt so bad that I couldn't get out of bed. Cramps were shooting up my legs every ten seconds, and my left shoulder had become so numb, so devoid of feeling, that it seemed as if my left arm was floating in mid-air. Not wanting to let down my mother yet again, I forced myself onto my feet and battled my way out of my pyjamas and into my clothes, having decided that I needed to get to Croxby by hook or by crook. '*Venga, venga, venga,* man,' I grunted through clenched teeth. 'You can do it, *compá.* Don't give in so easily.' However, on catching sight of my reflection in the three-quarter-length mirror hanging by the front door and noticing the dark bags under my eyes, I realised that I was only kidding myself. *I couldn't go to Croxby* – not in the state I was in. I therefore took off my jacket, lowered my frame unsteadily on the sofa and, after bringing out my mobile and taking a deep breath, called Connie Anne to tell her everything about my illness. Well, *almost everything* – seeing that, when I eventually got through, I downplayed my symptoms and made out that I'd soon be okay again. My mother, bless her, listened quietly to what I said, then treated me to one of her pieces of Yorkshire-inflected *llanito* wisdom: 'Okay, luv, don't you worry, luv, better to stay at home if you're not feeling all that great, luv – but please make sure you get t'doctor to explain why all this is happening when you see him to discuss your scan. These cramps of yours sound more serious than what you're making out, know *worrah* mean, luv?'

———————————◆———————————

The weeks passed. Instead of buying books from Amazon, I was now ordering CDs by Spanish bands and artists that I had listened to in my youth. Ketama, Jarabe de Palo, Rosario, Kiko Veneno, Juan Carmona, Camarón de la Isla. Most days I'd sit in my living room with my headphones on and several blankets piled on my knees, trying to block out the pain in my arms and legs by 'losing myself' in the music's lyrics:

> *Que bonito cuando te veo ay,*
> *Que bonito cuando te siento,*
> *Que bonito pensar que estas aquí,*
> *Junto a mí!*

What the music, alas, couldn't do was stop me from worrying about my rapidly worsening financial situation. Although I had worked for MSC Cruises for nearly two decades, I had spent my entire time with them on a rolling seasonal contract – meaning that I was only entitled to ten days of sick leave and an even measlier three weeks of statutory sick pay. This period of grace had already ended four months ago and since then I had been relying on what was left in my bank account (which, needless to say, wasn't much). Already stressed out on account of my medical problems, regularly making Amazon purchases I couldn't afford, I calculated I could stay afloat for another three or four months, after which God knows what I'd do to pay my household bills.

It was in this bleak frame of mind that I got called in one November morning to Southampton General Hospital to hear Dr Grierson, my Rheumatology consultant, confirm what my GP had suspected all along: I was suffering from rheumatoid arthritis. Mid-to-late stage RA, he said. Where the joints are bending out of shape and already pressing on some nerves. It was good that we had caught the disease somewhere between Stage 2 and Stage 3, he explained, because once we reach Stage 4 the joints fuse and then there are all sorts of complications, from pulmonary fibrosis to pericarditis to osteoporosis to different forms of vasculitis. I was to go on methotrexate, he said, a chemotherapy agent and immune-system suppressant. If after three to six months the methotrexate hadn't brought us *any joy* (his words, not mine), then we would switch over to biologics, a type of medication synthesised from bacteria, yeast and animal tissue cells. It was important not to give up, the NHS consultant said. Not to get too disheartened. With an individualised, treat-to-target approach we could slow down the progress of the disease and even mask some of the pain. Patience and a positive mentality – that, above all, was what was needed. Along with a healthy diet, plenty of fresh air and the elimination of all sources of mental and emotional stress. *If you follow these general guidelines and the medication works as it should, Mr Pereira, there's every chance you'll be able to lead a fairly normal life again.*

Remember when I was sitting in that London-bound train back in March 1999 and I ended up dramatically changing my plans after seeing an advert in a discarded newspaper? Well, something similar happened in the days following my diagnosis – with the difference that this time I was in one of the treatment rooms in the Department of Rheumatology at Southampton General Hospital. It must have been two or three weeks after seeing Dr Grierson. I am sitting on a plastic chair, rolling down my shirt sleeve. A Portuguese nurse called Cindy has just taken my blood pressure and is now asking me to grade each affected joint on a scale of 1 to 10 (1 representing no pain; 10 representing, as she puts it, 'the maximum pain imaginable'). She has already explained to me how methotrexate works (by slowing down the cells that cause inflammation, 'sort of like a parachute that stops you from falling too fast'), as well as forewarned me of its commonest side-effects (headaches, diarrhoea, vomiting, dizziness and hair loss ... 'although, let's be honest, the hair loss bit is never going to be that much of a problem for you, is it, mister Alex?'). As I rate the pain in my joints for her, I look at her eyes – those large, dark, emblematically Mediterranean eyes surmounted by two thick lines of downy brown. They are not traditionally pretty eyes, but there is something wholesome and pleasing about them, something completely at variance with our sterile, white-tiled surroundings. I try to think what this quality could be, but all that comes to me is a single word in Spanish: *alegría.* 'That's it,' I think seconds later, smiling in spite of my discomfort, 'that's what it is: *son ojos llenos de alegría.* There is no other way to describe those joyful eyes, is there?' Looking at them, I find myself remembering Mariadelaida Gonzalez and her proud walk up Castle Steps, I remember my father speaking tenderly to his potted *hortensias* in our tiny Castle Road patio, I remember Manu jumping up and down on the seat of his Bentley on the day of the riots, I remember the way he grinned at me when we came out of the cave in *la Isla de Perejil,* I remember him running out of Saint Bernard's School and sprinting around the tight corners in Abecasis's Passage as a seven-year-old kid, I remember sitting together with him under the old bridge linking Castle Steps and Macphail's Passage, I remember bringing out our bag of *colillas* and searching for the longest and juiciest butts, I remember watching our piss trickling down the sloping cement, I remember laughing so hard that my ribs hurt, feeling so happy that I could have forgiven my worst enemy – *venga, venga, Alex, mea más fuerte, compá, que el* trickle *mío va más rápido que el tuyo!*[61] And as I remember all these things, as they appear one after the other on the projection screen of my mind, a mellow glow ignites inside me. And as this warmth grows and spreads, as it envelops me and makes the outer world recede, I know that I am not going to stay here in grey, cheerless

---

[61] 'Come on, Alex, come on! Piss a bit faster! My trickle is going faster than yours!'

Southampton. Nor am I going to move in with my mum in Croxby, as she has been urging me to do now that she knows the full extent of my illness. No, I am going to pack my bags and use the last few hundred pounds in my account to relocate to Gibraltar. That's it, that's it, I tell myself, smiling at the nurse to distract her from the droplets of moisture now welling up in my eyes. I'm going to remove my earrings and my nose-studs and travel back to the place of my birth. *Where this story once began, that's where it will also end.*

As for the rest of my tale, well, you already know most of it, don't you? I returned to Gibraltar on 3 December 2019 with a three-month supply of methotrexate and, by one of those unnerving coincidences which sometimes occur in life, found a flat to rent in Chicardo's Passage, directly opposite my old school and a mere stone's throw away from our former Castle Road home. Once I moved into the property, I tried to register with a GP at the primary care centre – but I quickly discovered that the system here doesn't favour long-absent returnees. For the first couple of days, I wandered with my walking stick through Gibraltar's centre and old town, marvelling at how closely it all corresponded with my memories, trying to spot a familiar face from the Eighties and Nineties. But I only saw casual acquaintances and *conocidos de vista* – all of whom looked greyer, fatter and older than when I last encountered them (and who, in any case, I felt loath to approach in my current condition, fearing the avalanche of questions, grimaces and pitying looks that would surely come my way once I revealed my identity). On a handful of occasions, I ventured beyond the town centre into some of the newer residential and commercial developments, but I found the experience intensely jarring, the divergence between what I was seeing and how I remembered these locations triggering something within me resembling actual physical pain.

By the end of my first week, I refused to leave Main Street and its environs, preferring to stay in places upon which I could impose the template of my remembered past. I felt more comfortable in these old and familiar streets, less of an alien than at Ocean Village, Chatham Counterguard and the other areas that either hadn't existed or looked very different in the years of my childhood and youth. And yet it wasn't long before I also grew tired of Main Street, Irish Town and Cornwall's Parade – the simple effort of hobbling all the way down to town and back proving too much for my prematurely weakened body. From this point onwards, I remained largely at home, going out only when I needed groceries and other essentials, feeding my appetite for the past by means of this melancholy memoir. More than once I thought that I would never be able to finish this story, that I would keel over and be taken to hospital before bringing it to a conclusion. But thanks to the methotrexate I have somehow bumbled my way through to the end and here I find myself – about to type the closing lines of this tale.

What will happen with these papers of mine once I am not around is anybody's guess. My hope is that they will be taken to some evidence or storage room, where they will remain filed away until a coroner or a copper requests them and reads them. Most probably, though, this will never happen. Most probably they will be picked up by a Spanish cleaner sent to give the flat a good scrub. Let's call her Verónica, shall we? Pallid and unsmiling, mother to a fifteen-year-old autistic boy called Francisco and an eight-year-old girl by the name of María-Elena, living on her own since her *hijo de la gran puta* husband Santi ran off with one of her mates back in 2013, our indomitable cleaning lady crosses and recrosses the border every day to clean houses for one of Gibraltar's various rental agencies. She is a tough *señora,* resilient, down-to-earth, ex-*matutera*[62] and survivor of two three-year spells in jail, avid pro-lifer and moderately enthusiastic *cursillista,*[63] her difficult, trouble-scarred life attested by the numerous crosses, cobwebs, teardrops and Virgin Marys tattooed on her biceps, triceps and forearms. Due to her hard-working and uncomplaining nature, she is regularly sent by her Gibraltarian bosses to tackle properties after their tenants have died or done a runner. Arriving at my former flat, our Verónica will have a quick moan to herself about the state of the place, then get stuck in as always, whistling and breaking into song, displaying that legendary, slightly manic capacity for hard work which working-class *linenses* are justly famous for. '*Valiente guarro,*' she will repeatedly say, picking up a pair of dirty socks, or a sachet of Cup-a-Soup, or an empty wine bottle, or a wrinkled copy of the *Chronicle*, or whatever else she finds discarded on the floor. Perhaps, if she hasn't been able to scrape up the 120 euros for Francisco's next appointment with his private *fonoaudiólogo,* she will slip my old laptop into her handbag; perhaps, remembering the promise she made last year to Saint Jude to stay on the straight and

---

[62] Matutera – a crossborder smuggler (Spanish).

[63] Cursillista – a person who takes part in the RC Cursillo spiritual retreat (Spanish).

narrow, she will resist the temptation and place the laptop to one side. At a certain point she will see the bundle of A4 papers lying on the coffee table and, without a second thought, gather them up and put them in a bin bag filled with crumpled tissues, biscuit crumbs, cigarette butts and boxes of painkillers. Tying the bin liner with a double knot, she will carry it to the front of the flat and leave it propped by the door, next to the other rubbish she has already collected. At ten to five – ten minutes before her official finishing time – Verónica will remove her plastic gloves, take off her apron, bag her cleaning products, spray some deodorant on her underarms, untie the ribbon holding her greying hair, tidy herself in front of a mirror, apply some lipstick and eyeliner, lock up the property, and convey all the bin liners by the door – by this stage there will be at least nine or ten of them – to the rubbish bins at the bottom of Tank Ramp. One by one, she will toss the bags into the bin reserved for household rubbish – uttering breathy peals of satisfaction every time one of them clangs against the container's metal insides, enjoying the crunching sounds made by the shattering glass jars and bottles. This done, she will walk to the Arengo's Palace bus stop, ready to catch bus no 1 to Market Place and then bus no 5 to the frontier gates, desperate by this point to pick up Paquito and María-Elenita from her mother-in-law's. For the next two or perhaps three days the bag holding the papers will remain in the bin among other bags, slowly being crushed by the weight of the new bundles landing on it, *curianas*, *moscardas* and the occasional maggot darting across its tearing plastic membrane. Then one morning a rubbish truck will come lumbering up Castle Road and three men in blue overalls will transfer the bags from the bin to their vehicle. A trio of *machotes,* no doubt – pot-bellied, sour of face, routinely bellowing at each other over the lorry's engine. 'Mate,' one of them will shout to the driver, 'back up towards the wall, will you – these bins are full of fucking bottles!' 'Okay, okay!' the driver will yell in response. 'Hold your horses, will you? Let me at least switch on the frigging hazard lights!' In the old days the bin's contents would have gone straight to the incinerating plant on Devil's Tower Road, where they would have been vaporised into a foul-smelling toxic haze, but now that is all in the past. In this greener, more environmentally friendly era, Gibraltar's rubbish is transported to the Sur Europa landfill site in Los Barrios, about ten miles north of the border. There the bags will be weighed, deposited into lidless metal containers, sprayed with disinfectant and then torn apart by giant claw-like shredders, after which their contents will be first robotically and later manually sifted for paper, plastics, metals and other recyclable matter – a careful and methodical process which is supposed to salvage up to seventy per cent of the raw material arriving at the plant, but which, of course, it goes without saying, won't save any of the memories woven into the pages of my unread memoir....

So this is how this remembrance of things past will probably end – not in the hands of an appreciative or even a critical reader, but in a landfill site somewhere in the Campo de Gibraltar, buried among soiled nappies, used condoms and rolled-up sanitary towels. Quite a poetic conclusion, don't you think? Entirely fitting when you consider the wretched lives of those remembered in its pages. Ashes to ashes, dust to dust, and all that business. But before this happens, before

I print off this final batch of papers and switch off my laptop once and for all, before I entrust my story to its compostable fate, I'd like, as a way of wrapping things up and tying loose ends, to write some lines about an incident that occurred a few weeks ago at North Front Cemetery. It took place on 4 January 2020 – a day which dawned enfolded in a lovely *poniente* stillness, but which, from midday onwards, when the weather suddenly changed, was overrun by a windswept *levantery* gloom. I had been meaning to visit the cemetery, let me explain, since the day I arrived in Gibraltar – partly out of a sense of guilt for not having attended Manu's and John Dennis Leslie's funerals all those years ago, and partly to glimpse the place where I will one day be laid to rest myself – and that morning, seeing that the sun was shining, I called the Gibraltar Taxi Association from my UK mobile and requested a cab to take me to North Front. When I reached my destination three-quarters of an hour later, I made my way to the stone lodge by the entrance gates and asked the cemetery keeper where I could find the graves of Manuel Gonzalez and John Dennis Leslie Pereira – adding, as an afterthought, if he could direct me as well to the resting place of Mrs Mariadelaida Gonzalez, mother of the already mentioned Manuel Gonzalez. The cemetery keeper – a youngish, goateed fellow who was watching football on a portable TV – went very red in the face when I added a third name to my double request, but somehow kept his composure and logged into his work laptop, informing me after a quick search of his database that Mariadelaida and John Leslie were buried in Plot K, whereas Manu was in a small nook between the Presbyterian graves and the part of the cemetery maintained by the Commonwealth War Graves

Commission, not far from the runway. 'I've marked the three graves for you on this paper,' he said, handing me what looked like a photocopy of a hand-drawn cemetery plan. 'If you have any problems tracking them down, you can always ask one of the cleaners working on-site.'

I reached Mariadelaida Gonzalez's grave a short while later. It was decorated with one of those mass-produced *coronas* which are sold at Gibralflora and which are scattered, in various states of decomposition, all over North Front Cemetery. The wreath was lying facedown – probably having been blown into that position by the wind – and looked fairly fresh. With the tip of my walking stick, I flipped the garland over and saw a handwritten label pinned to one of the carnation stalks: 'For the lovely Mariadelaida. I will never forget you. Ephram.' As I wondered who this Ephram person was, it occurred to me that Mariadelaida – mother to Manu, partner to both Maikito and *el Pantera* – had stood head and shoulders above the men in her life, none of whom really deserved a woman like her around them. She had been a hero in a tale of villains and semi-villains, a star that should have shone at the centre of things instead of being condemned, because of her sex, age and lack of wealth, to shed its light from the periphery. 'Poor Mariadelaida,' I thought, shaking my head. 'You deserved so much more than this. And good on you, Ephram, too – whoever you may be – for tending her grave and treasuring her memory....'

My father's grave was plainer and less tidy than Mariadelaida's resting place. An FC Barcelona scarf lay strewn across its top slab, its random placement suggesting it must have blown over from one of the many scarf-bedecked graves in the vicinity. I stood beside the tomb for some moments, then brought out one of the Kleenex tissues I kept in my pockets. Crumpling it into a ball, I let it drop on the stone block and pinned it down with the tip of my walking stick. Slowly, awkwardly, leaning forward as much as my ailing hamstrings and lower back muscles would allow, I dragged the stick from one end of the slab to the other, keeping the tissue pinned under its tip. Instead of cleaning the grave as I intended, however, I only succeeded in causing even more of a mess, the squiggly furrow opened by the scraping ferrule merely highlighting the thickness of the accumulated dust. Even worse, during a second when I wasn't paying too much attention, a violent gust of wind suddenly tore across the cemetery and dislodged the tissue from under the walking stick, sending it twitching like a wounded bird into the air.

'Oh well,' I told myself, lifting my cane and taking a step back. 'It's not as if you were the tidiest of blokes when you were alive, were you, Dad? A little grime won't bother you, will it?'

I left John Dennis Leslie's place and hobbled over to the other side of the graveyard. The transition from *Poniente* to *Levante* was now almost complete and a powerful gale was funnelling its way between the monuments and headstones, toppling over jars filled with flowers and scattering petals like wedding confetti. Struggling against the headwind, I found myself thinking of those stormy strait crossings back in the Nineties, when Manu and I had come within a hair's breadth of capsizing out at sea. I remembered the fear, the wild adrenaline, the overwhelming sensations of relief that took hold of us once back on dry land – all those factors that had added such intensity to those night-time smuggling runs – then I thought of how things stood at present, with Manu dead and buried for years and me barely able to walk. 'Time doesn't just fly,' I thought, leaning on my stick. 'It spits in your fucking face!'

It took me another ten minutes before I reached Manu's tomb. Unlike most of the other graves at North Front, it was not part of a family vault and was only marked by a simple headstone. Bird droppings clung in scar-like streaks to its already veiny marble surface. Weeds were wrapped like coils of barbed wire around its base. I went up to the headstone, intending to rest my hand on its rounded exterior, but drew back when I saw an old man standing before a vault in the next row of graves. An elderly widower, I guessed, taking a quick look at the guy – one of those lonely, wrinkled *vejestorios* who shuffle over to the cemetery every day, come rain or shine. Put off by his presence, I remained where I was, staring at the grave while half-resting on the crook of my walking stick. Against my better judgement I thought about Manu's earthly remains, wondering what they looked like twenty-four years after his burial. Probably the flesh must have rotted off his bones, I reflected, wincing at the images entering my head. Or if it hadn't completely rotted, then it must have gone all hard and leathery – like a giant piece of salted *bacalao*. Alarmed by the increasingly morbid turn of my thoughts, I steered my focus away from his physical body and onto Manu's final moments, wondering if he had felt any fear or pain either just before or as he landed on that floating pallet. Surely, he must have, I told myself – if only during that micro-second that he careered through space to meet his untimely end. There must have been a ferocious surge of adrenaline, an explosion of raw, unarticulated helplessness. That's how these things always end: with a crash, a violent motion blur, a scream solidifying in one's windpipe. And yet, for all that, there was a certain majesty in his passing, wasn't there, a cold terrible beauty. No battles with sickness and old age for my friend. No seeing one's life sliced off cut by cut, stump by bleeding stump. Like a fugitive comet, he had briefly illuminated the night and then faded into the starless darkness. Emboldened by this somewhat maudlin metaphor, I took a step forward and, ignoring the presence of the old man, placed a palm on the freezing cold headstone.

'I know you'd have killed me had I said all this to you when you were alive,' I whispered, my words all but drowned out by the shrieking Easterly wind, 'but since you're dead and can do fuck-all about it, I'm going to tell you that you were my first and possibly greatest love. And if you don't like what I'm telling you – well, tough shit, *eso es lo que hay!*'

I removed my hand from the top of the gravestone and looked dejectedly at the ground. I could hear the sound of a plane landing on the nearby airfield, the roar of its engines just about audible over the wind. Pointlessly I patted down my thinning hair and dabbed at the moisture gathering in my eyes, trying to make myself look presentable. It was at this point, just as I was regaining my composure and readying to leave, that I caught sight of the old man weaving his way between the gravestones towards me.

'*Muchacho!*' the fellow hollered, coming to a stop behind Manu's tomb.

'*Sí?*'

'You're not a regular here, are you?' he asked, smiling in the manner of a *viejo* desperate to find somebody to talk to.

'No, no,' I replied, shaking my head. 'I'm just passing through, me.'

'I thought so,' the old boy said, smiling triumphantly to himself. 'I had a feeling I hadn't seen you before.'

'*Y usted?*' I shouted into the wind. 'Are you a regular here?'

'*Lo qué?*'

'*Usted?* Do you come regularly to the cemetery?'

'Oh, I come here almost every day. The ones I've got left out there don't talk to me. And the ones who actually meant something,' he said, taking his eye off me for a second to scan his surroundings, 'are all buried in this place. Here, there, by the runway, next to the Jewish cemetery, beside the entrance gates – they're all around us,' he yelled.

I looked at him for a moment – a pathetic old man with no teeth and hair which clung in long wispy streaks to the sides of his otherwise bald head – then, realising that I was probably in no better shape myself, dug my hands into my pockets and focused defensively on the Rock of Gibraltar looming behind us.

'By the way,' the pensioner blurted, stepping forward and grabbing me lightly by the arm, 'did you know....,' at which point he gestured with his eyes towards Manu's gravestone.

'Yes, we were friends. Many years ago.'

'Were you?' he asked, his eyes narrowing.

'Yes.'

'I also knew him,' he said, letting go of my arm.

'Did you?'

'Yes. We were sort of related, *sabes?*' To which he added with an unexpectedly roguish smile: 'You know what it's like in this fucking place: everybody is related to one another in some way.... But, tell me, *pisha*, was he as wild and crazy as they say?'

'Was Manuel as crazy as they say?' I smiled, an exhilarating idea forming in my head. 'Nah, not really. Sometimes he could be a bit impulsive, but deep down he wasn't a bad guy.'

'Just like his old man, then?'

I looked at him as he stood there before me, his eyes as veiny as the marble in Manu's headstone, his bony chin held nearly as high as in the old days. 'Yep,' I said, mustering a smile, 'just like his old man.'

With those words I turned around and walked away from Manu's grave. The Levanter wind was now whistling noisily through the cemetery and bits of debris (a scarf, a football shirt, a greeting card, a plastic poppy wreath) were hurtling past like tumbleweed in a Spaghetti Western. 'What crazy weather,' I thought, struggling to keep upright. Before I reached the end of the path and veered into the next track, I paused for a moment and, glancing over my shoulder, saw that the old man was now in front of Manu's grave. He was standing there motionless and with his head bowed, his long grey hair flapping against the nape of his neck, his hands held behind his back. 'Who'd have thought it!' I whispered, strengthening my grip on the walking stick and refocusing on the path ahead. 'Father and son together. The original Winston Boy and the one and only Marlboro Man! Maybe now, *amigo,* you can finally rest in peace.'

-The End-

Ah, meu maior amigo, nunca mais
Na paisagem sepulta desta vida
Encontrarei uma alma tão querida
Às coisas que em meu ser são as reais.
Fernando Pessoa

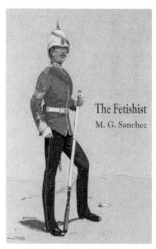

The Fetishist
M. G. Sanchez

The Fetishist

Nathan Holgado, admin assistant at Fernandez Funeral Services, loves all things British and military related. He is also obsessed with his Victorian English ancestor, his great-great-great-grandfather Private Edwin Baxter of the 15th Regiment of Foot. Looking at Google Street View one afternoon, Holgado discovers that the house in Yorkshire where Edwin was born is still standing. Filled with patriotic pride, he starts making plans to travel to the UK and visit Baxter's birthplace....

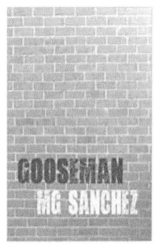

Gooseman

'If there is a date when my story begins, it is 13 September 1981. That day was not only my first day at school; it was the first time that I realised I was not like the others.' So begins ***Gooseman***, M. G. Sanchez's new darkly comic novel. Its protagonist is Johann Guzman, a cynical but quick-witted young Gibraltarian loner. Shunned by his schoolmates and bullied by his father, Guzman dreams about leaving the small-town atmosphere of his native Gibraltar and starting a new life in the UK. But when he finally overcomes his demons and cuts the umbilical cord tying him to the British Overseas Territory, things don't quite go according to plan....

'A must read for anyone who wants to find out what life is like for minorities living in Britain.' Dr Christine Berberich, Senior Lecturer in 20C Literature, Portsmouth University.

Crossed Lines

Crossed Lines, M. G. Sanchez's new volume of stories, focuses on three different, but equally troubled male characters. Jake Wallburger, stuck in a dead-end job delivering frozen fish to shops and supermarkets along the North Norfolk coastline. Graeme Kirkbride, holed up in a bedsit in the outskirts of Tokyo trying to forget about his past. And, finally, Paco Colomán Trujillo, a Spanish crossfrontier worker who pretends to love Gibraltar and its people, but secretly hankers for the day when the Spanish flag will fly from the top of the Rock....

'Future literary historians will see even more clearly than today's scholars can that the large and wide-ranging body of prose fiction and non-fiction produced by novelist, essayist, and anthologist M. G. Sanchez marks a crucial turning-point in the evolution of Gibraltar's post-colonial literary culture, as the growing attention being paid to his work by scholars in Europe and beyond already attests.' David Alvarez, Professor of English, Grand Valley State University, Michigan, USA.

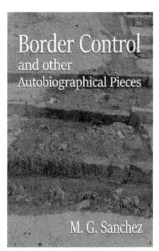

Border Control

Border Control and other Autobiographical Pieces focuses on topics as diverse as childhood bullying, border traffic queues, travelling through Spain, being pickpocketed in China, and life in post-Brexit referendum Britain — all of them filtered through the eye of one of Gibraltar's top authors.

'Until M. G. Sanchez appeared on the literary scene, no Gibraltarian writer had managed to capture the quiddity of the Rock's hybrid society and the complexity of its natural and cultural ecologies with as much psychological insight and writerly verve as are evident in every one of his many novels, stories, and essays. With his prodigious and growing output of prose fiction and non-fiction, Sanchez has gained Gibraltar admission into the world republic of letters.' David Alvarez, Professor of English, Grand Valley State University, Michigan, USA.

Past: A Memoir

In July 2013, just as a full-blown diplomatic row was erupting between Britain and Spain over the Rock of Gibraltar, Joseph Sanchez collapsed and died while cycling in Taraguilla, a Spanish village twenty miles north of the border. In this honest and sensitively written memoir Gibraltarian author M. G. Sanchez relates the hardships his family endured while trying to repatriate his father's remains during one of the most acrimonious phases in recent Gibraltarian history. Part-family memoir, part-act of remembrance, ***Past: A Memoir*** mixes personal reminiscences with political and historical commentary in a shifting, multi-layered narrative which explores – and vigorously upholds – what it means to be Gibraltarian.

'With Sebaldian elegance and candor, M. G. Sanchez's prose meanders through inner and outer geographies. Past: A Memoir *converses with photographs and personal memories as it crosses linguistic, cultural, national and genre lines.'* Professor Ana María Manzanas, Departamento de Filología Inglesa, Universidad de Salamanca.

Bombay Journal

Imagine that you come from one of the world's smallest micro-territories. And that you have a lifelong dislike of crowds.

Now imagine that you wake up one day and find yourself in a mega-city with eighteen million residents and a population density thirty-three times higher than central London.

Imagine the sounds, the crowds, the smells, the endless traffic, the mixture of exhilaration and panic coursing through your veins....

'M. G. Sanchez chronicles the highs and lows of his three-year residency in India with unflinching honesty, opening a novelistic window on India's maximum city.' Dr Esterino Adami, Department of Oriental Studies, University of Turin.

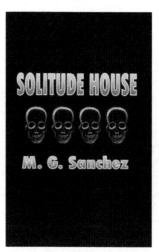

Solitude House

Meet Dr John Seracino, predatory ladies' man and born misanthrope. All he wants in life is a property free of any annoying neighbours. But Seracino has a problem: he resides in Gibraltar, where almost everybody lives in flats and where detached properties come at a premium. For the last few years he has been attending property auctions in the hope of bagging himself one of the old colonial bungalows that intermittently come up for sale. So far, though, he keeps getting outbid by lawyers and bankers, men for whom the annual £90,000 that Seracino earns as a GP are no more than small change. Then one day Seracino's luck changes and he manages to land himself an old colonial property in the Upper Rock area, the aptly named Solitude House. For the first couple of weeks the misanthropic doctor sits every evening on his newly refurbished veranda, looking out over the Bay of Gibraltar with a glass of his favourite alcoholic tipple. But events are about to take an unexpectedly nasty and frightening turn....

The Escape Artist

"So this, more or less, was how things stood for me at the end of 1981. I was twenty-nine years old and I was still on the lowest rung of the civil service pay scale and I lived alone in a three-bedroom government flat with twenty-four different sized statues of the Sacred Heart of Jesus...."

Spanning over ten years and moving between locations as different as Cambridge, Venice and Gibraltar, *The Escape Artist* (2013) is a novel about loneliness and broken friendship and what it means to be Gibraltarian in a rapidly changing world....

'A fascinating literary exploration of a Gibraltarian predicament newly relevant in the era of Brexit.' Ina Habermann, Professor of English Literature, Basel University.

Jonathan Gallardo

Jonathan is a member of the Bishop Audley Children's Home. He has been an orphan since the age of three. He is a strange kid – quiet and self-absorbed in some ways, but violent and ill-tempered in others. One day he slips halfway through a street fight and is repeatedly kicked in the head. From this time on he is beset by the strangest of conditions: he can hear voices near places where crimes and misdeeds have been committed in the historical past.... *Jonathan Gallardo*, M. G. Sanchez's third novel, is one of those books that defy generic classification. On one level it is the story of a working-class Gibraltarian kid striving to improve his lot in life ... but at the same time it is an exploration of Gibraltar's largely forgotten colonial history – or what the narrator of the novel at one point describes as 'an unrecorded history of division and conflict that wasn't supposed to exist but which nonetheless oozes like spectral mould out of Gibraltar's crumbling ancient walls.'

Diary of a Victorian Colonial

Diary of a Victorian Colonial and other Tales consists of three pieces centred on the themes of emotional and geographical displacement. The first and longest of these is set in late nineteenth-century Gibraltar, a British outpost known throughout Christendom for the intemperance of its military men and the 'contrabanding' conducted by its civilian classes. Into this fin-de-siècle world enters Charles Bestman, an Anglo-Gibraltarian returning home after twenty-five years of exile in mainland Britain. What is the infamous criminal stain that follows Bestman's name and why is he so reluctant to let anyone know about his past? The exilic connection continues in 'Intermission' and 'Roman Ruins', two modern-day tales which explore the problems faced by individuals when trying to recreate themselves outside their home environment.

'Relentlessly brutal, and utterly credible.' Professor John A. Stotesbury, Fellow of the English Association.

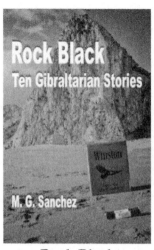

Rock Black

Rock Black: Ten Gibraltarian Stories, M. G. Sanchez's critically acclaimed short story sequence, takes us back to the late 80s and early 90s – a time when large quantities of tobacco were being smuggled from Gibraltar into Spain, the British government was threatening the colony with direct rule, and the Spanish authorities were subjecting the Gibraltarians to a concerted campaign of political harassment. Within its pages we find an almost anthropological gallery of 'types': reluctant tobacco smugglers, drunken English squaddies, small-town hedonists, Costa del Sol prostitutes, passing hippie travellers, as well as the constantly resurfacing figure of the jobless Gibraltarian teenager Peter Rodriguez.

'A necessary corrective after a prolonged period of silence.' Dr Rob Stanton, South University, Savannah, Georgia.

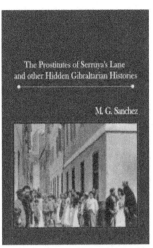

The Prostitutes of Serruya's Lane

'Smugglers and swindlers, pimps and prostitutes, grog-sellers and generals, soldiers, sailors and ship chandlers, all lived cheek by jowl ... within Victorian Gibraltar.' So wrote the British historian Ernle Bradford in his 1971 study *Gibraltar: the History of a Fortress*. Nearly forty years later, Gibraltarian scholar and writer Dr. M. G. Sanchez uncovers part of this lost world in ***The Prostitutes of Serruya's Lane and other Hidden Histories*** (2007), a groundbreaking new book of essays on smuggling, prostitution, racism and other little-known aspects of Gibraltar's Victorian history. If you want to know what life in a nineteenth-century British military fortress was really like, then make sure to pick up this book. You will never view the Rock again in the same light....

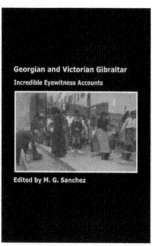

Georgian and Victorian Gibraltar

Drunken sailors, dandified English officers, hard-bitten Gibraltarian boatmen, polyglot Jewish rabbis, winsome Moroccan traders, moustachioed Spanish smugglers, cigar-smoking American adventurers, irascible Catholic priests, hoity-toity British military Governors – these and other emblematically colonial figures are to be found in *Georgian and Victorian Gibraltar: Incredible Eyewitness Accounts* (2012), a large collection of curious and surprising writings about eighteenth- and nineteenth-century Gibraltar compiled by M. G. Sanchez and published by Rock Scorpion Books.

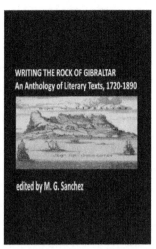

Writing the Rock of Gibraltar

Byron described it as 'the dirtiest and most detestable spot in existence'; Coleridge complained that the onset of the Levanter Cloud made him ill with 'a sense of suffocation' that caused his tongue 'to go furry white and his pulse quick and low'; the Scottish writer John Galt thought that the same was 'oppressive to the functions of life, and to an invalid denying all exercise'; Thackeray was entranced by the mixture of 'swarthy Moors, dark Spanish smugglers in tufted hats, and fuddled seamen from men-of-war' sauntering through Gibraltar's Main Street; Benjamin Disraeli thought that the Rock was 'a wonderful place, with a population infinitely diversified'. These and other comments about Gibraltar are to be found in *Writing the Rock of Gibraltar: an Anthology of Literary Texts, 1720-1890* (2006), a new volume compiled by M. G. Sanchez.

Printed in Great Britain
by Amazon

28713981R00185